Twenty77
The Secret Entrepreneur

Twenty77
The Secret Entrepreneur

Based on a true story

by Amanda Armstrong

ISBN: 978-1-78324-052-4 (paperback)
ISBN: 978-1-78324-053-1 (hardback)

Published by Wordzworth
www.wordzworth.com

"Everyone can close their eyes and listen to the sounds in their sanctuary; for some, it's a moment crushed by the distraction of pain and suffering. Others dare open them to the operant horror of their life, and for the few more fortunate, they open their eyes to their dreams. Let's not forget those that can only dream..."

—THE SECRET ENTREPRENEUR—

Contents

Authors Note

+2015+

There's a saying; when opportunity knocks, open the door.

I've been writing fiction for most of my life and in the last five years my books have been published, with a good degree of success, as I promote myself and my belief in my creative writing abilities. Occasionally, I'll write a short story and post it on my website, in the hope that somebody may just take a look and enjoy my words.

Well, it seems one day a certain somebody did…

In March 2015, I was contacted via my website by Ben Taylor; a retired entrepreneur who is very well known in his industry.

Now, there are moments in life when you meet somebody, through chance or fate, who has a story to tell. I don't know what drew me to this man but once I began to learn more about his story, the more excited I was to be the one to write it.

We initially spoke on the phone and, at first, he wouldn't give anything away, it felt almost as though I was being given an intense interview.

"I want to give my story to an unknown yet talented writer," he told me, "somebody I can trust." I swallowed nervously and nodded. I was certainly unknown, and definitely trustworthy. Was I talented enough though? Could I pull this off? This wasn't something I'd ever done nor even considered until now.

"I've read some of your work," he continued, "and I love the simplicity of your writing and your humour.

He paused as if weighing up his decision to offer me this oppor-tunity. "Do you believe things happen for a reason?" he asked.

My reply was simple. "Yes, I do."

He told me his real name and was adamant when he explained. "I must retain my own and my family's privacy," he said, "but it's important you tell my true story. I would like the title to be 'Twenty 77'. It reflects a date that harbours a secret; a secret I haven't yet shared with anyone."

"It may also help people understand the life of an entrepreneur where I own up to my own fears, insecurities, and of course, failings. It might even help future entrepreneurs. That would make me proud."

He waited as I considered his words, then asked, "Well, Mandy, would you like to take this on?"

I knew I had to be decisive here, this could be my destiny staring me in the face after all.

"Yes," I coolly replied. "Your story is truly inspiring. Perhaps I could dramatize it with my fictional writing skills. Kind of based on your true story, if you like?"

I held my breath, waiting whilst he contemplated my counter proposal.

"Yes," he finally spoke. "I like that idea. So, are you interested?"

Interested, I thought to myself, I can't wait to get started!

Whilst this is based on a true story, some names have been changed to protect identities and preserve privacy.

This book is unique in that I am also sharing my experiences as we journey through this project together. It is the story of Ben's incredible business career and an insight into what made him the man he is today, but it is in my own words and with a touch of my fiction.

It is also my story; my story of when opportunity knocked, and I opened the door...

Prologue

That would be the Stan factor

We first met in the Little Red Café which was to become our regular meeting place. It was quiet, tucked away in a little village beside a lake. There wasn't much passing trade during our morning meetings and usually only Doris, the sixty-something year old owner, was ever witness to them.

Armed with my notebook and with legs like jelly, I approached the café. I was early, deliberately so; I wanted to get a coffee and gather myself before he arrived.

I sat there for maybe ten minutes or so, my fingers nervously pushing spilt sugar remnants around the table, until I saw a man enter. He looked younger than his sixty-four years, slim and well dressed with a confident air about him.

"Morning, table for one?" Doris called out to him as she busied herself with the sandwiches she was preparing.

I stood up and cleared my throat, "No, it's ok," I smiled at him, for I knew it was him, "he's with me."

We shook hands and sat down opposite each other, making small talk until Doris brought his coffee over.

"So, Mandy," Ben looked at me thoughtfully as we got down to business. "I've created a website that counts down to the year 2077; the title of the potential book. Here." He turned his iPad towards me and I gazed in astonishment at the very professional website for a book that hadn't even been written yet, with mystical music and a countdown to 2077 set against a backdrop of a universe.

"So, what is it that's so special about the year 2077?" I asked, intrigued.

Ben's smile didn't quite reach his eyes but something else did. It was almost a flicker of fear which left as quickly as it had arrived.

"We'll come back to that." He sharply replied, and, having only just met him, I decided to let it go.

I sipped my coffee, opened my notebook, and grinned.

"So, tell me, Ben, how did it all begin?"

"Ah," he leaned back, a smile on his face as he clearly remembered fondly, "that would be the Stan factor…"

✦1974✦

"Mr Lenz will see you now, come with me," the pretty young girl smirked as she turned her lusty body and flicked her long brown hair down her back. She led me down a narrow, dingy corridor to the foot of a slightly echoic stairwell and ascended the stairs with me in pursuit. I was mesmerised by the graceful movement of her hips and wishing this wasn't a professional situation. I wanted to open a conversation, but just at that moment we reached the top of the stairs and she raised her arm to knock on the door. She hesitated, her hand on the door handle as she glanced back at me with a beautiful smile. Hopeful, I smiled back and cleared my throat, about to speak…

"Good luck, you'll need it", she raised her eyebrows with that smirk back on her lovely face again, and knocked. A gruff voice signalled permission to enter and she pushed open the door, ushering me in.

"Here we are," said the girl, "Mr Lenz, this is Ben."

The room was so heavily laden with smoke, it was nauseating. I blinked, trying to focus through the grey haze, holding in the cough that threatened to betray my composure.

Eventually my sight settled on Mr Lenz.

A well-built man in his early fifties, he sat behind a desk that was strewn with paperwork and an assortment of dirty coffee cups, as well as an ashtray that was overflowing with butts.

He looked me up and down as I stood nervously before him, not taking his eyes from me, expertly dragging on his cigarette.

It seemed an age before he eventually dropped his cigarette onto the ashtray and pushed his chair back to stand and shake my hand firmly.

"Hmm," he murmured, "take a seat, Ben." I hesitantly sat down.

This was my first real interview; my first job back in 1968 when I was sixteen years old was set up by my mum. She cleaned for somebody who owned a structural engineering company that built steel frames.

That job was as a print room boy in a drawing office and I earned £5 per week.

I worked hard and after a few months surprised my mum when I arrived home to tell her that I'd asked my boss for a draughtsman role and a pay rise.

Sadly, though Mum was surprised, she was not impressed by my boldness; she thought I should be grateful for the job I'd been given.

Within months, though, I was demonstrating my natural ability to draw and the company sent me to college where for one day and two evenings a week I studied structural engineering and architecture.

Now here I was at what was to be my first and last interview, with my distinction in architecture and construction being all that shone on my resume.

Mr Lenz settled back in his chair and I winced as he took another long drag on his cigarette before glancing down and flicking onto the next page. Gazing at my CV in front of this man, I noticed the name plate on his messy desk: STAN LENZ.

For some reason the name Stan resonated with me and I had no idea why it suddenly felt familiar.

Shrugging it off I concentrated on my interview, hating the awkward silence that filled the room. That and the smoke.

Finally, Stan looked up.

"So, Ben, I see you qualified as a structural engineer." He paused, "Hmm, and an architect." He raised his eyebrows, seemingly impressed that someone like me could have made such a grade.

"You worked with a company," another pause as he turned the page. He then looked back at me intently and fired the killer question.

"Why haven't you worked since September last year?" I swallowed nervously, my throat felt dry. I looked at Stan as he sat back awaiting my response and I couldn't help but notice the twinkle in his eyes. He was testing me.

I wanted to say I had been a hippy and a Californian beach bum; trying not to work but just write and play music. But I remember subconsciously spinning it and what came out was:"Oh ok, yes, well I have been travelling but I've gotten that out of my system now and I want to settle into a career."

Wow, did I say that? Well, yes. I mean, I heard myself say it, but was it a lie or was I discovering my natural talent to spin the truth?

Whatever my reason, it seemed to satisfy Stan. He smiled knowingly at me and I knew I already liked this guy.

I had the feeling he would have hired me even if I'd told the truth though, even if I had said: "Holy shit, Stan, this facility sucks and you smoke too much!"

But, of course, I didn't say that, and to be honest, there wasn't much about the conversation that led me to believe he needed to know whether I was really capable anyway.

Stan smoked one cigarette after another, launching into a long story all about the company, Onelock, which designed and supplied internal partitioning; movable walls in offices that came in all shapes and sizes.

He explained the draughtsman role I had applied for and told me how I would be wise to get on board now as the company was growing fast under the progressive leadership of its chairman, Maurice Newton; a man that Stan seemed to hail as some kind of cult hero.

As he talked, his voice faded out for me and I began to wonder why on earth I had left the United States to come back home to all this shit. *I should have tried harder to stay*, I thought, *where did I go wrong?*

Suddenly my subconscious kicked in and I decided I could just work for a few months and then go back to being a bum; a perfect plan.

I quickly focused back on Stan's explanation of how wonderful an opportunity this would be for me.

"Well, Ben, what do you think?"

I found myself nodding enthusiastically, even whilst wondering if I should have played more hard to get. Who was this subconscious person in my head making these decisions for me?

Stan suddenly (and probably quite fortunately knowing my big mouth) interrupted me from saying anything else.

"The starting salary, Ben, is £1940 per annum plus a bonus of course, and we can start you Monday as a draughtsman in a great little team led by one of my finest contract managers, John Stone."

When he finished speaking he regarded me with such intensity, almost as if he expected me to shout with joy and thank him profusely.

However, whilst my eyes grew wide and my mouth dropped open a little, it was not with happy surprise but sudden panic.

In that split second all I was thinking was; *Monday? Shit, but it's Friday today!*

Surely this wasn't how interviews worked? Hadn't anyone else applied for this job? Besides, regardless of all that, I needed time to relax, time to think, time to, I don't know, keep doing what I've been used to doing; bumming around!

After all, I was twenty-two years old. That's what you do at that age, you get a qualification and then you just bum, right?

I breathed out, trying to re-set my head.

Ok, let's formulate a plan here, I'll just work for a few weeks, get some cash and get the hell out.

Stan gazed at me expectantly, waiting for me to speak, and my mind continued to race.

On the one hand, I knew this job with Stan had to be a better move than what I had been doing for the past month since my panicked return from the United States.

Hell, I'd gone from sitting in the sun on a gorgeous Miami beach to freezing my arse off back here in England.

Huh, maybe I should listen to my rational side; it had heard how good the salary was and jumped right in.

Ok, I thought, *yes, let's do it.*

It was a no-brainer really and after weighing up the reasons why I couldn't take this job, my subconscious seemed yet again to have the answer ready and it spoke on my behalf.

"Yes, that works for me," said the angel on my shoulder.

Nooo! Screamed the devil on my other.

Stan smiled confidently, as if my accepting his job offer was never in doubt.

"I think you'll fit in well here, son," Stan reached across the desk to shake my hand. "Welcome on board."

And so it began...

Chapter 1
American Pie

The next time we meet, I am far less nervous and really eager to learn more about the business that made Ben the entrepreneur he became.

But hey, this isn't just about business; after all, all work and no play makes Jack…etc.

Today, Ben is clearly in the mood to talk fun and before I have even opened my notebook I look up to see him chuckling away to himself.

I smile too, his laughter is quite infectious. "What's so funny?"

✦1974✦

Just prior to that interview with Stan I had been determined to continue my lazy mindset and do nothing, but my dad had other ideas and, through his employer, managed to set me up with some cash-paid work doing casual labouring. I suppose he thought it was only right that I should earn my keep.

It turned out to be the hardest work I've ever done. I obviously wasn't fit and I hated the freezing cold. By the end of each day I'd be moaning that I had frost bite in my fingers and toes. Suddenly, such little things as short breaks for a cup of tea by the on-site fires were immensely pleasurable. The trouble was, those short breaks became longer and longer and I was soon pulled up on it.

That was a hard lesson learned and I knew then that working outside in the freezing English winter weather wasn't for me, so I surmised that the job with Stan would be just fine. After all, if I was going to be bored, at least I'd be bored *and* warm.

The weekend before I started the draughtsman's job felt like the shortest weekend on record. I spent much of it wondering if I'd made the right decision as I met up with friends to 'celebrate' my new job over drinks. Though it felt more like commiserating as we recalled some of the crazy things I'd gotten up to Stateside.

Monday morning came around far too soon and I found myself heading to work. Even the word 'work' freaked me out; I hadn't really worked for half a year.

I remember the drive, feeling scared and lost, wondering what I was doing and wanting so desperately to turn around and head home.

Nevertheless, I decided I would try and settle into this new job for now.

The trouble was, after a weekend of reminiscing about my travels, I had lain awake the night before with memories of all those adventures racing through my mind.

And all I wanted to do was get back there…

+ + +

Back in 1973, I'd had a yearning to travel to either Australia or the USA. I can't recall why those two appealed more to me than Europe or Asia. Perhaps I was uncomfortable with foreign languages.

Paul, a former colleague of mine, had wanted to emigrate to Australia and, apparently, it was easy. For a fee of ten pounds and as long as you were approved, it could be arranged through the Australian Embassy.

Paul had quickly signed up and I was literally within days of following his lead when my friend, Dave, persuaded me otherwise.

Dave was teaching me guitar at the time and he and his wife Di had decided to travel to California to live, so when they asked me to join them, with the offer of putting me up, I started to re-think my options. Something about travelling to the States appealed over Australia.

By now, Paul was already committed to Australia, so I asked my best friend, John, whom I had lived next door to since I was eighteen months old.

Obviously, he jumped at the chance, who wouldn't? We were young, free and ready to make our mark on the big wide world.

Dave and Di headed off and settled in Newport Beach, a coastal town south of LA, a few months before us and as John and I prepared to follow them, we were buzzing with excitement.

On an Autumn day in October 1973, with no fixed date of return, we set off to the airport to begin our amazing adventure, with no idea of where it would take us.

We were in high spirits as we boarded the Boeing 707 bound for Los Angeles and we didn't miss the disapproving glances we received from some of the more mature passengers.

We didn't care though; we were off to LA to live the American dream. I remember feeling so liberated, so excited at what life had in store for me and I turned to John as the aircraft rose into the sky.

"This is it, mate, no going back." My eyes glistened with glee and John laughed out loud and fired his fist into the air, "LA, here we come!"

We whooped and cheered and I'm sure more dirty looks were sent our way but we didn't notice. We were too busy enjoying ourselves.

We landed at LAX airport and when the taxi drove us past Newport Harbour, I got my first breathtaking view of Newport Beach. My heart began to race. This beautiful seaside city, with the sun constantly beating down on it, was now my home. I could hardly believe it.

I looked at John and his wide-eyed smile told me he felt the same.

Dave and Di welcomed us into their apartment with open arms and whilst we appreciated their hospitality, we knew we'd eventually have to get our own place.

But first we wanted to have fun.

On our first night, Dave and Di took us to a beach party. It was like something out of a movie; beautiful girls dancing in their bikinis whilst the boys did keepy-up with a football, trying to impress them.

Later, someone made a small bonfire and with the sun beginning to set, we gathered around it and Dave pulled out his guitar, striking a few chords before he nodded at Di.

"A long, long time ago, I can still remember..." Di's melodic tones rang out as we all cheered at hearing this familiar and recent hit song.

Despite the heat, I felt a shiver run up my spine and I looked around at the cool young crowd that I was now a part of, dancing barefoot on the white sandy beach. Glancing over at John, who had his arm around a pretty blonde girl, I raised my beer. Smiling, he returned the gesture and we all joined in the chorus, albeit rather more raucously then Di's gentle jazzy melody.

"Bye, bye, Miss American Pie!"

I sang out loud with the others, feeling a complete euphoria. This really was it, the American dream, and it would be my life from now on.

A few weeks after our arrival though, John and I were stung with a reality check. We had managed to secure our own small one-bedroom apartment in the same block as Dave and Di and it was perfect. It had a swimming pool and best of all it was located just ten minutes from the beach, but we had quickly begun to realise just how much shopping, laundry and cleaning cost.

It really made me appreciate how my mum had waited on me hand and foot at home; if I called out to Mum to put the kettle on, hey presto, there was a cup of tea. Everything else too; cooking, cleaning and washing, well it just seemed to miraculously happen.

Now though, the harsh reality of living on my own and being a grown up, albeit a bit late in life, had brought me down to Earth with a bump.

I woke up hungry one morning, knowing we had no food in the cupboards or fridge. We'd been champagne drinking on a beer budget and it was time to start earning a buck or two if we wanted to continue to do so.

Whilst our sole intention had been to simply bum around, we needed money in order to keep doing it.

Money, and a car.

So, with those priorities in mind, I got to thinking about what we could do…

"John," I walked out into the small living area where John was asleep on the couch, "I've got an idea."

Ignoring his groan, I sat down on the floor in front of him.

"I'm asleep, Ben!" John turned his back to me, thumping the cushion hard.

"Let's start up our own business."

"What? Shut up Ben, go back to bloody bed."

I wasn't wavering though and John knew it, he turned his face around and looked at me through his tired eyes. "Jeez, you're serious, aren't you?"

I nodded.

"We could wash windows, set a fixed price of say ten bucks. We'd only have to work a few days a week."

John groaned again, "We're supposed to be enjoying ourselves! Having fun, and bumming on beaches."

"But John," I reasoned, "it'd be a few days work a week."

John sat up shaking his head. "Nope, I'm here to have fun."

"So, you don't want to earn a few quid and maybe get a car?"

John paused and looked at me and I knew I had him.

"You know, John, with a car we could go anywhere across this beautiful country?"

I could see John's mind working overtime, which apparently was the only part of him that was willing to at that moment.

"What did you have in mind?" He finally said...

We called our new venture 'Sparkle Cleaning' and after dropping a free advert in a local paper, we waited for our first customer.

This would be my second attempt at starting a business; a few years before, my ex-girlfriend Janet's dad had introduced me to a range of biodegradable products called Golden Products which were sold on a pyramid scheme. I did earn some cash from it, but my heart wasn't really in it.

Now though, we needed the cash, and when we were suddenly, somewhat surprisingly, inundated with calls for our services, I thought this would be the perfect opportunity.

We quickly invested in a ladder, buckets and sponges and we were ready to rock.

However, our first lesson in business was soon learnt with our very first customer.

She was a sweet elderly lady with a typically large, one-storey house. We duly cleaned the windows, spending a lot of time to ensure we did a good job and gave a good first impression. Pleased with our efforts, we finished and asked for the ten bucks.

"Yes, yes," she said, "when you have finished."

I looked at John in shock and the look I got back, well, if looks could kill.

"Well, come on in, boys." She waved us in, apologising for the dozens of cats. "I'll make you boys some iced tea while you move the furniture," she smiled sweetly at us and gestured to the screened windows.

My mouth gaped open as realisation sunk in; apparently a window wash was expected to be inside and not just out.

"Brilliant, Ben, just brilliant!" John shook his head at me, taking one end of the antique drawers that were underneath the window.

"I wasn't to know she expected the inside done too!" I protested as I took the other end and we heaved the furniture away.

Every window had an inside screen to remove and it took us nearly three times longer than planned, but we were determined to see it through. By the end, we were shattered and holding our breath; the house literally stunk of cats and cat mess. Needless to say, she was not a customer we would keep. And wily as she was, she didn't even give us a tip!

It taught me an important lesson though when it comes to clients; always manage their expectations.

With that experience behind us we soon got into our stride with window washing but we set a new price; it was now twenty bucks a clean.

We only had to work a couple of days a week to pay our bills and when John also got a part time job at a record store we were able to set about sourcing a car.

With limited funds, we were introduced to some real wrecks, but one day, along came the opportunity to buy an old, white, slightly beaten up Pontiac Bonneville convertible. We made a quick purchase, snapping up what we thought was a good deal and we endearingly nicknamed her 'Bonnie'.

She was really cheap and for us it meant more independence. Not to mention the kudos as we cruised the beaches. There we were, John and I, long hair down to our shoulders and not a care in the world as we cruised along Newport Beach, the top down on Bonnie and the hot sun beating down on us.

Our English accents were loved everywhere we went, making us pretty popular amongst the ladies. It was such a blast!

I briefly took on a part time job, a paper-round, or route as they called it, but the early mornings didn't fit with my late nights of partying, and too often I would sleep through the alarm.

Needless to say, I was fired within weeks. That was fine with me, I still had the window washing business, but I still needed extra income. It was out of sheer desperation that I took a job as a structural engineer, earning in three days what we earned in a month washing windows. Alas, three days was all I lasted. It was proper work, hard work, so I walked out. I wasn't going to waste my travels by putting in any real hard graft.

By now I was also gigging with Dave and Di at parties and in local bars and whilst this brought in some valuable extra cash, I still wanted more.

It was at one such gig that I hit it off with a guy called Joe who shared the same love of music as me and he got me some part time work at a local supermarket. It was boring general duties; bagging up and carrying out groceries, but it was more money and that meant more freedom to maintain my hedonistic lifestyle.

It was Joe who came and got me when the famous actor of that day, John Wayne, came in to the store to buy a Christmas tree and gave me his autograph.

"Woah back there," I have to stop and interrupt Ben here. "John Wayne? Seriously?"

Ben nods, and I'm incredulous; John Wayne was a legend to my dad!

"Get off your horse and drink your milk." I quote and Ben guffaws into his coffee.

"Actually, I'm not sure he ever said that." Ben informs me and I roll my eyes, "Life is tough, but it's tougher when you're stupid. Now that's my favourite quote of his."

"And very true too," I giggle, tapping my pen on my notebook impatiently.

Those three months leading up to Christmas were pretty much a three-month long vacation. When we weren't washing windows, or working our other respective jobs, we would spend most of our days jamming with fellow musicians or swimming and bumming around on the beach.

One morning though, I woke feeling restless, like this just wasn't enough for me anymore. I jumped out of bed and quickly dressed, rushing out of the apartment without even glancing at John's sleeping form on the couch.

I took Bonnie down the coast road and pulled over at the beach, feeling a sense of peace just simply watching the sun break through the clouds and light up the lofty bend of the coast.

I had a sense of attachment to this place and dreamed of putting down roots here one day, but not now, not yet.

My wanderlust was stirring and I knew it was time to move on.

As Christmas approached, John and I talked and unanimously decided that since we had ultimately come to the States to travel, then that's what we should do.

We agreed on a route that would take us through ten US states and ultimately to Florida. It had to be Florida; I was on a mission to go to Miami.

Miami had a reputation as *the* cool place to hang out, so that was good enough for me.

For the next stage of our adventure we planned to sleep in the car and travel light, so we left our suitcases, full of clothes, with Dave.

We literally had no more than a couple of hundred dollars, some blankets and a hold-all and we were relying on good old Bonnie, who had no reverse gear and a torn roof, to take us some 4,500 miles.

We didn't care though, it was exciting, another glorious adventure, wasn't it?

Well, no actually. It was a poor, ill-thought through plan.

We were nothing more than a couple of English hobos, wandering without purpose and not much of a clue. We were ready for life to unfold day by day in whatever form it took, it was part of enjoying being young and free with responsibility only for ourselves.

Our first destination was Vegas, via a route through the LA mountains and then out across the Mojave Desert. There really wasn't much of a plan after that, other than track through the southern State borders where we would pick up the Panhandle and end up in Florida. It was childish to have such a fixation with Miami but when I was obsessed with something I usually made it happen.

The lack of planning hit us hard right on that very first January night.

We were driving through the mountain range around LA when the darkness set in and a thick fog began to swirl around us.

"Jesus, I can't see a thing," I muttered to a dozing John in the passenger seat. I slowed down, leaning forward and squinting into the darkness.

"John, wake up!" I nudged him and he looked at me, startled at my panic.

"You'll have to get out and walk in front of the car, mate. I can't see anything through this fog."

"But it's fucking freezing!" John complained and I slammed my hands on the steering wheel.

"Exactly! Which is why we have to get out of here, we can't stop and sleep up here, we'll perish!"

I was probably exaggerating a little in my panicked state, but I was truly scared; the swirling mist had taken on an eerie presence.

Reluctantly, John got out of the car, and with her headlights on full beam, I slowly guided Bonnie behind him.

In the early hours, we crawled our way into the Mojave Desert, cold, starving hungry and so tired that we could hardly keep our eyes open. We parked up in the wilderness, grateful that the thick grey fog soup was behind us, and finally slept.

By mid-morning, I had calmed down and, other than feeling cold, I was excited and ready to continue the journey. We both were, the adrenalin was pumping again.

I'll never forget my first sight of Vegas as it rose in the distance; a fuzzy haze in the middle of the desert, flagged by shallow mountains. It was a spectacle to behold.

There was a harsh beauty about the desert itself, despite the surreal aspect of Vegas as a city that stood out within hundreds of square miles of it.

I breathed a sigh of awe and looked at John.

"We're in Vegas, baby!"

He laughed and we high fived before heading into the bright light city.

Vegas was a crazy place; it could eat you up if you allowed it.

With the few dollar's we could afford we played the slot machines, hoping for a jackpot win, and like everyone else we found it hard to stop the feeding frenzy, consumed by the buzz of thinking that next time we'll win.

One night, with the constant, deafening ching-ching of those slots ringing in our ears, we headed to the bar. Shouting up two vodka shots, we hoisted ourselves into big leather chairs and grinned at each other as the barman placed them in front of us.

"To Vegas!" John shouted and downed his drink in one, slamming the empty glass on the bar and calling for another.

"Steady on, mate," I urged caution. John was a bigger drinker than me and we were already pretty low on funds.

John ignored me, threw the next shot down his throat as though it were water, and ordered another. The barman spun the vodka bottle behind his back, threw it up in the air and caught it, re-filling John's glass with a little flourish. John's wide-eyed delight made me smile and I relaxed. Sitting back, I scanned the room, watching the tense, serious faces of those playing the roulette tables and I started thinking.

"We could stay here for a few months, you know?" I looked at John intensely and he snorted before downing his drink.

"Ha, yeah right!"

"It's true!" I was animated now, "look at the earning potential out there." I gestured to the gambling arena before us and John stared at me, his face suddenly solemn.

"Nah, it's a mugs game." He was shaking his head but I was determined.

"We can beat the odds." My heart was racing and it had nothing to do with the vodka shots.

"If it's that easy, why doesn't everybody else succeed?" John screwed up his face, "You're full of shit, Ben."

"And you're full of shots, come on." I threw some dollars on the bar for the drinks and led John towards the sea of roulette tables.

"You see," I explained to a now drunk John, "You have to watch the pattern."

"The pattern." John repeated, nodding his head and rolling his eyes at me.

"Yes. Remember that hippy girl back in LA, she told me the number seven would be lucky for me?"

John laughed loudly. "Who, Shirley? She was off her head half the time!"

I swallowed nervously at his words, my fear at the memory of what Shirley had told me returning, and I hoped John was right that she was indeed off her head when she'd said some of the things she'd said. I said nothing.

"You seriously aren't gonna risk our money on a whim?"

"No, John, I'm not." I looked at John with a confident smile as we wandered amongst the tables. "I'm going to risk it on a win."

John groaned, "Why can't we just relax, Ben? Why are you always looking to the next big adventure? Let's go back to the bar."

"Just watch." Ignoring John, I approached the table where I'd spotted seven reds in a row. Perfect, I thought and I turned back to John. "Now we play."

With a reluctant sigh, John stood next to me and watched as I put ten-dollars worth of chips on black.

"Oh yeah," he muttered under his breath, "ten bucks, we're really going to make our fortune with that!"

When it came in, I took my ten-dollar win and looked at John. "It's all about patience. Let's go find another."

"Ben," John trailed behind me as I scanned the tables, the buzz of my win fresh and rushing through my body, looking for the next. "Ben, we could have washed a bloody window and earned more in the time this is taking!"

"Stop whingeing!" I joshed his arm lightly and stood at a table with six blacks in a row. "This'll do." I put down our ten-dollar win on red and we both watched, mesmerized as the ball spun in the wheel and sure enough landed on red.

Laughing, John slapped my back, "It really does work! Let's find another!"

So we did. Watching five reds come in, one after the other, I slammed my money on black and we waited as the ball spun around, almost in slow motion.

When it dropped into black, you'd have thought we'd just won a million.

"Genius, Ben!" John cheered loudly, gaining the attention of the other punters around the table, and in particular a young blonde lady.

Picking up her champagne glass with a sweet smile in our direction, she sidled up to where John and I stood at the table.

"Hey, I'm Melony," she drawled.

"Pleased to meet you, Melony," John drooled.

I turned back to the table to hide the smile on my face as I listened to John speaking.

"I'm John, that's Ben. But he's too busy to talk to you because he has a system."

Melony giggled and whispered something to John who burst out laughing and I searched the room looking for my next win.

With John and Melony in tow, flirting outrageously, I walked from table to table until I had studied one where seven reds came in. This was it, lucky sevens, just waiting for my money.

I looked to John, who had his arm around the giggly Melony, and placed ten dollars down.

"No, no!" John suddenly yelled. "Put all of our winnings on. We can't get rich on ten dollars!"

I hesitated, for just a split second, but it felt like forever. The faces around the table all looked at me questioningly, waiting for my decision.

And I put all of our winnings on black.

It was as if the whole room was spinning and not just the wheel. I held my breath, as did a now silent Melony and John beside me, and waited.

"Come on," I whispered through gritted teeth, willing the ball to drop into black.

"Boom!" John shouted prematurely, and with a click click click, the ball landed on red.

"Shit!" I thumped the table, ignoring the cautioning glare of the croupier. I felt sick, I hated losing. This was not going to beat me.

"That's it then, all our winnings gone?" John looked at me in despair but I smiled slyly at him and shook my head.

Reaching into my pocket I tantalisingly held up a ten-dollar bill. "It aint over till the fat lady sings." I grinned at John who was already shaking his head. "No, Ben. Enough's enough."

But nobody was going to stop me.

By now, clearly realising we were just a couple of bums with a badly flawed system, Melony had turned on her very high heels and sauntered off to find a *real* high-roller.

John shrugged at her departing back. "Ben, this is stupid."

"No, mate. *This* is what separates the men from the boys."

I bought some more chips and stood before another table, adrenalin racing through my veins as six times in a row the ball landed on red, and, remembering my lucky seven theory, I placed my chips on black.

Eureka! It came in and John and I screamed with delight, but by now I knew it was time to stop.

"Quit while you're ahead." I quoted to John and he nodded.

"What was with Melony back there then?" I asked John once we were back at the bar.

John chucked another vodka down his neck and sniggered. "Oh, she offered to make me happy for one hundred bucks."

I threw my head back laughing, "And where was that going to happen, in the back of our luxurious open air pad called Bonnie?"

We laughed and finished our drinks, deciding that tomorrow we would get the hell out of Vegas before it consumed us.

The next day, John and I finally tore ourselves away from the bright lights to continue our adventure and we headed up through the amazing Boulder Dam to the Grand Canyon.

Weaving our way to the South rim, we followed the route of

the little Colorado river, frequently stopping for photos of the fixating panoramic vistas that opened up before us.

It was astounding. The view that spread before us was magnificent, with a sky that after sun rise went from a scene of murky dust to a sea of colour. From the South rim, there were treks hugging the canyon wall that dropped one-thousand feet down to the Colorado river which cuts its way through the canyon base.

Now, it takes a good day to walk down to the Colorado river, but I'd had a bright idea.

We were in January and there was snow on the ground but hey as you'll soon know with me, nothing stands in my way.

"Let's hike down the canyon."

John looked at me as if I had gone mad.

"Ben, it's freezing cold, we only have t-shirts on and these sneakers aint for hiking." He pointed at his feet but I was laughing.

"So what? Let's do it."

John was shaking his head but I knew he would follow me.

Leaving the car park to begin the hike, I spotted someone up ahead and I squinted through the late afternoon air.

"Is that...?"

Before I could finish, John shouted out. "Melony? What are you doing here?"

"Oh my god, hey boys!" Melony's surprised face didn't quite convince me; was she stalking us?

I glanced at John, who, obviously still besotted by her blonde hair and good looks, clearly didn't find it at all odd that she was there.

"Did you tell her we were coming this way?" I hissed through gritted teeth at John who shook his head in genuine shock.

"No!"

My silence made him protest further. "Seriously! She wanted to charge me one hundred bucks for a good time, even if we had that sort of budget I wouldn't!"

I nodded and turned back to our blonde bombshell.

"What brings you here, Melony?"

"Well," she paused, tossing her fair locks behind her, her beauty was so much more fresh in this light of day; completely at odds with the vampish glamour we had witnessed back in Vegas. I could understand John's admiration, but still, there was something about Melony that unnerved me.

"What are you doing here, Melony?" I repeated, wanting to reach behind to John and lift his gaping chin.

"I'm meeting a friend but she hasn't turned up. That's Shirley for you; unpredictable." Melony sighed and shrugged her shoulders.

Just that one word – Shirley. The hair on the back of my neck stood up. *No, surely (excuse the pun) not Shirley?*

"Shirley?" I had to ask, this just didn't feel like a coincidence to me.

"Yes, my friend from LA." Melony looked around at the view. "Ah well, seeing as I'm here now, do you mind if I join you boys? It'd be a shame to waste an experience like this."

"Of course," John spoke before I could refuse and I sighed in frustration but turned to lead the way.

We stepped tentatively along the edge of the South Rim; the ledge was about nine-feet wide and slippery under foot. I trod tentatively along with John grumbling to a giggling Melony behind me as we walked.

"I can't believe we're doing this, Ben! You're off your head."

I chuckled but said nothing, inside I was beginning to realise this actually was a bad idea, especially when I looked over the edge at the one-thousand feet drop and above us the sheer canyon wall.

We carried on for another hour along the path which snaked in a gentle slope around a horseshoe bend.

I spoke over my shoulder to John and Melony.

"Make sure you stay on the inside when you pass anyone; people have been known to go over the edge."

John was quiet, I knew he was really nervous now. Hell, I was too! Strangely, Melony had also stopped babbling and the silence was beginning to feel a little eerie.

I'd just made the decision to turn back when…

"Woah!" Suddenly, as if the wind had taken him, John was slipping down the side of the canyon.

"What the fu…" I scrambled across the narrow ledge to get to him but Melony was already there, kneeling down, holding him as he teetered on the edge.

"Help me!" She screamed over her shoulder at me.

I panicked then, I'll admit. With my arms flailing I somehow managed to grab behind Melony and also get a hold of John.

All I could see, pulling my best friend from the edge of the canyon, was that sheer drop. And ultimately, his death.

We both pulled, Melony and I, and I'll never forget the terror in John's eyes. I was responsible for that. He hadn't wanted to even do this bloody walk.

My determination grew even greater; I was not going to let him die.

When we finally hauled him back up onto the ledge, gasping and breathless; the three of us huddled together in silent relief and the surge of panic left my body like a burst of adrenalin.

But the guilt set in.

"I'm sorry mate, I'm so sorry."

John actually smiled, whether at my words, the sheer relief that he was still alive, or at the beautiful Melony who was smiling down at him, I'll never know.

"My angel," he whispered with a beautific smile on his face for her.

"Christ, you saved his fucking life!" I stared at Melony. She didn't meet my gaze, simply staring at John, her chest thumping hard, her breath coming in short gasps.

"Hey," I gently grabbed her shoulder. "You ok?"

She nodded but said nothing.

"Come on," I said. "Let's get out of here. Go get a drink, yeah?"

"Halla bleeding lujah!" John exclaimed, and we all laughed.

Melony and I hauled a still shaky John up and then we began the slow walk back to the top.

I looked behind me, shuddering at what could have happened but I also took a moment to take in the view. It was natures aesthetic artistry and I was overcome with emotion, truly humbled by the panorama. I made a pledge to myself that one day I would return.

Later, once we'd arrived at a bar, I knew it was time to confront the Melony situation, she'd disappeared to the ladies' room.

"John," I tentatively began, "bit weird that she was there, right?"

John gulped back his beer. "Weird? She saved my fucking life!"

I nodded, I couldn't dispute that, but still, something played on my mind.

"You seriously didn't tell her that's where we were headed?"

John rolled his eyes and I said nothing more, but after about ten minutes, when Melony hadn't returned from the ladies, I decided to voice my fears to him…

I sit forward. "What fears? Is this something to do with that Shirley you mentioned?"

"At that time, it was purely coincidence that Melony had mentioned a friend called Shirley but there was just something I…"

"What?" Ben's face has paled and I'm slightly worried. He looks me straight in the eyes now and I hold my breath at his deadly serious expression.

"I think there was a reason Melony was there."

"Why was she there?" I ask Ben. I've not been to many parts of the States, but even I know it takes a good four hours or so from Vegas city to the Grand Canyon.

"Well, my initial instinct was that she was stalking us, but…"

"But?" I'm getting impatient now and Ben looks agitated.

"John and I waited for Melony to return from the ladies, I was dreading having to tell her that we really didn't want her hanging around us for the rest of our travels."

"How did she take it?"

"Well that's just it, you see. She never came back."

"She just disappeared?"

"At that point, yes…"

"What do you mean, at that point?"

Ben shakes his head, a strange look in his eyes.

So off we headed South in search of a warmer climate, but our lack of planning hit home again when the fuel crisis, quite literally, stopped us in our tracks.

"Wait a minute!" I interrupt Ben's attempt to continue his story and he looks at me sharply.

"Go back a bit. To you and John in the bar, what fears did you tell him?"

That darkness returns to his face and I freeze; a shiver runs up my spine.

"The gas crisis, yes go on…" I mutter to Ben, feeling suitably admonished, and I reluctantly return to my notes.

In 1974, the gas crisis had gripped the US as well as the UK, and whilst for us it was another part of our adventure, it was one that was set to be quite a challenge.

We were low on gas but fortunately had enough to get us to a gas station where we parked outside to wait for fuel. That night was one of the worst of my life.

In below freezing temperatures we had to sleep in the car with its ripped canvas and no fuel to start the engine and run the heater.

For me, I felt like I'd suddenly hit the lowest point of my travels. I could see John was struggling too.

"Well, Toto, it looks like we're not in Kansas anymore." I tried to chivvy him up but he just tutted and pulled his blanket tighter around him. I suddenly felt really immature. What the hell had we been thinking, just taking off on this road trip with no real thought out plan? It was stupid and irresponsible. I vowed I would never put myself in this vulnerable position again and, at some point, I shivered myself to sleep, dreaming of home and my bed with its proper blankets.

When the morning finally came, John and I were exhausted and numb from the cold, but at least we were first in line for fuel.

When it arrived around midday, the relief was exhilarating.

"Fill her up, Ben!" John shouted, and I can tell you, I've never been so excited to fill my car up in my life.

We continued heading South, but after a few hours I was struggling to keep my eyes open and wondered if I should pull over and sleep for a bit.

No, keep going. I kept saying it to myself but eventually it was John that made the decision for me.

Three hours later, having barely registered what state I had driven through, he suddenly sat up, his face a whiter shade of pale.

"Pull over, quick!"

I panicked, ramming the car into the side of the road and John flung open the car door, retching violently before throwing up.

I was despairing. I put my head on the steering wheel and wondered if things could get any worse. *Should we give up?*

As I comforted John, I suddenly felt that steely determination of mine well up. No, we would not give up!

When John felt able to, we set off again and while he dozed next to me, I searched my brain, trying to formulate a plan. There was no way we could spend another night in the car with John so ill and me so tired.

A couple of hours into that journey, I saw pink neon lights up ahead and I squinted through the navy-blue night to see what they said: *Bates Motel – No psychos please!*

Despite my dark mood, I chuckled, and with a quick glance at the sleeping John, I dropped the indicator and pulled in.

The next morning was a completely fresh start. Both John and I had gotten a good night's sleep and John was adamant he was feeling in tip top condition.

"Good," I told him, "you can drive!"

With the sun shining down on us, and feeling upbeat again, we plotted a route that was as direct South as we could go, heading for Houston and out across the Southern states.

We were doing fine, the top was down on Bonnie and music was blaring out as we made our way through Louisiana and Alabama, but then we were suddenly thrown another obstacle.

It seemed the local cops weren't too ingratiated with our Californian license plates and sailing down the road, my heart sunk when flashing lights and a screaming siren forced John to pull over.

"What the…"

Before I could finish my sentence, I was being yanked out of the car by a cop, while his partner looked on.

"Get your ass out of there, boy," he drawled in a Mississippi accent. I obliged. Well who wouldn't, the guy was six-foot four and built like a brick shit house!

Forcefully, though believe me no force was necessary for I was more than willing, he wrestled me round to the front of the car.

"Hands on the hood, hippy boy!" he demanded, pushing me against the car and kicking my legs apart. His breath smelt of stale coffee and tobacco when he spat the words in my ear and my stomach rolled over, disgust momentarily overriding my fear.

"Damn, you fricking stink!" The irony of his comment filled me with indignation, but he was right to be fair; the only ablutions John and I had performed were by swimming in the ocean.

Trouble was, since California, there'd been no ocean!

John was out of the car quicker than I'd seen him move for days and he stood in shock, watching as I was body searched with heavy hands for a weapon or drugs, his face a deathly white through his Californian tan.

"Don't you fricking move off that spot, boy," the cop snarled at me as he rounded the car and started on John. I was literally shaking. Were they going to shoot us? It felt like one wrong move from us and they would!

I suddenly missed home; this place didn't feel like paradise anymore. These cops were ruthless and crazed; angry, and certainly despising where we came from. It was like a scene out of a psycho hillbilly film. John was also body searched and it was my turn to watch as he half-heartedly put up a protest.

Finding nothing of interest on our persons, the cop opened the car and pulled out our bags. He looked at me suspiciously. "You got drugs in here, hippy boy?"

"No." I managed to stutter and he moved in towards me, pushing his open hand hard into my chest.

"It's no, sir, you piece of hippy shit!" Damn, there was that rancid breath of his again.

"No sir!" I barked back. He tore open our bags, rifling through them, checking each item before throwing them onto the side of the road.

The other cop stood there grinning, one hand on his weapon,

chewing on his tobacco. For the second time, he drew phlegm into the back of his throat and spat it out. My eyes couldn't help being drawn to the yellowy-green globule that glistened on the tarmac and I forced myself not to gag. If he was trying to make a statement that he was indeed a psycho capable of doing anything crazy, it worked, John and I were both freaking. There were no other vehicles on the road so the silence and solitude of that morning was eerie and disturbing. John and I looked at each other with the same thoughts in our heads and fear in our innocent eyes.

"No drugs, hey?"

I turned towards the voice of the cop. He stood there, a triumphant grin on his fat face, his hand in the air.

"Shit, Ben! What's that?"

My eyes widened as, confused, I looked at John and then back at the cop. In his hand, he held a small clear plastic bag with what looked suspiciously like white powder inside.

"What the?" I stepped forward, desperation in my voice. "That's not ours!"

I felt the hands suddenly forcing my arms behind my back.

"In the car, boy!"

The other cop had John in an armlock and John groaned, his head hitting the roof of the police car as he was bundled in.

"You boys are looking at a long stretch in the state pen, at least!"

I was thrown into the back seat next to John who looked like he was about to cry.

"Mate, it's ok. It's a misunderstanding, we'll get this sorted." I tried to reassure him but inside my heart was pounding and I really wasn't so sure myself.

"Oh my god, that's awful. Was it Melony who'd planted the drugs, do you think?"

Ben smiles. "That was exactly my thought at the time. I honestly don't know how the drugs got there, I can only assume it was the cops."

"How do you know it wasn't Melony though?" I'm confused.

"Well maybe I don't, but then something very strange happened…"

The cop car roared off and I ran my hands through my hair, shaking my head.

I looked at John, his expression was that of a deer in the headlights.

"This is serious shit, Ben."

I simply nodded. What else could I do? He was right.

At the station, the cops took down our details before John and I were hauled with heavy hands into separate holding cells.

The musty aroma in my cell was overwhelming and I looked at the bucket in the corner, nausea rising within me. I spewed the contents of my stomach into it and sank down heavily to the ground.

The hours ticked by and I sat on the cold stone floor with my head in my hands and despair in my heart. I couldn't believe we'd been set up like this. It had to be Melony, surely. But why?

I thought about my parents back home, what would they say about this? Would I ever be going home anytime soon? My thoughts raced through my mind until some time later the cop who had discovered the drugs came to my cell.

"Well, well, well, hippy boy, looks like you got you a roomie."

The door of the cell swung open and an old bearded man was shoved in. He fell awkwardly to the ground and the cop laughed loudly. "Sleep it off, Bert." He shouted and once again the cell door was clunked shut.

"You ok?" I went to the old mans side and he grunted with a nod.

I recoiled from the stench of booze that was wafting off him in waves and he looked up at me, his rheumy eyes blinking in the low light of our cell.

"Ah, home sweet home," he gave a little chuckle and pulled a quart of whiskey from inside his trouser leg.

"Want some?" He held the half full bottle towards me but I shook my head.

Shrugging, he unscrewed the lid and drank greedily.

"They keep me in overnight and send me on my way, every time. I've told them I'm happy to stay." He slurred with a chuckle.

"Why would you want to stay here?" I asked incredulously and Bert smiled, his glazed eyes twinkling at me.

"Aint got nowhere else to go, at least it's warm in here. Food aint too bad either." Bert snorted and took another swig of his grog.

Realising that Bert was clearly the local bum, I sat back, feeling cloaked in despair.

"What you in here for?"

I told him about the drugs and his eyes widened.

"Woah!" He whistled slowly, shaking his head. "You got troubles boy, them cops don't like you young travellers."

"The drugs weren't ours!" I insisted and Bert was nodding.

"I believe you, them cops have done this before."

I suddenly felt sick, what was he saying?

"You mean?"

Bert scratched frantically at his matted hair. "Yep, seen many a patsy gone down for this sort of thing."

"The cops planted the drugs?"

Bert belched loudly and my stomach turned, bile rising in my throat again.

"They aint got nothing better to do, other than pick up drunk bums like me. Makes life exciting for them."

"Jesus Christ." I muttered under my breath.

"They'd set him up too, given half the chance!" Bert roared with laughter, rolling onto his side, and I noticed the wet stain that was forming on the back of his trousers.

I stared at his huddled form on the cold hard floor and I knew that if I were to go to prison, I simply wouldn't survive.

Bert became silent and I realised he had fallen into a drunken slumber.

I felt alone once again. So alone, and terrified at my fate.

"It was the cops that had set you up?"

"According to Bert, yes." Ben nods.

"And you believed an old drunk homeless man?"

"I didn't want to, not at first. I was still sure Melony had something to do with it."

"So, what changed your mind?"

Some time during the night, I managed to doze off. The stress had taken its toll and to the rhythmic tones of Bert's snoring, I finally closed my eyes.

Bang! Bang! Bang!

"Wake up, boy!"

I started and sat up quick, my eyes suddenly wide as the cell door opened.

"Wasss garn on?" Bert mumbled groggily from the floor.

"Seems like hippy boy here found himself a reprieve." The cop, a different one, peered down at me.

"Looks like you boys have a guardian angel. You and your pal are free to go. We towed your vehicle to our lock up, you can pick the keys up from the desk when you sign out."

I was dazed, confused. Was I dreaming? Was this a sick joke?

"But..." I looked warily at the cop who stamped his feet impatiently.

"You better hurry up, boy, don't make me change my mind now!"

I scrambled to my feet and called a farewell to Bert, who muttered something incoherent, and I finally left that cold dark cell behind me.

The cop guided me out to the front desk and to my utter relief, there was John, looking as exhausted and confused as I was, but nevertheless unharmed.

"You punks have the lovely Melony to thank for this. Now get your sorry asses out of here!"

"Melony? What's going on?" I looked at John in shock, but he shook his head.

"Let's not question it, Ben. Let's just get the fuck out of here!"

Leaving that cop station, I thought I would break down into sobs of sheer relief but John and I held it together until we were reunited with our beloved Bonnie.

In the car, I put my head in my hands and gulped deep liberating breaths.

"Drive, Ben. Please just drive." John pleaded, tears in his eyes.

With our hearts racing and our heads in turmoil, we drove through the quiet, dark streets and headed for the highway.

"Melony again?" I gasp. Who was this Melony? And why did she keep showing up?

Ben looks at me. "I think she somehow got us off; saved us once again."

"Didn't you ask her how or why?"

"She disappeared again, and by that point we didn't care. We just wanted to get the hell out of dodge!"

The relief was intense when we sailed along the Panhandle and, finally, made it to Florida.

I fell in love straight away with Florida. After our experience in the Southern states, it felt almost as though we had reached a sanctuary. That feeling was enhanced on our first morning, driving towards the East coast where an intoxicating hint of citrus and pine filled the air.

We travelled down Route 1 before cutting back inland to visit the newly created Disney World and then heading back out again to enjoy some time at Cape Kennedy.

We got back on Route 1 towards Miami and enjoyed the breath-taking coast line and beautiful Floridian sunshine as we hit 4,500 miles on the Bonnie clock.

Ben pauses here, deep in reflection.

"Did you and John ever discuss the Melony thing?" I'm interested to know why Ben seems to be avoiding the issue.

Ben sighs. "We didn't want to dwell on it. We were just grateful to be free and back on the road."

"But, it doesn't make sense, none of it." I'm probably speaking out of turn here but I'm sure Ben is keeping something from me.

"Well sometimes there is no sense to things." Ben's weak response has me raising an eyebrow.

"Oh, come on," I say, "what really happened, Ben?"

His face flushes an angry red. "I don't want to talk about it."

Despite not wanting to upset the man I am working for I feel my own temper flare up.

"You don't want to talk about what you want me to write? That's helpful."

I can't help my sarcasm and I don't miss the flicker of irritation in Ben's face.

"Just not now, ok?" His sigh is one of weary resignation rather than real anger and I back down. He will tell me, he has to.

Just. Not. Now.

"So, you finally made it to Miami?" I change the subject and he nods.

"Yes, my ultimate destination." He smiles.

"Quite an experience you'd had getting there though!" I understate.

Fortunately, Ben laughs, and I feel better now that we are back on an even keel.

"It was an experience that I believe laid the foundation of my life. I grew up quickly, was forced to. It's something that I now look back on and treasure, but like all things, they eventually come to an end…"

My affinity with the US was not to end there but the moment came when we had to make a decision.

I was wading back out of the strong surf when a wave crashed into the back of my legs and swept my feet from under me. Laughing to myself, I fell to my knees and rolled over, laying for a moment in the shallow water and gazing up at the blue sky, the sun burning hot on my face.

This was how life should always be, I thought, just blue skies and sunshine. As if to remind me of the harsh realities of my daydream, a pain surged through my stomach and I realised I was hungry. I pulled myself to my feet and stretched upright, wading through the water and walking up the beach with the warm sand between my toes. It felt so good.

It was late on a beautiful Saturday afternoon on Miami Beach. The day before, we had been launching rocks into the palm trees in a desperate attempt to knock out a coconut. It was as futile as our other efforts to feed ourselves over the last forty-eight hours, for that was the last time we had eaten, using our last few dollars in the Pancake House to have breakfast.

Since then, all I'd had was so much water that my stomach was swollen. I was so hungry and things were getting desperate.

I sauntered up the beach and John threw a football at me. I caught it and walked towards him, knowing already what he was going to say and knowing too that, as much as I really didn't want to hear it, we really had no choice. I was already nodding with a resigned sigh as he said the words.

"We need to go home."

Our first experience upon arriving in Miami hadn't been the most positive to be honest. Our trusty beaten up old Bonnie had been our traveling home since we left California, yet each time we tried to get our heads down for the night in Miami we were moved on by the cops.

We once even tried sleeping on the beach but were threatened with jail if we were caught a second time and that was definitely not an option we wanted to re-visit!

It forced us to move around the city like vagrants, each night trying to find somewhere different to settle. Then one night, rather foolishly, we ventured a little too far south into Miami.

It was about 9pm and we were tired so we pulled into a local shopping precinct to get some sleep. The car park was full so we felt pretty inconspicuous parked amongst all the other vehicles. We were both exhausted from broken sleep and all the travelling and quickly fell into a deep slumber.

Some time into the night we were woken by flashing lights and loud voices. In our dozy state, we looked out of the window to find we were surrounded by two cop cars.

"Step out of the vehicle, sir." One of the cops ordered as he shone his bright torch light into the car.

"Oh shit," I mumbled, pushing open the car door, "not again."

I thought I was going to pee my pants when I found myself confronted with the cop, his gun drawn. He slowly beckoned me and John, who had also stepped out of the car, to spread our legs and put our hands on the hood. I think we were beginning to feel like old hands at this by now.

I was still groggy from my deep sleep and I was struggling to process the situation when the cop started to quiz me.

"ID," he commanded, not taking his eyes from me.

"It's in the bags," I muttered sheepishly.

"Drugs?" Despite my fright, I was tempted to reply, 'no, thank you' to his question, but I knew by now how serious these cops took themselves and now was definitely not the time.

"No, nothing," I replied honestly, not that that had counted for anything previously.

"Where you from, boy?" The cop and his colleagues stood poised, as if they expected us to run at any moment. To be honest, if it weren't for their guns or the fact that I was frozen to the spot with fear, I may well have considered it!

I hesitantly explained that we were from London, holding my breath, waiting for his reaction.

The cop shook his head with a rueful smile.

"You two guys have just had the luckiest break of your lives. This is a dangerous area," he explained, "two young guys here on their own at any given time of day could be robbed, or worse. You're lucky we spotted your car."

Spotted the car, I thought, *how, amongst all the other cars?*

It was then that I noticed the car park was empty, it was almost two in the morning and we stuck out like a sore thumb.

He was right though; we were fortunate.

We got the usual warning that if they found us again we'd be spending the night in the county jail.

We were still spooked after our experience with the Southern cops but despite that edgy feeling, we wanted to stay. We still wanted to 'live the dream'.

However, we had spent over two weeks looking for work in Miami, we didn't care what, just any work would do, from orange grove picking to washing up, but nobody would employ us.

And here we were, a couple of weeks in and starving hungry.

John's call that we should go home was a little late in the day though; there were no flights out on a Sunday. It was a case of either get on the Saturday night flight to London or we'd have to wait until Monday.

I turned to John. "You're right, mate, we either get that flight today or we'll have to steal to eat and I'm so hungry I'm willing to do that."

"No," John was shaking his head. "We've left it too late, the flight leaves in a couple of hours."

"We can still make it," I chuckled, suddenly feeling excited. Why do I always say *can* when somebody tells me I can't? "We can get that flight."

John smiled, he clearly also wanted some fun.

"Let's do it!" He cried.

So, still in our swimwear, we picked up our towels and ran up the beach towards the car. It was as we sped towards the airport that we began to question our decision.

We were still hatching a plan when we approached a toll. We didn't have a cent on us and John began searching frantically to see if we had any loose change on the floor of the car, but there was nothing.

"We'll just have to explain to the toll booth guy…" John began, but in a mad moment I made a quick decision and accelerated through the toll with all the bells ringing.

"You're crazy!" John screamed as we both howled and whooped with laughter.

We headed into the airport, parked up, grabbed our two, small hold-all bags and ran towards the departure building.

I briefly stopped to say a fond goodbye to Bonnie, our trusty Pontiac, and silently thanked her for taking us on our travels, planting a kiss on her torn hood.

Breathless, we got to the ticket desk with just one asset to our names; our open return tickets home.

We frantically explained our situation to the ground hostess, elaborating on our state of desperation, all of which was pretty obvious considering we were stood there in our T-shirts and damp swimwear.

"I'm so sorry," the ground hostess was sweet and apologetic, "I think they have closed the gate, but let me check."

She was on the phone for a few minutes and John and I stood there impatiently, silently both praying we could get on that flight, but inside thinking it was probably hopeless.

The hostess turned to us with a smile as she finished her call.

"That's great, thanks Melony. I'll tell them to hurry."

She put down the receiver.

"Ok, they have agreed to let you on." She printed off our boarding cards and looked questioningly at our confused faces.

"Melony?" I muttered to her.

"What? Yes, my boss. Now what are you waiting for, run!"

Running for the gate, my head was awash with thoughts of Melony. Would she be there waiting for us?

But when we reached the gate, there was only a smartly dressed man waiting to escort us on board.

"There's more than one Melony in this world, Ben!" John muttered, as though reading my thoughts and I nodded. I had to let it go. It was time to go home.

We walked onto the aircraft where everyone was already seated; they must have thought a couple of celebrities were coming on board.

Instead, there we were, still in wet swimwear, an embarrassment to England walking down the aisle to our seats. If I witnessed that now I would cringe, but we had no care in the world, it was all a big giggle. We sat down within minutes of taxiing out and looked at each other with relief as we shared another high-five and began to sing.

"So, bye bye, Miss American Pie, drove my chevy to the levy but the levy was dry..."

We laughed out loud, but deep inside we both had that deep sense of sadness that our adventure had come to an end.

"So, that was it, the love affair with the US was over?"
"For now..." comes his mysterious reply.

Chapter 2

There's Something about You

Ben arrives at our next meeting armed with documents.

"What's all this then?" I gesture at the stack of papers he places on the table and he shakes his head with a sigh.

"Oh, these are for my next meeting, after this."

"Aren't you supposed to be enjoying your retirement?" I ask and he gives a cynical laugh.

"Believe me, the more you get to know me, the more you'll understand. This is me, it's what I do. I simply can't stop working."

At that moment, as if to confirm this, he takes a call on his mobile with a quick mutter of an apology in my direction.

I sit and wait for him to finish what is clearly a business call, not that I'm eavesdropping of course, and I find myself looking forward to the next instalment of his career history.

+1974+

My adventures in the US soon became a distant memory in 1974 when I began my draughtsman job at Onelock.

Over the following months, I settled into my role; drawing floor plans and scheduling components to build internal walls. I was in a small team led by a contract manager, John Stone. His team consisted of a labour controller, thirty odd guys out on site erecting partitioning, an accountant and two other draughtsmen.

John's team was like a little company within a big company and I hated it.

Outside our team were four other teams doing the exact same thing and sprawled across the facility were three other teams; Accounts, Purchasing and Management and a huge warehouse where components were stored ready for delivery to site.

Each day, I arrived on time and left on time. I was always conscientious but I don't suppose I showed any real enthusiasm. In fact, I still dressed like the hippie from my bumming around days and probably seemed like a bad hire.

I often wondered why Stan *did* hire me but I still think to this day that he saw something in me. Maybe I had reminded him of his younger self, of when he had started his career full of hope and ambition. Or maybe he just thought I was a bit wet behind the ears and had taken pity on me, who knows?

As I went about my job from day to day, I was sure that I was giving something to the company and gaining experience for myself.

Things seemed to be going well until one day when John approached me, "Ben, can you stay back tonight? I need a word."

Oh no, I thought, *am I getting fired?* I mean, sure, I didn't particularly love the job, but it was a job all the same.

I spent the rest of the day fretting and feeling anxious about what John wanted to talk to me about and when everyone had left for the evening, he came to my desk where I had been waiting.

"Ben," he said, "a couple of things I need to mention. First, are you taking drugs?"

"Me?" I replied, shaking my head, my eyes wide in amazement, what was it with people always thinking I'm on drugs? "I've never even tried them, so no."

"Well, ok," John continued, eyeing me beadily, "I just needed to ask."

I chuckled at his incorrect suspicions, feeling relieved that it was all just a misunderstanding; he thought I was on drugs, I wasn't. That was it, all cleared up. I stood up to leave.

"Oh, hang on, Ben," John wasn't finished, "one other thing."

I quickly sat back down, my heart sinking just as fast.

"Have you noticed that everyone else in the team stays late and gets in early, you don't."

John always looked directly at you when he asked a question, it was quite intimidating and it would put you under pressure, as it did then.

"I, erm, I…" I hated that I stuttered then, but the piercing glare from John was enough to put anyone off their stride.

I tried to continue, to explain that just because I didn't work long hours, didn't mean I wasn't putting the graft in.

But John wasn't listening, or simply didn't want to hear it as he delivered his next words.

"It's a team effort here, Ben. We're earning a lot of bonus, and quite frankly, we are not going to carry you anymore, so…" I swallowed, my heart pounded in my chest and I waited for him to finish his sentence with a sick feeling of dread, "…so buck your ideas up or our next chat will be me firing you."

Whilst inside I was relieved I was still in a job, a part of me couldn't help but be scornful of John's words. *Oh, yeah right, the bonus, huh, that means a lot here I guess.*

As if reading my thoughts, John spoke again, rather excitedly. "Do you know how much the bonus will be this month?"

"I've no idea, John." I looked at him blankly.

"It's over six-hundred pounds." John snapped back rather sharply, waiting for me to digest this revelation.

I shrugged nonchalantly, feeling irritation well up inside me. "Well, six-hundred pounds across the whole team isn't really…"

John sat forward and looked me squarely in the eyes.

"It's six hundred each, Ben. Six hundred pounds each."

My eyebrows raised, I couldn't believe what I was hearing. That was three times my monthly salary and *that* was already far more than I'd expected.

I would be rich, well, richer than a bum. My mind began to whirl with thoughts; did I want to be rich or be a beach bum? Well I had enjoyed being a bum, maybe I could be a rich bum?

It had certainly stirred something inside me and I think that was the turning point; the moment when the entrepreneur in me became engaged. It was almost as though up to this point I had simply been drifting along not realising my potential and now I had suddenly woken up.

"I need you to change your attitude." John interrupted my moment of enlightenment, then he paused and looked at me for acknowledgement.

"Yes, yes, I will." I said, and by God I meant it!

The discussion had spooked me; just when I thought I didn't care whether he fired me or not, something had touched me deep inside. Suddenly I felt I had something to prove, not just to him but to myself.

"That was the proverbial kick up the butt that I needed," Ben raises his eyebrows at me. "It was also probably when I first discovered that I was motivated by wealth, by financial reward."

"Isn't everybody?" I ask, perhaps naively.

"You'd be surprised," he muses. "There are so many out there

that want reward of some kind, but it's amazing how few are actually willing to earn it."

I can't help but agree and Ben taps my notebook, ready to continue.

"Fortunately, I wasn't one of them…"

We hardly ever saw the other teams because we all worked in separate offices spaced out as small individual companies.

Stan rarely talked to me during that time, it was almost as if John Stone's team was his company and his call and he was always the first in line to shake a finger at.

The only thing that mattered outside of John's team was the chairman, Maurice Newton.

As I've said, Maurice was looked up to as some sort of cult hero, a celebrity status for some reason and I wondered why. I thought perhaps I should try and meet him; everyone I had ever spoken to had the highest regard for Maurice and his vision for the company.

After John Stone's little pep talk, I had decided to throw myself into my work and get more involved and I was interested in what made the bonus scheme tick, the numbers had me hooked.

There were always errors when we scheduled materials, which were in effect an explosion of many small components to make up the walls. Due to the number of components, it was quite complex and certainly challenging to get it right. In fact, it was unusual when someone achieved that feat, I hadn't at this point. Invariably the call always came in from the guys installing on site with a list of what was missing and another vehicle would be dispatched with the shortages, almost as a matter of course. I hated those calls, it made me feel so guilty that I had made mistakes and rightfully so. John Stone was always seething as he knew those errors cost us bonus, but strangely no one did anything about it. It was just accepted as being something too difficult to get right. I couldn't understand why everyone just accepted the errors, so I set to work on my idea.

I started to appreciate that our bonus was calculated as costed on the quote and that carried a premium for errors. So, any improvements in cost-saving by scheduling the materials correctly in one delivery would dramatically reduce costs and increase our bonus. In other words, the company was ultimately penalising us for having to re-deliver materials, and in most cases returning the labour to site.

The extra bonus that could be earned played on my mind and I started thinking about how I could get the materials right first time. Another factor that expanded our bonus was extras, for example, if a customer changed the specification. If we over-priced the extras we made a huge percentage of bonus on the profit; a practice that the company did not dissuade.

Maybe this was slightly unethical but I began wondering why a higher profit *should* be unethical.

After a few weeks, by trial and error, I had come up with a mechanism to go back and check the materials against a set of check lists. I made the check list so that it emulated the same format as the pre-printed components list. It was slick, and what's more, it was reliable.

I put it to the test myself on the very next project I was assigned.

Because it was a rarity to ever get a schedule of material correct, John came over as soon as it hit his radar.

"Ben, you did it, no errors!" Now John rarely smiled, but the broad grin on his usually grumpy face gave me even more incentive, so I repeated this process on my following assignment.

"Ben, you did it again, which seems unlikely to be a coincidence, how on earth are you doing that?" He leaned over my drawing board inquisitively.

"I have a system," I shyly replied and then I showed it to him.

"Hmm…" he pondered my formulation and with an enthusiasm he'd never shown me before, he said, "that wasn't an easy one to resolve Ben, but I've got to say it works."

He asked me to show it to the other two draughtsmen, to be sure they used it as well, and suddenly our errors were virtually eradicated and our bonus figures increased dramatically.

As a team, we were now standing out head and shoulders above the other teams. I was also racking up extras by over-pricing and at one point I remember our bonus coming in at five times our salary. I could tell John now really appreciated me and he finally shared his respect for me with Stan.

One day, when the office was abuzz with the usual activity, John took a call and shouted over to me. "Ben, can you pop up and see Stan straight away, please?"

Everyone in the team looked up at me with inquisitive faces; was Ben in trouble?

I dropped everything and bounded up the stairs to Stan's office, two steps at a time. I wanted to get whatever it was he wanted to see me about out of the way. If he was firing me, that was ok, I could deal with it. I knew I already had enough money for another ticket back to the States, which had always been my initial plan anyway.

Still, I couldn't help my nervousness as I knocked on Stan's door and waited for the big man to invite me in.

"Come in," Stan grunted, and I walked in, steeling myself and holding my breath against the smoke. God, I hated that room.

"Ben…" he paused.

For goodness sake Stan, spit it out!

"Maurice wants to have a chat with you."

I was confused for a moment, until he clarified further. "We've all seen the results which seem to relate to some sort of check system you devised, did you come up with that yourself?"

"Yes," came my hasty reply, then I elaborated, rather proudly I must admit. "I realised the impact any errors had on the bonus scheme and I was fed up with being moaned at by the works manager when trying to reschedule deliveries. It didn't stop there," I went on, "the site foreman would also rant about travelling to and from the site."

I stopped myself rambling for long enough to get a look at Stan's face, which wasn't easy through the screen of cigarette smoke that surrounded him.

He raised his huge eyebrows and nodded his head as if to acknowledge the brilliance of this system. Of course, there wasn't anything brilliant about it, it was simple common sense. Stan remained silent, he rarely said anything unless it was relevant, then he squinted and looked at me intensely. "There's something about you, Ben," he finally spoke, "if you will trust me, I want to work with you to get you on the right path. Let's just see where we can take it?"

I felt my mouth go dry, I swallowed hard and my heart raced. "Yes, that would be fine by me." I sounded calmer than I felt.

"Ok…" Stan tapped a pen on his desk thoughtfully as he watched me. "We'll start by having Maurice stop by to see you and we'll chat again next week."

"Sure," I nodded, and when he pulled another cigarette from its packet I took this as my cue to leave, but I couldn't help feeling his gaze on my departing form.

I jumped down the stairs like a kid on Christmas morning; *Maurice was coming to see me, how cool!*

Everyone looked up as I burst rather excitedly back into the office.

"Well, you're still here then?" My colleague Dave smirked.

"Yep," I chirped back, "all ok, it was only about the check lists. Stan just wanted to know how it was going, that's all."

Everyone was so focused on the job in hand that there was no further time for idle chit-chat as we were always at full tilt, so nothing more was said.

In a strange way, I was starting to feel comfortable in this routine, yet a month earlier I couldn't wait to get back to the States. John was already planning a trip back. This time he wanted to cover the Northern states and had invited his friend Gus to join us both, so I had been pretty much thinking my time here was just about up.

Today though, I wasn't so sure; something inside me had shifted.

I put my head down and went back to my work, a smile on my face and a new-found energy pumping through my bloodstream.

It's almost midday, the café will soon be occupied with lunch clientele so Ben decides it's time to go. I leave with him, both of us nodding goodbye to Doris.

I often wonder what she thought we were doing. She never asked, bless her. Just served us our coffee and exchanged comments about the weather.

As we step out into the rain, Ben smiles at me and taps my arm.

"Thanks, M," I'm only just getting used to his new term for me.

"For what?" I ask.

"For this, it's amazing what floods back to me as we do this. Things I had completely forgotten are resurfacing, and I'm quite enjoying it."

I smile back, feeling pleased with myself and he dashes off to his car; his mobile beeping, screaming for his attention, as always…

Chapter 3

Bordering on Broke

"Tell me something about your childhood."

I can sense his hesitancy; he had already emphasized prior to the start of this project that his private life should remain just that, private.

"I just want to get a sense of background," I explain, and I can see he is considering this.

"Ok," Ben finally nods.

⁺1958⁺

I was an only child, something that I think played a huge part in who I am today.

I often wonder if it was only child syndrome that brought about my materialistic side later in life, or was it simply because we had very little money back then. Maybe both?

We lived in a tiny little two-bedroomed council house; a dull-yellow, mid-terraced made of brick, with a tiny front garden that was screened by a dwarf wall.

There was no heat at all in the bedrooms and we only had electric blankets to keep us warm at night. In the mornings, I would stand in front of the gas fire in the kitchen to get dressed because it was so cold.

I dressed like a Victorian child back then, in a grubby white t-shirt that was two sizes too big for me. Torn, baggy jeans were held up around my skinny waist by a tatty elastic belt and I wore threadbare dirty plimsolls.

I stare pointedly at the words 'Hugo Boss' on Ben's shirt and he laughs.

"Ha, yes, I guess that inspired my love of good clothes. But these were the post war years, my parents were bordering on broke."

"That can't have been easy for them?" I cautiously pry.

Ben raises his eyebrows.

"Certainly not the best start in life." He agrees. "I guess it may explain some of Mum's little foibles."

I'm not a journalist but my ears perk up here. I take a deep breath and steel myself.

"Care to expand?"

He smiles wearily…

I have a very early memory of my mum shutting me in the pantry. There were no fridges in my young days and the forerunner to the humble fridge was a food cupboard; a pantry.

I was playing on the stairs for some reason and I guess Mum was having a bad day. I honestly don't know what exactly I had done to cause her temper, but she suddenly grabbed my arm, dragged me from the stairs and marched me into the pantry. I was crying and struggling to get free as Mum pushed me inside and shut the door, latching it from the outside. I was screaming so much that I was sure the lady next door must have heard me.

I can remember that pantry so vividly, it had a musty aroma; tainted with the earthy smell of vegetables, and just a tiny glass-block high above the shelves to let in a tiny crack of light.

My heart beat wildly as I thumped my fists against the door, desperate to get out of that dark, confined space.

I'm not sure how long I was in there for; it may not have even been an hour. But to my six-year old mind, it felt like an eternity. Eventually, exhausted from banging on the door, I crouched down on the cold, hard floor and sobbed.

"Mum, Mum," I called, tears streaming down my face.

I'm stunned and my heart goes out to the six-year old Ben. Despite this occurring almost sixty years ago, I get the sense this memory still disturbs Ben now.

"It wasn't that bad really, just oddities I sometimes dwell on, neither Mum or Dad ever beat me as such."

"As such?"

Ben dismisses my question with a wave of his hand and I quickly drop the matter.

I don't really blame Mum, we all have our moments, and she had endured and survived such unbelievable hardships growing up, I think she was entitled to blow a fuse every now and then.

When you're young and things aren't going right it's so easy to blame your parents for all those things that make you the person you are. The sins of our fathers, I believe the saying goes. But you can't dodge the truth; your genes, your upbringing and the people you surround yourself with all have an impact on the adult you become.

Personally, I realise my parents did what they could. They were who they were and I know they tried their best.

Although Mum and Dad were technically bordering on broke, I, like most kids, still had fun. There were seaside holidays where we would go rock pooling or play cricket on the beach until sunset.

I was allowed to roam free, wherever I wanted to, with all my friends. We went into the woods or played by lakes and occasionally over the viaduct towards the busy road.

There really were no restrictions and it was great, but who in their right mind would let their kids do that today!

Of course, the most outstanding, and I believe significant memory from my childhood was when I was fourteen years old. It was 1966 and England had won the World Cup.

> *I smile and raise my eyebrows as Ben looks at me.*
> *"Unlikely you'll ever see England win a World Cup."*
> *I nod and roll my eyes, Ben is probably right.*
> *"It's why I feel so privileged to have been around to witness such an historic sporting moment. I wonder if by the time my grandchildren read this, we'll have won another."*
> *I laugh, "I doubt that very much!"*
> *"True," Ben agrees gloomily and we continue.*

My mum and dad were definitely hard workers and their attitude and work ethic was first class.

They always had a strong desire to carve out a better life and my dad not only had his own decorating business but he also joined a self-build scheme.

Mum gave him full support, and together they spent nearly two years working weekends and evenings alongside their actual jobs, dedicated to the scheme.

I'll never forget their struggle to finance the build and I was sixteen years old when we moved into the three-bedroomed semi-detached house they had built.

That move may have been what inspired my own love of new builds.

Compared with our old council house, it felt as though we had moved into a palace.

Suddenly we were posh; we had new carpets, central heating, a modern kitchen and even a telephone, albeit a shared line. Good job Dad!

Years later, my dad's business partner was found to have been fiddling the books and the company went bust. Anything that was left was taken over by another company whom my dad served out his final years with as an office based employee, until retirement.

As a result of this, my dad suffered a nervous breakdown.

I suppose, in hindsight, maybe Dad was a little naive to trust a business partner with *all* the finances. Maybe things would have been different if, like me, he had had a business guardian angel.

"A business guardian angel?"

Ben looks at me and waits for me to make the connection.

"Ah," I say, as the penny finally drops. "Stan."

He nods.

Chapter 4

Read The Peter Principle

+1974+

After my last meeting with Stan, I was nervous and excited at the prospect of meeting Maurice Newton.

One afternoon, as the office buzzed with activity, all our eyes on profits and bonus, it finally happened; the door swung open and in strode the great man himself.

Maurice had a presence about him and I remember how the whole office fell silent. He didn't just enter a room he commanded it, with an almost hubristic nature.

"John," he bellowed, "may I have a word with young Ben here?"

John Stone practically stood to attention, "Yes, Mr Newton, of course."

It was very old school; no one would dare call him Maurice. He bounded over to my drawing board and shook my hand with a grip of steel.

"Pleased to meet you, Ben. You must be doing something right when I hear your name."

His body language was inspiring. He placed his hand on my shoulder, slightly tilting his head to one side and looked me directly in the eye whilst he spoke.

Despite my nerves at this visit by the great man, I felt exhilarated at being the object of his attention.

Maurice was just under six-foot with silver hair that was combed back and fell at the top of his collar. He was sixty-two years old, drove a two-seater sports car and regularly surfed. He looked the part, and by that, I mean the slick CEO of a public company. He was always smartly dressed, usually with a jacket, an open neck shirt and a cravat. He was so charismatic, there was an aura about him and, in that moment, I understood why he was so respected.

He quickly pulled over a chair and sat next to me so I turned my own chair to face him, hoping this would create an open, welcoming impression.

"So how have you settled in?" His first tact of making small talk was to make me feel at ease, but I was learning quickly, and with an air of confidence I didn't really feel, I looked him directly in the eyes and replied.

"I like the challenge," I grinned, "and the rewards."

Maurice chuckled. "Well that, old boy, is what makes everyone here so driven." Then, rather enthusiastically, he asked, "Now let me see, what is it you're doing, Ben?"

I took him through my system of checks and showed him that since we'd started using it as a team, we'd gone from an eighty percent chance of shortages to more than an eighty percent chance of getting it right.

"Very impressive, very impressive," Maurice murmured and I caught Dave winking at me out of the corner of my eye.

"Look, Ben." Maurice looked at me and I swallowed, my mouth dry. "I want to trial this with all the teams," he paused, "are you ok with that?"

In my mind, I replied. *Whoa Mo, yes, but I expect a cut of the other team's savings.*

Instead, which I was soon to discover was the correct response, I nodded enthusiastically.

"Yes, Mr. Newton, of course. I would be proud to have everyone use it."

What the hell was I thinking? There I'd been, sweating time and energy to hatch a money-making tool, and in an instant I was falling over myself to be subservient in giving it away.

I guess I was still growing out of my shy, naive phase but the truth is any other answer right then would have sent a different message and may have had a different outcome in the long term.

And so it was, the Ben Taylor system was rolled out to all the teams.

"Impressive," I say, and I am genuinely impressed.

Ben smiles modestly. "Probably, but there were other career options that, at the time, I wanted to explore too."

I raise an eyebrow, by now used to having to coax information from him.

"Such as?"

It was my third attempt at starting my own business. I'd wandered into a sports wholesaler called R4 Sports to buy some shuttlecocks and squash balls. R4 was a short walk away from the office and I would often take a quick lunch break, eating a sandwich while at the same time literally running around to the store.

The couple who ran the store were friendly and the prices were a fraction of high-street prices. They had a little warehouse stocked with all sorts of sportswear and equipment and it got me thinking. That entrepreneurial gene was kicking in…

The following week I went back and agreed a discount on volume purchases, and over the next few months I set up a trading company called 'Elizabeth Gold'.

I actually earned good cash by selling printed t-shirts for football clubs, as well as sourcing sports equipment; athletics wear, rackets, tennis balls and such for friends.

Of course, it wasn't to last. The lack of time and the pressure as my career began to take off meant I eventually had to give it up.

I was kind of proud of myself though, and whenever I had some rare spare time, my mind would wander back to my childhood days, trying to understand just where this kind of ingenuity came from.

"Where do you think it came from?"

He looks thoughtful and I wait patiently as he ponders my question.

"I suppose looking back there were shades of it during my school years. Although my real education came from learning on the ground, in the cut throat bear pit that was work."

"That and Stan," I smile.

"Yep, with Stan's guidance too, honing my natural drive. Though as a child, I think I had already begun to discover those rare moments of ingenuity."

Ben bursts out laughing as he clearly remembers one such incident and I pick up my pen…

I was, admittedly, a bit of a prankster, which earned me one or two spankings.

I would run home to my mum with a big red mark on my bum and she would just say, "You must have deserved it." I probably did.

I certainly deserved one when I sat my woodwork test at eleven years old.

By now I was fully aware of my lack of ability in wood work. We were tasked with building a stool which involved dove tail joints. Those joints were tricky and, for me, if felt like it was impossible to get right unless you were a born carpenter. So what do you do when you're up against it? Well, not what I did. Though, I must have been thinking outside of the box when I planed my friend's name off his work and replaced it with mine. Then, to finish off a genius piece of deception, I put Colin's name on my monstrosity. Upon inspection in the next lesson, the woodwork teacher grabbed my ear and dragged me over to my new masterpiece. He held it up to my face.

"Taylor, do you really think I'm so stupid as to believe you could create dove tail joints like this?"

"Erm, no sir." I respectfully replied…

I'm laughing too now. "That's outrageous!"
"But genius as well, right?"
And through my giggles I can't help but agree.

Back at work, under John Stone's leadership, I had become full of confidence and was intrigued as to what path Stan had engineered for me.

I was enthusiastic and ambitious but I felt things just weren't moving fast enough. I had so many questions, and with curiosity building inside my head, I asked Stan for a meeting. Mr Lenz, as I always politely addressed him, agreed to see me. He was Stan in my head but not in the office.

Bracing myself for the wave of smoke that would embrace me, I knocked on his office door. I had gone through, over and over in my head, what I planned to say to Stan, so sitting down opposite him I leapt straight to the point.

"Mr Lenz, you said you wanted to engineer a path for me, I'm anxious to know more detail."

Stan looked at me with a wry smile, and, I like to think, a little admiration.

"Ben," he replied, and as usual he paused. "If you run much faster you will fall over. I said I would take you under my wing and guide you, but Ben, you have to trust me on that. Patience is a virtue. You are not ready. You have barely been here a few months, drafting and learning about our products."

I gave him a puzzled look, not liking what I'd heard, and leapt to my own defence.

"But the draughtsman job is easy for me," I hastily replied, "and I know I can take on more."

Stan tilted back in his chair, lighting yet another cigarette so that I had to endure his usual slow response as the room filled with more smoke. I clenched and unclenched my fists at my side, my frustration building.

"Ben, if we move you too fast and you fail, we'll have a far bigger hill to climb."

For me it was always about the climb, like the song; *I can almost see it, that dream I'm dreaming, but there's a voice inside my head saying you'll never reach it.*

In my case, that voice was Stan. Did he no longer believe I had the gear?

Stan picked up his pen, scribbled a note and pushed it across the table.

"There," he said, "I want you to go and buy this book and read it thoroughly. It's 'The Peter Principal'. When you're done, let's chat again."

A book, I thought. *I want to forge a career, to challenge myself, and he tells me to read a fricking book!*

I sat there in stunned silence for a few seconds, wondering

whether to tell him to stick his literary recommendations, and his job, up his arse. He simply watched me, almost reading my mind, as though daring me to do such a thing, blowing his little blue rings of smoke into the air.

"Anything else, Ben?" His question hung heavily in the thick atmosphere of the room.

"No sir," I stood up, thanked him for his time and left his office.

Well that's it then, I thought, *there's no career here. He is making excuses but I know I am ready.*

I wondered whether this was a sign. Was Stan really to be trusted?

No, I decided. *I'm going to leave and go back to the States...*

"What is The Peter Principle?" I ask, but Ben is already shaking his head and standing up.

"Enough for today," he smiles wearily at me, "I'll tell you tomorrow."

As he strides out of the café, I watch his departing back and pick up my phone with a sigh.

"Fine," I mutter to myself, "I'll bloody google it then..."

...The Peter Principle is a concept in management theory formulated by Laurence J. Peter in which the selection of a candidate for a position is based on the candidate's performance in their current role, rather than on abilities relevant to the intended role.

Chapter 5

That's Where Mary Comes In

The following morning, Ben breezes into the café, clearly in good spirits as we settle down with our coffee and continue.

"So, did you quit and go back to the States after that meeting with Stan?"

"Well, no," he smiles fondly, "you see, that's where Mary comes in…"

+1974+

Despite my misgivings with Stan after our last meeting, I still harboured hopes that he really was trying to guide my career path, that maybe, somehow, he really was my business guardian angel. So, I decided to get my head down and work hard to prove to him I was capable of more responsibility.

During this time, my good friend and footballing buddy Barry had invited me to join he and his girlfriend on a blind date with her friend, Mary.

I remember standing at the bar of our local pub with Barry

when the two girls walked in. I'd never been nervous with women before but when I took my first look at Mary, the attraction hit me like a bullet train. Her dark hair and deep soulful eyes had me completely floored and it took me a few minutes to gather myself before I could finally muster up the confidence to talk to her.

"Would you like a drink?"

Her dark eyes gazed at me shyly and she nodded, asking for an orange juice.

We sat down in a far corner of the pub with our drinks, the four of us making polite small talk until Barry and his girlfriend started smooching each other.

"Get a room…" I muttered, rolling my eyes at Mary.

The delicate tinkling sound when she giggled lifted my heart, and in that instant, I knew I was smitten. With the ice broken between us, we talked and talked and we didn't realise how much time had passed until the bell rang for last orders.

"Where did that time go?" I looked at my watch in surprise and Mary smiled.

"I guess time flies when you're having fun." She looked at me, a rose-pink blush forming on her pretty face.

"Can I see you again?" I suddenly asked, all my composure gone. I simply had to see this girl again.

"Yes, I'd like that." The relief I felt at Mary's reply surprised me.

Keep it together, Ben! I berated myself, but actually I was enjoying the warm feeling that seemed to have ignited from within me.

Over the following months, we began to see each other more and more frequently, but in the back of my mind, I felt I should exercise caution.

My friend, John, was still making plans for our return to the States, and I had enough to buy a ticket. I mean this had been my game plan all along, hadn't it?

Now though, I had doubts. On the one hand, I knew John and I would have a blast travelling the US again, and with my faith in Stan slightly shaken this seemed like the perfect time.

On the other hand, though, I still felt like my career wasn't done yet, that I had so much more to give and prove, to myself and Stan.

Aside from that, I had really fallen for Mary and the thought of leaving her behind tore me up inside.

It brought back long since buried memories of a previous girlfriend, Janet, whose family had been in a cult religion.

Janet and I had fallen in love and enjoyed a memorable Spring/Summer relationship. I really had thought she was the one.

However, by the Autumn, Janet had decided to join the cults secret organisation and go abroad, which meant she could have no more contact with the outside world.

When she left, it broke my heart, I was devastated and knew there and then that it would take a special woman for me to ever fall in love again.

And here she was, Mary.

Could I really pass up this chance of love and happiness?

It was decision time, should I listen to my heart or my head?

We are both silent as I finish scribbling and look up at him. This really is the closest Ben has got to talking about his personal feelings and I can sense it isn't something he is completely comfortable with.

"Did you...?" I swallow and clear my throat, not sure whether I should push him any further today. "What did you decide?" I finally stammer.

At that moment, Doris, bustling behind the counter, drops a plate and the startling chink of broken china makes us both jump.

"Sorry, my lovelies!" Doris shouts across to us and we both smile, but the moment is lost and my heart sinks as Ben stands up.

"I'm done for today." He smiles mischievously at my frustrated sigh, loving how he keeps me hanging, then with a shout of thanks to Doris and a nod of his head to me, he is gone.

By now I am used to these abrupt endings to our meetings but I still can't help feeling disappointed that he doesn't quite seem to completely trust me yet. It confuses me, sometimes he is so open; almost enjoying sharing his memories with me. Then other times, like today, he will instantly become a closed book; an enigma that almost feels too exhausting to work out.

I drain the last of my coffee, pick up my things, and with a resigned farewell to Doris I also leave, vowing to myself that when we next meet, Ben isn't getting off that lightly again.

Fortunately, when we do meet again, he is in an open mood and happy to pick up where we left off…

It was with only slight ruefulness that I finally told John I wouldn't be joining him in the Northern Territories. I had made my decision…

I really had been captivated from the moment I saw Mary. She wasn't just lovely on the outside, she was a thoughtful, caring and loving woman, and most of all, she understood me. She knew what made me tick, knew how to calm me when I was feeling under pressure and she made me feel happy.

The realisation came one night when Mary and I were fooling around on the sofa.

She was laying across me, gazing at me with her beautiful dark brown eyes; I got lost in those eyes, and as she swept her long brown hair to one side, it hit me. It was one of those surreal moments. I just knew that I wanted to spend the rest of my life with this woman and I wanted to be the one to make her happy, forever…

John took it well, was happy for me even, and he set off to the States again, this time with Gus.

With my decision now made, and feeling very grown up and responsible, I went out and bought the book Stan had recommended; The Peter Principle.

Once I'd read it, what Stan had said suddenly became much clearer to me. He was pointing out the importance of taking small steps, of allowing me to gain experience in every role and then for him to be sure, with his experience, that I could handle the next level of responsibility. The point was that there were two levels of responsibility; one being your own, ensuring you're ready for the responsibility yourself, and the other being of the company, to follow their own due diligence and make absolutely sure the role is right for you before offering promotion.

With this revelation, my passion and excitement for my career was re-ignited and I felt ready to throw myself head first down the professional and personal paths I had chosen.

Starting with my decision to propose to Mary...

I clap my hands and squeal here and Ben rolls his eyes at me.
"What?" I ask indignantly, "I love a bit of romance!"
He chuckles and shakes his head good-humoredly. "I can assure you, M, it was far from romantic."

I was still slightly lacking in confidence emotionally, after my previous rejection by Janet, so I think I deliberately approached it as a business proposition, just to hedge my bets.

"If I asked you to marry me, would you?"

Don't get me wrong, it wasn't quite as formal as it sounds, I was gazing lovingly into her eyes at the time.

To my amazement, and relief, Mary said yes and I remember my heart swelling with love whilst at the same time my head raced with thoughts that with marriage came parenthood.

How would I compare to my parents?

"Were you close to your dad?"

Ben takes a moment to think about this. "Sometimes, I suppose," he replies, clearly reflecting.

"We had some things in common; Dad was also into his music, although he liked brass bands, not really my cup of tea. He actually played the trumpet and the bugle, and on each Remembrance Day he would play 'Last Post' at the church."

Ben pauses in contemplation and I give him a moment to gather himself.

"On Dad's eightieth birthday, through the pain of the cancer that was killing him, he played his last post. That music touches me still now, every time I hear it."

I smile sadly at Ben. "He sounds like he was one hell of a strong man."

Ben nods animatedly, "Dad was a pretty tough guy, a former boxer."

"You never got into boxing?"

Ben chuckles, "No, I didn't, not for Dads lack of trying."

He sighs wistfully now.

"No, for me it was simply football, football, football…"

For me, football was and still is the greatest game on Earth. There really is no other sport like it.

My passion began and was encouraged when my dad took me to my first ever match at a London based club when I was just four years old. From then I was hooked and just wanted to spend any free time I had playing it. I'd play it out on the streets, which back then were somewhat emptier of the cars that adorn any average street now, or on any available green space. My friends and I would simply drop our jumpers on the ground to use as makeshift goalposts.

When I first played during my infant school years, everybody kept telling me how good at it I was. So, by the time I'd failed my eleven plus and gone to secondary school, I was convinced I would be a professional football player.

It was in my first year that the PE teacher lined us all up during a lesson and asked us to each, in turn, knee the ball back to him.

When it came to my turn, he threw it straight at my midriff. It took a couple of knee jangles but I kneed it straight back at him.

He caught the ball and looked at me. "What's your name, son?"

"Ben," I replied sheepishly.

"Do that again for me, exactly the same, hold it up and knee it back, ok?"

I nodded and he threw the ball at me again, I kneed it twice and then straight back at him.

"Perfect!" He clapped his hands and looked at the other lads. "Now that's what I want to see from all of you."

It was a strange moment but one that made me further believe in my own skill.

The trouble was, apart from Dad, who was useless at football, I had no real coaching or encouragement from anyone.

Sure, Dad tried to make me tougher in the tackle, but then he'd been trying to toughen me up ever since he had me punching the life out of a four-foot high, blow-up Yogi Bear from aged four! Not quite the same, but nice try Dad.

We both smile.

"So, did your footballing career ever take off?"

He shrugs here, "I think maybe it could have, if I'm honest. But we'll come back to that…"

His mobile rings and Ben rolls his eyes at me as he takes the call, which is clearly of an urgent matter because when he ends the call he stands up to leave.

"Sorry, M, urgent business. Laters!" He darts out of the café and I stare open-mouthed at his retreating form.

"Where's he off to in such a hurry?"

I turn in response to Doris, "I honestly have no idea." I shake my head as Doris chuckles away to herself and then I open my notebook and begin to write.

Chapter 6

It's All about Your Mindset

I was gradually becoming somewhat used to Ben's elusiveness and evasiveness by now, as well as with the way he likes to be in control of this process; of what we discuss and as to when he feels ready to talk about certain areas of his life.

This was fine with me; with each meeting, I was gathering more and more detail and insight into what made Ben, well, Ben.

Every evening I'd pour over my notes, taking out what I didn't consider relevant and keeping aside what I did, ready for when it was time to shape it.

However, I was impatient, and Ben was a busy man so couldn't afford me as much time as I would have liked.

When I next see him, I explain that I am finding the slow pace a little frustrating.

He smiles, "I understand that, M, but this will take time. It's not something to be rushed, and you know..." he pauses, a huge grin on his face as another memory comes to him, "patience is a virtue..."

✦1976✦

Back at work, time just flew by as I worked from early in the morning till late in the evenings, grafting hard to forge my career. I was still anxiously waiting to see what Stan had planned for me, but by now I wasn't dwelling on it as much and was resigned to the fact that Stan would let me know when it was time.

We still had our regular chats where Stan would deliver his words of wisdom and I soon became reliant on his teachings.

Then, finally, one day Stan called me in for another chat. On this occasion, however, it wasn't simply for more guidance talks.

The atmosphere felt different from the moment I stepped into that smoky old office of his.

I could see he was busy, distracted even. Or maybe he was just excited about his next words to me.

"Ben," he was eager, gone were the usual long, thoughtful pauses in between chugs of his cigarette. "I reckon you are now ready for the next role. You read The Peter Principal, right?"

My heart leapt in my chest. This was it; my moment. I nodded.

"And you now understand my previous caution?"

I wanted to scream, to shout, "Yes! I get it! Now tell me, please!"

Instead, I nodded once again and I watched Stan's face; even he couldn't betray his feelings.

"I have created an opportunity for you to take on the responsibility of financial controller."

My heart missed a beat as I digested his words.

"As you've seen from within your team, it's a very different role, but it will give you an immediate insight into accounting," he continued.

I was already nodding my approval, "I am sure I can handle it."

Stan smiled. "Yes, we are too. Which is why you're starting tomorrow. We're moving the current financial controller, Alan, to another team, so you can spend the rest of this week handing over from him."

My mind was working overtime as I took in his words and one question was in my head that I couldn't suppress, so I jumped straight in.

"Is there more money for that responsibility?" Well come on, you must know by now, I'm motivated by money, anyone that says they aren't is a liar, or poor.

Stan smiled and gave his usual nod.

"You see, Ben, that's why we think you'll do fine. You're motivated by your career and its rewards and you're not afraid to admit it. I like that."

I smiled, though in my head I was thinking, "That's all very well but cut to the chase, Stan, more money or not?"

As if reading my thoughts, he lit a cigarette and looked me squarely in the eye.

"The short answer is no, not straight away, you need to prove yourself. Do a good job, Ben, and I will review you again in six months. Meanwhile, we will have our regular chats and make sure you're not drowning. How does that sound?"

Of course, I was disappointed that the rewards were not to be immediate, but I could also see that this was a fantastic opportunity for me.

The role of financial controller was to send out valuations and invoices, chase outstanding money and calculate the monthly profits and loss; a far cry from real accounting but it was to give me some insight into it.

Whilst it was very different from my current role, I was excited but still rather nervous.

Did I really want to be in management? At this stage in my career I wasn't convinced that I was cut out for all that. But no one was going to tell me a job would drown me! By even suggesting that, Stan had lain down the gauntlet, and well, you know me when it comes to a challenge…

"Ha ha, never tell you that you can't, hey?" I smile.

"It's like a red rag to a bull with me." Ben admits with a laugh. "Can't do means will do."

I study him and I realise this is true. He really is a determined man, somebody who will not give up without giving something his all. As I slowly begin to understand the man I am working for, a few of his personality traits stand out for me.

It is clear that whilst he is a very private person, he is also generous in nature, fair but firm, somebody who will back you one hundred percent. Cross him, however, and that's your lot.

Fortunately, I haven't crossed him yet.

Meanwhile, a year had passed since our wedding on a cloudy Saturday afternoon. It had been a frugal affair; neither of our parents had the resources to make it a grand occasion, but Mary and I were happy and in love.

I had stood there in my cream suit, with John from my travelling days cracking jokes to calm my nerves, and it felt like I was having an out of body experience. I was tense and nervous but at the same time incredibly excited.

When the church organ began to play and the chatter in the church died down, I turned to look back up at the aisle. And there was Mary, with her proud dad by her side. My heart felt like it would burst with pride, she looked absolutely stunning.

As we took our vows, I'd never felt more emotional.

The reception was at a local social club with Mary's mum and my mum providing the home-cooked buffet.

After a brief stay with my parents whilst it was being built, we now owned a small but brand new semi-detached house which was local to work, and I often thought in astonishment at how my life had changed.

From simply wanting to bum around on Miami beaches, I was now married with my own home and a prosperous career ahead of me.

The career part, though, wasn't going so great. I never admitted it to anyone at the time, barely even to myself, but I was finding it tough.

Whilst I loved adding up the profit, I hated the balancing and the chasing money side of it and I was already desperate to move on to what Stan had next in store for me.

It was through that finance role that I met the head of finance, Peter Coleman.

There are some people in this world that you have an immediate connection with and there are those you don't. Peter came in the latter category for me; he had the face and mannerisms of someone I just knew I was going to dislike.

Now, I'd made mistakes by judging some people too quickly in the past, so I was prepared to reserve judgement, although, nine times out of ten, the chemistry that someone gives off is enough. Coleman was in his late thirties, tall with short fawn–coloured hair and he wore lightweight, steel–rimmed glasses that sat forward on his grumpy looking face.

With his oversized shirts that he always dressed with narrow bland ties, he had no real dress sense whatsoever. His limp hand shake, which to me showed a sign of weakness, was contradicted by his tone when he spoke; sharp and commanding.

Stan always said never judge people too quickly and he had taught me to deal with it slightly differently.

"Ben," he'd said one day, "we have to change your submissive body language. You have a good firm hand shake but I detect shyness, weakness and a lack of confidence as you come into my space."

My eyes widened at the time. *Wow, thanks Stan, I sound really pathetic!*

But Stan drove into me just how important first impressions were in business.

"You need that look in your eyes, a confident opening smile with a firm handshake and a dominating first few words."

He'd often have me doing role play; practising my stance and my demeanour until it was what he considered as, 'in the shop window'.

Then he went to work on my mindset.

"Ben, what's in your mind when you first meet someone?"

I hesitated before admitting that I just got an immediate sense of whether I liked somebody or not.

"Yes, yes exactly!" he said enthusiastically, "but now I want you to have a different mindset.

You need to be indifferent as to whether or not people like *you,* you need to see *them* as an arsehole, no matter what they portray on the outside or the inside."

I stuttered in amazement. "An arsehole?"

Stan chuckled at my shocked reaction.

"Yep, from now on, everyone you meet should now be in that category until they earn your respect." I was laughing too at this stage as he went on, "And until they earn it, they stay an arsehole."

Which leads me nicely back to Peter Coleman; he *was* an arsehole, and unfortunately that's how he would remain.

Coleman disliked me intensely and the feeling was mutual. He was full of arrogance and showed me unnecessary hostility from day one. I don't know why, maybe he thought I was a young upstart who needed putting down. He certainly wasn't one to encourage me, in fact I'd go so far as to say he was a bully, constantly trying to intimidate me.

As I've said previously, my dad had taught me from an early age that all bullies deserved was a bloody nose. What I didn't know at the time is that I would later be engaged with one of the worst kind of bullies; a devious nemesis.

Now though, I was about to learn a very different, more mature tactic.

Business was yet to unfold some ugly challenges, some of which to many may seem insurmountable.

"He sounds awful." I shiver.

Ben nods, "It was quite challenging for so early on in my career. But like with all things, you use them as a learning curve."

"So, what happened, what did you do?"

"Well don't forget, I had Stan in my corner…"

By now I was unloading on Stan like he was my therapist.

"Ben," he would say, "this is business. If you don't design your own life plan, the chances are you'll fall into someone else's plan. And guess what plans Coleman has for you?"

Well he hadn't needed to ask that, that was plain as the nose on Stan's face. Coleman wanted me out.

Stan looked at me intensely. "Seriously Ben, if you can't cope with the likes of Coleman, you'd better go back to drawing."

I knew he was testing me, pushing my buttons, knowing full well that I'd never go backwards. I'd never gone back on anything in my life and I wasn't about to do so now.

I decided to stand up to Peter Coleman, I had no choice if I wanted to progress within the company.

He continued trying to put me down, but on reflection it simply made me stronger

I knew I had a short temper, like my dad, but Stan taught me to control it, to use it as an asset. He encouraged me to look for the positives in any situation, to take a step back and be patient. I quickly discovered that by distancing myself for a while from a situation, I could control and use my temperament to be ruthless in a productive and authoritative way.

"It's all about your mindset, Ben." Stan repeatedly told me, and he was right. I became tougher as a result, some might say ruthless even.

I hadn't found Maurice to be particularly ruthless and I wondered how he operated, so one day I asked Stan.

Stan disagreed with me. "Maurice is not only *extremely* ruthless but he's tactically clever and calculating. He's a gentleman and a motivator. He is passionate, enthusiastic and has a deep desire to succeed at all costs. You really wouldn't want to see the switch in him if someone crosses the line."

My eyes widened. "Wow, that's what I want to be like!" I exclaimed. "Can you teach me to be like that?"

Stan burst out laughing. In fact, he laughed so much, he had a coughing fit.

I blushed bright red and inwardly cursed myself for my eager puppy moment, then Stan composed himself and smiled.

"What Maurice has is a natural talent," he said solemnly. "It's rare to have that and if you haven't, we can only sharpen what you *do* have."

I nodded, feeling enthusiastic again, but Stan's expression changed in a flash.

"If you don't have what it takes, you're going back to drawing, Ben."

Stan had these moments where he was tough with me and I knew it was his way of making me 'man up' but in that instant, my heart missed a beat. One sign of weakness from me, and I wouldn't be moving on to the next level.

"Well you obviously did?" I say, always enjoying hearing about Stan. That guy seemed like he had really wanted Ben to do well.

I wonder what happened to him and make a mental note to ask Ben one day soon.

"Perhaps I was too eager, if that's possible." He ponders.

"No such thing as too much ambition, surely?"

"Well, no," he agrees, "but don't forget The Peter Principle. You read it, right?"

He is watching me intensely now and I blush slightly.

"Well, I erm..."

"Tut-tut, M," he's teasing me. Again.

"I googled it," I finally admit with a little laugh and to my relief he laughs too.

"So, you understand the concept, and why Stan was keen to make sure I was prepared?"

"Yes, of course. Though, I think Stan had your back from day one."

He seems almost surprised by this and he looks at me quizzically.

"You're right. It's strange, with Stan there was never any personal relationship. No asking how the family were or anything like that. But he really did believe in me, career wise."

"And how were the family at this time?" I probe with a sly smile on my face...

Mary and I had talked about starting a family and with my career going from strength to strength and us settled in our home, now seemed the perfect time.

On the day we became three, I was a wreck.

I stood in the operating theatre, shuffling from one foot to the other feeling completely useless as chaos seemed to unfold around me.

I was struggling to breathe and felt myself starting to faint. Get a grip, I repeatedly told myself, watching the doctors and nurses going about their work.

I'll never forget the moment our daughter entered the world; a beautiful little baby with a mop of black hair

Up until this point, my priorities had been Mary, of course, and my career.

The moment you become a parent though, that changes. Everything you've done, everything you thought you wanted to do is no longer important. All that matters is that precious child that you are now responsible for. As I gazed into the eyes of our daughter, she blinked up at me and I felt an overwhelming feeling of joy as well as the weight of responsibility. I just wanted to hold her in my arms and protect her forever from the big wide world that awaited her.

"I'll look after you, little one." I whispered, cradling my first born. It was a vow I would keep.

I wipe my eyes with my sleeve. "That's so beautiful," I sigh.

Ben also appears to be quite choked up and I almost laugh at his awkwardness.

As always though, the moment passes and he slaps my arm playfully, "Man up, M! As Stan would say; let's get back to business!"

Chapter 7

Never Trust Anyone

+1977+

Over time, I'd really settled into the role of financial controller and I felt I was ready for the next stage. I rather boldly requested a meeting with Stan and announced to him that I felt I was ready for the labour controller position. The labour controller was responsible for the total planning and organising of an on-site team spread across middle England which was made up of about forty guys and a site supervisor.

I never expected for one minute that Stan would agree and I was pretty much ready for the brush off.

To my amazement though, Stan, after lighting a cigarette, nodded and said, "As it happens, Ben, I have a new team being set up next month."

I waited with baited breath for him to continue.

"I've been wondering whether to put you into that team as labour controller." He nodded to himself as if satisfied that he was making the right decision.

I realised then just how right I had been to push things.

Without good timing, and my own determination, I may well have missed this window of opportunity. It was another valuable lesson learned.

Stan waited for me to say something and I was suddenly hit with the reality of the situation.

What about the bonus? Would this new team make a bonus?

Stan, ever perceptive, raised a questioning eyebrow. "Well?"

"That's erm, great," I stuttered, "but..."

"You're unsure now, aren't you?"

"No, no," I quickly recovered myself. "It's fine, I'm just wondering about the bonus."

Maybe I shouldn't have said that but hey, this was my business guardian angel, he was on my side, wasn't he? I continued nevertheless.

"I've worked hard with that team to set up our bonus." It sounded like a pathetic argument but it was true.

Stan replied without hesitation. "Then you will work hard in the new team to achieve the same." I understood that but I still had to fight my case and I jumped straight in.

"You promised me more salary if I could handle the responsibility." I was calm, trying not to sound like a petulant child and I think Stan could see that.

"Leave that with me," Stan replied after a pause, "I'll take a look at it."

My heart was quite literally racing. Had I just behaved like a bull in a china shop by not thinking things through? Or was I just following my determined plan to climb my way to the top?

That night when I took the news home to Mary, she was excited for me, for us.

"But what if I'm forcing things too quickly," I sighed, sitting at the dinner table with my head in my hands. As always, Mary was the calming influence.

She sat down opposite me and took my hands within hers.

"You're ambitious and determined, Ben," she smiled encouragingly at me as she squeezed my hands, "and it looks like it may be about to pay off."

She was right. For the first time in a long time, I was involved in something that meant a lot to me, something I wanted desperately to succeed at. Something I had started to feel I was

good at...

+ + +

On the first day of my new role, I took a deep breath and pushed open the office door.

The sight that greeted me was not pretty; the office was pretty basic, old desks with papers strewn across their surfaces and a grubby worn carpet. It looked like, and actually was, an organisation in chaos.

Bracing myself, I walked in and a casually dressed young guy with short dark hair and black-rimmed glasses stood up to greet me.

"Ben" he shook my hand enthusiastically, "good morning. I'm Jim Castle." He had a well-spoken soft voice and a firm handshake. I immediately warmed to him.

Jim briefly showed me around and I quickly realised that the set up was identical to that of my old team, albeit with three draughtsmen and a finance controller.

Gesturing to a desk opposite him, he smiled at me. "Well, there's the hot seat, let's get started."

I sat down at my desk and swiveled around in the chair with a silent shout of triumph, a huge proud grin on my face.

The pressure was now on for me to succeed on the path that Stan had engineered for me.

"Stan had every faith in you though, didn't he?"

Ben shrugs, "Neither he nor I knew for sure that I would cope. In fact, the more I think about it, the more I realise that Stan took quite a gamble with me."

I had come a long way in just three short years under Stan's guidance.

Stan had explained to me at length that this particular position was one of huge responsibility and that he had given much consideration as to whether, at my tender age of twenty-five, I could cope.

He had questioned whether I would be tough enough, whether I could hack the stress, and whether I had it in me to carve out more profit from each project.

As my role evolved, in fact it never stopped evolving, I began to question where my own level of competence might be. I became filled with self-doubt which made me feel vulnerable.

On the outside though, to Stan and everyone else, I was demonstrating total confidence.

Those first few weeks were probably the toughest I had faced yet and I think Stan had prepped Jim to take me under his wing, to keep me from the wolves.

Jim was a very quiet and unassuming man, yet he was extremely confident and capable and I was in good hands.

I soon began to appreciate the power that I had within my role. It was my call as to where the site guys would go and what jobs they would get. I had forty odd guys that were split into a dozen teams of three or four men, led by a foreman who reported to me on a project by project basis.

However, these guys, or wolves as I had begun to think of them, were seasoned professionals and knew how to play the game. They all obviously wanted the best and most profitable jobs, as well as those closer to home, and I found myself very quickly running up against them as they bayed to control and manipulate me.

It became a battle ground; of logic, will, ruthlessness and negotiation. I had to learn so many skills and ensure that they were perfectly executed.

It demanded so much of me and initially I really struggled. On many an occasion, I would look up from a conversation with one of the 'wolves' and Jim would mouth quietly, "be tougher!".

As time passed though, I discovered my hidden strengths and I started to use them.

My confidence grew more and more. It was hard work but I soon found I was beginning to enjoy it, even though at times I'd look at my workload and just want to cry.

Jim would be there though, supportively telling me: "If you can't get it right, just get it done."

That statement summed me up perfectly. I would work at a thousand miles an hour, eating up ten tasks to anyone else's two. If I had four unfinished tasks, I was still three times more productive and I began to surpass myself with my thinking, planning and organisation skills.

Sure, I made mistakes, who doesn't? But Jim and Stan were always there to pick me up.

"Move on, Ben, we all make mistakes." Stan would reassure me. "What's critical is that you stop and learn from them, and that you don't make the same mistake again."

Ben smiles, "I can still hear him saying that now."

"And what's the biggest mistake you've ever learned from?" I want to know.

"DIY!" His instant answer makes me almost spit my coffee out over the table.

"Ha ha, DIY?"

"Ha ha, yeah, I once built a garage with my neighbour, Greg. I say built but it was a complete bodge-job. My DIY skills were awful, which surprised me as my dad was a hands-on plumber and my mum could easily turn her hand to a bit of DIY."

"So what happened?" I laugh.

"Well, the floorboards that had been taken out upstairs when the piping was put in collapsed and the garage continuously flooded!"

I am shaking with laughter as he regales me with more DIY disasters and then he becomes suddenly pensive...

"It was actually those little mishaps that made me determined to be in a position one day where I could afford my own DIY person, and I began to keep a diary of my dreams; my plans for the house I wanted to build, how much land I sought and the car I wanted to drive.

I had a passion and, I think, a flare for designing spaces. I have always liked drawing, and ever since my parents had designed their own self-build house, I had been intrigued by plans and planning. I can sit and look at good house plans for hours, they mesmerise me.

Strange then, that my career had taken itself in the direction of management, and I wondered if it would satisfy my desire to create..."

Before I knew it, I had been in my new role for almost a year and it had taken that time for the team to earn the same kind of bonuses I had been enjoying in my previous team.

By now, I had settled right in and really grown in confidence. I had surprised myself and I wondered if maybe Stan was making it sound harder than it really was.

I was eager for more, so the next time Stan called me in for a chat, I decided to put it to him.

"Mr. Lenz," I began after we'd made our usual small-talk. "I now know I am ready to be a contracts manager."

I was anxious not to come across as too pushy but I also wanted to portray my confidence in my ability.

Stan, used to my determination by now, showed no surprise and I knew he was about to roll out the old, "slow it down," speech.

He took in a deep breath, looking deliberately thoughtful as he spoke.

"Well, Ben, I can't deny that Jim thinks you're doing an amazing job."

I smiled and nodded, "I like Jim, he's been good for me, really encouraging and teaching me how to focus my short temper."

Stan laughed, "Yes, so I've heard."

I didn't ask him to elaborate for fear of straying away from the conversation I needed to have.

"Well, all I know is I'm ready now."

Stan leant back in his chair, studying me with a slight smile on his face. I was used to his mannerisms now and knew he was about to enlighten me with wise words.

"It's one thing having Jim there watching over you," Stan paused, of course he did, "but it's another being on your own. And that's the difference between taking full responsibility and letting Jim take the strain at the moment."

I had to concede Stan made a very good point, but it didn't take away from my initial disappointment.

My silence obviously made Stan pick up on that disappointment, and, as if to encourage me, he sat forward and slapped his desk.

"Tell you what, Ben, let's see where we can take this," I gasped with a smile and he continued, holding his hands up as if trying to reign my excitement in.

"Hey, I'm not promising anything but I've a meeting with Maurice next week."

I was like a nodding dog by now. "Absolutely Stan, erm, sorry, Mr. Lenz."

Stan chuckled as I left his office and went back to my desk, where I relayed the meeting to Jim.

I was a little deflated when he told me that he felt I needed to spend more time doing what I was doing, it felt a little like he was pissing on my parade.

I wasn't sure whether that was because he knew I was doing a great job and didn't want to lose me or that he genuinely thought I wasn't ready yet. Maybe it was both, but Stan had long since drummed it into me that I should never trust anyone in business.

"Keep everybody at arms-length," Stan had always said. "Never trust anyone."

At this point in time, I wondered if this applied to both Stan and Jim...

I'm astounded. "Seriously?"

Ben nods, a grim look on face. "I was beginning to feel a little paranoid. The buzz, adrenalin, call it what you will, was taking over. I was loving the pressure, thriving on it even. But believe me, Mandy, it can make you doubt even your biggest allies."

I shake my head, "But not Stan, surely?" I feel cheated myself, surely this man who had been the constant in the early career of my entrepreneur wasn't like that?

Ben's next words make me sigh with relief.

"No, never Stan. I had been wrong to doubt him."

A couple of weeks had passed since our last meeting when Stan asked to see me.

"Maurice has plans for you, Ben." My heart leapt in my chest as Stan continued, "but Maurice is also guided by my judgement."

I leaned forward, "Yes, of course." I agreed, desperate for him to go on.

"You need to trust us both on this, ok?"

Hang on a minute, I thought to myself, *you told me not to trust anyone.*

Now I was confused, I had learned to trust Stan, but Maurice and Jim?

Stan broke my train of thought. "The idea we're pushing around between us, Ben, is to get you in the London team."

I nodded, even though panic surged inside me. The London team was the hardest team with the most responsibility; everyone knew it was a bear pit.

"We are creating a new role, something we'll trial for six months, an assistant contracts manager position for you, reporting to Bernard."

Bernard ran the London team and was Onelock's top contracts manager. They were earning some serious bonus.

"You will be our first ever assistant contracts manager."

Stan sat back in his chair, a smug smile on his face as he waited for my response.

"Ok, but what happens after six months?" I was excited, intrigued as to what plans Maurice and Stan had carved out for me.

Stan nodded and picked up the phone.

"Yvonne, bring some tea up here," he ordered and I shook my head with a bewildered smile.

Tea with Stan, brought to us by his lovely assistant, Yvonne, could my day get any better?

"Ok," Stan slapped his desk and reached for his cigarettes. He leaned forward and spoke in a conspiratorial whisper.

"You are sworn to secrecy here, but all I can say at the moment is that we have a project waiting for board approval. It's to computerise our whole operation through automation, all of the drawing and scheduling. Think of it as taking your check schedules and making the process super-fast and guaranteed error free."

He stopped speaking as Yvonne arrived with the tea and I sat processing the information. This sounded like a challenge, and it was one I knew I had to accept.

Stan waited until Yvonne had left before he spoke again.

"Ben, there is not a word to be spoken about this outside of the office, and that includes your position with Bernard."

Fixing his eyes on me, he prodded the desk with his fingers. "Do I make myself clear?"

I smiled, enjoying being party to this secret plan, then I picked up my tea and nodded at Stan.

"You have my word," I promised.

It's late and I'm sitting at my computer typing up my notes when my email pings. It's Ben, cancelling our scheduled meeting for tomorrow.

With a sigh, I reply: "Ok, fine, when can you do? Plus, why are you up so late?"

His response comes in a few minutes later. "Not sure, busy with planning stuff…"

"Aargh!" I slam my hands on my desk and put my head in them in despair.

What planning stuff? He's never mentioned this to me before and I feel frustrated at his cryptic message.

And worse, I now have no idea when I will be able to find out from this elusive entrepreneur of mine.

Chapter 8

Keep Your Eye on the Ball

It is about a week later that we meet again and as soon as Ben arrives, I can see he is stressed. He looks tired and is clearly distracted, his phone to his ear as he sits in front of me.

I feel a surge of disappointment, I'd planned on discussing some personal things today but now I'm not so sure he'll be up for it, he seems totally wired.

Ben finishes his call and apologises to me, as he always does.

"So, that call, M, was our local councillor pushing me to prepare a traffic survey."

I'm puzzled, but pleased he is telling me. "Is this the planning stuff you'd mentioned?"

He nods, just as his phone starts ringing again. Quickly checking the caller ID, he declines to answer it. Hurrah, I think, we're making progress.

"Yes," he continues, "over the past two years we have won all seven of our hearings with greedy developers."

I raise an eyebrow, "But you're a build freak. Why would you oppose development?"

Ben laughs, "Yes, I am, but one that wants the building to work not only on the inside but on the outside too, with supporting infrastructure; things like roads, public transport, schools and health services."

I can't disagree with that and Ben, clearly on his soap box now, becomes excited as he talks.

"This country's infrastructure has been neglected by past governments, and in most towns and villages it's at breaking point."

I love hearing Ben's personal and political views but I'm beginning to think if I let him rant any further this book could end up being the size of War and Peace!

"So," he concludes, "we're now facing three more appeals. Honestly, M, it's like David and Goliath."

I laugh at his words and realise what it is that makes him tick.

"You still desire a challenge, don't you, you need to be pushed to the limit?"

"It's an in-built mechanism, I think." He pauses and laughs. "It's funny, I'm learning as much about myself as you are, M."

I laugh, but inside I disagree. I still feel nowhere near to knowing him.

+1978+

Stan was true to his word and a month later I was leaving Jim's team and establishing myself with Bernard as the assistant contracts manager.

Bernard had been briefed about the short six-month stint and he let me have control of the team. He took a step back, almost as if to test me, to see if, as per the Peter Principal, I may exceed my level of competence.

The pressure came thick and fast; it was an intense environment. This wasn't just extreme pressure to plan and organise, I had to pull out all the stops.

It was a whole new ball game and the resentment from some of the team members was my first obstacle.

I suppose they saw some trumped-up kid being promoted above them and as some of them felt they were more worthy they began to create barriers; plotting to undermine my judgement both in the office and on site.

There was a constant underlying current and though I grappled to establish respect, I have to admit, it started to get me down. Not that I ever let it show.

When Stan called me in for another chat, I put on my brave face.

"How have the team been with you?" Stan asked and I quickly replied, "Yes, they've all been fine."

Stan looked at me with a fixed gaze. "All?"

He had a way that put you on the spot; a way to extract the truth there and then and I chuckled nervously.

"Well yes, ok," I finally admitted. "There's been a few that aren't happy."

Stan nodded with a wry smile. "If you can't deal with them, Ben, then you've reached Peters Principal."

I bit my bottom lip and paused for thought. Had I reached my level of competence? I felt suddenly angry, both with the bastards that were making me doubt myself, and with myself, for not believing in my own abilities. Right then and there I decided I would turn this around.

"They aren't a problem for me, Mr. Lenz. I have things under control and I will win them over. I just need time." I stood up with a confidence that I was, at last, beginning to feel, when Stan gave his parting shot.

"Ok, Ben, but remember…" I paused at the door and turned to face him, "time isn't on your side." He sucked on his cigarette and gestured for me to leave.

My heart was thumping; Stan could do that to you.

He was reminding me that he was the master and he was now turning the screws.

Ben looks angry now as he remembers.

"Throughout my career, I recall comments from some work colleagues that I was arrogant. Do you find me arrogant, M?"

I sit up straight, surprised at his question and as I formulate my answer, that I don't at all, he continues to talk.

"I never thought of myself as arrogant, I saw myself as confident. Confident in my ability to make the right business decisions. Even though it helps to have rewarding comments or a coach to keep your feet on the ground, as I did Stan, you also need to believe in yourself. To know when you are good at something."

"Deep," I mutter when Ben finishes.

"Sorry, M. It still riles me sometimes. Hey if this ends up being some kind of self help book for others, I'll say this: Encourage failure as many times as you can take it because it's failure that can build success, but only if you learn from it."

Over the next few months, although there were gradual signs that the team were becoming more reassured of my ability, the back-stabbing wasn't subsiding. They ridiculed me behind my back, made little jibes in front of me, and I found myself fighting every day not to let it get to me.

This was no place for weakness though and I reflected that if I hadn't been so head strong in my earlier demands for promotion, I would have failed in getting it. I had to adopt that mindset again.

When Stan called me into his office again I was expecting a grilling as to how I was getting on. Instead, as I walked in, I was greeted with a cheeky grin.

His left arm was stretched out across the desk, his hand upturned, and in the palm of it he held an orange stress ball.

He tipped back in his chair, took a long drag on his cigarette and rigorously pumped the ball. I discreetly held my breath as he exhaled; the room couldn't take anymore smoke and it hung like a stale cloud threatening to engulf me with its toxicity.

Suddenly Stan leaned forward, dropped his cigarette in the ashtray and pointed to his eye. Then he opened his left hand with the stress ball in its palm and pointed to it.

"Ben," he said calmly, "keep your eye on the ball."

My eyes widened, I was confused, was Stan about to show me a magic trick? This was just weird.

He grinned, "Now, pay attention."

Attention, I thought, *I am riveted with anticipation. I am not taking my eye off that ball!*

"You need to look carefully at every tough situation for that one idea that is the key to a solution." I nodded slowly, wondering where this was leading.

"You'll be confronted with a number of potential solutions but there is always only one that will stick in your mind, waiting for you to refine it. That key solution is the ball, Ben, and though you may amend your strategy, you must never take your eye off it until you have a result."

"He was like Yoda, with his wise words and clever displays," I smile as I picture Stan imparting his wisdom to a young Ben.

"He was. I always enjoyed Stan's words of wisdom, but that was one piece of advice that I absorbed and have carried with me through life for the many difficult challenges I have faced."

"Look, Ben," Stan smiled, "let me put you to the test?"

I gulped at the thought of being put on the spot, but nodded for him to continue.

"Ok, how about your situation right now, with Bernard's team?"

Stan looked at me quizzically and I tried to think on my feet as he waited for my answer.

"Yes," I eventually sighed, "that's a tough one and I can't say I know the way through it yet, other than to just do what I do well."

Stan shook his head in disbelief at my pathetic answer. "Doing what you do well is one thing, being an entrepreneur is another. You need to be a thinker, a strategist, someone who is capable of playing the game and, if necessary, changing tactics."

I stared at him, not quite grasping what he was trying to say.

"Where's the ball, Ben?" Stan demanded to know as I gritted my teeth. I preferred to play these games where I could go away and analyse things. Being put on the spot was not one of my strengths.

I had no answer right at that moment and I felt like a fool. When Stan excused himself briefly, I sat with my thoughts.

Come on, I begged of myself, *what is the ball in Bernard's team?*

I desperately wanted to impress Stan with an answer by the time he got back but my mind went blank and I felt myself beginning to drown under the pressure.

"Tell you what, Ben," I jumped as he strode back into his office. "Seems to me you're struggling to find that ball. I'll give you till tomorrow morning."

I sighed with relief, grateful for this small reprieve, but panicking at just how little time I had to find that bloody ball.

Stan's wide grin seemed to suggest he didn't think I had a hope in hell of finding a solution by morning.

But I wanted to prove him wrong and I went away determined to find that damn ball.

Later that evening, I continued to dwell on my issues with Bernard's team and as I racked my brains, desperately searching for that ball, or any ball for that matter, I thought about the process. It made sense, but that ball I was looking for felt like a needle in Bernard's haystack.

That night I tossed and turned until Mary eventually had enough and switched on the bedside light.

"Ok, what's up?" She asked gently and I shook my head, not wanting to worry her.

"Nothing, just a work thing," I muttered. But Mary was having none of it and my attempts to play it down went awry.

I explained the problem and my conversation with Stan and I found I was doubting myself again. Maybe I wasn't up to it, maybe I was clutching at straws.

I felt desperate, and, though Mary tried to soothe me with supportive words, I felt like a failure. My last thoughts before I finally fell asleep were that maybe my good old subconscious would tell me by the morning.

When I sat bolt upright the next day, the early morning sunlight peeking through a crack in the curtains, it was with the sinking dread that there was still no ball.

It was ridiculous, I had come up with absolutely nothing and that just wasn't me. It takes a huge amount of imagination to find your way through dark times in business, and right then, I was sorely lacking.

So, it was with a negative frame of mind that I swept into my early morning meeting with Stan and, without really thinking, I announced rather bluntly that I hadn't been able to find the ball.

"I tried so hard last night, Mr. Lenz, but I can't do it. I can't find the ball!" I cringed inwardly at my pitiful words, but felt relieved that I'd gotten them off my chest.

Stan looked at me, I'd never seen him so angry. His face was bright red and I worried he was going to burst a vessel.

"Well, Ben, maybe this is your 'Peter' moment; your level of competence. Maybe I was right testing you with the junior role, because you obviously couldn't handle the pressure that comes with a senior position."

Stan had never spoken so fast and when he finally stopped, he sat back, gesturing a response from me. I put my head in my hands in dismay. I felt sick, bewildered and close to losing it.

What the hell had just happened in the past twenty-four hours?

I had crashed from hero to zero. It was like seeing my football team go another goal down with no time to respond.

I was drowning in self-doubt faster than a sinking ship.

"That's awful," I say, feeling a sudden flood of sympathy for the young Ben, "so much pressure for someone so young, and now to have lost your biggest supporter in Stan too."

Ben shook his head. "Things aren't always what they seem, M. Not where Stan was involved anyway."

Ben has no time to explain further, he has another meeting to go to, so he bids me goodbye, adding that he'll be in touch soon.

At this point, I wasn't to know that 'soon' would turn out to be a fortnight later, as a few days after that last meeting, I receive an email from Ben explaining that he's had to fly out to the States for an important meeting.

I sulk for a few days before replying with a curt response, "Fine."

To which Ben replies a few hours later, "It's clearly not, M."

I chuckle to myself despite my anger but I know I need to make him aware of how I feel and I resolve to mention my frustrations to him when we next meet.

+ + +

When we finally do meet, back in the café after his return from the States, I'm feeling a little anxious about raising the issue of his sudden disappearance, but I say my piece nevertheless.

"I know, I know," he raises his hands in defence. "I'm a busy man though, M, you know that."

"Yeah, I know," I say dejectedly, knowing I'm coming across as a petulant child.

Ben sighs, "Look, let me try and explain a little to you about why I'm so busy, why I need to be busy. Ok?"

I nod and wait for him to continue.

"I think a lot of Stan's teachings were to prepare me, so that I would learn how to adapt to change, whatever that change may be.

When I retired, I knew it would give me the opportunity to run my affairs at my own pace. But I also knew that I would still need to be constantly challenged, I still needed that buzz of adrenaline, you know?"

I nod, "And do you have that?"

Ben laughs, "Christ yes, in spades! I always accept the most extreme challenges, if there is something I think I can win easily, it's not enough, it bores me."

"But look at you," I gesture at his mobile phone, which for once, incredibly, is silent. "You're constantly busy!"

Ben picks up his phone, "Look." He holds it up to me.

I look at the screen and my mouth drops open at the number of unread emails.

"They're all work mails?" I ask incredulously.

"Kind of," Ben throws his phone on the table with a sigh, "different projects and planning stuff, these ones are just the low priority ones."

I shake my head at Ben.

"So, you see, M, whilst I am enjoying creating this biography with you, in fact it's my more favourable project right now, I do have other priorities too."

I look at Ben, grateful that he has taken the time to explain why he can't commit to our project as much and as frequently as I would like, and finally I think I understand.

"Ok," I concede, "I'll let you off. Seeing as you said this is your favourite project."

Ben snorts with laughter and we go again.

What I didn't know was that this was all in Stan's plan, another one of his games to push my boundaries and manoeuvre me to the edge, only to grab me and haul me back before I jumped. It was a bit sick maybe, but so effective, well, effective as long as I could regain my confidence.

At a meeting with Stan the following day, he went some way towards explaining himself.

"Ben, never say I can't to me again. I saw a loser in you yesterday, I hadn't seen that before."

I felt myself redden and swallowed my disappointment that I had let Stan down. Maybe he thought I was coming to the end of the road?

He pointed at me aggressively and went on.

"Never give away the fact that you have been defeated. Hold your head up, portray confidence and convince people you will win."

I was dumbstruck and embarrassed.

"Do I make myself clear?" Stan asked authoritatively.

My voice was unsteady as I replied that yes, he was perfectly clear, and he irritably waved me away. He had every right to be annoyed.

I continued to fight desperately with myself over that bloody ball, with Stan's words coming back to me, and I began puffing out my chest to try and put on a confident act. I'm not sure who I was convincing but it obviously had the desired effect on Stan when he approached me one morning in the car park.

It was incredible really, after all he had put me through over that damn ball and he just came out with it.

"Ben, your ball is Tom."

My mouth gaped open in surprise and Stan chuckled. "He is the most disruptive, conniving and influential individual in that team and he presently stands in your way. I've talked privately to Bernard about what's going on and we agreed to see if it would play out in its own time. Tom is your ball, Ben, keep your eye on that ball."

He strode away and I simply stood there with my mouth open. Of course, he was right, and it annoyed me because it was so simple, but now at least I had Tom on my radar.

Tom was the accountant in Bernard's team; a tall skinny individual with a mop of ginger hair and an outgoing personality.

He was certainly talented but he had a tendency to be extremely disruptive, which he seemed to make as priority over his responsibilities.

Bizarrely too, he was able to rally support from the other team members.

As it happened I didn't have to work out how to play him, but simply how to expose his destructive attitude, and one day he handed me the opportunity on a plate...

At this time, I was overseeing the project for a large power station in the Medway. The project was so large that every month we would put a valuation against completed work so that we could claim payment from the client. That valuation stood as credit for our bonus.

Tom was pushing to get as much invoicing done in the month as he could, but the foreman and the supervisor advised me that, in their view, we had overvalued the power station and should rein in any further valuations. The supervisor had warned that they may stop payments if we kept over-valuing and that was enough for me.

When I told Tom that there would be no more valuations that month, he completely lost it with me.

In front of everyone in the team, he exploded. "You're out of order, Ben, you're just shutting down our bonus potential!"

He was making me out to be a villain, and I knew it, but I stood my ground and tried to explain that the site staff surely knew better than anyone and that we should exercise caution.

Unfortunately, my reasoning fell on deaf ears and Bernard took the view that I was too new in the team to call the shots on a project that had been already been running for a couple of years. He overruled me, and Tom claimed it as his victory.

It was no surprise to me then that the next month we weren't paid the valuation by the power station and they assessed we had been over-valuing for three months.

This was a catastrophic moment for the team and for our bonus, as it meant we had to issue credits; credits were penalised by the company scheme so we were now facing a few months without any bonus.

I was shocked at how the team blamed Tom and he quickly became the villain. Bernard was hauled in front of a raging Stan and, I think in a twist of good fortune, was told to hold Tom accountable.

After further investigation, Tom was dismissed. It turned out the project had been over-valued by some six months and Tom had been responsible for forcing valuations to increase the bonus.

It was a day I celebrated, and well worth those few months without a bonus to finally see justice done.

Ben stretches his legs out in front of him and yawns. "Let's go for a walk!" he suddenly says.

"A walk?" I look up from my notes. "Where?"

"Summers wood, of course!" Ben stands up with a laugh and I hastily begin to scrabble my things together.

"What's Summers wood?" I ask. He is animated now, practically dancing around the café in good spirits and it's catching. It's a beautiful day outside, why shouldn't we enjoy it?

"Summers wood, my dear M, is mine and Mary's very own wood." He chuckles as he waltzes out of the café and I trail behind him, muttering to myself as I shake my head.

"Well of course you own a bloody wood…"

I knew Stan would call me in to ask about Tom and when his call came I was excited to share the story with him.

That day he was in good spirits.

"Ben," he smiled jovially. I liked that he always began by saying my name, he'd once said you should always begin a conversation by addressing someone personally as it immediately improved the connection.

"You need to expand your thinking, Ben, it's too one track." I nodded and waited for him to continue.

"You need to clear your mind, to reset the buttons. Then, imagine a solution and reverse engineer it."

After a short pause, he pointed to his eye and to the stress ball in his open fist.

I smiled, "I've got it, Mr. Lenz."

"Yes, but is it the right ball?" Stan cocked his head to one side inquisitively. "If it's the wrong ball, Ben, your chasing a lost cause. Make doubly sure you have the right ball and then keep it in sight as though your career depends on it. Because, trust me, it does."

"I've got my eye on the ball, don't worry." I assured him and Stan smiled.

"You've come through this better than I could have hoped. Perhaps you're a natural after all. I need to ask though; did you really plan that tactic with Tom or did it just happen? Be honest Ben."

"Yes, I did," came my proud reply and Stan nodded in appreciation. As I left his office, I felt finally that I had redeemed myself to him.

"Well done, Ben," I murmur with a silent clap of my hands.

We are walking through Summers wood and the sun is beating down on us.

There is a violet blanket of bluebells covering the ground, and that, coupled with the vibrant lush greens, astounds me. It's so peaceful here, so picturesque.

"This is stunning," I gesture at the wonderful nature around us as we reach a clearing. Before us is a field of daffodils and I am instantly reminded of my favourite poem by William Wordsworth.

"Oh yes, it's another one of my projects," Ben tells me and I roll my eyes good humouredly; when would this man stop?

"The plan is to renovate these sixty acres back to their natural beauty, with tracks, bridges and nature walks. I'm also in the process of gaining permission to rename it Taylor's Woods. We want to leave it to our grandchildren but also thought it would be cool to enjoy it with them and our kids right now."

I love how he speaks about his grandchildren. They mean the world to him and I voice that to him.

"Our grandchildren, of course yes, as well as our children." Ben bites his lip, clearly a little emotional.

I say nothing as we continue to walk, and then the serenity is interrupted by the ringing of his phone...

+ + +

So, I'm up late again, trying to put my notes into some kind of order, when my email pings.

If that's Ben cancelling again, I think, I'm gonna...

It's not though, it's a guy calling himself Jack Bourne.

I chuckle as I read his mail:

"I've been appointed as your agent by a Mr Ben Taylor, I am experienced in marketing and promotion, and I think you could use my help. Ben will confirm me to you. You may find me a little eccentric at times, but trust me, I am working for the good of you and Ben."

I sit back with a surprised laugh. What the hell was this?

I want to contact Ben but I know it's late and don't want to disturb him.

Is this a joke?

I don't reply to Jack, I shut down my computer and go to bed. I can't sleep though, I'm too wired, what the hell have I gotten in to?

Chapter 9

I Think You're Going to like This

As he walks towards me, Ben is smirking and I roll my eyes and shake my head.

"Morning, M," he chirps and Doris looks up with chuckle; I think she has a crush on him.

"You didn't bring Jack then?" I raise a questioning eyebrow and he laughs as he sits down.

"Ah yes, about Jack…"

"Who is he?" I'm still unsure as to whether Ben is winding me up with this Jack Bourne character.

"He's your agent," he's serious now, "well, mine too I suppose, though he obviously doesn't know my true identity."

"Really?" I'm excited, I've never had an agent before and I'm flattered that Ben thinks I am good enough to warrant having one.

"Yep, if this takes off Mandy," he's definitely serious if he's using my actual name, "we're going to need Jack, and believe me I've done my research; he's one of the best."

I squeal with delight, clapping my hands, and Ben smiles at my childlike behaviour.

"Is that really his name though, I mean Jack Bourne, come on!"
I start giggling and Ben shrugs with a snort.

"Who knows, M. But then, who knows who anybody is these days?"

"You have a very good point, Ben." As I emphasise his name I can't help but agree, then I decide to tease him.

"Although, Ben," I smile cheekily, "what would you do if some-one offered me a fortune to tell them who you really are?"

Ben looks up with raised eyebrows and slowly smiles at me.

"Well then, M, I would remind you of our contract."

"Ok, ok!" I giggle, "I'm not going to tell, don't worry!" I'm suddenly worried that I may now have planted some mistrust in Ben for me but he leans back with a grin.

"Good," he nods, "because you'd also have Mary to contend with!"

✦1979✦

Over the next few weeks and months, I noticed Stan was keeping his distance and I wasn't sure whether he was busy with another secret project or if he was just leaving me to it, to see whether I could handle it. Bernard was there of course, less engaging than Jim, but always supportive.

Then one day Stan requested a meeting with me.

After so long of not hearing from him, I wondered if he had some exciting news to impart.

However, after a few minutes of him making small talk, I started to wonder if it was bad news and he was just putting off telling me. When eventually he spoke, without smiling, my heart was in my mouth.

"Ok, Ben, look…" I held my breath and waited. I couldn't think of anything I may have done wrong so…

At last Stan grinned, "I think you're going to like this, Ben."
I sighed with relief, though at the same time I wanted to whack
him for making me panic.

"Now you'll know that the trust you placed in me has paid
off, when I tell you this is perfect for you." Stan paused and I tried
not roll my eyes.

Ok, Stan, just get on with it.

I was tired; some crisis had kept me late in the office the previous night and I wasn't in the mood for games but I waited, as I
always did for Stan.

He went on to explain that the board had approved Maurice's
plans to computerize the drawing and scheduling, his excitement
was contagious and I sat forward, eager to hear more.

"Maurice wants it all up and running within eighteen months,"
Stan spun his pen in his hand and shook his head, "and when
Maurice wants something, Maurice gets it, you understand?"

Stan looked me square in the eyes, "Don't be late on this,
Ben."

For a moment, I was suddenly acutely aware of the challenges
ahead but I absorbed everything as Stan explained they would be
setting up a team, to be led by Alan Palin, the purchasing director.
The plan was that he would gradually take a step back and allow
me to take the responsibility.

As I took all of this in, I began to wonder if Stan was saying
what I thought he was saying.

His next words made me almost sure and I wanted to fist
pump the air.

"That means a key management role for you, Ben."

I'm pretty sure I was beaming at this point but as Stan continued, the realities of the task ahead began to sink in.

"We've decided to add to Alan's team; besides yourself, there'll
be John Devlin, who has already been recruited as computer

manager, and Paul, who is a draftsman and computer programmer in his spare time."

Wow, I thought, *I'm still climbing, but there is no sign of the summit. This feels like we're just setting up base camp.*

And oh, how right I was…

The more I heard about Ben's steady rise to the top, the more I sought to know if he ever looked back in later years and thought, wow, I did that!

I ask him one day and his eyes glaze over, as if he is lost in his own little world; a place he calls his sanctuary.

"There was a moment back in Autumn 2012…

It was that time of year when the English Summer had said goodbye to the last of the steely blue sky, but I wasn't ready to.

So off we headed for a Miami Autumn.

Autumn evenings in Miami are wonderful; the evening light lingers in the humidity, making the days longer.

I remember one such evening just feeling so grateful to be savouring all of this and my mind drifted to the previous day, spent picking fresh oranges in the groves, the hint of citrus hanging in the air.

Right then I felt a moment of pure contentment and thought how lucky I was that I had chosen the path that I did. Things could have been so different, why weren't they?"

I am struck by how grateful Ben is for all he has. It's not often you see that in someone so successful but then again, he has worked bloody hard for all that he has now.

When I mention this to him, he explains;

"I believe passionately in democracy. I've always appreciated the democratic platform that gave me the opportunity to create wealth and I've never had an ounce of jealously towards wealthy individuals. For me, I looked up to them in awe and it did nothing but motivate me to emulate their talent. I'm not sure everyone around me shares *my indulgence in wealth, we are who we are. What annoys me more are individuals that, from a distance, form a view of how corrupt too much wealth is, but when it touches them, they can't resist embracing the benefits..."*

As I prepared myself for my new role, I considered how back in Bernard's team I'd felt like I was on a merry-go-round, this however felt far different.

Even though in the space of four years I had taken on four very different roles that had been completely alien to me, this one felt the most daunting, and I didn't even know what *this* was yet.

The room they had allocated to the new team was tucked away from all of the other teams. It was like a large classroom, sparsely furnished and totally soulless. The shabby blinds filtered dull light into a room that smelled of musty body odour, and the carpets were worn and dirty. Not the most welcoming of work spaces.

I'd arrived early, as usual. I had a thing about punctuality, it was something that my parents had drummed into me since I was a toddler; be on time or pay the penalty. The penalty usually being a slap on the buttocks. Not that I was expecting Alan to do that of course.

I stood there in the middle of what was to be my new office, taking in the huge marker board on the wall, the flip chart in the corner, and I felt a sick sense of unease and utter disappointment.

At that moment, the door swung open and in strolled a chubby, scruffy looking man with long hair and a beard.

He was late, and as he casually strode towards me, I deliberately glanced at the clock and stepped towards him authoritatively.

"Morning, I'm Ben." I shook his hand firmly; it was limp. "I'm Paul," he introduced himself.

The door opened again and Alan appeared in a puff of smoke that trailed behind him like a steam train.

"Good morning!" I cringed inwardly as he bellowed out a greeting without even introducing himself.

Alan strode to the marker board and without saying another word, he wrote, 'VAX 11/780', drawing a big circle around it as he stared at us expectantly.

We turned when, at that moment, John entered the room, his casual manner as though it didn't matter what time he turned up. He was smoking a cigar and I groaned silently; I was already holding my breath from Alan's smoke, now a cigar! Right at that moment I'd have given anything to be back in Bernard's bear pit.

John was polite and friendly and he shook our hands, his was a slightly firmer hand shake, before joining Alan at the marker board.

Paul and I sat down in front of them.

It all felt very surreal, like I had been transported to a parallel universe, as Alan and John proceeded to talk at us for the rest of the day.

They were already well up to speed on the project, but Paul and I were bamboozled with technicalities and intricate details on how we were going to tackle this project, whilst they reiterated that we had just eighteen months to deliver it.

By the end of the day Alan began setting us tasks and you could have knocked me down with a feather when he turned to me with mine.

"Ben, you'll go with John next week to meet John Nelson, CEO of Dex Inc, the software company we've spoken of."

I spoke up tentatively, "But aren't they based in…"

Before I could continue Alan interrupted me. "Boston, yes. Problem?"

"No, no problem," I shrugged nonchalantly, as though business travel was something I did all the time.

Inside, however, I was thinking wow!

It seems I was off to Boston…

I couldn't wait to get home and tell Mary the news. I was excited but at the same time I felt a little guilty at leaving her to cope alone.

Mary, as always, took it in her stride. "It's work, Ben, if you have to go you have to go. We'll be fine. It's only a few days after all," She chuckled and my cheeks began to redden.

"What?" Mary had noticed my blush.

"Well, it's actually for a couple of weeks," I mumbled.

Mary's smile faltered slightly but she quickly recovered herself and turned to me.

"Like I said, it's work. We'll be fine."

She smiled brightly at me and I wondered again at my good fortune in having this wonderful

supportive woman as my wife.

It gave me the further determination to succeed at this project, wherever it would take me...

Today I got to meet Mary.

Strangely, I felt a little nervous; Ben had told me she wasn't at all keen on this project as her family's privacy was paramount, and I prayed there would be no animosity.

My prayers were fortunately answered and I felt relaxed and comfortable within seconds of meeting her.

Weirdly, also, she was exactly as I had imagined her; dark and attractive, and instantly likeable.

"I'd love to get your take on things; how you coped with Ben working long hours and travelling." I half joked.

Mary smiled knowingly, "Oh, I'd have plenty to tell." Her kind but firm gaze told me this was a no go area.

During the flight to Boston, John Devlin explained more to me about the guy we were meeting and why we had chosen that software company to partner with, over some of the larger UK competitors.

This John Nelson we were meeting was a Harvard genius who had developed a computer system that enabled you to draw on the screen. It was called CAD, or, Computer Aided Drafting. Apparently, Nelson had left the elite Harvard Business School with the design and he now ran a small team of six programmers. He had taken the software further to develop a CAD system with a small database aimed at managing large companies space. Like mapping in a helicopter view of all the offices and meeting rooms etc.

John's biggest client was a huge computer company based in the Eastern seaboard of the U.S. called DEO. I knew the plan was to take his software and write our own routines, in other words apply our own pigeon programming, to create a custom application for Onelock's sole use. The exciting bit for me was the creative involvement, the idea of drawings and plans and the anticipation of delivering something quite ground breaking. The eighteen-month delivery I wasn't so sure about though, but I put it to the back of my mind.

John Nelson greeted us at the airport. In his early fifties, he was over six-foot tall and bald, with a smooth American accent. He seemed warm and friendly, though the cynic in me assumed this was because we were his clients. But then, maybe that was Stan getting into my head again; *"Let the niceties go, never trust anyone, Ben."*

I smiled to myself; *Everyone's an arsehole to begin with eh, Stan?*

And after that first night in Boston, that was pretty much my initial impression of Nelson.

The Chinese restaurant he took us to was dimly lit, creating a soft and warm ambience around the stark white of the table linen. The staff were polite and welcoming as they showed us to our table, exclaiming delight at our English accents as they seated us.

Nelson seemed a little flustered and I wasn't sure if this was just his manner or if he was agitated about something. I was later to learn that he simply struggled in social environments but as we sat there, pondering the menus, I could feel the tension radiating from him.

The food was good and we talked business as we ate what seemed a never-ending flow of it when course after course it kept coming.

Finally, with our stomachs full to bursting and John Devlin and I feeling the wearying effects of our journey, Nelson asked for the the bill.

Whilst he studied the check, the waiter bantered with John and I, asking where in England we were from. Funny, I always find it easier to say London.

"Ah, Arsenal? Chelsea?" The young Chinese man began to reel off the London football clubs, all except mine of course. Typical.

"Thank you." Nelson slammed a handful of notes onto the silver plate with the bill and the waiter bowed gratefully.

"Oh," Nelson suddenly said, "here."

John and I stared in disbelief as he flung one cent onto the plate.

The waiter stood there, clearly confused at Nelson's gesture, as were we.

"It's your tip. That service was shit!" Nelson said coldly and stood up to leave.

The waiters face flushed a furious red and my heart lurched as he lunged at Nelson from across the table.

A flurry of staff appeared amongst the ensuing chaos when Nelson squared up to the younger, shorter man and the staff pulled them both apart.

"Just get out!" A man, probably the manager, shouted at us, "and you no come back!"

We hightailed it out of there, both John and I feeling so embarrassed as well as sorry for the poor waiter. I was also beginning to wonder just who Nelson was and whether he was always as ruthless as he had just portrayed to us. Was this a flaw in his character that I would later fall foul of?

The following morning, we arrived at Nelson's offices to meet his team of programmers.

He didn't say a single word about the previous night and I wondered if it was because he was embarrassed. If he was he showed no sign of it and he simply introduced us to his staff.

Every single one of them was a complete introvert and his secretary gave the impression she would run a mile if you so much as raised your voice an octave. I wondered why Nelson had created this team of individuals with such extraordinary intellect yet absolutely no social skills.

Throughout the trip, we delved into the detail of the project and the task ahead soon became clearer. By now, I had forgotten all about that incident in the restaurant as I became more and more impressed with Nelson and his technical knowledge. I guess that was my first mistake.

This project was enormous. It wasn't my remit to know the investment that Onelock were making in terms of computer hardware and software, but I'm pretty sure it would have made my eyes water.

My task was simply to make it work for them to get a return on their investment. I say simply, but by now I was starting to understand the responsibility on my shoulders.

The trouble was, I was short on time and long on incompetent team members…

+ + +

Back at Onelock, Alan Palin was orchestrating things whilst John Devlin was ensuring everything came together technically, so that left Paul and I to be hands on.

Paul was lazy and without an ounce of get up and go. I didn't suffer fools gladly and I vowed to myself that he would never be in any future team I led.

The months passed quickly by in my isolated world of technology and Onelock went public and secured an investment in some new, nearby premises to help fuel their continued rapid growth. The new facility was a large one storey unit with offices around the perimeter of a huge warehouse.

We were located only two-hundred yards away from it, so it was convenient to drop by and see how the renovation was going and watch the steady progress of the computer room being constructed, with its deep false floor, miles of cabling and massive air conditioning units.

We got to see the finished article in an official tour. It was an impressive facility and one of the first computer installations of its kind. The computer room spanned some eight-hundred square feet and housed a monster Digital VAX 11/780 main frame computer.

In effect, it was a huge grey box with flashing lights, and it still strikes me as incredible to think that the power and storage in my iPhone right now is far superior to that which spanned the computer room.

John Devlin spent most of his time focusing on getting the computer and equipment up and running. The main frame was also being used to accommodate the companies accounting system, so John's duties were pretty varied.

Paul and I, having had training from Nelson's team, were now busy writing code and I hated it. Our task was to use a simplified version of Fortran4, a programming language using 'what if' statements to write code. Using my knowledge of the Onelock product, we would tell the system, via code, to pull together specific components for whatever product types were selected.

We would compile the code we'd written each day and the system would automatically analyse and de-bug it overnight, using one of Nelson's clever routines. Those routines checked the logic and ensured the accuracy of what we had written. Although it wasn't my bag, I liked the way you could write an instruction and then, as if by magic, out came the list of components. It had a rhythmic sense to it, like it was flowing along collecting components but at an alarmingly fast rate. It was so gratifying when it compiled without errors.

As I typed in what if, I wondered what if you could programme your journey through life, but actually you can, you do, I was!

Paul was as sloppy and slow as I was demanding and we constantly clashed, but there was no time for resource changes. It was another lesson for me in utilising what resources I had to get a job done.

It was full on over the following twelve months, but as Stan kept reassuring me, it was a means to an end and I would appreciate the end. That was about all that kept me focused.

By now, the main frame Vax Computer system was being used by accounts and it was time for Alan Palin to step away.

I was given the grand title of Computer Operations Manager and took on full responsibility. I did consider whether that was Alan's way of walking away from any blame if Maurice's target wasn't met, but I felt confident so it didn't bother me.

I had to report into a new board member, a young astute guy called Bob Pearce who was from finance. I liked Bob and we got on well. Being in finance was convenient too as he had no idea what we were doing and fortunately didn't interfere.

By this time the system had evolved, and as more superior elements had come on line, Bob asked if I was ready to bring clients in for demos.

I was excited and wanted to shout about this project whenever I could. No one had seen anything like it, impressive was an understatement, it was state of the art.

I confirmed he could, and later that day Bob popped his head around the door.

"Ben, 11am tomorrow. Maurice wants to bring in one of our top clients and show them the system," he looked worried. "If you're not ready, don't do it. This is Maurice, after all."

I nodded, I already knew Maurice wouldn't suffer anything less than success.

I took a deep breath, adrenalin kicking into my system.

"I'm ready," came my confident reply but Bob still looked concerned so I gently slapped his arm, "it'll be fine!

Of course, the system wasn't ready to go live yet, but I had nailed the demo and loved the theatre of it.

At 11am the following day, right on cue, I heard Maurice's voice booming down the corridor and warned Paul to get ready. Paul always needed warning.

Maurice strode in alongside three smartly-dressed city gents, all with very posh voices, and we were quickly introduced.

Whilst Maurice had seen parts of the system, he hadn't yet seen a full-on demo, and, as by now I was used to doing them, I had choreographed some real show off features.

Don't forget this was the beginning of the eighties, people had rarely heard of, let alone seen a computer and what I was about to showcase was, in those days, pure magic.

Ben is animated. "See, back then, this was groundbreaking stuff. Imagine if…" He picks up the sugar bowl on the table, "I simply

*pressed a button and this suddenly dropped through the table and
onto the floor or floated up to the ceiling."*

I raise my eyebrows, "Well, yes I'd be pretty impressed."

"Exactly! It truly was like a magic trick."

I loaded up a drawing of a floor plan onto the computer screen and
popped a print of an office floor plan onto a large electronic tablet.

I explained to my rapt audience that a draughtsman would go
through the process of scanning in the floor plan and as he did so,
the details would show up on screen.

I then moved to a huge TV screen, like an old cathode ray
tube, CRT TV. On the screen was the floor plan that I had
shown mapped on the tablet. I selected from a menu and drew
in some internal walls representing our own internal partitioning. Touching the screen with the pen, I picked up the partition
wall and dragged it across into another space, showing how easy
it was to move.

Before I could even look up to see their reaction, they were
gasping in amazement.

It was as if they were watching England score the winning
goal in the world cup; the whole room exploded in euphoria.
One guy stepped back and grabbed Maurice by the arm, "I can't
believe what I'm seeing! Bloody hell, this is something, Maurice."
As he patted him on the back, Maurice beamed from ear-to-ear.

I continued the demo, pointing out the ease of moving walls
around and showing the components for those walls and different
partition types.

I went on to impress further by explaining that just those few
clicks would have taken hours for a draughtsman to draw and
schedule.

"More importantly," I added, "a draughtsman's manual schedule would be full of costly errors."

They all spontaneously burst into a round of applause, they were literally swept off their feet. I felt so good. In fact, scrub that, I felt fricking amazing!

Maurice put his arm around me and whispered in my ear. "That was so good, thank you, Ben, thank you."

With that they left and I allowed the adrenaline to run through my body.

I wanted more, and so apparently did Maurice…

✦ 1981 ✦

Back at home, Mary was getting used to me bringing home my stories and career updates. She was excited for me and delighted at what may evolve but she had her hands full. Our daughter had colic and Mary was exhausted. I needed sleep to be sharp for work so Mary took most of the burden. It only confirmed for me just what a supportive woman I had married. She didn't complain, knowing that as my career took off, so the long-term benefits could be reaped. I was doing this for my wife and my beautiful daughter, my family.

And we were about to become four…

When our son entered the world, Mary and I were elated. This was another proud moment for me. Finally, a son to complete our little unit and to carry on the Taylor name. I looked down at his trusting little face, and felt again that feeling of incredible love and the overwhelming need to protect and guide.

He was such a happy little chap and our daughter, nearly three years old, loved fussing over her baby brother.

Mary and I were a great team; she took full control of bringing up the children, and I concentrated on my career.

It was full on for both of us with our mortgage pushed to its limit, but we dug in, working together to give our children a secure future.

I'd made a vow to myself on the day my son had been born that I would never impose my views or interests on him. I wanted him to feel free to make his own choices, to discover his own likes and dislikes. Including which football team he would support...

"Ah yes," I interrupt Ben, "about that. Tell me about your footballing career."

Ben chuckles, "I knew you'd ask. Well it wasn't so much a career, very short lived if so."

There are some games of football you play in when you feel you have magical powers and you can do nothing wrong. They are rare though and for me there were only a few but when they happened they were like treasure.

I was playing for my school in one such game against our biggest rivals. We were psyched.

Our PE coach had pumped us up and told us to win this for the school.

"Put it out there, and leave it all out there!" he rallied us and I felt readier than I had ever been before.

I was playing right wing but kept straying out of position to influence the game with my enthusiasm and touches. I felt I could do no wrong. I was naturally a right-footed player and had a knack of crossing the ball to pinpoint accuracy.

We were playing on a slight slope, attacking downhill, when we won a corner on the left side. Unusually for me, I moved quickly from my right-hand position, across the left side of the penalty box and lost my marker. The ball swung towards me as I ran onto it and for the first time I hit it on the half volley with my left foot. It was a one off, but it couldn't have been sweeter. It just rocked into the top left hand corner of the net.

Everyone was astounded and at half time the opposition coach came over.

"You're one hell of a player, lad," I blushed at his praise, "well done, you're gonna be a professional, that's for sure."

This was enough to buoy me up further and in the second half I carried on where I had left off. I sprinted up the right wing and cut in to my left, to fire another left-foot goal from just inside the penalty area.

That would be the first and last time I would score two goals with my left foot but what a game that was!

On the flip side, the worst game I ever had was at a county league club when I was sixteen years old, and I broke every bone in my right wrist.

It was at that club that I was spotted by a scout and invited to train with the team he represented.

I hadn't even been at their training ground for five minutes though when I found myself at the receiving end of some very stern words.

"I wouldn't even put you in training," came the devastating words of the coach, "you'd be killed out there, you're way too fragile."

He didn't hold back, didn't hesitate and didn't even want to see my skills.

I was instantly dismissed with the soul-destroying words: "Go away, get yourself some weight on and then come back and see me."

It was a far tougher game in those days and despite my feelings of rejection, it didn't dent my confidence. Maybe I do have to thank my dad for being tough with me, because although I was gutted and felt like I had failed without even getting a kick at the ball, it hadn't phased me.

However, over the next year or two, despite my best efforts to put on weight, my footballing ambitions just seemed to drain away.

Football had also begun to punish my knees and I was frequently in pain when I played.

I finally had to accept my football career was over when I was told I needed a cartilage operation. All of those years of kicking a water-sodden leather ball had finally taken its toll on my knees.

Now my football experience would no longer be playing, but watching, and the London football club that I supported is where I would go...

Ben rolls his eyes here. "It's just dire at the moment though," he groans and shakes his head. "We have to force a change of ownership."

"Can you do that?" I ask and I notice Ben is looking at me with a hesitant smile on his lips and a mischievous glint in his eyes.

"What?" I'm intrigued. "Do you know something I don't?"

"Let's just say," he whispers mysteriously, "that Stan may have offered me a final ball to throw at this."

I'm confused but I ask no further questions. His talk of Stan has reminded me of why we're here and knowing Ben as I am beginning to, well, sort of, time is precious...

Chapter 10

Forget the Flashy Title, Is This Progress?

+1983+

I was spending a lot of time working with Nelson, grinding out changes and moving the development of our customized system forward, and my relationship with him was growing nicely.

Then one day, he confided in me a conversation he had had with Maurice. He claimed Maurice and Bob Pearce were keen to close a deal for Onelock to exclusively sell Nelson's CAD software, called AEC, in the UK. AEC stood for Architecture, Engineering and Construction.

He went on to explain that he was going to agree to their terms and the news would be announced alongside the launch of our project.

I was so thrilled at the prospect and wondered whether this could lead to yet another opportunity for me.

When Nelson came to the UK, primarily to meet with Maurice and Bob, I formulated a plan to hijack some of his time to iron out a host of issues on our project.

For the first couple of days Nelson was pretty tight-lipped.

"Ben, honestly, I'm sorry but I can't say anything," he replied when I asked for news, "it's pretty exciting though and you will be invited to the next meeting."

I was impatient, frustrated at not knowing what was going on and eager to find out.

Finally, I got a call from Bob who had now become Maurice's errand boy, asking myself and John, the computer manager, to meet him in the board room. We were literally shaking with anticipation as we entered the room. Everyone was on such a high, you could almost smell the adrenaline in the room, not to mention John's cigar.

Maurice couldn't wait to get started and as everyone hurriedly seated themselves, he paced around the conference table like a cat on hot bricks. His enthusiasm for this project was obvious and he was clearly falling over himself to spit out the news.

"Well, lads," his huge grin made us all smile too, and we hadn't even heard the news yet!

"We are delighted to have struck a deal with John Nelson here to be exclusive UK agents for the AEC software." He paused, allowing us to take this in and, I imagine, to enjoy our wide-eyed reaction. I think he may have suspected Nelson had spilled the beans and was keen to be the bearer of such good news. I should have won an Oscar for my feigned surprise.

Maurice continued, "We will be selling the AEC software in the UK as soon as our own system goes live." He looked straight at me with beady eyes as he said this and I nodded, I knew what that look meant – Yes, Ben, make that happen, and quickly.

His news hadn't surprised me, but what came next did.

"Ben, John," We both sat up straight and nodded as Maurice addressed us, "we have already set up another company called Dex UK. It will be 75% owned by Onelock and 25% by Nelson's US company, Dex Inc. Bob will be managing director and we would like you two to join the board of directors."

My mouth dropped open. It took a few minutes to digest the news and get over the shock. Me, a board director?

Wow! Just seven years in, who would have thought? There I had been, striving to be contracts manager, which had actually eluded me, and now I'd jumped to a board director.

Who would have thought back in those heady Miami days that I'd go from beach to boardroom!

Suddenly, it was as if Stan was in the room, I could almost hear him.

Ok, yes, this is good Ben, but don't get carried away with yourself, forget the flashy title, is this progress? If so, what responsibility do you have?

I quickly analysed the situation, wishing Stan would stay out of my head for a moment.

Jeez Stan, at least let me enjoy this for a minute before you piss on my parade!

I did suddenly wonder though whether I had actually jumped anywhere, but I ignored that thought as things began to sink in.

I was on the board of a company; Dex UK. I whispered the name, wanting to hear it from my lips, and I suddenly felt an immediate deep sense of love for that company.

It was as if I was being told at that very moment to look after this company as it was my vehicle to the future. I'll never forget the feeling that day and I couldn't wait to tell Mary and, well, anyone else who would listen!

"That's remarkable, you'd only been there seven years!"

"It was a pretty rapid rise," Ben admits, "the beginning of exciting things to come and a proud moment indeed."

"I bet Mary was so proud…"

"Oh yes, of course. We had Nelson and John Devlin around for a celebratory dinner.

I remember I had a really good vibe. It felt like the start of a great relationship between us all."

Ben sighs deeply and I look up at him questioningly. "Wasn't it then?"

"At the start, yes…"

With a month to spare on Maurice's deadline for completing the project, I was ready. Onelock's teams were all scheduled in for training and whilst some had a sense of trepidation, most were excited.

Of course, when it was announced, Alan Palin and Bob Pearce stood up and took the credit, but it didn't bother me, I wasn't looking for a pat on the back.

Each step I had taken on my journey had come without credit so I had gotten used to continually moving onto the next goal.

During the next few months we gradually bought all the teams up to speed and they started using the system to its full potential. It was proving a huge success and I was proud of myself but I don't remember stopping to enjoy that moment.

I should have.

Instead, as I seem programmed to do, I started to wonder what was next.

It was then that we were suddenly hit with news that would change my world forever and put everything we had worked for at risk.

"Want to take a break here?" I look at Ben who shrugs.

"Doris, another latte and a cappuccino, please." I call out and Doris nods from behind the counter.

"With a…"

Before Ben can finish, Doris shouts, "Yes, I know! A cold side of skimmed milk!"

Ben laughs and I shake my head.

"She's getting too attached to us." Ben says with a smile in Doris' direction. She catches his smile and beams back at him.

"To you, I reckon!" I say to Ben with a wink.

Ben gives me that withering look that he does so well, and after our fresh drinks are served, by a very giggly Doris I must say, he continues with his story.

It was a shock to everyone when PI, a subsidiary company owned by Onelock, literally went bust overnight.

Rumour had it that the extent of its losses could pull Onelock to its knees, in fact many were saying it wasn't going to survive.

Within days, Maurice called everyone into the warehouse for a company meeting.

We were all anticipating the worst, expecting Maurice to say we had all lost our jobs.

I'd never been so tense, so frightened. I just felt so helpless and completely vulnerable.

Where was Stan when I needed him? It had been a while since I'd seen him and I could have used one of his pep talks right then.

I started to wonder at the unfairness of it all, how I'd come so far, so quickly. Was I about to have the rug pulled from under me? I couldn't believe this was happening. But it was and I had no control over my destiny.

Maurice stood, circled by over a hundred employees, as he prepared to address the company.

Standing just ten feet away from him, I could clearly see his face was saddened with despair. The charismatic guru was gone and in it's place was a broken man; a shadow of his former self. It was a reminder of how finely balanced life is and how the best of us can be brought down to earth.

I looked at Maurice and thought about how he had focused on the wrong ball. How could he have missed something so significant that it threatened to bring down the company?

A shiver went through me at the realisation that potentially it was all over, and I felt close to tears.

Maurice's voice was trembling as he tried to deliver his well-prepared speech from the piece of paper he was holding. Then he paused, folded up his notes, tucked them in his jacket pocket and spoke from his heart.

He spent some time explaining what had gone wrong; the management of the subsidiary had raked up huge losses amounting to over £1.5 million and it had impacted Onelock.

He stopped and picked up his glass of water with a shaky hand.

He took a few seconds to compose himself before he spoke again and in that short moment I think we all lost our own fear and just felt for him.

In the eerie silence, we waited anxiously to hear his next words, a lone pigeon fluttered up in to the eaves of the warehouse, the atmosphere was intense.

Maurice cleared his throat. "We can only survive this if we quickly lay off staff." There were no gasps of surprise, just sighs of sad acceptance and Maurice continued.

"By reducing the work force we are sure we can recover strongly." I could sense the relief in the room, coupled with nervous anticipation at the thought of being laid off.

Maurice went on to explain that it was going to be an extremely painful year with redundancies amounting to more than half of the work force.

I knew I had to be patient and stay positive, after all I had half a chance of being kept on. I'm sure wherever the hell Stan was, he would be telling me; *Ben, you're an asset, why would anyone let you go?*

I kept repeating that in my head like a mantra but at the same time the negative thoughts found their way into my thinking.

I don't think I've ever seen so many people so unmotivated, it was such a difficult time. As management, I felt a responsibility to try and keep everyone lifted but that wasn't easy as I was overwhelmed with thoughts of the risk this was to my own family.

The whole process must have been a nightmare for the directors to sort out but gradually those dreaded meetings with the staff, to rehire or fire, started to take place and a pattern quickly emerged.

The executives at Onelock explained that everyone would have short, one-to-one interviews over the next few days where we would learn our fate.

At home, Mary was trying to be as upbeat and positive as she could but I knew she was worried too. What would this mean for us? Mortgaged to the hilt, with two young children, and now the possibility that we could lose everything.

"Where was Stan?" It has occurred to me as Ben has been talking that Stan hadn't featured for a while, and I haven't missed the comments about his absence during this time.

"It's strange," Ben frowns, "I'd seen him after the creation of Dex UK."

He chuckles softly, "I remember I was so excited and couldn't wait to tell him."

"I bet he was delighted for you." I smile, my eyes shining at the thought of Stan hearing about the success of his young protégé.

Ben nods but his face tells a different story. "He was of course pleased and excited for me, but I got the sense he was slightly subdued. He looked at me and said, 'hold on to that, Ben, it's going to be good for you.' Then he looked like he was about to say something else but instead he repeated, 'just hold on to it, Ben.' It was very odd."

"Very odd," I agree, "didn't you ask what he meant?"

Ben shakes his head with a rueful smile, "No, Stan and I didn't have that kind of relationship. I wished we had, but Stan never let anyone get too close."

"But he had let you get close." I'm confused, the way I see it, Stan looked on Ben almost as though he were his own son.

"Stan liked me and despite not knowing him on a personal level, I liked him. What we did have was a great respect for each other. And I'll always be grateful to that man, wherever he is."

I'm surprised, "You don't know?"

Ben looks slightly ashamed and more than a little emotional as he replies.

"No, I don't. That was the last time I saw him…"

It was like some sinister culling, as, one by one, individuals were called in. We huddled in groups, protecting ourselves with humour as each name was called. No work was done, we just sat around chatting. For us, it seemed the end of the world had come and consuming coffee would help. We cheered each employee as they went down for their news, trying hard to encourage them as they sauntered off, slouching down the corridor with their heads down.

When they came back we could see the result on their faces and would surround them like hounding press hungry for a story. Out they came, one by one, some with tears in their eyes. They picked up their belongings and most hardly had the voice to choke out a goodbye. By now, we'd got the gist that all those leaving were being told first, so we waited for the first employee to come back and say it was all ok. But that didn't happen, and all that day they kept falling like lemmings. I was getting disillusioned, the shock of so many I had worked with saying goodbye and the thought of what it must be like to go home and have to tell your family hit me. I felt sick, my mind was thinking of the worst-case scenario, and my breath was coming in small gasps.

I stopped and closed my eyes, trying to breathe normally. I could feel tears gently rolling down my cheeks. I wondered where Stan was in all this mayhem, there was no sign of him but he was in my head, taunting my negative thoughts. *"What's the worst that can happen?"* he would say. *"Ok, now plan for that as contingency, anything better is a bonus."*

Well, I thought, *the worst that can happen is I'm left without a job. I have a family to support. My contingency is to get another job, and quick!"*

The next morning the pattern repeated itself, and one by one our colleagues marched down the corridor only to be told they had lost their jobs. Then, after lunch on the second day, I finally got my call.

"Ben, you can go down now," called out one of the guys who had come back to clear his desk. He was angry. He thumped the wall with his fist. "Not fair," he shouted, "not fair! This sucks, I've been here twenty years, they have no right to do this. Sorry Ben, get ready for bad news, I think everyone in this team is going."

I felt a sensation move down from my chest to my stomach and I clenched my fists to regain some composure.

Making the long walk to my already decided fate, I tried to rationalise the situation, but I could only draw the conclusion that business is just darn right cruel and it takes no hostages.

I felt angry at the situation I was in, and it suddenly occurred to me that my anger was at myself, because I'd left myself, and therefore my family, vulnerable.

I pushed open the door and gasped inwardly. Brilliant, there sitting with Bob Pearce was Peter Coleman. Now I definitely didn't want to be there.

Right in front of me was one small ally in Bob, and one huge enemy in Peter.

I wondered whether to turn and walk back out again, I knew Peter would be campaigning for my departure.

When Bob spoke, Peter remained silent and I couldn't even look at him.

"Ben," Bob began, "first of all, let me tell you that you're staying."

My mouth dropped open and my stomach swept back up into my chest. The sheer relief was exhilarating.

Bob smiled understandingly and continued, "We are forming two new contract teams and we've chosen you to be contracts manager of one, with Vic Underwood the other. You'll have the largest team; ninety on-site staff including two supervisors and an in-house team of seven, including an assistant contracts manager."

I swallowed my shock and composed myself, before thanking Bob for the privilege. Coleman was staring at me as I stood up to leave and I could sense his disapproval.

He suddenly spoke.

"Obviously, these decisions have been collective," he smirked, or was it a sneer? "But both you and Vic will report to me."

And there it was, with those words he was telling me this wasn't his choice. He really needn't have bothered though.

Still, he continued. "The reason you have the bigger team is because we want to continue with the computer system, it also runs our accounting system and payroll. Bob here will retain responsibility for any computer issues so you'll report to him on those, but contracts are *mine*," I didn't miss his emphasis on the word mine but had no chance to respond when Bob spoke up again.

"Maurice also wants to keep Dex UK operating, Ben, so your position in that company as director remains, albeit your primary focus is now contracts."

"So," Coleman was smug, "that had better not affect what you're delivering in my team."

I looked into his weasel-like eyes as I delivered my parting shot, "I'm disappointed you would even think that, Peter."

Leaving the room, I could feel his hatred burning into me and it made me all the more determined; I might not be in control right now, but I was going to find a way to beat Coleman.

"Eurgh," I shiver, "I hope karma came back to bite him!"

Ben laughs, "Do you believe in karma then, M?"

"Absolutely," I nod my head vigorously, "what goes around comes around!"

Ben studies me with a smile on his face.

"What?" I ask, uncomfortable under his gaze.

"We're quite similar, you and I."

"Are we?"

"Yes," Ben nods slowly and thoughtfully, "yes, I think we are. I just hope karma isn't going to bite me."

The mysterious look on Ben's face suddenly reminds me of his secrecy about the year 2077 and I give him a curious frown, but he quickly looks away.

Chapter 11

I'll Never Be Good Enough in Your Eyes

Two weeks have passed since our last meeting and I'm getting used to Ben's odd absences.

It doesn't stop me feeling frustrated though; until I have more material, there's nothing more for me to do on our book.

I pour a glass of wine and decide to do some proof reading; somebody else's novel.

I curl up in my pyjamas and read a few pages about vampires before I fall asleep on the sofa.

My phone buzzes, thankfully waking me at the point where Dracula is chasing me.

"Yeah?" I'm still half asleep but worried at getting a call this late.

"M," comes a familiar voice. "Meet me at the red café tomorrow at ten. I have more for you."

I'm too sleepy to argue. "Sure."

I put my phone down and sigh, "Here we bloody go again!"

As I close my eyes though, I can't help but smile...

✦1983✦

What a bizarre way for me to finally, but unexpectedly, get the contracts manager position.

I'd gone from thinking I'd made a jump to director to going another step back and once again trying to earn the trust of someone who would never accept it; my nemesis, Coleman.

Stan would have said, be patient and the follow up pays off. But patience was no longer my biggest virtue.

As the weeks passed, I thought it was time to call on Stan again. I was in need of some advice and reassurance from my business guardian angel.

When his secretary told me he'd gone on long term leave, my heart almost stopped.

"What exactly does that mean?" I could almost hear her brain ticking over as she tried to think of a response. Mine was too. Where was Stan? Was he ill? Was he coming back?

"I'm sorry, I can't disclose any more information," came her curt reply.

I asked around, nobody was saying anything, but Bob later confirmed he had taken early and immediate retirement. If only I could have seen him to thank him, to say goodbye.

This business was tough, but in a strange way he had even toughened me up to deal with his departure, almost to treat it as just another event I had to just move on from.

Stan was a hard task master but soft inside, he taught me with care and made me feel what I was doing really mattered. Stan's teaching proved invaluable, the source, as I now recognise, of the best advice I ever got. He was calm but calculating, motivating, an astute intellectual, my business father, and my friend.

Stan would never be forgotten.

"No!" I can't believe it. "He just left without a word?" I feel bereft, Stan had done so much for Ben. It was almost as though he'd guided Ben, taught him. And once he felt he was ready, he let him go off into the big wide world, alone.

Ben looks sad. "It felt like quite a loss at the time. Made worse that he didn't even say goodbye. But then that was Stan's way; make your mark and walk away. It's another thing he taught me, I suppose. All I know is how grateful I was, and still am for my business guardian angel."

I feel so sad at Stan's sudden departure, just as Ben seems to be by just recalling it.

"It's unlikely now, but if he's reading this; thank you, Stan, from the bottom of my heart."

One weekend, Nelson called me at home. Considering he'd just tied up the exclusive agreement for Dex to sell his software in the UK, he wasn't happy about the situation at Onelock, especially as Maurice hadn't disclosed the PI crisis.

I couldn't disagree with his concerns and told him we would talk again once I was settled.

I arrived early on the Monday after the weekend refurbishment so that I could familiarise myself with the new office space. I was to have a small in-house team of seven working with me and we had acres of space.

I was keen to get stuck into Dex UK but this task ahead with the new team was huge, not least because I had Coleman to contend with, and he was determined to bring me down.

I was on my own here, with Stan gone and Maurice with all sorts of problems of his own, I had no allies. It was time to grow up quick.

I kept thinking about The Peter Principal and whether this, once again, was my level of competence.

I had been desperate for the contract manager's role and now that I had it I wanted the Dex UK role.

I felt like I had gone backwards.

The Coleman situation was my first real test to find a way through a tough situation without Stan. A situation that would demand the use of his, 'find the ball' psyche.

This was it. I was faced with a huge challenge, one that could take me down, so I really had to find that ball, and fast.

For days, I dreamt up different scenarios, but it seemed the more I thought about it, the more the answers eluded me.

It was only after I put it to the back of my mind, hoping for a light bulb moment, that it came to me.

It was a few days later when my trusted assistant, Terry, and I were talking about our profit for the month and how we could defer some revenue on a job that wasn't finished. It was just those three words; profit on deferral, but they jumped out at me.

This was just a technical way of arguing for profits to be rolled into the future, based on the potential threat of unforseen costs. In other words, it was accounting smoke and mirrors but that was my ball. The only way I was going to defeat Coleman was by continuously making more profit than Vic.

See, Stan? I found the ball all by myself!

I was smug with myself, thinking perhaps I could make this work after all. Now I had to follow it up with some tactics.

I decided to have Terry go undercover to look at Vic's profit. If we could beat him each month by adjusting deferred revenue, I could show consistent results by keeping our profit just ahead of Vic's. Thereby saving excess profit for those months we may need to play catch up.

Over the course of the next few months, I knew I was becoming swamped, as the contracts, coupled with the inevitable computer problems, started to take their toll.

I was taking the bonus scheme calculations home every month, which would take me a whole weekend just to keep on top of things. I was still also giving the odd demo's but I had no time to follow them up and Peter was on my case, winding me up at every given opportunity.

Looking back, it was good for me. I got stuck in and stopped thinking about Dex UK for a few months, determined to get better results than Vic's team. Peter couldn't argue with the facts.

I think it was at this point that I quickly learned the art of delegation, which gave me time to think, time to plan and focus on efficiency and profit.

As I begun to continuously overtake Vic on bonus, Peter would just nod at me. He couldn't bring himself to say anything like, 'brilliant Ben, well done.', or anything motivational. It just wasn't him.

But that nod was good enough. In my head, that nod was a punch of victory.

And there it was, right there, victory, proving that my level of competence as contracts manager was yet far from reached.

I was so chuffed with myself, though saddened that I couldn't share it with Stan.

I wondered where the big man was and whether he was ok. It felt like the end of an era, but as Stan always said; turn the page and move on.

I had a whole book of pages ahead of me to turn and I was now the one turning them, but I knew I needed more control.

"I still can't believe Stan just disappeared." I shake my head, "did you not try and track him down?"

"I thought about it," Ben says, "but if Stan had wanted to stay in touch, he would have."

I'm suddenly excited. "I've got an idea!"

Ben looks bemused, "M…"

"Let's try and find him and…"

"Now M, that's not a good idea, some things are best left…"

I stand up and gather my things, not missing the irony that, for once, I am the one leaving our meeting.

"M?" He calls after me as I giggle and leave the café with a cry of, "Laters!"

I swear I can feel him shaking his head at my departing form.

+ + +

Earlier today, I had the pleasure of meeting my agent, Jack Bourne.

I arrived at his swish London offices and waited in reception for him.

I was expecting someone fairly young and so was a little taken aback when he appeared in front of me.

"Amanda?" I hate being called by my full name, it reminds me of being in trouble as a child.

"Hi," I stood to greet the silver-haired man in his late fifties who had a confident smile on his tanned face.

"Good to meet you," his hand shake was firm and I thought briefly of how Ben would approve of this.

As we took the elevator up to his luxurious office that overlooked the city, he talked animatedly about what Ben and I were doing.

"Do you think I'll ever get to meet this secret entrepreneur of yours?" Jack had a twinkle in his eyes as he stared at me waiting for an answer and I felt myself blush.

"Erm, no," I stammered, "He's very private."

Jack burst out laughing at my awkwardness and patted my arm gently.

"Fair enough, then that's the stance we'll take."

I was confused, "Stance?"

Jack nodded, "Yep, we'll play up the secrecy. Keep people guessing and wondering. It's a winning formula, Amanda."

He winked at me and I giggled. He really is quite a charmer.

Despite his assured cockiness, I found Jack to be astute, and enthusiastic about our project.

He outlined what he would be doing for us; marketing and promoting the book via social media as well as with endorsements from some influential personalities. When Jack then began to explain that he would have my interests at heart and would be the buffer between myself and the publisher, I began to feel more and more comfortable with him.

I also began to feel a real sense of excitement. This was really happening.

I couldn't wait to tell Ben about today's meeting and it made me smile, it was almost as though Ben had become my Stan.

Speaking of Stan, I haven't given up on my search for him yet, but right now, I need to get on with Ben's story…

Throughout the next year, I was well organised and in control and was even starting to earn some revenue from the demos that were beginning to turn into small orders.

Nelson's software was harder to sell because the outlay with computer hardware was extremely expensive, so I focused my attention on turning the impressive demo into an offering to provide drawings through a service bureau. It worked so well and I began to build up a few clients.

Coleman was still trying to undermine me at every given opportunity and I considered I'd done pretty well to keep him at bay with my results.

Or so I thought.

When Peter called me into his office, I immediately suspected he'd found yet another nit-picking issue, but no.

"Ben, you need to sit down on this one." His expression was serious and emotion welled up in me yet again. Had Peter finally found a way of getting me out?

He certainly looked as though he was enjoying the moment.

"The company is still struggling with the debt and cash flow from the collapse of PI. I'm afraid we're having to cut back and let more staff go."

I took a deep breath and let him continue. "Maurice wants to limit the redundancies, but in doing so it may continue for a few more months, well, until we're in the clear."

He pressed on, not waiting for me to respond.

"In your team, I have to lose twenty outside staff, including a supervisor, and two inside, so come back to me with your recommendations."

That was it. There was no small talk with Peter. He really was a despicable man.

"Ok?" he said coldly, waving his hands at me in a gesture to shoo me out. "Well go on, get on with it."

I left that meeting wondering how Coleman had broken The Peter Principal by being promoted to a level of incompetence and yet, by some kind of miracle, stayed in the role. I was numb, angry and frustrated. Not just with Coleman but also now with Maurice.

My team were doing so well and making good profits; we didn't deserve this.

I suddenly felt an overwhelming determination to take back control. I refused to be undermined anymore.

I thought about what Stan would want me to do and I took a step back and began to plot.

I was angry, but that was good, because now I was fired up and in the right frame of mind to hatch a plan.

The way I saw it, Onelock was potentially dying on its feet. I figured with Coleman representing it, the company would definitely fold. Maybe it was time to jump ship?

I requested several meetings with Coleman to discuss things, but all I got were excuses as he kept putting me off; he really had no time for me.

One afternoon I caught him though and I wasn't about to be fobbed off again.

"Peter, can I have a minute?" I strode confidently into his office, shutting the door behind me.

"What, right now?" he practically rolled his eyes at me but I stood firm.

"It won't take long." I glared at him, he'd pushed me too far now.

With a shrug, he extended his arm to the seat in front of him but I was already sitting down and I couldn't help notice his frown.

"The thing is, Peter," I felt in control, I had nothing to lose. "My results speak for themselves, but I honestly feel no matter what I do I will never be good enough in your eyes."

I sat back as he smirked at me, a typical Coleman mannerism.

"Well, Ben, this is awkward," he was nodding, "but yes, you're right."

I almost laughed out loud. There it was, and he didn't even care to defend it.

However, I was ready for this reaction, he had now crossed a line with me.

I pushed my chair back and stood up calmly.

"Yep," I nodded, "I thought so."

I looked down at him, enjoying the vantage point of standing up.

"Well, Peter, I guess any awkwardness disappears if I also disappear."

He narrowed his eyes, clearly wondering at my meaning, and for a moment we stared at each other.

Then I walked out.

I felt good though, like I had regained some power. Coleman didn't believe in me, but I wasn't going to let one person shatter my confidence. In fact, Peter had actually done me a favour, he had set me free.

And now I felt ready to fly…

"So, had you just threatened to quit?" I ask, "I'm confused."

Ben throws his head back and roars with laughter, "And that's exactly how I wanted Peter to feel."

I was now holding my own with most aspects of the business, and, in seven years I had learned far more than I would if I had gone to university. Here I was without a degree, poor schooling and a handful of fairly meaningless qualifications, but I knew I could rely on what came naturally to me and *this* came naturally.

I was smitten with Dex UK and passionate about the potential. I felt I could now exercise some structural and stylistic freedom and create something special

Mary and I had often discussed this scenario and we both agreed now that the time was right. I was ready for the unthinkable; ready to leave.

Stan was in my head guiding me. *Assess the risk, Ben.*

So, I began to plan, to strategise and to weigh up the risks. This, I realised, was another gift that had surfaced through my training; my ability to focus on what I wanted the final outcome to be.

That outcome was ultimately some control in Dex UK, so I concentrated on that goal, which would mean prizing it away from Onelock. They still owned 75% and Nelson's Dex Inc the other 25%.

Obviously at that point Onelock's attention was elsewhere, in their moment of weakness now was my time to strike, and I hatched a cunning plan.

I put my plan to John Devlin and got him on side, and when Nelson next came over John and I presented him with my proposal.

Nelson was very enthusiastic.

"Let's just play this out, see how it unfolds," I commanded, "don't say a word to anyone else."

They both looked questioningly at my last statement so I quoted another 'Stanism'.

"You don't interrupt your enemy when they are making a mistake."

Devlin smiled and puffed on his big fat cigar, nodding his understanding and Nelson shook his head with an admiring smile at me.

To convince Onelock to let go I needed to make Bob think I was going to walk, so that Nelson could add pressure by threatening to pull out of the Dex operation. His reason for this being *because* of my departure.

Yes, we were bringing the new venture to its knees before it had even got wings, but the company had brought it on themselves.

I knew Nelson and I held the ace cards; it would be impossible for Onelock to allow me to walk away so quickly. I was, after all, key in the short term to their thirst for continued profitability as well as stability of the computer system, so together we had leverage.

Once Nelson and I had got Bob in a check-mate situation, he had nowhere to go.

As planned, Nelson offered Bob an olive branch of compromise. He explained that he knew how excited I was about the software and that he would offer me employment with him.

This meant that I would stay to do a three-month handover, and Nelson could ensure it was clean and swift as well as continuing to support the current computer system.

Part of that stipulation though, was that Nelson would do so only if he took over Dex UK, giving one-hundred percent ownership to Dex Inc.

It was a pincer move, leaving Onelock with nowhere to go.

Stan would have been so proud of me.

When Bob sat me down one day, I was poker faced.

"Ben," Bob was solemn as he spoke, "I will support you on this one."

I kept a straight face as he continued. "I've actually wondered if you have manipulated this situation, but I must say, if you have, you deserve a bloody Oscar."

I smiled calmly but inside my heart skipped a beat as I delivered my line. "Bob, I'm no actor, but I *am* a business man."

Bob took Nelson's proposal to Maurice with his blessing so we had no doubts he would approve it. Maurice had far too many pressures at that time and he agreed without hesitation.

Nelson, Devlin and myself had secretly agreed that once the deal was done and Dex Inc had bagged Dex UK, then Devlin and myself would take 75% of the UK company, split equally. In return, we would both put up £10k of our own cash, which at that time was equivalent to 30% of my mortgage. A financial risk, but it was a brilliant initiative and thankfully we executed it perfectly. Well deserved, Ben, Stan would have said, you do deserve a bloody Oscar!

"Very cunning," I say admirably.

"It was, and it made me reflect on when I had first shown such duplicity."

"Go on…" I urge Ben.

"Well, it sounds silly but there's a memory that sticks with me. I recall at eight years old playing hide and seek in the woods near our home with my friends.

'It's your turn, Ben,' shouted Ray. I ran off deep into the woods that stretched for a mile from a farm to a quarry.

I made out that I was running towards the quarry but then deceptively doubled back to where they were counting and squatted behind a bush no more than thirty feet away from them.

'I saw him head towards the quarry!' Ray declared when he'd finished counting and I giggled quietly to myself as they ran off in the direction I had originally set.

As they disappeared into the distance, I stood up, a big, proud smile on my face.

They obviously couldn't find me, and eventually I had to go hunting for them before it got dark.

I think even at that age I was beginning to discover tactical skills and the ability to implement them quite impressively."

Chapter 12

Do what You Hate to Get what You Love

+ 1984 +

It felt so good to be a part of Dex. It was like it was a part of me, especially as I was about to own 37.5%.

Mary and I were mortgaged to the hilt by this time, since we had moved house a couple of years earlier. We managed to borrow £10k to buy the shares, but the risk and responsibility to keep up the repayments weighed heavy, especially as my income was unchanged.

I duly handed over the reins to Terry, my number two, so that I could focus on Dex, with the promise that I would be on hand to support him.

It was agreed that the hand over would be completed within three months.

As expected, the redundancies continued a month later and Coleman, who had no appetite to use the computer and software we had worked so hard to commission, agreed with Bob to let it lapse. Now that man deserved an award for incompetence!

This meant that upon my official exit we had the computer and equipment to ourselves.

Bob also agreed that Nelson could let Dex continue, providing it paid a peppercorn rent to use the main frame computer and office space. It was perfect.

"You wily bugger!" I exclaim and Ben grins proudly.

By December 1983 we were completely isolated from Onelock and using the door into the main computer room as our own business entrance. I set myself up in one of the offices and created a meeting room in the other.

Our offices were so frugal that I had to beg for chairs and desks from Onelock, which, let's be honest there were plenty of spare, after all the redundancies.

So, we were set, the business was ready, now we just needed sales.

The romance of gaining company ownership and taking the grand title of Managing Director was soon to fade into raw reality though.

John Devlin was there as technical support for the main frame computer and the associated equipment we used, but the sales side was down to me.

It felt as though everything was down to me to be honest. I was in effect a one-man band, without the sales the business would fall at the first hurdle.

It was a lonely existence at times. I was used to a team and an office buzzing with activity and pressure.

Now there was simply a silence that was only broken when I picked up the phone to make another cold sales call. I worked through the telephone book, making my pitch to sell the services of the system on a bureau basis and trying to reel customers in for demos.

I can seriously say I absolutely hated every call I made. I

would grind out the calls all day long, forcing one after another. Sometimes, a week would go by with nothing but rejection and it was a completely demoralising time, but I continually learned from mistakes. Whenever I felt myself getting down though, I'd let Stan's words back into my head to lift me.

Sometimes you have to do what you hate to get what you love.

To break up the week I started to canvass local businesses; knocking on doors and dropping leaflets I had prepared.

I felt so far outside of my comfort zone and I seriously considered quitting on numerous occasions. It was a horrible time and I really had to dig deep to motivate myself because I couldn't face failing and letting my wife and family down.

Those few moments when a customer would commit to a demo were like an injection of adrenaline though and enough to keep driving me forward.

Very gradually, I established a few customers and began to earn a regular monthly income and gain some stability.

Meanwhile, Nelson was supportive of my efforts, but back in the USA his sales weren't too impressive. His main customer was DEO and he relied purely on them ordering additional software as they rolled the system out to more sites. Nelson knew how to create quality computer code, after all, having been educated at Harvard, one could say he was a genius.

The trouble was, his strengths did not lay in managing people, being customer facing, or pretty much anything to do with the business side of the company.

This was through his own admission as well as my perception and one of the reasons why such an amazing product was being held up in a small office with just six programmers.

What drove me first and foremost was the fear of going broke and I had to keep overheads to a minimum even when we gradually began to accumulate profit.

The software, though, was something I was in awe of and I never stopped believing in it. Whenever I performed a demo, I couldn't get over the reaction and I just knew AEC was a winner.

I also knew my destiny was in my hands alone and I was determined to reach the next stage where I could afford to employ someone else to help support the demo's and the sales.

My big break came with a couple of clients who were interested in buying a system rather than renting a service and Nelson did actually come over to help me close the deal. Things were starting to take off.

It wasn't until we bagged a major insurance firm though that I knew we were really on our way.

The rich insurance giant known as Londex were moving from their old facility across the street into a new build that was in the throes of being completed.

The building was an innovative glass structure that looked like a giant petrochemical plant but was the talk of the city. I stood ten feet tall and this became the project I would talk about to help close every new deal.

It was a huge coup, my revenue at the time was about £20k per year and this order, with hardware and software, exceeded £140k.

I was beside myself with excitement and tempted to increase my salary to take the pressure off our family finances, but I knew I had to invest in the longer term and take more risk.

That decision came from my head and not my heart. One day, I promised myself, I would take that investment back into my family, with profit from selling the business.

+ + +

Despite all my training at Onelock, one thing I hadn't been involved in, besides sales, was the recruitment of staff.

My first hire was a young kid called Alex and it was his first job. Alex was a bright, technical enthusiast who was a programming junior and lived and breathed computers, so I knew I could fast track him.

We weren't recklessly throwing money at new people or breaking the bank, I still wanted to take a cautious approach.

One morning, a beautiful, brand new Jaguar pulled up outside our door. In those days, it was rare to see such an iconic car so we were all eyes.

"Maurice has sent in the cavalry," Devlin shouted above the noise of the computer when a smartly dressed man stepped out of the car.

We all watched as our visitor opened the rear door of his Jaguar and pulled out a long tube.

He swiftly walked into our office and I stepped forward, wondering if perhaps he was lost.

"Brian," he introduced himself confidently, shaking my hand with a firm grip. "Onelock sent me round."

I didn't introduce myself but simply let him explain.

"I sell microfilm, it's useful to store all of your drawings."

Smiling at Brian, I proudly gestured to the main frame computer humming away behind us. "Yes, but so does this."

Brian looked bemused but I could tell he was interested and when he began to ask questions I found him to be quite engaging; he had a presence about him and, with his dark hair combed back, he reminded me of Maurice. I found myself wanting to tell him about what we did and when he listened intently, I couldn't help but like him and I gave a quick demo.

I was confident of the reaction I would get to my magic show, and, as expected, he beamed with excitement and disbelief.

"Look," his enthusiasm was evident, "I've just sold my business and I am now consulting on my own. I've kept contact with my city customers and I could make some introductions." My heart soared but I stayed calm, Stan was in my head again. *"Body language, Ben. Don't let the enemy read your every move, treat it like a poker game."*

This was perfect though, exactly where I was hoping the conversation would go, this could be my sales person.

But then reality hit home when it occurred to me that someone of his calibre would be way out of our league. Thinking on my feet I pointed out we were a start-up and couldn't afford to employ anyone but that we could offer him a generous commission if he closed a deal. Seeing his slight hesitancy, I followed this by mentioning my success with Londex and I knew I had him hooked.

He held out his hand to me. "I'd like to get together and work out some detail, but I'm in."

I shook his hand and we arranged to meet again soon.

I couldn't believe it: I had built my team quicker than I could have ever imagined and I was looking forward to great things to come.

Another late night, and I'm writing Ben's story, storming away you might say, when I get a message, from Jack.

"Can you stage a picture of your cat sitting on your laptop and tweet it?"

"What?" I reply incredulously.

"Everyone loves animal pictures; it'll get a lot of likes."

Christ, I run my hands through my hair, he's actually serious.

With a sigh, I save what I've been working on and shake my head at what I'm about to do.

"Matilda!" I call my cat.

The social media frenzy it seems, has begun, and I'm ready to go…

Over time, Brian began to bring his city clients down and I would work my magic to keep them keen and build up strong prospects.

Meanwhile, I was hatching a plan to offer something in between the high cost of a system and the service bureau. There was a vast chasm between our offerings. I discussed with Nelson the viability of extending the bureau over a lease line so we could put the equipment on the customers site linked into the main frame at our offices. There was little effort needed technically, so within a month we had added it as an option and it got immediate interest, and results.

One of Brian's city bankers signed up with their building in Croydon.

The deal was worth about £2k per month and we had three months of capital to fund into the equipment, so month four was profit. This became my first lesson in cash flow as I quickly understood the power of cash in the bank to leverage opportunities like this.

Then in came another surprise order for a full system. I had been bidding for the business of a furniture giant for some time but without a track record I didn't think we stood a chance. The two guys that were sourcing a system for saw the potential to not only procure our outstanding software but to also tie up a deal to offer bureau services similar to ours.

We all connected well, it was people chemistry working its magic.

The order was significant because it was in their prestigious London head office. We were also particularly excited at the prospect of them rolling the system out to other dealerships around the country at a later date.

DEO in the UK was also a prospect I had been chasing for a long while as Nelson had secured all of their business in the US, and things started to move when two of their guys showed interest.

One was their European facilities manager, who wanted to procure the system for the UK and Munich, and the other was a guy who intended to break away and set up on his own. Phil wanted to set up a bureau in partnership with an architectural practice. We secured both orders, although the business with Phil's newly formed venture needed a carefully constructed contract to ensure they didn't take bureau business from us.

I'd always thought it was important to listen to customers, to understand their needs.

It was a skill that, coupled with my background in construction, was an asset when I set up an independent user group.

The plan was to encourage our customers to decide a committee and elect a chairman.

I would then be invited to sit on the committee which would give me an insight into our customer's view point. I was fully aware that this venture could turn into a pressure group and a vehicle for customers to complain. However, I wanted satisfied customers, so complaints would be listened to and corrected where necessary.

Our team were driven to provide excellence in terms of software and after-sales support, so I was confident. Nothing keeps you in check as much as when you argue a 'why we have to' point and somebody delivers a superb example of 'why not though', but this was fortunately rare.

It was the facilities manager of Londex who agreed to be our very first chairman and our first user group took place in their very prestigious 1986 building. It was a proud moment, not only having such a well know city institution as a customer, but holding the first user group in such an iconic building.

As much as I hated getting those crowded trains into London, I did love walking through the city and savouring that sense of pride that ran through me as we passed building after building knowing our systems ran many of them.

Another morning in the Little Red Café, and I'm regaling Ben with Jack's tweeting mission from the previous night. He's distracted again though and I can't help but notice he is tapping his fingers on the table top.

I've seen him do this a few times when he is deep in thought and I decide to ask him about it.

"Hmm?" I bring him out of his revelry with my question and he smiles. "Sorry, M. Yes, I have a song in me."

I laugh but stop quickly when I see he is actually serious.

"I've had this beat going around in my head for years and one day I intend to get it into music and lyrics."

I'm stunned. Just when I think I'm beginning to know this man, he surprises me with another revelation.

"As you know, my other passion, after football, was to be a musician. However, I had neither a musical education or the support from my parents. In fact, my dad was so anti pop music that when I begged for a guitar at the age of eleven he remarked that The Beatles were just long-haired hippies and there was no way I was going to be one of those.

No wonder I became one!

At twenty-one, when I'd worked with Dave and he'd tried to teach me guitar, I grew to love writing songs, lyrics seemed to come naturally to me.

The guitar though wasn't so natural, even with Dave's expert tuition, and when I got onto the music scene, I realised my musical skills and my voice just weren't exceptional enough.

I did believe in my lyrics but that wasn't going to give me a career, although I wrote a number of songs and even had one published. It was called 'Californian Concert' and was inspired by my exit from the States. The record sold next to nothing and I probably still have the only copy left in the world!

So, there it was again, the story of my life. Just as with football, every time I wanted to carve out a career in something I was passionate about, the realities of life came home to roost."

"Well, you never know, Ben," I say quietly, "it could still happen."

Ben chuckles, "You're right, M. Maybe I'll find a musician to make my song a hit. Just like I found a biographer, you, to write my story. As the great man, Stan, would say; 'play to your strengths.' I really envy people who can make a career out of what they love."

Ben nods at me here and I realise he is referring to me. He's right. I'm suddenly overwhelmingly grateful that I am here, making a career out of my writing, something I love. Well done me, I silently congratulate myself.

"I think it was then that I decided all I could hope for was, that one day, I would discover a talent that I could shape and hone. I deeply yearned for that greatest gift of all, love of my work."

"Is there anything you haven't done, or don't want to do?" I tease him.

"Ha ha, plenty M, believe me!"

But I don't believe him. Never have I met someone with so much drive and ambition, even after his so-called retirement. He puts me to shame and I've barely even started!

I can only hope some of his traits will rub off on me...

I was by now used to, and in fact embraced, the surprises that came with every new day, that's what business does.

Sales were now strong and Brian wanted to invest and take a salary so John Devlin and myself agreed to Brian investing £10k for 10% and we would dilute to 32.5%.

We also agreed Brian would be salaried and we took that notion to Nelson in the U.S.

Brian and I did all the travelling, as Devlin had to maintain duties running the computer system, more on Onelock's behalf than ours.

When we met up with Nelson, he seemed to be in complete awe of what I had achieved in the UK in such a short space of time and insisted I take a salary increase.

I agreed, and although I accepted less than Nelson had suggested it was very much welcome; at that stage Mary and I were really struggling financially.

Nelson was obviously impressed with our management and he finally requested some support from us. He suggested that he would run the software development and I could mastermind the rest of the US business. This, I knew, would be a real challenge, but we agreed we should afford the time and investment to emulate in Boston what we had achieved in the UK.

When we returned home, John Devlin took a dim view to my salary increase, despite the fact that he too had been given a rise. I was pretty bemused; Devlin was on only slightly less than me with nothing like the responsibility, so his complaint made no sense, in fact, his whole attitude irritated me.

I decided to let it go, little did I know it was to become a problem he couldn't get over.

By now, computing technology had already moved on and Digital Equipment released a mini version of the Vax main frame, called Micro Vax.

It was a fraction of the size of the mainframe, like a filing cabinet, and was to be the first step in allowing me to pull away from Onelock.

The thought of total independence spurred me on and I decided to re-locate the business.

Within a short space of time I found the perfect facility just a mile away. It was a square blue-glassed building with warehouse space on the ground floor and carpeted first floor office space, in total about two-thousand square foot.

It was perfect, but with the rent at £28k per annum and a

lease that meant twenty-five year's commitment, it was also a huge risk.

I knew that if we could sustain the orders of the magnitude we had recently enjoyed, it was doable. Just.

I was confident, Brian was confident, and Nelson was supportive, but Devlin still couldn't get over my salary increase and he tendered his notice.

I bought back his shares which gave me a controlling interest of 65%, leaving Brian with 10% and Nelson still with his 25% holding.

Devlin worked his notice respectfully and without any problems, and we eventually moved into our new offices nearby.

"Do you realise how incredible that sounds to me," I ask Ben, "in such a short space of time, you had gone from being pretty much an office junior to now owning your own company?"

Ben shakes his head, "On the one hand, M, all of your admiration is making me cringe a bit."

"Charming!" I exclaim.

"But when I think back," Ben ignores me, "it does sound pretty incredible to me too. I suppose back then I was so caught up in the business, I never took the time to stop and consider just what I was achieving."

"I guess that would have meant taking your eye off the ball, hey?" I make reference to Stan with a twinkle in my eyes and Ben smiles.

Chapter 13

This Was My Dream

With the lease signed and the rent stretching our budget considerably, we had to fit out the first floor pretty frugally.

This was where having a furniture supplier as a customer proved useful; we were able to obtain a discounted quote to install internal office partitioning and furniture on the first floor.

Onelock allowed us to take away the peripheral computer equipment which Coleman had decided not to use, and we invested in our own new Micro Vax computer so we were no longer reliant on Onelock's main frame Vax.

We were self-sufficient and it felt so good.

Don't get me wrong, I felt the weight of the overheads immediately, but by now we had some solid revenue.

As I negotiated loans on hardware, the office refurb, and an overdraft with the bank, I was aware that it was my head, and therefore my family's, on the line for any consequences.

On the first morning after the refit, I arrived before everyone else came into the office. I wanted to take it all in. I wanted to have a rare moment to myself and to stop and think about what had just happened.

My whole body tingled as I pulled into the newly created business park which housed a dozen or so brand new, blue-tinted, boxy buildings, all linked together like terraced units.

I parked in my personal space and, with a racing heart, I strode across the red-paved car park that was skirted with shrubs amid the little areas of lawn.

I couldn't help but beam a proud smile and felt almost as though I were having an out of body experience; that all this was a dream.

I stood before our newly fitted out facility, with anticipation building.

This *was* a dream. It was *my* dream.

This was Dex, the company that back in 1983 I had known was my destiny. This caterpillar had finally formed its beautiful red wings and now it must fly into the future.

I walked the few steps up to the glass fronted door. The morning was befitting the experience, with the sun bouncing off the front of the building. I unlocked and pushed open the heavy entrance door and glanced up at the stairwell that was filling with morning sunlight which highlighted the sleek lines of the grey steel stair case. Walking up the stairs, I looked at the huge grey wall in the stairwell and envisaged hanging a huge company mural. My heart was thumping with excitement as I pushed open the office door and breathed in the rich smell of new carpet.

I was in absolute awe, I loved it.

The offices had been designed to skirt the perimeter of the square building, creating an open plan area in the centre. The internal walls were decorated in a light wall paper and the aluminum trim was anodized in red.

Beside each solid wooden oak door was a foot wide, full height side panel in grey smoked glass, finished off with smart venetian blinds for privacy.

The attention to detail had been worth the effort. I walked into my office and the hairs on the back of my neck stood up. I shivered as I spun around to take it all in. It was surreal.

My desk sat against one wall with a high back blue covered executive chair on castors. In the corner of the room, beside a white board, was a round meeting table with three blue sleigh chairs.

Despite my frugality, it had all come together perfectly, and it looked amazing.

Caught up as I was in these exciting times, part of me wanted to push the envelope and keep investing whilst times were good. Fortunately, though, I was learning caution. Just as well really, because hard times were on the horizon.

Alex was working on servicing the bureau projects and with more flowing in, the lease work was expanding.

Around the lease line we had created a product that could be packaged to include the software, hardware and an operator, and we were selling that system with options of either purchase or rental, stand-alone or lease line. Alongside that we would train customers or provide onsite staff and we were quickly getting into our stride.

I had sole responsibility for the accounts and I'd take the books home with me in the evening or at weekends to keep them up to date. Those days as a financial controller had paid off.

I'm wondering at this point how Mary must have felt. Ben obviously had his hands full trying to make his business a success, but it must have been difficult for Mary, managing the home and the children. And whenever Ben was home, he was working.

I don't say anything but I think, not for the first time, what a remarkably strong woman she is.

We had moved the software into some diverse and huge UK corporations and were beginning to put a lot more pressure on Nelson's team, wanting more from the software than even his own US operation demanded. I wanted excellence and Nelson was capable of delivering it but I wondered whether he could tolerate being pushed so hard. It would have meant him increasing his staff, and with his operation simply surviving on sales to DEO, he didn't have the funding to do it. In the past two years, we had accumulated a lot of sales and cash, whilst Nelson was struggling.

These were danger signs, but before I even had a chance to discuss it with him, Nelson pushed again the idea that we try and replicate in the US what we were doing in the UK, which I thought was rather positive if a little unexpected.

By the time Nelson came over to discuss his idea with Brian and I, I had a plan.

Nelson didn't have the cash or profit to operate the US business in the same vein as the UK one, he needed investment.

We agreed to use our UK funds to invest in the US and I set out a tough but fair stance to create a holding company which we called Tech Group.

The new company would wholly own both Dex Inc and Dex UK. The negotiations that followed were critical. At that point Nelson currently owned 100% of Dex Inc and 25% of Dex UK.

I convinced him to give up control so that, between Brian and myself, we had 60%. There was no real financial justification to this other than Nelson knew his operation was struggling and ours was booming.

So it was, I had 40%, Brian 20% and Nelson 40%. In just three years from the start up, I had clawed my way from being a non-shareholder in a UK agency to owning 40% of both the UK and American operation.

It was a sweet move and though there wasn't much time to stop and digest it, I felt pretty bloody proud of myself.

I didn't realise just how shrewd my plan had been until late 1986, when there was a profound shake up in the city.

The old boys network of regulation was abolished by Maggie Thatcher to allow competition to flourish. It had a profound impact on city institutions and they scrambled to invest in technology.

Of course, there wasn't anything more innovative than what we were doing, and in order to sustain our innovative edge I encouraged those little grey fabrics of ideas as they appeared.

In the period before and after Christmas, we were taking an order a week for six consecutive weeks.

It was one of the most exciting times, Christmas had, quite literally, come early for us.

Orders followed from great companies and our prestigious list grew and grew.

We were on a roll and I like to think these weren't just lucky breaks but the result of some really good preparation merged with hard work and determination.

I'll always remember a conversation I had with a guy from one major company.

"Ben, we love the system! Get us a quote and remember, profit isn't a dirty word." His words resonated with me. I mean I knew all that, but how very refreshing to hear it.

I took the revenue and invested, starting with staff.

We increased the sales force under Brian, as well as our services staff, to cope with bureau work, and our technical support team.

Most of my thinking time in terms of strategy was late at night or weekends and it was at this time I hatched a plan to charge for hardware maintenance.

We already charged for maintaining the software and this,

together with rental income, gave us a solid and smooth income stream.

With an increase in staff salaries and rent to pay we still needed cash so we set up an increased overdraft facility of £250k, all supported by my personal guarantee.

Once again, I was signing my life away to guarantee the overdraft as well as making shrewd investment decisions with the personal assets that Mary and I held. Whilst we were both excited, Mary and I were also nervous at the increasing debt and risk.

This experience made me appreciate that when I was employed by Onelock the same thing was going on with owners and management there. As a humble employee, why would I care about the stress and debt they were harbouring? The worst that could have happened to me was losing my job.

I guess when you're not the one taking that kind of pressure, not the one with debt, it's not so important. As the owner, though, all of the pressure, and debt, is yours.

It weighs heavy, but then again, if you get a return on your investment, so too are the rewards your own, which is why entrepreneurs should get more recognition.

As I've mentioned, it's without a shadow of doubt that one of the biggest motivators is the fear of going broke. It's not just about the opportunities we are given but what we make of those opportunities.

For any entrepreneur, seeing an opportunity and making it work must come naturally.

This very mechanism was being repeated up and down our country, giving rise to and creating employment, and encouraging people to seek opportunity and reap the rewards.

By now I was learning fast that cash is king.

There's a fine balance in keeping yourself within those overdraft limits and investing more to grow the business. I was beginning to appreciate just how much cash needed to be spent before we could recover it back from sales.

When my bank manager pointed out that more businesses go bust through over trading than under trading, I latched onto his words and exercised some caution.

But we drove the business into its third year and it felt like our infant company was growing up; we now had twelve staff and were filling the spare seating I had originally created.

What's more, our success was driving more programmers and support staff into the US office, so Brian and I planned a visit to the US to check things were running smoothly.

As we boarded our flight, I looked to my left at the wide reclining seats, the champagne being passed around to the passengers, and I wanted that.

Brian nudged me in the back. "Economy lands at the same time as first class," he pointed out.

"So what?" I replied. "When I can afford it, I'm going first class all the way. I want to feel like I've landed first. I want to feel fresh. I want to feel like I've finally arrived in the world."

Ben has been busy for a few weeks with his planning projects and something to do with saving his football club. I'm still not quite sure what the latter is about, he's been very mysterious about it, simply saying he can't disclose anything until he has firm confirmation. He's excited about it though. The last time we met, his eyes were bright and he was in good spirits…

I told him what I'd managed to find out about Stan thus far. This being exactly nothing.

"I just think he played such a huge role in your early career that I, and I'm sure our readers, want to know what became of him."

Ben had nodded, "Unlikely he's still alive, but still, I've often wondered myself…"

As I sit here typing from my notes, I think again of the relation-ship between Stan and Ben and the similarities with my relationship with Ben. He's certainly not a father figure, but it does feel a little like he's become my mentor.

Just as with Stan, there is no real personal information shared. He knows little about me.

I'm not sure if that's because he doesn't need to, because I hav-en't shared anything much, or because Ben is simply just wired to business.

Either way, as this project has evolved, I am continuously grateful that he has given me this opportunity, and my respect for him and what he has achieved increases with every chapter of this book...

When Brian and I met with Nelson to discuss the running of the US office and the plan to integrate with the UK arm, he seemed to have lost his appetite for growth. I got the impression Nelson felt uncomfortable at the thought of more staff around him, so we agreed that I would handle recruitment for his admin and bureau staff and Brian would recruit and manage his sales staff. Nelson would remain CEO of the US operation, but by reducing those other duties it would free him up to focus on developing the software.

Over the next few months, Brian and I made a couple of trips over to recruit and train the new staff. Under my wing was Joan, the admin manager, and Terri, training as bureau manager.

Brian managed the new sales manager, Diane, and brought in another sales person, Topsy.

With Nelson increasing his programming and technical staff, that brought the total in the US office to seventeen.

Over the course of that year the effect was almost immedi-ate and the US sales rose sharply. The problem was Nelson was struggling to come to terms with this rapid change, and as his three new managers settled in, his attitude towards them became something of an issue.

"Oops, the cracks were beginning to show?"

Ben nods glumly, "Don't forget Nelson was a techy geek, he didn't really do people. As for people management," he sucks in his breath, shaking his head, "forget it! Brian and I had to do a lot of hand holding during that period."

"That's pretty tough when you had the UK office to run too."

Ben starts laughing. "It was a pretty crazy time!"

"Go on…"

Chapter 14

We've Got
Competition!

"Have you ever been skiing, M?"

With no idea as to where this is heading, I tell Ben that I'm more sunshine than snow, but I know this is leading somewhere so I humour him...

+1987+

I'd never been skiing before, so when, on one of my many trips to Boston, Nelson asked me to join him and his two children on the slopes, I jumped at the chance.

I went straight out and bought all the gear; ski goggles, thermals, ski suit, boots, several scarfs, gloves. I was prepared and looking forward to another thrill-seeking adventure.

"Hey John," I called out when I met up with Nelson at the bottom of the slope.

To my astonishment, he took one look at me and burst out laughing.

"Jeez, Ben, this is Boston, not the frickin antartic!"

My heart sank when I looked around me at the other skiers, all in ski suits, yes, but not quite the winter wonderland outfit I'd trussed myself up in.

Ah well, I shrugged my epic fail aside, I was excited to get going.

The journey up to the first ski slopes in the white mountains was something I will never forget. The trees had started losing their vivid colour and were developing a starkness, in readiness for the cold winter.

We headed further North where the landscape became more volatile, the hills topped with white snowy peaks. We climbed higher and higher up the mountain range towards our resort destination and before me was one of the prettiest sights I've ever seen.

I had a fire burning in my belly; pure anticipation of racing down those sleek white slopes.

"Ben, this is Tom, he'll be your instructor for today." I was confused as I politely shook the younger mans hand, not missing his smirk at my ski get up, and I looked at Nelson.

"But…"

Nelson smiled kindly, "Ben, you need a few lessons on the bunny slopes before you take on the runs."

"I'll be fine!" I insisted, but Nelson and the instructor, Tom, were shaking their heads.

It was with a sinking feeling and the urge to stamp my feet like a petulant child that I watched as Nelson and his kids disappeared up the mountain to enjoy the black runs.

"Ok, ready?" Tom gestured for me follow him.

Tom spent a couple of hours teaching me to bend my knees as we practised traversing and safe falling sideways, as well as, of course, the all-important breaking to stop or slow myself by pointing the tips of my skis together.

It was all very enjoyable but I wanted to be up there on the mountain, I was too impatient and I'd been told those dreaded words; You can't.

When we met up for lunch, I tried to convince Nelson I was ready to get the chair lift and take a run down the huge wide slope.

He raised his eyebrows, "Really?" He looked pretty doubtful. "You've barely had a mornings lesson."

"Ah come on!" I felt so ready, "Let's cancel this afternoon's lesson, I'll come up with you."

Nelson didn't seem overly enthralled, obviously wanting to be doing the tricky runs rather than ski down the big slope with me.

I realised then that whilst skiing was fun, it wasn't very sociable if you're on different skill levels.

Still, I duly cancelled my lesson and joined Nelson on the big slope.

As we queued for the ski lift, Nelson kept repeating, "Remember, just zig-zag, watch out for other skiers, and when you can't turn just fall on your side."

I can do that, I thought, course I could. What was the big deal here?

I looked at the lift that ran parallel up and down the mountain. On either side there were tall pine trees laden with snow. It was a spectacular sight but I wasn't here to sight-see, I was on a mission. The adrenaline was pumping and I wanted to ski my first run.

"See you up there!" Nelson called and he and his children took the first two chairs.

I was on my own. I panicked a little as I clambered awkwardly into the seat but I pulled the safety bar down and rested my skis on the top.

It was mesmerizing and I was completely lost in the experience, taking in the blanket of brilliant white snow all around me.

As the lift trundled its way up the mountain, I looked down at the many skiers traversing down the slope and I began to hum one of my favourite pieces of music – White night by Ludovico Einaudi.

With hindsight, I should have been concentrating on how the skiers got off the lift at the top, but I was in the zone, imagining what a rush it would be to just ski straight down that slope.

It was a steep slope and ended in a gully, gently rising up again to where the queue for the lift was.

Minutes later, we'd arrived at the top of the mountain and I waited for the lift to stop so that I could get out.

As the skilled skiers around me pushed up their bars and began to ski off to the side, the chair lift rose quickly and then began to descend. It only occurred to me then that it was on a loop and would not be stopping any time soon.

There wasn't much time to make my move, and my God, I needed time.

My moment came and I tried to lift the bar but for some reason it just wouldn't raise up.

"Come on!" I willed it in frustration, desperately yanking on the stupid bar to release myself. Too late, I realised it was my skis resting on top of it that were hindering me!

The chair lift was rising again and in that instant I wondered whether I should jump, but by now my moment was gone.

The chair lift emptied of all its occupants but me and rose back up the mountain and I could hear the hoots of laughter from down below.

"Yeah, very funny." I muttered through gritted teeth, preparing to face my fellow skiers and knowing that I was quite clearly now the main attraction.

As expected, when I finally arrived back at the bottom, the lift still in motion, I was greeted to a round of applause from the other skiers, including Nelson and his kids.

"Hey, I was enjoying the view!" I laughed along with them, even giving a flourishing little bow. Oh, I took it in my stride alright, but I'd be lying if I said my pride wasn't a little wounded.

The lift began its ascent and back up I went, feeling my growing unease.

Right, I thought determinedly, this time I'll be ready.

As I prepared myself for those few seconds I'd have to ski off the chair lift, I could feel my heart thumping, my cheeks were hot and I was struggling to catch my breath. I suddenly had visions of me riding the bloody thing until someone switched it off to let me off.

It cranked and clattered and I steeled myself for my moment. When it arrived, I lifted my ski's and forced the bar up.

The chair swung and swayed as I pushed myself off it.

Ok, I can land this, I thought ambitiously, just before I fell flat on my face in the snow.

As you can imagine, peals of laughter rang out around me, but I didn't care, I was off that darn lift.

"First time skiing?" A young couple helped me to my feet, their mirth evident, especially when they clocked my outfit.

"How could you tell?" I dead-panned and they began to giggle uncontrollably.

"Do you want us to help you ski down?" they kindly offered through their laughter, but I still had some pride, just.

"No, no, thank you. I'll be fine."

Nelson and his children were nowhere to be seen, so I stood at the top of the slope to take in the beauty of my surroundings.

It had just started to snow and across the top of the slope I spotted a small shack selling hot chocolate. I fumbled around and grabbed a dollar from my zip pocket, this I had to try.

I stood there sipping my hot mint chocolate with the snowflakes falling around me amid the stunning mountain views.

I could have stayed there longer but I knew it was time to face the dreaded ski down.

The slope looked like a ski jump with the gully way down in the distance. I could barely make out the skiers queuing for the lift. It was a pretty daunting view and steeper than I had thought. Tentatively, I traversed across one side to the other, becoming a target for the skiers that were hurtling down the slope.

Oh, this is ridiculous! I thought. Let's get that thrill!

I figured that if I just skied straight down, the gully would slow me at the bottom. Right?

Wrong!

Off I went, whooshing down the slope. The problem was, I hadn't reasoned at just how steep the slope was and the speed that I would reach. It was exhilarating, don't get me wrong, but it was difficult to enjoy it all when I suddenly realised I was going too fast.

I frantically tried to remember what my instructor had taught me in my brief morning lesson and I bent my knees, keeping my skis together.

Well, he definitely would have said, "If you bend your legs and keep your skis straight, you'll go faster."

Christ! I was now hurtling towards the gully at the base of the slope, a queue of skiers right in front of me as I headed straight for them.

It was as though it happened in slow motion; gradually they all began to notice me racing towards them and they panicked, scattering apart as I left the top of the gully, flew a few feet into the air, and finally ploughed into about three of them.

By now my pride had left the building anyway, so seeing that nobody was hurt I gave in and accepted what had clearly been great entertainment; me. I lay there in a heap in the snow amongst roars of hysterical laughter and I laughed like I would never stop.

I did venture up the mountain a few more times after that but I avoided the straight run.

Strangely, I never saw Nelson and his kids again that day…

I am literally crying with laughter, as is Ben. I like this side of him. He genuinely doesn't take himself too seriously, it's one of his nice qualities.

Another being his generosity, as I was about to discover…

I had built a solid and regular income base from our existing customers but growth had started to slow and any new business was being undermined by a new kid on the block.

It was a system called iCAD and it offered similar computer aided design, or CAD features, but on a PC platform, rather than ours that was main or mini frame based.

CAD sat at the heart of our AEC system, but we offered much more than just that; we held data about other aspects of the facility.

In those days, we looked at PC's and laughed; the power they had was nothing in comparison to the mini computer. What we didn't factor in though, was that many other applications were being built on PC's because the authors of iCAD were encouraging developers to integrate with the clever strategy of providing open code.

It was catching on, and the PC and iCAD quickly gathered popularity with multi-purpose computing.

It put extreme pressure on us; iCAD came in at the very low starting price of £2.5k whilst our software was more than ten times that. The hardware was also a fraction of the price.

All we had going for us was a database and performance. I knew there had to be a fundamental shift, so I immediately launched a product which we called AEC packs; aimed at breaking down our software into more affordable modules. That was the short–term solution of course, in the long term we were in trouble here. We had competition!

It was fairly easy to create and we launched within a few weeks, but I was becoming increasingly concerned at the impact iCAD was having on our sales.

It was a bold move, but after much thought I decided it was time to drop our CAD system in AEC and rewrite our software around iCAD.

I reflected at the time on how this market changed so rapidly when new technology took off. The problem was, unless you were the one creating that new technology, it was impossible to judge what exactly *would* take off.

My proposal, as part of our integration with iCAD was for us to become a dealer and developer with what was essentially the competition. I understood what our clients needed and had always seen our business model eventually changing from CAD driven to data driven so this was in fact a positive opportunity.

I recalled those 'wow' demos I'd given in previous years and I wanted to recreate that within iCAD.

This proposal was not welcomed by Nelson, however; he still saw AEC as his panacea.

About a month later, Nelson visited the UK for a routine meeting with Brian and myself. It felt a little frosty, Nelson was still standing his ground not wanting to give up the AEC/CAD element and integrate with iCAD, but he finally succumbed and therefore it was agreed, or so we thought.

Despite our disagreements, the negotiations seemed fine, with no sign at all of just how nasty things were about to get...

"Oh no, what happened?" I'm intrigued, on the edge of my seat, wanting to get all of this down.

"Patience," Ben tells me with a smile, "we'll get to that. Now..."
He leans back with a confident smile, "I have a proposal for you."

I raise a questioning eyebrow as he tells me that he is leaving the following day to visit one of his homes in Miami.

"I'll be gone for a couple of weeks," he explains as I nod politely, desperately trying to hide my disappointment that our interviews will be on hold.

"Ok, I have plenty to be getting on with anyway."

"Well, that's what I was going to suggest," he smiles at me and I hold my breath. "Why don't you come with Mary and I?"

Chapter 15

This Is the Life

✦2016✦

Well there I was, on my way to Miami, and I was determined to enjoy every minute. I chuckled to myself at being flown in Ben's private jet. Just who the hell did I think I was? First class wasn't good enough for me. Haha, dear God, perhaps I'm turning into Ben if I'm starting to think the best is not good enough!

I shook my head and stretched out my legs, a huge smile on my face as I accepted a chilled glass of champagne from the flight attendant and snuggled under the duvet. I almost wanted to pinch myself. Instead, I quickly opened my notebook, desperate to record this experience as it was happening.

I had arrived in heaven, and just when I thought things couldn't get better, my space was quickly transformed into a first-class dining area, with linen table cloth, silverware and an a la carte menu that made my mouth water.

"How cool!" I declared, picking up the little solid silver airplanes that were the salt and pepper pots, and one of the crew members sitting across from me smiled.

I blushed; keep it cool, Mandy, keep it cool.

But I couldn't. This was the life, well, actually this was Ben's life. This was how he travelled, not me. I gave a silent nod to whatever God had blessed me with this good fortune.

It only seemed as though I'd been in the air for a few hours before I was miraculously being fast-tracked straight through customs, like a celebrity, to where Ben's chauffeur was waiting for me in arrivals. He asked how my flight was as he took my bags from me and we walked out of the smart air-conditioned building into heat which hit me like a brick wall. I felt like an electric blanket had suddenly smothered my body and it filled me with contentment and excitement.

"Is Ben at the house?" I asked as I got into the back seat of the limousine.

"Mr Taylor will join you later, madam." Was his polite reply.

"Madam?" I chuckled, "No, no, call me Mandy," I insisted, to which he didn't respond but nodded politely.

"How far is the journey?" I tried to make small talk, feeling a little uncomfortable with his stuffy attitude.

"About twenty-five minutes, madam," As he deliberately ignored my previous request, I rolled my eyes and sat back against the leather seat, deciding to just enjoy the ride. I watched the scenery fly past me and before I knew it, we were confronted with a gate house that was teaming with security.

Good Lord, I muttered to myself, was Ben part of some kind of mafia mob?

As Ben's chauffeur was waved through, my eyes grew wide and my mouth gaped open. The long road ahead was a stunning avenue of tall palm trees and to each side of the road there were lawns swept with manicured tropical shrubs, all amid the backdrop of a pine forest.

"This is simply beautiful," I murmured softly.

"Indeed it is, madam." The chauffeur smiled at me in the mirror, clearly enjoying my first impressions.

We passed a huge waterfall and I gazed in amazement at an adjacent footbridge that looked like something out of Grand Designs. I don't ever want to leave, I thought, I've barely arrived and I don't want to leave this place.

Snap out of it, Mandy, I berated myself, you're here to do a job, just focus!

Get lost, my naughty side chipped in, just enjoy every minute!

We pulled up to two huge gates which opened automatically onto a wide road lined with some of the most beautiful homes I have ever seen. Ben's mansion was the first on the street and as we pulled in I felt as though I had been transported to Italy; it was an impeccable Italianate design with soft colours and lines, dressed with Italian cypress trees and stunning red Bougainville that popped out from an array of other tropical plants.

I'd barely had a chance to dwell on the beauty of this home, when I was swept in through two huge great doors by the caretaker, who introduced himself as Charlie.

"Welcome," he stood back to allow me to take in my surroundings. "Ben and Mary will be back shortly."

Stepping into the great room, my eyes fixated on the view outside. It was truly breath-taking. The infinity pool neatly dropped off to reveal a lake beyond and across to the right was a huge seating area set around a fire pit.

"Beautiful, isn't it?" I jumped, I was so stunned by the sight before me, I'd forgotten Charlie was still there. I nodded as my ears suddenly pricked up and I listened to the classical music that was softly filtering through the house. Above me, a beautiful chandelier hung, circled by a huge galleried landing that was accessed via a huge spiral staircase tucked to one side that led to the upper floor.

I stood there, drinking in the detail, embedding it in my mind, in case this was a dream and I might suddenly wake up. Just at that moment, Ben and Mary walked in.

Mary rolled her eyes, fondly greeting me with a kiss on the cheek. "I see he's staged the scene for you." She meant the music that flowed gently from every room, the lighting, the scented candles. Ben had already told me this is what he does for every guest. He too kissed my cheek and asked about my journey and as I began to squeal like an over excited puppy, I quickly reminded myself that first class travel is no big deal to Ben. Keep it together, Mandy, I silently ordered myself.

"Let's go and eat," Ben suddenly said and I nodded, even though I wasn't very hungry. "We'll introduce you to our club house."

"Club house?" I looked at Ben and Mary and they smiled.

"It's exclusive to the folks who live here…"

Of course it is, I thought to myself, an exclusive club house, I knew that.

I rolled my eyes and followed their lead. The walk to the club house took us alongside the lake, where the landscaping looked like it had been manicured just minutes ago, everything was so pristine. On the other side was a pine forest and as we walked, Ben pointed out a little deer scuttling through it.

"Oh wow!" I crossed to the edge of the lake to get a better look at the deer, who, sensing she was being watched stopped still in her tracks.

"It's teaming with wild life here," Ben called out proudly as I stared, fascinated, at the wide eyed little doe. She edged back, her anxious gaze fixed on me. "You look a bit like how I feel," I whispered with a little laugh, before walking back over to where Ben and Mary were waiting.

After a short walk, we arrived at the club house, a beautiful Spanish style building with a long sweeping drive, and we were greeted by a team of concierge.

It was such a warm welcome, as though Ben and Mary were family and I watched as Ben bantered with the staff who were clearly very comfortable and familiar with him and Mary.

Then he introduced me. "This is Amanda."

I shivered at the use of my proper name, that fear of being in trouble as a child washing over me again.

"Amanda is a famous author," he announced with a smile in my direction, "well, she will be soon."

I smiled gratefully as my heart leapt in my chest. Could it happen? Would I be famous? Would this kind of life ever be mine? I didn't know, but right then, anything seemed possible.

"Here to eat, Ben?" A young man who Ben introduced as Jed asked, and he and Ben fist bumped each other.

Ben nodded. "Absolutely, is Tracey in today?"

Jed walked us through to the bar and dining area and seated us at our table. "Yep, I'll let her know you're here."

I sat and took in my opulent surroundings, feeling like Alice in Wonderland, transported to another world.

"It's so quiet here, where is everybody?" I asked Mary.

She smiled, "It's pretty exclusive, it gets busier during the peak season, but most of the home owners here might only come out once or twice a year, so it's like having our own personal restaurant, most of the time."

As if to confirm this, we were joined by the chef, Ricardo, who greeted me warmly when Ben introduced us. He was flamboyantly Italian as he kissed both my cheeks and told me to choose from the a la carte menu, but that if there was nothing I wanted from that, he would cook me whatever I wanted, if he had it in his kitchen.

I shook my head in wonder and laughed lightly with a whisper to Mary, "And a personal chef too?"

Mary chuckled as she perused the menu and then we were joined by a bubbly young girl, Tracey.

"Ah, Tracey," Ben stood to hug her, "this is Mandy, my biographer."

"Wow, cool!" Tracey enthused, pulling up a chair next to Ben.

They immediately began an animated conversation about football, or soccer, as Tracey calls it.

Mary nudged me, "Tracey is almost as mad about football as Ben." She rolled her eyes good humouredly and we both looked over to the pair, engaged in a heated exchange.

We chose our food and I was quite simply amazed at the swarm of waiters and waitresses on hand to tend to our every need. It was just outstanding service, made even better by the warmth and friendliness of the staff.

Later, we began the short walk back to the house. Mary and I were lost in conversation when Ben suddenly interrupted us.

"M, you're about to see paradise descend into dystopia!" He gestured to the sky which had suddenly darkened around us and I looked at Mary with wide eyes.

"This is Miami," she shrugged, and at that moment the heavens opened and the rain came down.

"Run for it, girls!" Ben shouted from ahead, and Mary and I picked up our feet, giggling away, despite the soggy messes we had quickly become.

Within an hour, the rain had stopped and the sun burned bright through the sky again. I accepted the martini that Ben offered to make me once I'd settled myself beside the pool.

"Lovely," I murmured, breathing in the warm sunshine and stretching myself out on a lounger…

+ + +

I'm laying here right now, and as easy as it would be to just chill, I need to write, I want to capture the here and now again.

Ben has returned with my drink and we sit in silence for a while, simply enjoying the late sunshine and the peace and tranquillity surrounding us.

"This is great," I gesture my surroundings.

Ben nods, "We love it here, especially when the grandchildren are with us."

"Your grandchildren really mean the world to you, don't they?"

Ben's face softens at the mention of them.

"There really is nothing like being a grandfather."

"Or a grandmother." Mary joins us and sits down next to Ben. As they talk, the love and pride for their grandchildren and their children is evident and it makes my heart swell.

They regale me with lovely stories of their young grandchildren.

"You sound like dream grandparents," I say, laughing at their stories. "Were your parents the same with your children?"

"Oh they adored each other," Mary says and Ben suddenly looks serious.

"It was strange really, that in the space of five years, we lost all four parents but had gained four grandchildren. I guess that's regeneration for you."

We all become pensive and sip our drinks in a comfortable silence, the cicadas in the forest our only soundtrack.

+ + +

It's my second evening here in paradise. We've finished our meal, prepared by Ben's personal chef, and Mary has suggested that Ben and I take our wine outside to the huge terrace that wraps around the pool. It has been a warm day and even now that the sun has faded, it is still so humid. Despite this, Ben bizarrely lights the fire pit, I suspect this is more of his scene setting antics and I move forward towards the dancing flames. He sits down next to me and sighs contentedly.

"This place is beautiful," I gaze up at the stars.

"It's my zen-like sanctuary," he murmurs as he too focuses on the navy blue night sky.

"One of many." I tease, feeling relaxed, and maybe a little tipsy. The wine has fired my confidence it seems. Ben smiles at me and I take another sip of my drink as we sit silently for a few moments.

"I worked hard for this," Ben suddenly speaks, "and wonderful moments like this."

He looks out across the lake, deep in contemplation. It's grey and choppy, and on the far side a storm rages over the pine forest, creating lightning flashes that light up the dusky sky. Ben is lost in the moment, fixated on the storm.

"What are you thinking about?" I bravely interrupt his revelry.

"Ah, just life and the universe." Ben sighs. "You know, I have a real obsession with the universe, and a parallel universe or multiverses."

"Multiverses?" This all seems a bit deep for me but when Ben is in a mood to talk I like to grab the opportunity whist I can.

"Yes, I'm not a believer in a God of such. I'm more science and technology. I believe in the theory that there is a set of finite and infinite possible universes."

"Freak!" I joke and Ben laughs.

"You think I am, you'd be surprised."

He takes another sip of his drink and I notice his hand his shaking slightly.

"Ok, M. You remember Shirley?"

"Argh! Finally, you're going to tell me? Go on."

Ben takes a deep breath and nods to himself, almost as though confirming his decision to continue.

"In the apartment that John and I shared in Newport Beach, we had a neighbour, Shirley."

"You followed her lucky seven advice in the casino." I remember.

"Good memory, M. Anyway, she, for some reason, got evicted and John and I kindly allowed her to stay with us till she got back on her feet."

"Oh yeah?" I raise my eyebrows with a smirk but Ben is laughing and holding his hands up.

"Not like that!"

I splutter into my wine glass and Ben continues.

"No, she was a bit spaced out, a bit of a hippy I suppose. But one night she told us about her ability to Astra-travel."

"Astra-travel?" I'm howling with laughter now and Ben has to shush me with a nudge.

"Seriously, M! She reckoned that she could have out-of-body experiences and assume the existence of an astral body. She claimed she could pass between parallel universes and into the future."

"Are you sure you weren't taking drugs?" I tease Ben and he rolls his eyes.

"Don't you start! No, John and I were sceptical, but Shirley, well. She actually believed she had left her physical body and really did travel in an astral plane."

"Did you believe her?" I ask. I'm still laughing but Ben looks contemplative.

"Well, at the time I laughed but she turned to me, a deadly serious expression on her face as she said: 'Ben, you won't be laughing when at some point in your life the number seven plays an important role and Stan comes to your aid.'."

I feel the hairs on the back of my neck stand up as Ben looks at me, a solemn expression on his face.

"Seriously? She mentioned Stan, before you'd even met him?"

It suddenly hits me. "So that's why his name seemed familiar when he first interviewed you?"

Ben nods. "She also told me a lady with the intial M would feature in my life."

I gasp. "Mary?"

Ben smiles sadly. "That's what I want to believe, it could also be you. But don't forget about Melony, how she bailed us out when she kept turning up? Perhaps Shirley sent her to guide me?"

"Oh my God." I put my hand to my mouth, stunned.

"Let's just say, M, I can't not believe what Shirley told me. There were too many coincidences."

I go to speak but Ben suddenly leans forward, his face is so serious that I almost recoil in fear.

"M, there's something else Shirley said."

I am reminded of the flash of fear I thought I had seen in Ben's face at our first ever meeting, but the look on his face now is not simply fear, it's sheer terror.

I know now that my initial instincts were correct; There is something Ben isn't telling me. Is it to do wth 2077?

"Ben, you're really scaring me now." I whisper.

Ben stares at me, blinking in the darkness, then he picks up his drink. "Sorry, M. Too much of this talking." He shakes the glass, shrugging his shoulders with a light laugh but I can see through his bravado.

"Ben, please. What is it you're not telling me?"

Ben drains the last of his drink and places the glass on the table.

"M, honestly, it's nothing. John was right, Shirley was off her head most of the time."

I don't believe him though and later as I lie in bed I think about that conversation. A part of me finds it ridiculous, but another part of me considers Ben's words and that comment about Stan. How could this Shirley have known then that somebody called Stan would play such a vital role in Ben's life? And Melony too, why had she followed Ben and John?

If it's not yet proven, it also means it's not disproven too, but it's just too weird to contemplate.

And what else was it that Shirley said that has frightened Ben so? I need to find out and I am suddenly nervous that I may have become an unwilling party to something terrible.

My dreams that night see me travelling the world, spanning Thailand to Japan, back to Europe; parts of Italy and areas of Spain.

All of this while my body lies firmly in its bed. A dream, of course?

+ + +

"Morning, M," I glide down the beautiful swirling staircase like a character out of Dynasty to be greeted by a smiling Ben and Mary.

"Gosh, have I overslept?" I ask in a panic.

"Not at all," Mary assures me. "You're on holiday!"

"Well, I'm not really," I quickly look at Ben but he's shaking his head at me with a smile.

"We're just planning tonight's drinks, it's early yet."

I inwardly breathe a sigh of relief.

"Oh. Where?"

"Here," Mary says. "Just a few drinks and nibbles with our close friends out here."

"Cool!" I say and Mary is already shaking her head at me, albeit with a knowing smile on her face.

"It's a private party, Mandy, not an interrogation of our friends."

Both Ben and I laugh as Mary stands up, rolling her eyes at us. "Coffee?"

When Mary leaves the room, Ben looks at me. "You need to relax more; this is a holiday as much as some working time you know."

I sit down on the huge white leather sofa opposite him and I retort, "You're telling me to relax!"

Ben chuckles. "I always try to relax on holidays. Especially now. I had far too many family holidays when I was in business that were interrupted by conference calls or phone calls with various issues that needed resolving."

"I can imagine," I say as I tuck my feet under me. "Well seeing

as I'm supposed to be in vacation mode, why don't you tell me about your holidays?"

Ben smiles. "Where do I start? Of course, there have been many trips. In fact, we once took a trip back to Newport Beach where I re-visited those heady beach bum days with John back in the seventies."

"That must have been interesting after all those years?"

Ben nods. "You know our old apartment was still there? I was expecting the area to be bull-dozed and unrecognisable. But no, it was still there, thirty-two years after I'd made it my home. I felt so moved, I think if I hadn't been with others, I would have cried."

"Incredible," I say, as I consider what an interesting life Ben has had, still has. "And that was where you met Shirley?"

Ben gives me a warning look and I understand, sort of. I stand up and address him, "Back to business?"

Ben heaves himself up from the sofa with a groan. "Ok, M. But let's take it outside, it's too nice to be sitting indoors and I fancy a swim."

We head out to the pool, my notebook tucked under my arm.

The day after our meeting with him, Nelson had a mid-morning flight home.

As was our usual custom, I drove him to the airport and walked him through to customs where we said our goodbyes.

In hindsight, he had been unusually quiet on this journey but at the time I had seen nothing wrong.

It was only when we shook hands and I felt a piece of paper nestled in his palm that alarm bells started to ring. He pressed it into mine, pulled his hand away, turned and strode off.

I was slightly stunned as he walked away.

"John," I called after him. "John, what's this?" He ignored me and carried on walking.

"John?" He didn't look back and I quickly unscrewed the crumpled up single sheet that I was holding.

I quickly read the hand-written note and my heart began to race. By now, Nelson was through customs and out of sight. I wanted to run after him and ask him why?

I was panic stricken and I began to shake at the content.

Guys, I'm really sorry but I can't do this any longer. This isn't what I want and I need to go back to doing my own thing. I'm taking back the software and won't be supporting you anymore. I wish you well in whatever else you do. John.

I ran to the nearest phone booth and called Brian.

"Brian, I'm on my way back, don't go anywhere!" I yelled, and within ten minutes I'd arrived back at the office to find Brian pacing outside.

He jumped in the car and we sat there, out of sight of the staff.

"Is it Nelson?" Brian was anxious, "Is he ok, what's happened?"

I took a deep breath and handed him the screwed-up note.

During the ten-minute journey back to the office, I had already mulled over the enormous impact Nelson's actions would have.

He was basically shutting us down. Without the software source code and the control to update it, we would no longer be able to sell software or, worse still, support our customers. This was the end of the road for us.

All I could hear at that moment in time was Stan in my head. *Well, Ben, you didn't fail because of business, you, my lad, took your eye off the ball. You were sloppy, I told you not to trust anyone and you trusted Nelson.*

Damn you Stan!

At best, we were bankrupt, and at worst we would be sued for negligence by our clients. Everything I had was seemingly wrecked with one moment of madness.

"He's bloody well lost his mind," Brian swore, "what did he say to you, Ben?"

"Nothing," I sighed, "he didn't even have the decency to talk about it, he's a coward, he literally ran away. And now he's closed our business."

I put my head in my hands.

"No, he can't do that, we have controlling interest." Brian said sharply.

"Legally, he can't," I agreed, "but he has full control here because he has the software source code and our business evolves around that source code. There is no way we can get access to that."

At that moment, I wondered why on earth I had been so trusting. I'd been so naive not to have had a copy of the source code. I'd screwed up.

"Ok, we have to put this right." I finally said decisively.

"Ben, there is no getting away from it, we have a legal right to get that source code back." Brian was positive there was a solution to this and we talked for hours that afternoon, before deciding to discuss it again the following day after we'd slept on it.

Sleep didn't feature as you can imagine. We really were in a very difficult situation.

The next day Brian called up one of London's top lawyers, and, suited and booted we met with him in his swish offices. His PA collected us from reception and walked us into his huge office. He was dressed in a navy-blue pin striped suit and had combed back dark hair.

In a well- spoken voice, he ushered us to a leather seating area. I must admit I took an instant dislike to him, but he looked the part and at this moment in time, he was our lifeline.

We gushed out our story and handed over the company documents which he flicked through, every now and then simply giving a little, "hmmm".

He quizzed us as he tried to establish the authenticity of Tech Group and our controlling ownership of both the UK and US arms of Dex.

He kept nodding at our questions and, from his mannerism, I could see he wasn't interested in our case.

He sipped his coffee and sat back in his leather chair, ready to sum up, and I sensed there was a but coming.

Brian and I leaned forward intently as he spoke.

"It's not good news," he began, as my heart slid into my stomach. "Look, if I were you guys I would just go and start up again. You're only a small business."

We sat there in stunned silence as he continued to explain his crazy rationale.

"You see, if we raise a lawsuit against Nelson and, of course, you have every right to, it gets far too complicated. I fear you guys would just be throwing good money after bad. I am sorry," he said with a rueful smile, "as unfair as it seems, I just can't see you getting justice on this one."

With that dismissive attitude, he outstretched his hand and offered our papers back.

As we walked out of that office, I could feel myself welling up with tears but I didn't let Brian see it.

I just wanted to be alone.

We got back to our offices and I got into my car.

I waited till Brian drove off in his, and then I broke down.

With my elbows on the steering wheel and my head in my hands, tears streamed down my face. I looked heavenwards and yelled to the great man.

"Stan, where the hell are you? What do I do now?"

I felt consumed with loneliness as I sat there in my car and wept. I was inconsolable. I was so disappointed in myself, and the thought of letting my family down and being bankrupt engulfed my entire being with an ache I had never experienced before…

> *"My God," I almost feel like crying myself as Ben finishes speaking and I can see that it has left him pretty emotional too.*
>
> *"That's still not an easy memory to recall," he explains and I nod my understanding.*
>
> *I'm suddenly exhausted, Lord knows how he must be feeling. Drained, I should imagine.*
>
> *"Hey," I nudge him gently and gesture at our surroundings, "it all worked out ok in the end though, didn't it?"*
>
> *He smiles tiredly and nods his agreement. "Eventually. Fancy a dip?"*
>
> *I shake my head no as Ben stands up. "You go for it."*

Chapter 16

The Redcoats Are Coming

+1987+

Brian and I concluded we weren't giving up yet, it just wasn't in our DNA, and the only way forward was to try another lawyer.

Most of the time, Stan's eye on the ball analogy was easy to recognise, but when tough situations like this came along, it became difficult to see the ball and it took the edge of my ability to solve problems. I had been pretty sure the ball in play this time was the lawyer, in fact I'd been convinced it was the lawyer, how had I got that wrong?

As I began to question and doubt myself I suddenly had a lightbulb moment.

I did have it right! It was the lawyer, just not the UK lawyer.

Right then I knew I had the answer. I needed a Boston lawyer.

During my training with Stan I would often ask how he dealt with so many problems at once. "File them in order of priority,"

Stan would say, "pick them off one at a time, don't let anyone force the pace, don't panic, just solve what you can."

I got to work, researching Boston's biggest lawyers until I very quickly found what I was looking for; a company based in the heart of Boston City.

Expense had no bearing on my thinking at that moment and I obtained a telephone number and shut the door of my office to make the call that could potentially save my business.

Excitedly, I dialled the number and explained that I needed to talk to an expert about company law to do with a US company.

The receptionist asked me to hold and then connected me.

"King speaking," came the voice at the other end. Did I hear that right, King? And wasn't my very own motto, cash is king?

I introduced myself and summed up briefly what it was I needed help with, just to be sure I had the right person.

As it happened, I did.

The King was short for Kingston and I spent the best part of the next half an hour pouring out my story to him. He listened intently, enthusiastically even. He knew exactly how to communicate, using my first name, making me feel positive, full of support.

When I'd finally finished, I couldn't wait to hear how he would sum up.

"Ben, I can help you", he paused and I held my breath, "in fact, do you know what fella, we are going to do this for you, don't worry."

The relief, just to hear those positive words, was enough to lift me ten feet in the air.

What a contrast, from the impossible to the possible. It was a lesson on never giving up on anything.

Kingston then went on to explain that we would need to get the US company articles, which wasn't a problem.

Then he asked if, when the time was right, I thought we could get Nelson out of his office. I wondered where he was going with that one but I acknowledged that, yes, we could.

"We have some loyal staff that report to me, so it's possible," I told him, knowing deep inside that I'd have to move fast as Nelson would be firing the lot of them soon!

King explained. "The thing is, Ben, I always say that control is nine tenths of the law, if we can get that control we can nail it for you."

I took in his words, wondering what his plan was.

"Get me the paperwork," he finished up, "and call me next week."

When I came off that call it was as if I had just won a huge order; I was elated. Of course, it was nothing more than a step in the right direction, but it was one I wanted to take with a giant leap. Suddenly I could see a win and I wasn't going to be stopped along the way. I discreetly obtained the paperwork through Joan, my US admin manager, making sure there was no way Nelson would know. Joan knew nothing that was going on at this stage and I asked her to trust me and not say a word to anyone back in the US office.

As I heard myself say those words to Joan; 'please just trust me', I thought about the fact that, after trusting Nelson, I was adamant I would never trust anyone again in that way. But thankfully, Joan *did* trust me enough to get me that paperwork

On my next call with King he already had everything organised.

"Ben, we can do this," he reiterated. He explained that he would draw up the legal paperwork that would have to be issued to Nelson. Those papers would be the basis for us to take control and leave Nelson to fight us from the outside.

"Ben," King was suddenly very serious, "this is important. You will need to get Nelson out of his office. I want you to issue him with the legal papers, say at the airport, and then you need to get back to his office before he does." I almost laughed out loud, what was this?

But King continued, "That way you will have control, remember what I said about control." He also suggested we have a security guard at the office and our hotel to deal with any repercussions.

My mind was going crazy with questions, but now was the time to take Joan and Brian's sales manager, Topsy, into our confidence.

If they spilled the plan to Nelson it was over, but fortunately they disliked him so much it was easy to ask them to stay silent and they were actually excited at the opportunity to get one over on him.

King sent over the papers we needed to issue to Nelson. They essentially stated that he was fired from his CEO post at Dex Inc, as well as his board position in Tech Group. He was also being given a court order to stay away from his premises. Of course, he remained a shareholder in Tech Group with 40% equity and had every right to legally contest our actions and try and get reinstated.

King said if we stormed the office and got control of the staff, the cash, and the source code, we would essentially have control of the fort.

King insisted we had extra security at all times, reminding me that we were putting Nelson in a vulnerable position and a desperate man would go to any lengths.

This didn't sit easy with me, Nelson had once been a friend, I didn't want to break him.

The more I digested what we were about to embark upon though, I told myself Nelson deserved it. Well he did.

All we had to do now was set the trap, but would Nelson fall for it?

I called him and played him the line that we realised it was all over, but we wanted to come over and chat as we had to close out our customers in the UK.

Nelson was reluctant, as you might expect, saying he didn't see the point, and for a moment I felt it was all slipping away.

I pleaded with him, explaining how hard it was to come to terms with and that he owed us at least this much.

I told him we would literally fly into Boston, meet him at the airport and fly out again, and finally he agreed.

"Wow, Ben," I rudely interrupt, "a second Oscar winning performance!"

Ben nods, "I certainly had to act up for that cause."

All we had to do now was hope he would turn up, that Joan kept her secret, and that we pulled the trap. The plan was that when we met Nelson at the airport, Joan and Topsy would be there in disguise, watching us. They would be ready to grab Brian and I and rush us back to the office before Nelson got there. Meanwhile, armed security would be posted at our hotel and at the office.

So, the sting was all set and we now had to hope it would play out and Nelson wouldn't break down and do something silly.

Mary was understandably nervous and though I played it down for her, inside, I too was nervous, as was Brian. We had every right to be; I remembered Nelson when I had first met him, in the restaurant ready to fight the waiter.

I had to tell Mary that I didn't know when I would be home and that it could be weeks getting control and sorting out the U.S. office. As usual, she was amazingly supportive and never once did she let me know anything other than that she would cope at home on her own with the kids.

The flight to Boston seemed to drag but Brian and I used the time to discuss just about every scenario. We checked and double checked we had the issuing papers. We couldn't help but think about the enormity of this meeting. If we got this wrong, there was no plan B.

When we came through US customs, I thought this must be what it's like to stand in the tunnel of a big football game, I was shaking with nerves.

I just hoped that the girls were in place, and that Nelson would even show up.

I took a deep breath and looked at Brian.

"Let's do this." I said.

"This is mental!" I exclaim, incredulous at what Ben was about to do, in his story.

"Ha ha, it all felt very surreal at the time, I must say," Ben swims another length and I wait for him to come back to the end of the pool that I am sitting at.

"I'd have been terrified," I call out, as he emerges from the water.

"I bloody was!" Off he goes again, diving under the surface.

I shake my head with a smile, "Hey, Ben," I shout out, once he comes up for air.

"What?"

"You should write a book about this!"

As he splutters and laughs in the pool, I pick my notebook back up...

As we walked out into the arrivals area of the airport, I scanned the sea of faces, desperately looking for Nelson. Then I saw him, standing there with a solemn look on his face.

My heart was quite literally thumping in my ears and I rubbed my sweaty palms on my trousers before shaking hands with Nelson.

"Good flight?" Nelson enquired politely.

Good fricking flight? Christ, he was acting like we were old friends and not the poor bastards that he was trying to do over! I resisted the urge to smack him one when I caught Brian's warning look with a small shake of his head.

"Let's find somewhere more private, shall we?" Thank God Brian was being calm, I feared opening my mouth to say anything at this point.

We made our way over to a fairly quiet seating area and I scanned the airport looking for the girls. *Shit, where were they?*

I needed to know they were close by but I couldn't see them, and, this being in the days before mobile phones, I had no way of contacting them either.

Brian, sensing my agitation, placed a hand on my arm to calm me.

"John," Brian began, "are you sure this is really what you want?"

Brian and I had previously agreed that we would try and convince Nelson to reconsider, but I knew he wouldn't and the determined shake of his head confirmed that.

"I can't do this anymore, like I said."

Brian sighed and I could feel my rage boiling over. Then I suddenly noticed Topsy, hiding under a huge floppy hat, and my agitation began to subside.

That was enough to spur me on.

"There's nothing we can say to convince you to change your mind?" Brian tried again and again Nelson shook his head, his jaw set in a determined frown.

To be honest, if he'd agreed, I'm not sure where we would have gone from there. He'd crossed the line with me; the trust was gone.

"I've made it perfectly clear," his cold tone was in stark contrast to the man I thought I had known. "Now, I'm a busy man. What is it you wanted to discuss?"

I could see that even Brian was struggling to hide his anger now, his fists clenched at his side.

I was feeling ruthless, and, right at that moment, I admit I really did want revenge.

As Brian softened things up, explaining what we had put into this venture, both financially and emotionally, and that we had a huge customer base not only in the UK but also the US too, Nelson was switching off. He shuffled his huge feet and picked up his brown leather satchel.

Brian handled it well though. "Bear with me, John."

I gritted my teeth, wanting to give Nelson what for. This guy had put my family at risk, I actually wanted to punch him one.

"We've come a long way for this short meeting." Brian unclipped his brief case and Nelson sighed, I swallowed hard but I could feel the adrenaline rushing through me.

This was pure theatre; I would pay big money to watch this.

I glanced over to make sure Topsy and Joan were still close by. They were, clearly excited and giggly. I suppose not many employees get to witness and be involved in something as bizarre as this.

Brian lifted out a pile of papers and looked up at Nelson as he delivered his lines to perfection.

"Well, regrettably John, we cannot accept your judgement on taking the software and essentially closing down the UK business. We are therefore instructed by our lawyer to issue you with instructions to the contrary and ensure you understand what we are doing."

Nelson leaned back, stunned into silence for a moment, and I thought he was going to get up and leave.

He didn't say a word, and in a gesture of resignation, he put his satchel back beside him and just sat there.

I was mesmerized as Brian went on to explain that Nelson was being released of his duties both in Dex Inc and also Tech Group.

Brian passed over more paperwork which confirmed that the warrant being issued would legally prevent him from visiting the office. He went on to explain that the office was already under our control and currently being guarded by armed officers.

Nelson shook his head, reeling from this information, but he didn't utter a word.

"Ok, I think we're done." I said, watching Nelson stand up and slip the papers into his brown leather satchel. His face was bright red, screwed up with anger, and he shook his head for a final time, then turned to walked away. Before he did, he took one final look at us and pointed his finger.

"Don't think this is the end of this!" He stabbed his finger angrily into the air and Brian and I stepped back in fear he would hit out at one of us.

Instead, with a resigned shake of his head, he picked up his satchel and disappeared into the crowd.

We quickly dashed over to where the girls were waiting, and, with no time for small chat, we legged it to the car.

"Jesus Christ!" I shouted as we squealed out of the car park, "Floor it, Topsy!"

We assumed that Nelson would be heading straight for the office so we had to get there before him. The office was some thirty miles away, and good old Topsy drove like a woman possessed, loving every minute of it.

When we got to Nelson's offices we were confronted by two armed-security guards. They checked our ID, and satisfied that we were who we said, let us into the office. How many times as a child had I played out those cowboy and Indian games, trying to claim the fort when I was younger? And here I was, emulating that in real life.

I felt an enormous sense of relief, I had control and I didn't care what the consequences were, but I should have.

Sometimes when you fall you have to trust the fact that maybe, just maybe, you can fly.

The staff, about fourteen of them, were grouped together in the middle of the open plan office, almost as though they were hostages. I suppose they were in some ways!

They all looked up anxiously as we walked in with the two girls; rumours had clearly been rife. I explained very calmly to them that Nelson had been fired and we had taken control. I told them all to go home and that tomorrow I would be having a one to one with each of them. I also re-iterated that their jobs were safe and we would be continuing to invest in the US. Despite their obvious shock, I could also sense their relief; Nelson clearly hadn't been a popular CEO.

The security guards were rotating throughout the night so we felt it safe to leave the office and head to our hotel where we would be greeted by even more security.

The next morning, after a restless night, we were buzzing, and I just wanted to get back to the office and get started.

I was working my way through the staff sessions mid-morning when Brian interrupted.

"A word, urgently." I quickly excused myself and Brian explained that Nelson had called and wanted to come by the office that evening to collect some personal belongings.

"No way!" My first instinct was to outright refuse but I decided to call King to see what he thought. He suggested we let him in but have the security guards there, although in disguise, so as not to agitate him further. King thought if Nelson took this to court it would look more favourable on our part if we'd shown compassion in allowing him to pick up his personal items.

Brian called Nelson and suggested he visit the office at 7pm that evening.

We ran through a plan with the security team and decided they would be disguised as technicians working on the computer when Nelson arrived. That way, he wouldn't be spooked by their presence but at the same time, we'd be protected and safe.

Safe, I thought, nothing about this meeting felt safe at all!

That evening, right on time, Nelson drove into the empty car park and we watched him from our view point on the first floor.

He opened the rear door to his car, pulled out his worn brown leather satchel and fumbled around with it.

The head security guard looked on from the first-floor window before he turned to his colleague.

"Len, look, he'll have the gun in his satchel."

My eyes widened as I looked over at Brian.

"Never trust a man with a satchel," Brian quipped to cover his nerves.

"Sir, I suggest you take this seriously and look out for your-self." The security guard glared at Brian and he looked suitably ashamed.

I was scared stiff, we both were. It had suddenly hit home that the culture amongst US citizens was to carry a gun for their own protection. We had a serious situation on our hands.

I went to the kitchen, took out a knife and slipped it into my pocket, deciding not to take my hand off it at any time.

Nelson was here, and I was ready, but was I really prepared to use that knife?

As I greeted him coolly in reception, I saw the pure hatred in his eyes and for a moment I felt a pang of regret that it had come to this. But I had to focus on the here and now, this guy had crossed a line with me and there was no coming back from it.

I had to keep that in mind; it gave me strength, and as I curtly asked him to follow me into the office, my gaze remained fixed firmly on his satchel.

When Nelson walked into his old office, Brian explained why the 'engineers' were there, but Nelson had no interest, he knew.

I asked him to put on the table what he was taking away as I wanted to check the items did not belong to the company. He said nothing, simply shaking his head in disgust. His silence felt threatening though and I was expecting him any minute to draw a gun and finish us both off. I'd never felt so vulnerable and I wondered whether this was worth it all for the sake of business or whether events had overtaken us and we had gone stark raving mad. If I got shot now it would have all been pretty pointless.

My mind was running riot and I struggled to focus, knowing that I needed to get through this moment, no matter what.

Nelson seemed to be taking his time and I began to wonder if he was deliberately delaying for a reason, but at last, he bagged his belongings and walked out.

We all stood in silence, not trusting that he had really left. For what seemed an age, we gazed at his car in the car park, willing to see him get in it and drive off.

But as the minutes ticked by and there was no sign of Nelson, I could sense our security guards getting agitated. I glanced nervously at Brian who blinked in the stillness of the office.

"Do you think he's waiting for us?" My question made Brian and the guards jump and both the guards were nodding their heads solemnly.

"I'll call for back up to..." Before the guard had even finished speaking, Brian shouted and pointed to the glass panel that led out to the reception; "Fucking hell! He's back!"

We all looked and there he was, Nelson, a murderous look on his face.

"Shit! You guys get in the kitchen and push anything you can find against the door!" The security guards were already heading towards Nelson and, terrified, Brian and I raced to the kitchen.

My heart was pounding in my chest. I knew Nelson was volatile but shit, I hadn't really been expecting this.

Slamming the kitchen door behind us, Brian unplugged the small microwave and placed it against the door.

"What the...?" I stared at him, "How's that going to hold anyone off?"

Brian wiped the sweat from his brow. "Well, what the hell else do you suggest?"

I looked around me, panicking, and my gaze fell on the small fridge-freezer.

"Here, help me," I pulled at the appliance and Brian took the other side as we tugged and shoved until it was firmly against the door; our only protection from the chaos that was happening on the other side.

Crouching in the corner of that kitchen like scared hostages, we waited, straining our ears to hear what mayhem was ensuing outside in the office.

"We're sitting ducks," Brian whispered and I felt the bile rise in my throat. "If Nelson gets to us, we have no weapons, nothing to protect us. We're finished."

I sat up, pulling the knife from my pocket that I had armed myself with earlier and with a shaking hand I held it up to Brian who gulped. "Shit, I can't believe it's come to this."

He tentatively reached across to the small cupboard next to him and pulled out a saucepan. Despite my terror at the situation we were in, I couldn't help but chuckle. "Seriously, a saucepan?"

Brian shrugged at my raised eyebrows. "If he gets in, I'll bang on this to distract him and you stick him with that knife."

"Jesus Christ, it's like..."

"Something from a movie?" Ben finishes for me, "It certainly was, M. It was the most surreal situation I've ever been in."

"So, what happened?"

We waited for what seemed an eternity, neither of us speaking. The only sound in that small kitchen was our shallow breaths and racing heartbeats.

Suddenly we heard the wailing of sirens.

"Jeez!" Brian looked at me wide-eyed. "The guards must be in real trouble if they've called for back up!"

I swallowed nervously. This shit had just got real.

"There's gonna be a shoot out," Brian exclaimed, "we'll be all over the f'ing news!"

"No such thing as bad publicity." I dead-panned and Brian rolled his eyes at me.

"It's all clear guys!" The sudden knock at the door made Brian and I gasp and I scrabbled to my feet.

"Wait!" Brian hissed, "It's a trick, that sounded like Nelson. Don't open the door."

My mouth was dry, my hands trembling as I considered Brian's warning.

On impulse, I dragged the fridge to one side and whipped the door open, ignoring Brian's pleas.

I stood in the doorway, peering out into the office, wondering if this would be my last view. Was I about to be shot or was this nightmare finally over?

With Brian clambering to his feet behind me, I called out. "Anyone there?"

A sudden movement took my breath away and with a flood of relief I saw Len, the security guard, standing before me.

"It's ok, guys," he said with a sympathetic smile at our terrified faces. "It's over, the police are here."

I felt as though I were about to pass out and, clutching one of the desks, I sunk into a chair whilst Brian leant against the wall.

"Did that really just happen?" I muttered, more to myself than anyone else.

"Dear God…" was Brian's simple reply.

"So, what had happened, what had Nelson done?"
Ben sighs and I shudder, feeling a shiver go down my spine.
"He got hold of Len, put a gun to his head. But by that point, the other security guard had dialled 911."
Ben pauses.
"So they arrested him?"
With a shake of his head, Ben finishes the story.

The police arrived, and once they realised this was a hostage situation, they brought in the feds.

They ordered Nelson to drop the gun and release Len several times apparently, but Nelson was standing firm.

They had no choice but to storm the building.

"And then they arrested him?"
Ben draws a shaky breath.
"No, M, they shot him. Dead."
I gasp.
"Really?"
Ben is laughing now, winding me up again.
"No, they arrested him." He's still laughing and I shake my head at him but I'm laughing too.

Once the police had finished questioning us, we were allowed to leave. I felt an overwhelming rush of emotion and no sense of pride for what had happened to Nelson, as well as an outpouring of complete and utter relief that it was over.

My first call was to Mary to let her know that all was ok and the mission had been successful.

Mary's relief was audible at the other end of the line and I felt a sharp stab of regret that she had been put through all this worry, and, despite some remorse, anger at Nelson for being the perpetrator of that.

I rarely drink, but that evening I downed a few piña-colada's in the bar with some of the staff, trying to relax under the watchful eye of a security guard. Joan summed it up perfectly when she said, "We always said the Redcoats were coming, but this time you were victorious!" It was a perfect analogy. It had been an aggressive, calculated and bloody British victory.

Later that evening, in a quiet moment to myself, I let my tears flow, all remnants of my Britishness gone.

> *"I never wanted it to end that way for Nelson, but he'd brought it on himself. He served a few years for that, from what I heard, but I've no idea of what became of him after."*
>
> *"Do you want to know?" I'm curious but Ben shakes his head adamantly.*
>
> *"No, M. That is one man I really don't want to think about again."*

After all the upheaval, I still had to deal with the day to day back in the UK office as well as now rebuild the US business, but years of learning to soak up the pressure and be at the top of my game at Onelock had prepared me well.

It wasn't long though, before I realised that Dex Inc had a cash crisis that Nelson had cleverly kept from us and I estimated that, going forward, the company would need an injection of £160k. It was a huge amount and it also meant that any investment would have to be met and guaranteed by all of the shareholders.

I met with our US bank to see if we could get their support in a loan form but as expected they were reluctant to bridge the gap. Brian decided to waive his right to invest and I decided to raise the funding myself with a combination of more personal loans and guarantees.

It was a huge undertaking but by now I was committed to and didn't want to let our loyal US staff down.

Brian wanted to protect his own wealth and I understood this. There was high risk at stake and it meant a heavy dilution of share ownership from him.

It meant that with my investment I would now own 94% of Tech Group, the holding company.

Despite the risk being enormous, I didn't flinch at taking it on. I had control and with that came confidence. The workload to recover would be arduous and I was now in debt for far more than our home was worth, but I couldn't allow myself to be scared.

This felt like the fight of my life but it was one I was happy to take on, even though it felt as if, against my own will, I had been sucked into some crazy kind of vortex. I guess, in reality, that's just business for you. Well, that's what I kept telling myself anyway.

Against all the odds we had secured a future, feared for our lives and uncovered a debt that held the threat of unhinging both companies.

It occurred to me in a deja vu moment that this was a similar scenario to that of Maurice and the PI collapse. Would I have fallen into the same trap if this had continued? I had certainly taken my eye off the ball with the software but also, as it appeared, Nelson's cash flow.

Another lesson learned I suppose.

It was almost four weeks later that Brian and I finally arrived back home, both exhausted.

For me it was a flying visit as I had to return to the US with Alex. I had promoted him to take over the reins and access the software development status, and he was delighted with his new appointment.

At the time, it struck me that I had probably just broken every rule in The Peter Principal but it brought into question that it was all well and good in the perfect rulebook but in the real business world, rules got broken. The key point was to be aware of the risks when breaking the rules, after all, look at the risk Stan took with me.

We're having cocktails on the terrace and Mary introduces me to some of her and Ben's close friends; Gary and Di and Ray and Gill. I feel instantly relaxed around these lovely people and we chat comfortably.

Ben approaches us and joins in the conversation and I 'screen shot' this moment in my mind; the sun setting in the pink skies, the tinkling of laughter and clinking of glasses.

I breathe a sigh of contentment and Ben smiles at me.

Just then, more guests arrive.

"Ben," a voice booms out across the pool, "wanna share a Bud Light?"

As the gathering of people erupt into fits of laughter, Ben takes my arm.

"M, let me introduce you to Lewis."

I cross the terrace with Ben to meet Lewis and his wife.

"Good to meet you, Amanda." Lewis greets me warmly, a twinkle in his eye, and I shake his hand.

"Nice to meet you, too, Lewis." I say with a cheeky smile, "I've heard a lot about you, and it's not all good."

Ben chortles, "She's got your number, mate!"

We all laugh and I watch Ben and Lewis banter back and forth, clearly enjoying the same dry sense of humour, which I realise is much like my own.

Later, Ben and I sit by the fire pit. It's been a great day and I have met some genuinely lovely people. I'm tired but I want to get some more of Ben's story down before bed.

Ben starts to speak but his phone pings and he looks at the text as I roll my eyes.

"I saw that, M," he mutters without looking up and I feel exasperated.

"Well, come on!" I throw my hands up in the air, "I know you're busy, and I get that but it's frustrating getting any momentum here."

"That's just it," he sighs, "I don't think many people do get it, M."

I'm puzzled, "Explain it to me then?"

Ben is shaking his head, "It's complicated, and I'm tired." He yawns as if to confirm this and I wonder how Mary puts up with him. He can be so exasperating!

"How on Earth do you expect me to write your story when you're such a closed book?" I know I am probably speaking out of turn, and as I feel the tears forming in my eyes, I struggle to compose myself...

"Mandy..." he begins, but I've had enough.

"I'm done," I stand up, shaking my head. "I can't do this anymore."

He grabs my arm as I turn to walk away. "Sit down!"

I look at his face, there is no anger there, despite his sharp tone.

"Sit down," his voice is softer now, "please?"

I sit down and wait for him to speak.

"Dear me," Ben gives a little laugh, "that was reminiscent of Stan and I just then!"

I smile lightly, "How so?"

"You with your self-doubt..."

I interrupt him, "Hey! I have no doubt about myself but..."

He laughs and I know he is teasing me again. I'm relieved and ready to get back on track.

"There really is no such thing as retirement where wealth is

involved. When you've created wealth, you've generally done it because you're wired to do it, it's in your DNA. The fact is, when you do have wealth, nobody realises just how much time and effort comes with managing it. You know, I'm so obsessed with being in control and love spreadsheets so much, I actually have an 'end of life cash flow'."

"A what?"

Ben smiles and nods, "Yep, with contingencies too. I'm a lover of economic finance."

"Dear God," I mutter, not for the first time. Or last.

Ben chuckles, "I call it Benomics."

"I see what you did there," I reply, rolling my eyes.

"Seriously though, sometimes it's like I'm still managing a small company."

"So why do you continue to involve yourself in more and more projects then?"

He rubs his eyes wearily before he looks at me.

"It's who I am, M, it's what drives me."

Ben looks shattered, and stressed, and I feel sorry for him all of a sudden.

"It's late," I look at my phone, "get some sleep. We'll start again tomorrow."

He smiles gratefully and I pat his shoulder as I pass him on my way up to bed.

I know as soon as I am gone he'll be back on that bloody phone of his again though and, sure enough, when I glance back, there he is, tap tap tapping away.

+ + +

A new day dawns and we are having breakfast; a wonderful array of pastries, fresh fruits and of course an early Bucks Fizz.

Ben is quiet and Mary and I look at each other in concern. I wonder if he has told her about our near argument last night.

"Aren't you hungry?" Mary looks at Ben's still empty plate as he shakes his head.

"Just coffee for me this morning, I had rather a lot to eat last night."

I glance anxiously at Mary but she simply shrugs, she is obviously used to Ben's more contemplative moments.

"I'm not that hungry either, actually," I say as I refill my coffee cup, "shall we begin?"

Ben groans, "Not today, M, I have other things to do."

I swallow nervously, is he still cross with me after last night? I decide to say nothing and I stand up from the table, give a nod of thanks toward Mary for the breakfast and take my leave.

I have a whole day to myself, I may as well enjoy it, so I head to the beach. I can do contemplation too, Ben, I mumble to myself tetchily.

Setting out my towel I retrieve my notebook from my bag and begin to think about who Ben really is.

I need to get into his mind, to work out what makes him tick, and I'm just not sure how to do that or whether anybody is even capable of that, let alone little old me.

Have I taken on too much here? He approached me after all. But can I do this?

A thought suddenly strikes me; does he still want me to do this?

I wonder if I should consider heading back home, to leave him here in his sanctuary to relax and decide if he wants to continue this project. I've only been here a week but perhaps it was too much too soon.

I lay back, enjoying the feel of the warm sun on my body and, taking a deep breath, I make my mind up. When I get back to Ben's this afternoon, I will tell him I'm leaving.

Chapter 17

That over-Rated Term; Work Hard, Play Hard

+1989+

With software re-writes and the fixing of glitches, we now had to take some risks because we were running out of time, and what with the integration of iCAD, I wondered how we would do it without one of our greatest technical assets, Nelson. At the same time, we were trying to stave off the threat of losing business using our new AEC pack products.

I decided to launch a product called 1992, which bundled stand-alone hardware, software and support into a £1992 rental cost per month. The 1992 concept took off and we started to sign up some new deals. It was a respite, but I knew it wouldn't last long, iCAD was chipping away at our core business. Despite this, I had seen to fruition, my plans to convert the ground floor warehouse into more office space.

I'd charged Alex with managing the software and the US team of programmers as well as access our integration with iCAD and he had started well, undertaking his duties with confidence. My main objective state side was to get the US back into profit so I introduced a combination of ideas for cost cutting and ways of increasing sales. It was a difficult period for the US company and our loyal US staff but we had demonstrated our faith in them by investing so quickly and they were grateful.

It was now apparent I would have to split my time between the US and UK operations so I set myself a regular schedule of six weeks in the UK and two weeks in the US. I desperately needed another me to be CEO of the US operation!

"That can't have been easy for Mary."

When I got back from the beach earlier, Ben had greeted me with much more enthusiasm than he had shown at breakfast. It made me wonder if Mary had said something to him.

We've been continuing with his story for over an hour now and I have yet to tell him of my plans to leave tomorrow.

"Mary was incredible; I'll never forget her support during those difficult times."

I'm unused to Ben speaking so candidly and endearingly about Mary so I take the opportunity, figuring I have nothing to lose now anyway.

"You and Mary are a good team and it seems you have been for a long time," I gently probe Ben and of course I'm not surprised with his sharp response.

"I know where you're going with this, M!"

Shit, why am I always on the defence here?

"Ok, ok," I hold up my hands up, "I should probably tell you now I'm going to go home tomorrow."

Ben looks up surprised, though I don't know why. He clearly doesn't want to work with me right now.

"There's no need to be rash," he is calm but I can see he feels a little awkward.

"I just wonder if my coming out here was a mistake," I explain. "This is your place, where you come to get away from things, my interrogating you can't be relaxing." As I finally say my piece, Ben is smiling apologetically and nodding.

"I've not made it easy for you, I'm sorry. I'm just under some pressure right now."

"I understand," I say solemnly, though I don't, not really.

"Look, M, stay a few more days, as you can see, I hardly get away from things!"

"Ha, true," I concur, "ok, let's get some more done."

I inwardly breathe a sigh of relief that he does want to continue after all and I am about to ask him to continue with the business line of his story when Ben speaks first, and incredibly he talks about Mary.

"Mary supported me in the best way possible; letting me be myself, believing in me, and allowing me to express my ambition. I realised some time ago that this was quite something and I hope when she reads this, she will realise that it was because of her that I was able to achieve what I did."

I'm touched by his fond gratitude to his wife and allow him to continue whilst he is clearly on a roll.

"I guess I also did the same for her, by not interfering with her day to day routine as she brought up the children. She has been an unsung hero."

"She deserves a lot of credit." That's an understatement, I think, as I say this. "But you did spend time with them?"

Ben laughs, "Of course I did! We were both always there for the children but there's no doubt Mary bore the brunt of it. It's only now that we have the grandchildren that I can appreciate how hard it is."

I chuckle and look around his office at the family photos on the wall, noting how cute the grandkids are.

"Yep," Ben continues, "Mary was a class act as a mum and our kids have turned out to be fine examples of adults; we're both so proud of them.

I stay silent; this is the most Ben has ever opened up to me about his private life and his family. I watch him, quietly waiting, gently encouraging him, not wanting to push him too far.

And he continues. Wow! I'm feeling pretty proud of myself, ha ha!

"I sometimes feel sad that I didn't have the time with my own children that I do the grandchildren, but I guess Stan was wiring me for wealth, and the kids wired Mary for parenthood."

"Yes," I say, "but you both wanted the same thing, you just each took your own role, right?"

"Marriage is a long road, fraught with many challenges; family issues and financial struggles," Ben explains, "it makes you wonder how any families get through it all."

"But you came through it," I smile.

"We've had our moments, but yes, Mary has always stood by me and together we've come through it. We are complete opposites which I think in a strange way is why we work so well. You don't realise these things until you get older but it's almost like we compliment each other."

"How so?"

Ben laughs to himself, "Mary is too nice, and I am not nice enough…" He takes a moment to contemplate his words. "But we've made everything work."

As if on cue, Mary knocks on the door and with a smile tells us the car will be here in one hour to take us to the restaurant we are dining at this evening.

As she closes the door, Ben looks at me and we both smile in a sudden moment of understanding. Ben has given me more insight

*today then I think he ever intended to, and I give him a look of
assurance; this is enough...*

✦ ✦ ✦

In order to keep costs down we purchased a small condominium
in the US to save on hotel bills.

The UK services, thanks to the 1992 rental system initiative,
were flying, so I decided to invest in more infrastructure to continue our growth.

Despite there being talk of the UK going into recession, I
couldn't see any signs, and I guess I believed we were immune to
things like that. Would a recession really bite us?

As part of the new infrastructure, I wanted to separate Dex
as a software developer from the services and I created a new
company called Res X. I moved all the services side of the business into that company and left Dex to develop and support our
software.

I had ambitious plans for Res X; to include recruitment, consultancy, outsourcing and more. If it worked, I would emulate the
idea in the US. It was at this point that I realised my decision to
leave the draughting side of things to embark in management had
been the right one.

In management, I was now able to satisfy my thirst to create,
and it felt fantastic.

By this time, I was, as you can imagine, juggling a lot of balls,
and not the Stan kind of balls, so Brian and I agreed to bring in
some help. One of his old business contacts; a self-made, multi-mil-
lionaire called John Westin fitted the bill perfectly. John lived in the
Cotswolds so it was agreed he would commute twice a week to
run the admin team for me. He was fantastic, smart and articulate,
and he became a real asset.

As a bonding session, and to give them a better understanding of the UK operation, I brought over the three principal managers from the US; Joan, Terri and Carol.

US sales were flagging because we were missing the technical back up and I was becoming exhausted, what with balancing the two companies and travelling every other month.

With a good management team being built up in the US following the UK blueprint, we knew we had to recruit a CEO and we found our man, Lawrence, through another of John's business contacts.

Back in the UK, I had head-hunted the facilities manager from one of my clients, Mike, and I made him CEO of Res X.

I put my faith in Lawrence and Mike to take the two businesses forward.

This was a big opportunity and whilst on paper, the structure of my idea was promising, as always it was about the people, would they deliver in practice?

Tech Group was the holding company; owning Dex, Dex Inc and now Res X, of which I was chairman, with Brian as sales director and John Westin, board director.

I was also managing director of Dex, Lawrence was CEO of Dex Inc and Mike Ide, CEO of Res X.

So, the scene was set, investment was made, and my expectations were now on delivering results and believe me, I drove those guys so hard. I could literally smell the success in that infrastructure.

"Did you ever stop evolving and growing that business?" I ask with an incredulous laugh.

"You can never stop, M, not if you want to stay in business. As I'm sure you're gathering, it's the proverbial roller-coaster."

"Well, I guess you have to work hard to reap the rewards?"

"Ha!" Ben exclaims, "I wished I could have felt comfortable with that over-rated term, work hard, play hard. I constantly promised myself that I would play hard when the job was done, but like so many entrepreneurs, the play hard part was always on hold."

"Yes, so I can see!" I tease Ben.

"I think," Ben is thoughtful, "one of the defining examples of an entrepreneur is that moment when you're faced with a tough decision."

"Go on," I sense Ben's need to reflect and he continues.

"When there is split opinion, when you can feel support waning, you have to work harder to convince others of your argument. You have to stand up and be counted and you have to stand firm. That, to me, is the difference between being decisive, and potentially divisive, or simply selling out for an easy life."

"I can't imagine you ever backing down!" I retort as Ben laughs.

"Don't get me wrong, I always understand there is another view and I listen. But to be honest, once I've made my mind up, that's it."

"Yes, I kind of noticed that..." I mutter this under my breath and fortunately Ben doesn't seem to have heard.

"Just consider this, there are only 65% of entrepreneurs that have created wealth from nothing."

"What's your point?"

"My point, dear M," he smiles slowly, "is that I'm very grateful to live in a democracy where I was able to pull myself up from a poor background. Sometimes," Ben says, "when I do ever get time to sit and relax, I like to read the Sunday papers to satisfy my curiosity about other entrepreneurs."

"How so?" I ask and Ben smiles.

"Oh, all sorts but there's always an article each week, almost a Q and A type interview that asks different individuals basic questions about their lives. I find it really insightful."

Ben is quiet and thoughtful and I suddenly have an idea.

"Let's do one then, on you!"

Ben splutters with laughter, "No, it seems far too indulgent, almost narcissistic even."

"Ah, come on," I plead. "It's just a bit of fun."

Ben thinks about this and I just know he's going to agree.

"Go on then, M." He finally chuckles, "What do you want to know?"

I clap my hands joyously, "Ok, here goes; how much money do you have in your wallet?"

Ben is shocked, "M! That's a bit personal, isn't it?"

I am laughing away at his surprise for my impertinence, "Just answer the bloody question."

He shakes his head but he's smiling as he obviously decides to indulge me.

"About one hundred and fifty pounds and a couple of hundred dollars right now."

"What credit cards do you use?"

Ben is getting into this now, I can tell, and he answers directly.

"Virgin Amex, I don't need to, obviously, but I collect the air miles. And I always pay off the monthly debt. I hate debt."

"Are you a spender or a saver?"

"Absolutely without a doubt, a saver."

"Do you invest in shares?"

"Yes, I bought into banks when they crashed in the 2008 recession, knowing that in the long term, they would come back strong at some point."

I raise my eyebrows at Ben.

"Not that it's going to be anytime soon!" he chuckles, "Now get on with it."

"How do you think others perceive you?"

Ben snorts with laughter, "Not normal probably!"

"Ha," I laugh, "seriously though?"

Ben considers this for a moment. "Maybe just that I like to be different and surprising."

"You're certainly that," I mutter under my breath.

"Oi, I heard that!" Ben cries indignantly and I giggle.

"Who do you consider has had the most influence on your life?"

Ben sucks in his teeth here, "Ooh, that's a tough one, there's been lots."

"Go on," I urge him and he ponders my question a little before answering.

"Well, there's been Mary of course, without her things could have been so different."

I smile at Ben, glad to see he has his priorities right and he rolls his eyes once again at my romantic notions before he continues.

"Then, obviously, there's my kids, and grandkids and of course, Stan."

"Of course," I nod.

"Then there's Maggie Thatcher, and now you."

I look up from my note book in surprise, a huge beam on my face, and Ben smiles back.

"Have you ever been hard up?"

"Yes! When I started work and then again when I started my business, borrowing to invest."

"And what's been your best investment?"

"My banking shares of course," Ben laughs, "no, really it's my business."

"Do you support any charities?"

Ben ponders this before answering. "Yes, we do, but in circumstances worthy of donation as opposed to generally donating. We prefer to support individual cases."

"What's your financial weakness?"

"Mercedes, Hugo Boss, land lots and new builds." I roll my eyes but continue all the same.

"What's the most important lesson you've learned about money?"

"That it's so darn hard to get in any real quantity, and even when you do it's not a passport to happiness but it can be incredibly rewarding in lots of ways."

I sit back and put my pen down, I'm all out of questions but Ben carries on.

"It's important to step away from the frantic over stimulation of what life throws at us though. To find happiness by filling your senses, not just your pockets."

"Your senses?" What is Ben on about now?

"Yes, sight, sound, touch, scent. To feel emotion and, just as we're doing here, stimulate the imagination and leave a lingering sense of hope."

"Christ, Ben," I chuckle, "that wasn't a Q and A answer, that's our next book!"

Ben roars with laughter.

"That was fun, M!" He sits forward and peers at me. "Now let's do it on you."

"Erm, no," is my stern reply.

Thanks to the services, in particular the rental side of things, regular income was helping to fund our investment.

Mike brought in two more experienced facility managers and was able to split his services into three teams, with a facility manager looking after operators in house and on site. By now, we had eighteen operators, most of them on site, to provide the hands-on running of our client's systems.

Alex was working hard to replace our CAD engine with iCAD and as it was nearing launch, we decided to use that opportunity to forge a partnership with the authors of iCAD.

They encouraged developers to participate in adding value to their bland CAD based drafting tool by adding specialised areas, in our case, building management.

The list was huge, any application you could think of with CAD at its heart and we were just one of hundreds of developers.

My vision was to drive the emphasis more towards the database than the CAD system and eventually have some separation, but iCAD's author had the opposite vision; their primary goal was to sell volume copies of iCAD, and that didn't fit with my vision of a separate database.

For now, this suited us both though as, for us, it meant we could arrest the slide of software going to iCAD, and iCAD's authors would gain business by selling more iCAD software to our market.

It was a forced relationship, in truth, my version, iCAD in particular, and the up-swell of the PC muddied the water.

But business is all about survival of the fittest and we learned a lesson; if we had have stayed with the mini-computer that Nelson was clinging onto, we would have died alongside it, for it wasn't long before the age of the PC saw off the main frame and mini computers for the mass market.

I did contemplate how difficult things could have been if we had stayed with Nelson's software, in fact I didn't see any way that we could have survived.

I decided to relaunch the AEC software with another name and I came up with BIM, a name I loved. It perfectly embraced our market and iCAD.

We took our BIM system to iCAD's authors event in San Francisco called DEVCAMP to show off our proud development and it was met with astonishment.

All we had done was swap our own CAD system for iCAD, but they hadn't seen anything as slick as our database software before.

✦ ✦ ✦

Mary and I raise our eyebrows as we hear Ben's raised voice from his office whilst we are sipping iced tea by the pool.

"He doesn't stop, does he?" I smile nervously at Mary.

"Huh, he never will!" Mary shrugs and sits forward conspiratorially, "Look, knowing Ben as I do, he's going to be working on this current problem all night. What say you and I go out?"

I nearly fist pump the air, I don't though. "I'd love that!"

Mary smiles, "Let's go and get ready then."

I stand up with her and as I walk away she calls my name.

I turn and she fixes me with that look again.

"This is not for the book though, ok Mandy?"

I smile. I don't need to say anything, because I am beginning to feel that I'm gaining Mary's trust too.

Chapter 18

Never Stop Believing in Yourself

When I catch up with Ben the following morning, he asks if Mary and I had fun the night before, clearly pleased that we are getting on so well.

"I'm sorry I couldn't join you," he adds, "things have taken a bit of a downturn in one of my projects and to be honest I kind of enjoyed having a bit of space."

I don't ask Ben for any detail, knowing by now that if he wants to tell me he will.

It's apparent that he doesn't when he says, "Anyway, I've got through worse. Shall we?"

I nod and pick up my notebook...

+1990+

A year into the company restructure, things weren't working out with the two new CEO's, Lawrence and Mike.

Both Dex Inc and Res X were losing money and my overdraft was marching towards £200k, practically at its limit.

I had invested my money, my time, and I'd been supportive of them, patient even.

Well it seems I'd been too patient and now I was angry. Even I wouldn't want to mess with me when that line had been crossed.

I couldn't pedal the business any faster and with bank loans that far exceeded our mortgage, we had signed over everything we owned in assets as guarantees to the bank.

I felt like I'd sacrificed most of my leisure and family time as well as put my family at financial risk, and I wondered if, if I had the choice again, would I have still done this?

I didn't think so, well not in that way. I guess that's hindsight for you and you learn from that.

Once again, something Stan had once said came back to me:

"When, like Maurice, you own something Ben, you too will feel the pain. But you must keep driving and believing in yourself. Know that you deserve the gain, recognise when the opportunity is there, then take it."

"Stan was still such an influence in your life even after he had disappeared, wasn't he?"

"He still is, M, if I'm honest. Even now."

"Keep your eye on the ball," I repeat the mantra and Ben nods.

"Yep, even when people expect you, or actually want you, to fail."

His words resonate with me, "Ha, I know that feeling." The words are out of my mouth before I can stop them and I blush as he looks up at me enquiringly.

He doesn't press me on this though and I'm grateful.

"So," I quickly move on, "who wanted you to fail?"

He smiles knowingly at my swift subject swerve and shakes his head.

"It's a general thing really. In my view, in the US, entrepreneurs are respected for their risk taking, for their blood sweat and tears.

It's acknowledged that they create employment and career oppor-tunities. When they grow wealthy as a result of their success, it's widely accepted as a real achievement, and, in the most part they are entrepreneurial hero's.

In the UK, we've grown to be a little too envious of success. We like to build up losers and when we get them on a pedestal, we are quick to knock them down."

I think Ben has a good point here, it's sad really that so many people find it difficult to applaud hard work and ambition.

I would often take time out to strategise and analyse the things I could be doing better.

It was during one of these moments that I took a long hard look at myself instead of just the business.

What was this really all about? Was it about how much money I could make or was it about the control, the power? Or was I simply trying to prove to myself that I could do something extraordinary?

Where was my level of competence? Now I was in control, did The Peter Principal still apply? I asked so many questions of myself as my self-doubt kicked in.

Was I only worthy of running a small team or was I about to preside over a bankrupt company?

I had to shake myself, to remind myself of what I had achieved so far, and under extreme circumstances.

I was still learning and I took another lesson from Stan in my head: *"Never stop believing in yourself."*

This wasn't over yet, so on we go…

In tough times, I don't think many people say; "Hmm, now would be a good time to invest."

Perhaps if I'd had the cash I would have, as times were about to hit us hard, and the thought of investing when everyone else was cutting costs stuck in my head.

In late 1990, the recession started to take an effect on the UK and I discovered we weren't so immune after all. It was my first taste of a recession and I realised I had no real concept of just what it would do to us; it came so fast and furious, it was ruthless.

The first sign was when three contracts with customers that had secured twelve CAD operators on site were cancelled, all within a three-month period. It was a huge blow, with at least two thirds of our service work drying up.

One customer, with four of our operators on site, didn't even give the conventional three-month notice. They simply broke their contract and told us if we didn't like it, we should sue them.

I'll let that company remain unnamed, but as a huge PLC corporation, they should be ashamed.

It was a chaotic time, but I wouldn't let anyone pressure me into making a decision, I liked to step back and think things through.

And by now, I had thought things through and made a decision. It was a quick reaction and whilst it was a tough decision to make, at the same time it was easy. Easy because it felt right.

I just needed to convince others.

John was really supportive, Brian less so, but I had made my mind up.

I'd been taught that, in business, it's not personal. It's a game you have to win at all costs; survival of the fittest if you like.

And now it was time for another lesson for me. The lesson in how to dismiss staff, not only because they had not performed but because we also had to survive.

I fired Mike and released his two managers, and without any contracts coming in, I had to let some of the CAD operators go too. Those key members of the management team had had their chance to change things and they hadn't.

The upside was that we got to keep the strongest in the team. I had to be ruthless for the good of the company and, although there wasn't much of it, clearing out the dead wood was a start. Don't get me wrong, this wasn't a cool breeze approach, it was more like a hard frost. I was determined to make recovery cutbacks just this once, the answer as to whether it would be enough, was about to be revealed.

It soon became apparent that I had no choice but to focus wholly on the UK business.

I thought about how Maurice had let PI almost bring the Onelock Group to its knees; that wasn't going to happen to me.

It was time to let go of the US and it was with a heavy heart that I decided to sell Dex Inc but I couldn't allow my emotions to overrule my rationale.

I was so critical of and disappointed in myself. Between the UK and US we had built a growing company of forty staff and now we were pulling back to half of that in order to survive.

It felt once again like déjà vu, a mini version of what I had experienced at Onelock with PI. Would I learn from this? Was the cycle of life repeating itself?

I was constantly beating myself up about where I had gone wrong, which I knew was wrong, the recession after all had taken this out of my hands. But still I anguished too much over whether I could have prevented this. It had to be a lesson learned for the next recession.

My PA, Liane, was a high flyer and she decided to move her career on, I wish I could have kept her but I knew it was right for her. There we were bunkering down to weather a storm and there she was ready to fly high. This, I suppose, was the flip side to The Peter Principal; a company unable to keep pace with the growth of their employees.

In the book, The Peter Principal, it talks a lot about individuals being promoted to a level of incompetence, but the episode with Liane reminded me that a company also needs to keep in sync with an individual's career. If the company falters and the individual grows it's always in the best interest of the individual to move on, but it was hard losing her all the same.

With the decision now made to sell Dex Inc, it was now down to Alex to take back what he had developed in the U.S. and rebuild it within the UK team as a continuation of this process.

With that plan underway, I flew to the U.S. to inform Lawrence of my decision.

Although my decision was based upon us having to cut costs as opposed to his performance, Lawrence seemed almost relieved as he admitted it had become a struggle for him.

This reaction confirmed to me that what I was doing was right; he knew he was failing, yet I felt disappointed in myself for not choosing the right man for the job.

The management team were obviously really upset and unsettled with yet another change.

They tried to convince me to let them run the company, but the risk was too great; failure would bring down our UK operation.

Over the coming months, as we advertised Dex Inc, I had a mind to sell it all off and tie it into a dealer contract with us. To be honest, my whole focus was to urgently consolidate, bunker down and get back to the U.S. when, and if, the time was right.

There was very little response to our advert, in fact only one investor came forward with a serious offer and after some discussions, we eventually agreed a deal. Richard Dell would take 100% equity in Dex Inc for what we invested in it, which was about £160k.

I seriously considered keeping some equity but eventually convinced myself that to have 100% ownership would be much more motivating for Dell. I knew where my priorities lay and aside from that I didn't want to fleece him. That company would need a lot of Dell's cash and I had structured the deal so that the more successful he grew, so too would we be rewarded further.

It was a good way forward; Dell would operate as an autonomous dealer. This was a great opportunity for him to build a business and potentially sell it back to us in the future.

We had our lawyers draw up the paperwork and set a date to fly over to complete contracts.

It was planned that I would fly in one day, get the papers signed and fly out the next day, with Alex coming along to finalise the release of the last programmers.

I was finally starting to feel as though I had regained control of what was a potentially damaging situation. Though I wasn't getting too comfortable just yet, we were still in a recession after all.

Alex and I were on a tight schedule; due to arrive in Boston at 5pm, my meeting to complete the contracts with Richard Dell was the next morning and then we would be flying out at 7pm that evening. As we began our descent into Logan airport though, the captain's voice came over the intercom system.

"Ladies and gentleman, I'm afraid we're having trouble getting into Boston due to fog. We will be circling for a while to see if we can make another approach."

Alex and I looked at each other but didn't think too much of it until the captain spoke again.

"Ladies and gentleman, I'm sorry but we will be making our way to Montreal where we anticipate a short layover while we refuel before making a return to Boston later this evening. I do apologise for the long delay."

"Shit," I muttered to Alex, "we're already tight for time."

Time, however, became the last of my worries, when we began hurtling towards the runway in Montreal at break neck speed.

"Jesus Christ!" I shouted, clutching my arm rest as all around me passengers gasped, and Alex, his eyes shut tight, said nothing.

It was a heart stopping moment, oxygen masks fell out and loose items in the galley went flying as we tore down the runway, breaking hard. I seriously thought we had crashed.

Even the stewardess, professionally keeping everybody calm, a fixed smile on her pretty face, looked pale.

Just over an hour later, Alex and I breathed a sigh of relief as we took off again, heading for our third attempt into Logan.

There was nothing but fog as we began our descent into Logan and we seemed to be flying for ages. The longer we flew the more we worried. Neither of us particularly enjoyed flying but flying blind through cloud or fog was even more unnerving and after our recent experience in Montreal, we were pretty on edge.

Eventually the captain spoke again.

"I'm sorry folks, we are going to have to return to Montreal. There will be a replacement aircraft to fly you back to Boston tomorrow."

As most of the passengers groaned, I began to panic. How were we going to get our business done in time for our flight home tomorrow night?

That evening in the hotel I went back through the contract documents in detail and spoke to Dell on the phone to get a heads-up of any of his queries, we wouldn't have time for them tomorrow.

We finally flew back to Boston at lunchtime the next day and had literally just two hours to sign the contracts before catching our flight back to the UK.

At the check in desk, I mentioned that we had been on yesterday's twenty-four hour delayed aircraft.

"Oh, you poor dears," the check in hostess smiled apologetically, "let's upgrade you."

With Dex Inc sold, we flew back to the UK in business class, and although my heart was heavy from the sale, I wondered if that was a sign.

"A sign?"

Ben runs his hands through his hair, "Yeah, it was weird. I was obviously feeling deep sadness at giving up the U.S. company, and initially, I'll admit, the delay into Boston seemed to me to be fate, maybe delaying my decision to sell."

I smile sadly, it must have felt awful, after all that hard work he'd put in.

"But you see," Ben smiles, "when we got upgraded, I saw it as a new sign. We had left the toxicity behind in order to upgrade to pure luxury."

I look at Ben as he sits and reflects, and I think I'm finally getting him.

Am I?

He stands up and stretches, "I need to walk for a bit."

I say nothing, but as I watch him go, his shoulders are sagging like he has the weight of the world on them. Why, when he has just relayed another successful business decision? What is it that pains him so?

No, I realise, I don't get him. I don't get him at all...

Chapter 19

"Seventy Mill," I Said without Hesitancy

+1991+

My cost controls were still in effect but at the same time I wanted to take advantage of investing.

Despite the loss of a lot of my on-site operating staff because of the recession, I still needed to forward think and knew I had to get a handle on the accounts.

My accounting role in Onelock had been invaluable but I needed an in-house expert working alongside me; someone who could guide my overdraft away from its limit.

When I recruited Jessica, we were £240k overdrawn and at risk of the bank calling in the loan. She proved to be the best recruit I'd ever undertaken and together we embraced the phrase 'cash is king', as we worked towards our debt free target.

Meanwhile, we had established another big order from our furniture supply customer.

The MD, Gary, reminded me of a younger version of Maurice.

He was a good looking forty-year old who was very well spoken and always smartly dressed. He had real charisma.

I must admit, when I first met Gary, I saw him as a bit of a challenge. I'm not sure why, maybe because I found him a little dismissive of me when we first met, and I wanted to change that.

The company were planning to create key dealerships in different parts of the country that would be exclusive dealers.

It meant another system sale for us and quite a significant one. With some of that profit, I also purchased 5% of one of their companies, which at £5,000 was yet another huge risk for me, but by now I wasn't shy of risk. As it happened, I had to pull that £5k back a year later, but I don't regret having what one could call a bet.

Over time, I had struck up quite a good relationship with Gary, once I'd got past his steely exterior. I like to think the feeling was mutual.

On one occasion, I was in a meeting with him and two other guys when he asked us all.

"What is it you want from your businesses?"

As the others guys talked intelligently about growing and running an empire, I smiled knowingly, then Gary turned to me.

"How about you, Ben?"

"Seventy mill," I said without hesitancy. "I want to sell out for seventy million pounds."

Gary gazed at me as he processed my answer and I could see the gaping mouths of the other two men.

"You didn't hesitate," Gary smiled, "why seventy mill?"

"Why not?" My answer had come from my heart and not my head, but sometimes it's the heartfelt ideas that you build on. I was here to create wealth, for myself and my family, there was no point in dressing it up as anything else.

"You knew what you wanted and you were determined to get it, weren't you?"

Ben nods, "Absolutely, there's no point in aiming low, have a goal, make it a big one and aim for it with every fibre of your being, and…"

"Never take your eye off the ball." We say in unison and fall about laughing.

"Have you heard any more from our friend Mr Bourne?" Ben suddenly asks and I shake my head.

"No, it's weird. Every now and again he'll tweet something about our book, but then he just goes missing for days."

Ben chuckles, "Very elusive."

"Yes, very elusive," I agree, "in fact his latest tweet was to suggest we turn this book into a film."

Ben roars with laughter, "I wonder who would play me?"

"Ha ha, it's not as ludicrous an idea as you think." I put this to him and he sits back thoughtfully.

"It's funny," he says, "I've watched a few awful films and thought my story would be box office compared to them."

"Well then, maybe it could happen?"

Ben is lost in thought as he speaks.

"In fact, I've also read a few books that made me think I could write better, hence, I suppose, why I began writing my story."

He stands up and I assume this is the end of today's session but Ben holds out his hand to pull me up.

"Come on," he says as I stand up, "I want to show you something."

I follow him to the far corner of the terrace and he stops in front of two blue lounging chairs.

"What?" I ask, confused.

"This," Ben relaxes into one of the chairs and stretches his legs, "this is my favourite place to explore my love of writing. To simply sit and create."

I settle into the chair next to him and I can see what Ben means, this is a dream spot. The sun is behind us and the lake in front of us is flooded with the rich reflective sunlight. A cool breeze blows the scent of Bougainville over us and the sound of the waterfall on the pool provides a calming sound.

"I didn't realise you wrote that much."

"Oh, M. There's lots you don't know about me."

"Telling me!" I snort and he turns to me with a grin.

"Yes, why not become a writer, I thought. That's what led me to thinking about an autobiography. I would often tell friends about things that happened in the business and they would be wide-eyed."

"Well yes, obviously."

"The trouble was, my family were, understandably, uneasy about it, which was why becoming the secret entrepreneur seemed perfect. They and my close friends would know my identity but to anyone else I was just another successful entrepreneur providing what I hope is a good story."

"It is a good story!" I exclaim and Ben continues.

"As I started writing, I realised just how much I loved it and how inventive it could be.

I would write for hours when I felt the content was good and stop when it wasn't. I didn't care about grammar or spelling, I just wanted, no needed, to get it out of my head.

It felt quite therapeutic as, every day, I would find my mind wandering back to different parts of my life as more and more detail returned and I tried to bring it to the page.

I would grab my phone and drop myself an email when something inspired me or if I suddenly remembered a name from the distant past.

I was encouraged by how much I remembered about my business and how, when you get back in that zone, the memories flood back."

"So why did you ask me to write it for you?"

Ben turns and looks at me.

"I love writing, M, but you, it's in your DNA; you live and breathe it and I chose you for a reason; you're a class act."

I blush at the compliment but I say nothing. I don't need to.

We both sit in silence, gazing at the lake, watching the wildlife dance over the water.

Over the course of the following year we began to extend the business with our first European relationship.

I received an enquiry through one of my UK contacts from a German company. As with many of our overseas enquiries, we trod cautiously, not taking the interest too seriously.

It seemed though that this one had more to it.

The company were a well-established architectural based tech company and its owner and CEO, Herbert, was determined to acquire our technology.

After a few telephone conversations, I flew over to Munich to meet with him and I committed to writing an interface for them which converted BIM into a German version.

As part of this deal, we would also be training up Herbert's staff, which was a new experience for both companies. Herbert and I connected very well and I liked him a lot, so when he invited Alex and I to his special 50th birthday celebrations, I was honoured.

It was all designed as a bit of a long mystery weekend; we were sent tickets to fly to Verona on a Thursday, returning the following Sunday.

I was trying to make sure all my weekends were spent with my family as my weekdays were full on, but I made this an exception.

We were met at Verona airport by one of Herbert's staff. He was tight lipped as he drove us to a small hotel Herbert had taken over, where thirty other Germans were also staying.

"Guten tag," Alex and I pigeon Germaned as we greeted the other guests; we were the only English invited and again I was touched that Herbert had included us in such a personal event.

No sooner had we checked in, when we were told we had to board a coach.

"What's going on, do you think?" Alex whispered excitedly to me and I shrugged.

"Well, it's a mystery, isn't it?"

We both sniggered as we boarded the coach, with no idea where we were heading.

Two hours later we arrived in the heart of Venice and it was magical.

We were told to go off and do some exploring before meeting back up at the dockside by 5pm. Alex and I had absolutely no idea what was planned, and if anyone else knew, they certainly weren't letting on.

It didn't matter though, here we were in Venice, and we wanted to explore this beautiful city.

We took a gondola through the Grand Canal thoroughfare that is lined with Renaissance and Gothic palaces and laughed at how absurdly romantic it was.

"If you think I'm going to kiss you under the Bridge of Sighs, think again." I muttered as Alex snorted with laughter.

Later, after a quick beer in the central square; Piazza San Marco, we stood at the agreed meeting place.

We were excited and curious to know what was in store, guessing correctly that we were about to be taking a boat somewhere. We boarded the small but well equipped vessel and joined in the delighted sighs of the other guests.

"Wunderbar, wunderbar," they enthused at the scene before us; the boat had been lavishly set up for dinner, exclusively for us.

We left Venice as the sun set on a glorious warm evening and Alex and I clinked our glasses. I felt like pinching myself. It felt incredible to be part of this, and there was still more to come.

As the evening wore on, the drink took over and some serious partying began, it was crazy!

Think Wolf of Wall Street but without the naked girls and the drugs, yet it was still a great party!

There were drunk Germans everywhere, some were jumping overboard, splashing and frolicking in the warm water, it was surreal.

We arrived back at the hotel at about 4am, with instructions to be ready by 9am. Now when the Germans say 9am, they mean it.

So, with hardly any sleep and running on pure adrenaline, we boarded a bus bound for Verona.

First up was the Castelvecchio museum; restored by the architect Carlo Scarpa between 1959 and 1973. With my love of all things building, I could appreciate the unique style that was visible in the details of the doorways and staircases. Even down to the furnishings, it was breathtaking.

Next, we headed for the famous Verona arena; a huge 1st- century Roman amphitheatre, where we were treated to an evening showing of Aida.

Then, as if that wasn't full on enough, we were treated to a late-night meal at one of Herbert's favourite Italian restaurants, eating and drinking merrily before arriving back at our hotel at 2am.

Thankfully the next day was a rest day and pretty much everybody slept in late, but later we all met up in a pizzeria to watch Italy, who were playing Brazil in the World Cup Final.

When Brazil won, we witnessed the Italians sobbing in the street and I wondered if England would ever give us another opportunity to cry at a final!

On our last day, we were taken to a huge Italian mansion where Herbert was launching the opening of his new refurbished Italian offices.

We travelled by mini bus that afternoon, heading out into the beautiful Italian countryside. It was a sight to behold, with typical honey hue homes scattered in the rolling hills of olive groves.

We turned off the road with the last of the afternoon sun behind us, highlighting the long straight road ahead; an avenue of tall, whispery, Italian cypress trees.

As we drew around the turning circle in front of the house with the sound of the wheels on the gravel drive, I gasped. The house was everything you could imagine of an Italian home; stunning architecture draped in pink and white bougainvillea and creeping vines that twisted their way up to the grey slate roof. In that moment, I knew I wanted this. I vowed to myself that if I ever got the opportunity to design and build my dream home, this would be my inspiration. It was so very romantic and set so perfectly in the landscaped grounds, an elegant tall figurine neatly located in the manicured lawn. The entrance was flanked with high, aged clay pots that flowed over with beautiful blossom, and there was Herbert, the perfect host, ready and waiting to greet us. He was accompanied by two smartly dressed, attractive waitresses, in starch white jackets and tight black skirts holding silver trays of champagne. The air was heavily laden with the scent of the purple trumpet flowers and soft classical music echoed from the open doors like a melodic tapestry. I gazed at my surroundings, drinking in the moment and enjoying the stimulation of my senses. I felt like some important dignitary as we enjoyed canapés in the beautiful Italianate gardens, and I realised I liked that feeling.

It seemed we'd barely had time to catch our breath before we were heading to the airport for our flight home. What an experience that was, made even better in that Herbert had just opened the door for us to Europe...

+ + +

Changes were not only afoot within the business; at home, we were on the move.

We had spotted a new-build Tudor style house in a select development within our village with far more space inside and out than we currently had.

As I've said, Mary and I share a love of new-builds, as well as similar tastes for interiors, so we set about designing our house together, not in a move to make money but to create a family home that we would fall in love with.

This love, however, quickly became costly when interest rates rose sharply to 17%, making our mortgage repayments excessively high, whilst at the same time house prices fell, and in our case, by about 20%.

Accustomed to high risk and used to the financial pressure as I was, this only fuelled my desire to drive more from the business in order to balance our lifestyle.

Over a few years, it had become increasingly evident that Brian was struggling with his sales role.

It had become much more of a technical sales job, due to purchasers wanting to be shown exactly what our product could do.

Despite my constantly encouraging Brian over the years to spend time learning the technical side and practicing demos, he seemed unwilling to.

So, as he struggled under the pressure, we had to source an operator to work alongside him for each appointment.

I think in truth Brian probably wanted out at this point; feeling vulnerable in an environment that he was rapidly losing touch with, so I confronted him with an ultimatum; step up and commit, or leave.

When the weeks passed and he did neither, I knew I had to take the difficult decision myself. I let Brian go.

He was devastated, believing the support he had previously given should see him in good stead to continue with the company, no matter what. But I explained, quite firmly, that no one could be carried, that everybody needed to show productivity and be at the top of their game at all times.

I reminded him that we had been suffering this same conversation for years and he had shown no appetite for change. There was nothing more to discuss and, needless to say, it was not a happy departure.

In the space of seven years I had lost four of my key management team; Nelson, Mike, Brian and John. It was now time to start rebuilding from within.

I duly promoted the two people within my team that had shown the most promise, the most loyalty and dedication. I chose Jessica as Finance Director and Alex as my R&D Director.

I also, in what I considered a generous but motivational gesture, awarded them both shares; fifteen each or the equivalent to 1.5% of the company group.

It was around this time that I began to feel stressed like I'd never felt before, and emotional too…

Ben stops and I'm expecting at any moment that he'll stand up and walk away. He doesn't though. He runs his hands through his hair and I wait for the 'let's do this later' speech but again, he surprises me. "Let's go get a beer."

I raise my eyebrows in surprise, Ben doesn't really drink, but I'm not about to argue, I could use a beer myself at this point.

Mary declines to join us, and an hour later we sit in a bar nursing our bottles of Bud, Bud Light in Ben's case. Ben continues with his story…

"Normally, I could handle the stress, my God, after the situation with Nelson, you'd think I'd seen the worst!"

"Well, yes. I must admit, after all that you'd already gone through, why would this be any worse?"

Ben drains the last of his beer from the bottle and shakes his head, signaling to the young waiter.

"I think it was a combination of things, everything that had gone before in business, maybe turning forty too."

I grimace, I've recently entered my forties, and Ben laughs. "I'm sure you'll cope, M."

"Ha, did you?" I ask him seriously.

I'd gone through so much more before, but this time, for some reason, it had gotten the better of me.

I couldn't share it, I couldn't explain it, and I just couldn't shake it.

I was a forty-year old man, and men don't do emotions, do they?

Especially under circumstances when 'man up' was the only thing on the agenda. Yet here I was, wondering at my purpose and beginning to doubt the business around me. I just couldn't let go of that fear. As much as I tried to hide it, I felt like I was in a pressure cooker and about to experience a burn out. It was as if my ability to multi task had suddenly vanished. I was used to mulling over one issue whilst two others conversed around my head. Now, I could only hear one.

One of my attributes, or so Stan would have had me believe, was my obsession with something; obsession, that's me to a tee. But, like a temper, it can be damaging unless harnessed.

Maybe, having reached forty, some kind of chemical trigger had gone off in my body, perhaps even some kind of mini breakdown. I had just lost my maternal grandma, whom I'd been close to throughtout my childhood, maybe that had some bearing on how I was feeling. All I knew was at this time in my career and life, a change had happened and I was feeling my control slipping away.

> *I puff out my cheeks, Ben has been very deep today. "Another beer?"*
> *He asks, and I nod but he's already gesturing the waiter again.*
> *"Are you ok, Ben?" I ask tentatively.*
> *"No, not really, Mandy." He smiles sadly. "I will tell you about*
> *it, just let me get my head around it first, ok?"*
> *I nod as we get back to business…*

Even as I was totally in control, I felt so out of control, and these feelings fostered my compulsive retrospection and introspection.

It was another moment in my life when I wondered, what if?

What if I can't handle this?

I'd had so many of these moments that could have changed the course of my life and of those around me. It felt like I was living in some kind of weird parallel universe, or had I just crossed a line? If so, boy was I having trouble getting back to the other side.

Leading up to this moment, I admit, I'd cried to myself on a few occasions, in particular when I thought I would let my family down by being fired from Onelock and especially when Nelson looked like taking the business.

But I'd also cried with joy on many other occasions; business and pleasure, the birth of my children being the most memorable.

This felt different though. *I* felt different.

Chapter 20

I'm in a Terrible State!

I was sleeping on the floor, cold and uncomfortable. I felt exhausted but I needed to stay alert. In the deathly silence, all I could hear was the hum of the computer. I'd thought about working, after all I was in the office, but I'd drifted off to sleep.

Suddenly I woke to a noise outside and I sat up, my heart racing as I readied myself to fight.

Three days earlier I had arrived at the office to find the doors broken down, we had been burgled. There were no alarms in those days.

I assessed the office, noting that, other than a few missing computers, there was no real damage and all the furniture was in-tact.

I was angry though, this was yet another setback. Who the hell could have done this?

The police were very supportive as they dusted for finger prints and took details of the missing computers. When they asked for the names of current and past employees, especially any that might have a grudge against us, I felt totally confident that it wasn't any of my staff.

It was a difficult time because everyone was suddenly under suspicion, but never from me, I never once doubted them, even those who had recently left of their own accord.

The police warned me to be extra vigilant as in the majority of cases the thieves would return, especially when, as they thought, they had been disturbed.

We were insured and had organised replacement computers and repairs, but they would all take a few days and it worried me as to how we would keep things ticking over.

It was then I had decided to protect what we had myself and sleep at the office for a couple of nights. Was this over the top? Maybe. Or was I subconsciously aware that another setback could break my spirit completely?

Now, startled from my sleep by the sound of rolling milk bottles outside, I leaned forward, peering into the darkness for my intruder.

With my breath coming in shallow gasps, I fumbled for the kitchen knife I had kept beside me and stood up, frozen to the spot with fear.

For a tense, few minutes, I strained my ears to detect any noise from within the office, my fingers poised on the phone to dial 999.

There was nothing but silence, was my mind playing tricks on me?

I waited a good ten minutes, scared senseless, before venturing tentatively out into the stairwell and down the stairs, my arm outstretched holding the knife.

I was shaking as I stood again waiting for the faintest of noises, but the only sound was my pounding heart.

I unlocked the front door and peered out into the early morning dawn into nothingness.

And there really was nothing, except the milk bottles that had rolled over when the milkman had delivered them some fifteen minutes before...

Ben and I are strolling back from the bar and his story sends goosebumps up my spine.

"My God, that sounds terrifying!"

"It was, and with the stress I was already under, I seriously thought I might lose it."

"You didn't though?"

"I managed to keep it together, somehow. Just as well really."

"And did you ever find out who'd broken in?"

Ben laughs and nods sadly. "Ha, yep the police later discovered the missing computer at the home of a former employee."

"No way!" I stop and stare at Ben in surprise.

"Just goes to show how right Stan was eh, M? Never trust anyone."

"All hail the big man," I agree and we carry on walking.

Ben seems a little more relaxed now so I ask him if during the whirlwind of business, he ever had any downtime.

"You know, any time for yourself?"

He takes long slow strides as he ponders this. "Well, any spare time I had, I of course spent with Mary and the kids, but yeah, I had hobbies too."

"How did you find time?"

"Lord knows; you just do I guess. Things were always so full on though. I sometimes wished I had a passion for gardening, you know? Something in which I could just potter at my own pace."

"I'm sure," I muse and Ben speaks again.

"Oh, and there was another passion of mine." He laughs at my surprised look and enlightens me.

"Straighten your legs," bellowed the instructor. "Arch your back, pull, pull, pull," he screamed ruthlessly.

I was so tired I could hardly respond, but the thrill was exhilarating.

"Give me more, Ben" he demanded, his voice deafened by the howling wind.

I was leaning out at full stretch, trying to catch my breath from the speed, my eyes were watering and my feet were flat, as I tried to leverage goodness knows how much weight back upright.

Then I heard it.

It started with a gentle vibration that turned into a violent shudder. After a few seconds, the shudder subsided, to be replaced with a welcome humming sound as the hull of our little sailing dingy caught the air under it and started to plane over the water on a small cushion of air. Ah, it felt incredible.

"You took up sailing?"

"Ha ha, I did! It was a great outlet for me. It gave me a sense of adventure, almost a frisson of unease as the wind clanked the sailing rigs. I actually entered a few races."

"Seriously?" Here we go, yet more surprises, I think, though nothing surprises me anymore.

"Yep," Ben nods proudly, "some with my sailing partner, Emma. Jeez, now that woman was crazy! She was a plane junkie and constantly capsized us. I think we must have had the capsize record! Still, I went on to achieve my level two credit and pushed for my level three, although there were a few other, ahem, mishaps along the way."

Ben cringes and I laugh, only briefly though.

My instructor elected to take me out in, what could only be described as, risky weather. I had been taught that when the waves on the reservoir had white tips we were at force four, which meant it was time to dock, not sail. That is unless, like me, you need the ultimate thrill.

The reservoir was bridged by a huge concrete dam at one end and was three miles long by a mile wide, so plenty of water to create waves.

I remember being so excited in that moment I was screaming with joy at reaching the plane, but at the same time I had lost focus. As my dinghy capsized, I was thrown violently into the freezing cold water and it shot through my body like an electric bolt. All I could see was the white water that churned from the wipeout and I took in a gulp. I was struggling to breathe and panic set in. When the dinghy collapsed on top of me, the sail pressing down on my body, trapping me in my potential watery grave, I became totally disorientated.

I desperately struggled to keep my head above the water but as I disentangled myself from the gib ropes, I went under again.

I tried to launch the dinghy off me and push myself to the surface. I was panicking and thrashing out but I was trapped under the sail and my body began to feel heavy as I drained the last of my energy.

I had little breath remaining, but I was suddenly overcome by a surreal sort of calm; almost an acceptance.

Was I going to die here? If so, where were those moments that are supposed to flash before your eyes?

It was all so quick; *It's ok,* I told myself. *If this is my time, then I must let go.*

"Jesus! You could have died!"

Ben bursts out laughing, "I'm being over dramatic probably, the next thing I knew I was being hauled into the rescue boat, dumped on my side and was spewing water and sick everywhere. I guess it was my lucky day."

I shake my head crossly at Ben, "All for the sake of a thrill?"

He raises his eyebrows at me. "Would you expect anything less, M?"

As I roll my eyes, he nudges me gently. "I saved a few lives too, you know?"

"You hero, you," I mutter sarcastically, but I'm smiling because I know he's going to tell me about it and I like this new sharing Ben.

Every year members were put on a rota and required to run rescue duty. It was the Easter following my near-death experience and my turn to witness the madness of sailors claiming a plane, from the perspective of a rescue boat.

This was, however, some of the worst Easter weather anyone had known.

The waves were white tipped, so we were at force four before the race even got started.

Within an hour though, it got even worse and became so serious we didn't know which dingy to recuse first. It was like a battlefield; broken masts, upturned hulls and scarcely a sailing dingy upright.

This kind of thing was so far outside of my comfort zone but it was strange, I don't recall being frightened, just totally absorbed in wanting to get everyone on board the rescue boat and back to safety.

Trying to manoeuvre the rescue boat alongside the upturned boats in the water was no easy task and I'll never forget the last two people we picked up.

The high waves were sweeping their dingy towards the dam and I managed to get up next to them.

My co rescue-worker swung down to haul one of the sailors from the wreckage of the dinghy; it's mast was broken and the sailor was clinging on to the upturned hull which was about to be smashed into the dam.

We lurched several feet above him, screaming at him to get into the rescue boat, just as below us, in the swell, his boat suddenly caught a wave side on.

As he disappeared under the water, we were yelling, feeling helpless in this frantic situation. Then all of a sudden, he bobbed back up in the water, coughing and spluttering for breath as he grabbed the keel of his dinghy. He shouted something at us which, above the wind noise, was hard to hear but then he shouted it again, "I'm staying with my dinghy!"

My colleague and I looked at each other in desperation. What could we do? He shook his head and shrugged sadly, but I wasn't giving up, not yet.

"Take the rudder!" I screamed, and we quickly swapped places, the rescue boat rocking as we struggled to stay upstanding. All that was driving me at that moment was saving that man from drowning for the sake of his dinghy.

"Pull us around!" I commanded of my colleague, but much as he tried, attempt after attempt seemed fruitless and we were washed against the dam time after time.

It was beginning to look like we were going to lose this guy, until suddenly, we paired up with the dinghy.

Somewhere deep inside me, an explosion was ignited.

"Get in this f'ing boat now!" With strength I didn't know I had, I hooked him and screamed at my colleague to reverse as we dragged him away with us.

So we got our man, and our story was told in the level three classrooms and many others for years to come.

As was the story of my near drowning, but I erm, like to think I'd redeemed myself after that…

"Haha, wow! You're a bit of a dark horse, aren't you, Mr Taylor?"
I tease Ben, and just as he guffaws and starts to reply, his bloody phone rings.

I see the concern and stress return to his face as he takes the call and despite knowing it's morning back in the UK, I feel sad

*that Ben is taking calls after midnight on what is supposed to be
his vacation.*

*We arrive back at his home and Ben tells me to be ready at ten
o'clock tomorrow morning, he has a surprise for me, he says.*

By 1996, we seemed to be easing out of the recession and I was
beginning to look forwards again. It was like I had just ridden the
worst storm imaginable and, somehow, I'd come through it.

Despite having posted some shocking results over the last few
years, I was still looking to invest and I'd recently seen a plot of
land for sale.

It was almost an acre, with planning permission to knock down
the old residential property and build a small commercial building
of 2,500 square feet.

It was called The Shambles and that perfectly summed it up;
the old building was literally derelict. The gardens were completely
overgrown and in the corner of the lot was a run-down barn, but
to me it was perfect.

The problem was we were only ten years into a twenty-
five-year lease, with no break clause. It felt like a prison sentence
because I knew we didn't have the cash to buy ourselves out of it,
but of course, to me it became a challenge.

I wondered if I could somehow convince my landlord that we
were going under. After all, we had certainly come close and the
results we had just posted showed our losses and debt to the bank.
These facts couldn't be argued with, so I decided to use that data
and put a spin on our untenable future.

I met with Roger, the agent selling the land, and explained
our dilemma; telling him I wanted to purchase the land but could
only do so if he helped us exit the lease.

As luck would have it, Roger had a client who was interested
in renting our ground floor space, which would strengthen our

case, so he agreed to be a go-between and pose our situation to the landlord.

I was on tenterhooks by the time Roger called back.

"Ben, it's bad news," I felt my heart sink, "this is a huge pension fund, they aren't going to move. Your committed for another fifteen years and they aren't buying it, I'm sorry but they'll want a buy-out of half a million pounds."

"Shit, Roger, that's totally unreasonable!" I exclaimed and though he agreed, Roger explained that nevertheless that was the case.

"Ok, Roger, let me think." I dropped the phone, I needed to think.

As usual, my attention was taken up with my day to day business so I had no time to dwell on an alternative strategy until later that night.

That was usually when I did my thinking and I was always amazed when things came to me so late, when my energy levels were at their lowest.

It occurred to me that in business there are lines you have to cross when your conscience tells you it's justified. To some it may seem an interpretation that can get blurred, but to me, justification lay between those hardened in principal and those willing to take a risk and give things a different spin.

And right now, this was the time for risk, for crossing that line, and I was determined to free us from the lease on our hi-tech building at any cost. So off I went with Stan's find the ball analogy and it didn't take me long to find it.

The synchronicity to this was the land lot I had fallen in love with and the demise of my business, and as my creative juices started flowing, I suddenly got it. Stan, you absolute genius!

Our accounts reflected a state of bankruptcy, subject to my own injection of cash, so technically we were bankrupt. Fact. And there it was, my mojo was back!

The next morning, I eagerly picked up the phone to our accountants to explain our dilemma and gain their support.

"Woah, Ben," My sensible account manager was quick to bring me down to Earth. "How are you going to keep the company afloat, purchase land, and invest in a new build?"

I was quick to answer.

"That will be funded separately from my pension fund," I had it all worked out.

"Risky, Ben, very risky," I could hear his brain ticking over, "Ok, but it's more of your own personal money at risk though."

All I heard was the word ok. The risk part was only a risk if I didn't believe in my product, and I did.

So, with their support behind me, I was ready to play the game.

As soon as I had my accounts lined up, I called Roger.

"Ok, Roger, we have a plan and it's a hard ball."

"Go on," his said, rather enthusiastically, as I explained.

"Roger, you have to digest this as what's actually happening in order to present it. The truth is the facts don't lie, and that's what we're using, fact."

"I hear you," he chuckled and I continued.

"We're going into bankruptcy; our accounts can verify it and my accountants letter now backs it up too. I have stopped the standing order to the landlord for rent. Basically, they either lose the rent owed and search for a new tenant, which could leave the building unoccupied for more than a year, or they can agree an immediate release which, we will claim, after much restructuring will keep us in business."

I could hear Roger take in a deep breath at the other end and I carried on.

"That means we could arrange a loan and pay them one-years rent in advance, and you can hand over a new tenant. Now they have to access reason; a new tenant lined up for them and the advanced rent. But, Roger, the clocks ticking on this. They have seven days."

There was silence for a moment and I thought Roger had hung up, but to my relief he spoke:

"That works for me. I don't know about them though, Ben. They may still call your bluff."

I smiled from my end of the phone as I listened to his words.

"Well that's why you need to digest this and convince them, Roger. Because you also want me to buy that lot."

It was brilliantly executed, even if I do say so myself and less than a week later they agreed to release us.

Roger was in awe; not only because he didn't believe they would buy it but he also got his sale.

I personally funded the land purchase with my pension and became my own landlord; preparing to finance the build then return that investment with a rental income.

With a year to build before we had to exit our lease, there was no time to waste and I awarded the building contract to a local builder.

The overall investment was £350k with £220k budgeted to build.

"Wow, I'll drink to that!" I giggle as I raise my champagne glass and Mary and Ben also toast the air.

Ben has hired a private boat, it's a beautiful warm day and the sun sparkles off the water as we sail around the coast of Miami.

We've just sat down at a table laden with wonderful fresh food that Ben has hired the caterers from his private club to prepare; lobster, scallops and other delights.

As surprises go, this has to be up there with one of the best ones. Not least because Ben had remembered my once telling him of my love of water and had arranged this most perfect of days for my penultimate one here in Miami.

Yep, I am due to fly home tomorrow, leaving Ben and Mary to enjoy another week here.

Ben and I have had our ups and downs on this trip but to give him his due, he has really tried hard to open up more to me. To be fair, I can be as stubborn as him, as my little tantrums have shown, but now I feel Ben and I have a mutual trust and understanding of each other.

It feels good to leave things on such a high.

Because of the strict planning constraints, I was unable to change the layout within the building, but that didn't stop me pushing the boundaries.

I designed the roof to be open eaves and boarded with a proper staircase, claiming it gave us more accessible roof space for storage. Later we would apply for it to be converted, at relatively little cost, into third floor office space.

Although the build was completed on time, the heating system was ineffective. The builder had designed a cheap, and as it turned out, flawed system of delivering heat.

I withheld their final payment, sighting it was their responsibility to heat the building, but the company ended up going broke so we were forced to install independent heating anyway.

Despite that little setback, myself and the staff were so excited at the prospect of moving into our new offices. Set in an idyllic location, overlooking farm land with a lovely westerly facing aspect for sunsets, we would soon become oblivious to the noise of the aircraft.

The facility was filled with architectural intrigue and delight.

It would be a proud place to work and things, finally, seemed to be running smoothly.

One of iCAD's largest distributors was a company called Softspace, and they wanted to license BIM to sell it through their network so Alex and I set off to the states again.

We had a full agenda, arriving in Boston and then traveling to New Hampshire the very next morning to meet Dave, the president of the company.

We'd been given directions and a note telling us that, with traffic, we should allow 3/4 hours. We set out that morning, giving ourselves an hour, which we thought would be plenty of time. The roads were clear and as we didn't want to be late, we floored the accelerator, at times exceeding well over one-hundred on the open roads. We arrived and commented to the team that met us that we weren't sure how anybody could do that journey in forty-five minutes.

They all gaped at us in total disbelief and Dave took the directions that I was holding from me.

"Three to four hours, not three quarters of an hour," he pointed at the note. "How the hell did you do that in an hour?"

He shook his head incredulously as we all laughed. It actually really broke the ice.

That meeting was really productive and I closed the deal on an upfront non-refundable payment of £50k for them to stock BIM and sell it on through their network of dealers. The next forty-eight hours were going to be a tough call though.

I had a meeting in Newport, Rhode Island, which was a one-and-a-half-hour drive south of Boston and then I was on to Albany in New York state, heading north west on a near four-hour journey.

Being mentally prepared was key, but the driving, together with the meetings, was exhausting and I didn't leave Albany until 11pm. That left me with a three-hour drive back to Boston and, at best, two hours of sleep before I had to go to the airport for a 6am flight to San Francisco and another DEVCAMP event.

I was so high on coffee that I didn't feel sleepy at all on that long drive back to Boston. The road emptied after midnight and with two hours to run, I found myself heading along a straight freeway as far as I could see without another car in sight.

It was lonely, solitary and in the pitch black of the night, actually quite scary. It felt safe to speed though so I pushed the throttle to the floor in the little red saloon that I was driving. I couldn't get back to Boston fast enough.

Then a twinkle of light caught my eye in the rear-view mirror.

When I looked again though, it was gone. I blinked into the darkness, wondering if perhaps I had imagined it, when there it was again.

It was definitely car headlights, but there was no way that car could be catching me; I'd been constantly touching 120mph!

But it was. It was still some way off in the distance and I braked, slowing to ninety then seventy as the headlights bore down on me.

Thinking that I'd just let the maniac go past me, the car suddenly shot past and braked in front of me.

"What the…!" As the car slowed up in front of me I pulled over and then, seeing the flashing lights, I manoeuvred in behind it with a sinking feeling.

The cop got out of his car and walked towards mine, his torch-light shining through the windows.

"Where you headed?" he asked when I'd wound down the window, and I told him.

"I was in the central reservation back there when you passed me, you were going so fast you rocked my car! Do you know how fast you were travelling?"

"I'm sorry," I looked suitably ashamed as I explained myself. "I'm from England and I have an early morning flight to catch from Logan airport."

"This isn't an autobahn with unlimited speed," he warned me, obviously not realising that we don't have them in the UK either, but I saw an opportunity so I took it.

"Yes, I'm sorry. I think it's cause that's what I'm used to."

"I could issue a fixed penalty," he told me as he checked my ID, "but I'll let you off."

As I sighed with relief, knowing that time was ticking and I'd miss my flight at this rate, he continued. "Somewhere between here and Boston, I will be ahead of you waiting. If I catch you even one mile per hour over the limit, you're booked."

I finally drove off ahead of him and all the way to Boston I observed that speed limit, though I did wonder how he could have actually got ahead of me. Still, I'd learned my lesson.

I made it back in time for about two hours sleep before I had to leave for San Francisco.

It was yet another crazy schedule and after the flight to San Francisco, that evening's meeting felt like the longest I'd ever had. I just wanted to drop my head into my food and sleep. I don't think I have ever been so tired and I slept for a straight twelve hours before the show the next day.

This event was where the authors of our CAD engine, iCAD, brought their developers together. There was never much down-time in the office, so these sessions were good for development, bonding and sharing ideas.

It was at one of these events a few years before that I had met Lewis and his business partner, Mike. We'd all hit it off immediately, shared technology with with each other and swapping business stories. Lewis and I clicked instantly and on another trip to Boston when Lewis was in town we decided to have a few late drinks back at my hotel.

"I'll have a Bud light," I told Lewis, who sniggered at my lightweight ways when it comes to drinking. I dropped my jacket on the seat next to me and stood to get some air. I'm not sure if it was the hotel bar that was too hot, or if I'd had too much to drink, that being one more than my usual, erm, one.

It was nearly 1am and everyone else had gone to bed, but Lewis and I were batting on.

"I'll make this my last," Lewis said as he reappeared with the beers and handed me my drink. "I've an early morning flight back to LA."

"Well, I've got all night." I raised my bottle and chugged the cold beer down my throat; my flight wasn't until later the following evening.

We finished our drinks and I headed up to my room, feeling a little light-headed but not drunk as I collapsed on the bed and slept.

At around 5am I suddenly sat bolt upright, my subconscious had been hard at work all night it seemed, and had finally awoken me with a thought that immediately filled me with panic.

Where was my jacket?

I leapt off the bed and checked the closet and then the bathroom, and in those few seconds I remembered I'd left it next to me on the sofa in the lobby bar.

Grabbing my room key, I raced down the stairs as though the hotel was on fire.

You see, it wasn't just my jacket. My wallet was in the inside pocket and I'd foolishly stuffed it with my airline ticket, passport, credit cards and $400 in cash. Stupid didn't even cover it.

The lobby was deserted and, as I had suspected, my jacket was nowhere to be seen.

I ran over to the front desk and explained my predicament to the receptionist.

"Oh dear, sir, that's awful. Let me call security," She was very calm, clearly seeing my panic as I digested that without my passport I wouldn't be flying home anytime soon.

Not only that, by this time someone may have already used my cards and cash. I wiped the perspiration from my forehead, how could I have been so stupid? I paced the floor, waiting for the young girl to finish her call to security.

She was nodding as she put down the receiver and smiled at me and my heart raced with excitement.

"Good news, sir, your jacket has been found and security are bringing it down now."

I almost passed out with relief but that was soon to be short lived.

When the security guy handed me my jacket, I immediately reached into the inside pocket and froze.

"Something missing, sir?"

I gulped, feeling sick as I nodded.

"Yes, my wallet."

"Oh no!" the girl on reception looked up, "he had his passport and money in his wallet."

I sank on to a nearby sofa with my head in my hands.

"My boss just came on duty," the security guard patted my shoulder, "let me go get him."

A few minutes passed until the head of security appeared and introduced himself, reassuring me that he would sort everything out. He was brilliant.

"Right, let's start with cancelling those credit cards, sir." I nodded numbly. "But let's do that in the privacy of your room."

I followed him mutely as we took the lift up to my floor and walked to my room.

I sat on the bed while he called the first credit card company and then once he had explained, he handed the phone to me.

"Good morning, sir," came the sympathetic female American voice as I took the phone. "I'm so sorry for your problem. I just need to go through some security questions, ok?"

I nodded dumbly, then remembering that she couldn't see me, I muttered, "Yes."

"Ok, sir, great. Now, what state are you in?"

I rolled my eyes, "I'm in a terrible state!"

I realised she was laughing and when I saw that, so too, was the head of security, I suddenly saw the funny side.

Despite that moment of light relief, I was angry at myself and resigned to going to the UK embassy first thing the next morning, but to my surprise I received a call just before I left.

"We've had a call from a guy," said the head of security, "he says he found your wallet. There's no cash in it but your credit cards and passport are."

As I took my flight home later that evening, I thought at how, once again, I'd gotten myself out of another fine mess.

Credit too, of course, to The Marriott Hotel in Copley Place, Boston, you guys were amazing!

I've just sent an email to Ben and Mary, letting them know, as promised, that I've arrived home safely and thanking them for their wonderful hospitality.

I'd used the flight home to type up most of the notes I had taken during the trip, so I sit in front of my computer now, slightly nervous at what I am about to do and feeling a little trepidation at what I might find.

"I'm going to find you, Stan." I whisper, as I type his name into the search engine...

Chapter 21

Well He Took His Eye off the Ball, Didn't He?

+2016+

Google throws up a myriad of Stan Lenz's for me to investigate and I start by ruling out the obvious non-contenders.

Such as Stan; the bodybuilder from Daytona beach, or the Stan that has been recently appointed as judge at a county court somewhere in Denver, Colorado.

I sigh and sit back. This could take some time.

"Think, Mandy!" I say out loud and my cat jumps up onto my desk, purring and wanting attention.

"Not now, Matilda," I push her away gently, before she takes up residency on my laptop and I curse Jack Bourne for having made me encourage her to do so in the first place.

I need to think. I need to start small, and a google search is not small.

I troll through Twitter and Facebook, but come up with absolutely nothing. I'm starting to think that, short of putting out an advert in the Times, I'm not going to find him.

As I am pondering this, it occurs to me I am looking for that ball. But where is it, Stan?

I decide to sleep on it tonight, surely there's some way of finding him. I have to, I feel like I owe it to Ben and Ben owes it to Stan.

As I close my eyes, I vow that I will leave no stone unturned until I find Stan.

And that's when it hits me!

A week later, after some exhausting, and quite disturbing, searches on social media, I think I finally have my lead.

I have located the son of John Stone, Ben's first manager back at Onelock, on Facebook, and messaged him asking him to contact me with regard to a mutual friend.

After three days, of which I am constantly checking for a reply, Ian finally responds and I explain to him what I am trying to do. He seems genuinely intrigued at my project but tells me that his father is now in a home for the elderly.

I quickly message back, asking if John is able-minded enough, and willing, to speak to me.

To my relief, Ian replies almost immediately and tells me that his father is still very astute and that he'll ask when he sees him next if he would allow me to visit.

Two weeks later, I arrive at The Poplars elderly care home and ask to be taken to John Stone.

This all feels very surreal, I am about to meet Ben's first boss, who to me, is still a middle-aged man since I last wrote about him.

Now though, John is nearing his eighties and very frail, but he greets me with a friendly smile as I sit down beside him on one of the mismatched armchairs that circle the TV room.

I thank him for letting me visit and John asks how Ben is and what he's doing. I fill him in on as much as I think Ben would allow, then I explain my reason for wanting to find out about Stan.

"I can understand that," John nods, "He and Ben always had

quite a unique relationship." John chuckles, "I used to feel quite undermined at times."

I smile, "I get that. How close were you to Stan?"

He shakes his head, "Not particularly close. He was my boss and I respected him greatly but I was always slightly envious of the guidance he gave to Ben. Could have used it myself at times."

John doesn't sound bitter, more reflective.

"But you do know what became of him?"

John looks hesitantly at me and is silent for a moment. I sense he is wondering how to tell me something.

Sadly, I'm right.

"Stan took early retirement from Onelock due to ill health, I'm afraid, Mandy."

Tears fill my eyes as John continues. "I'm afraid his heavy smoking habit took its toll on him, he was dead within six months."

I don't know why I feel so stunned at this news; after all there was always a chance Stan wouldn't be around now anyway.

I think it's just the finality of hearing it. Hearing that this man, who was once such a supporter and guide to Ben, died so soon after he lost touch with him.

John pats my hand sympathetically and I smile through my tears and thank him for his time. As I stand to leave, John reaches out a shaky hand to touch my arm.

"Please, do give Ben my regards, won't you?"

I nod that of course I will, and as I walk away I suck in my breath; Ben!

I would have to be the one to break the news about Stan to him…

✦ ✦ ✦

I'm back at The Little Red Café and the inclement weather outside is quite befitting of my somber mood.

"You alright, love?" I look up in surprise as Doris calls across the empty café.

"Yeah, I'm ok," I sigh with a sad smile.

"Stood you up, has he?" Doris is teasing me and I laugh at the cheeky glint in her eye.

"Get me another latte, please Doris." I say with a false sternness.

"And mind me bleedin' own, I get it." She cackles away to herself as she prepares my drink and I sit back to wait for Ben.

I'm certain Ben wouldn't have expected Stan to still be alive now but I'm dreading telling him when and how he died. It's like the end of an era I suppose, and I don't want Ben to stop relaying the Stan teachings as we go forward from here.

He strides into the café, looking tanned and well since his return from Miami, and I wonder if I should maybe hold off being the bearer of bad news.

"Here he is!" Doris shouts, "The proverbial bad penny."

Ben sits down laughing, shaking the rain from his coat. "Nice to see you too, Doris. Looking lovely as ever, I see."

I smirk at the banter between these two and roll my eyes.

"How are you, M?" Ben smiles brightly at me and I fake an equally bright grin, which of course he sees right through.

"M?"

"Here you are, my lovelies." Doris places our drinks on the table, giving me a few seconds to steel myself.

"I'm good," I finally say to Ben. "How was the rest of the trip, how's Mary?"

"Wonderful, though I think she missed her co-conspirator." He teases me and I can't help giggling. "Hey, we had fun!"

Ben nods, serious now. "And now, have you been having fun? What have you been up to Mandy?"

He's almost showing fatherly like concern as he waits for me to reply and I know now is probably the time to tell him.

"So, I did some digging."

Ben takes a deep breath, "Stan?"

"Yes." My face, my watery eyes and my trembling lips give it away.

"Tell me, M. What became of the great man?"

"Well he took his eye of the ball, didn't he?" I blurt out, and it's now that I let my sobs come, for a man I have never met before, but for whom I have grown such an attachment to.

Strangely, it is Ben comforting me as I spill the details that I got from John Stone.

"Wait," Ben smiles, "You met John? I'm impressed M, how is he?"

I gather myself again and tell Ben all about my meeting with his former boss.

"He sends his regards," I add as I finish my story.

Ben sits back and regards me with a smile, "What a long time ago that all seems now."

He shakes his head sadly, "And the big guy is gone, for some time it seems. I always thought the smoking would be the end of him."

I sit there, the seconds seem like minutes as Ben absorbs everything he has just learned.

He'll leave any minute now I think to myself.

But he doesn't. He clears his throat and sits forward.

"Stan didn't help himself, with the cigs. But what a horrible disease that C word is."

Ben looks down at himself, back up outside the window, and finally he looks me square in the eyes, his pain obvious.

"I just found out my best friend has it too."

"I'm so sorry." It suddenly occurs to me that it was this and not any football or planning project that had made Ben so distressed during my time in Miami.

"It was crap, that afternoon I found out," He is speaking as though he knows my thoughts but is now with his own.

"I stood in the shower and cried my eyes out, the shower is the best place to cry."

Ben is still processing the information about Stan, the thoughts of his former boss, John, and now his best friend, Barry. I should leave him to it, but it seems he wants to speak...

"One minute he was ok, the next he was short of breath. Within three weeks, he has had scans, a collapsed lung, an operation, and a prognosis that I can't bear to think about."

I don't say anything, I just let Ben talk.

"I've known Barry since I was nineteen. With Mary and Jill, Barry's childhood sweetheart, we would hang out a lot together as a foursome; remember I told you it was Jill that introduced me to Mary.

Of course, as is life, the years go by, and as my business consumed me, I regretfully drifted from many close friends.

Since retiring though, those friendships have been rekindled, especially with Barry.

We meet every other week for coffee, to put the world to rights, both of us loving this fairly new concept of retirement.

We talk football, business, the universe and the most heart-warming of topics, our grandchildren."

Ben blows out his cheeks.

"It's now a case of doing what we can to make his life as positive and comfortable as possible and to be sure his family have everything they need. Christ, M!"

Ben slams his fist on the table in angry frustration.

"He's just sixty years old, this should be the time for him to be enjoying his life, not..."

Ben doesn't finish his sentence; he doesn't need to.

I nod my understanding and he whispers an apology.

"Sorry, I, this is just heart wrenching."

His voice is shaky and I want to cry at the emotion he is clearly feeling.

This has been such an emotional rollercoaster already for me, too. I never thought when I first agreed to do this that I would feel so much for people that I have never met. They are a part of Ben's life, not mine, yet, now I suppose they actually are in my life.

And it's such a privilege.

As we leave the Little Red Café, with yet more banter between Doris and Ben, he touches my arm.

"Thank you, M."

"What for?" I shrug, I'm desperate to get home and have a good cry.

"For making me feel." Ben simply replies and I watch him walk away, a small smile on my face.

Dear me, are we actually making progress here?

Well of course not, because the next time we meet, it's business as usual.

Chapter 22

There's a Chemistry Clock between People

+1997+

There was always a freshness about our company and part of that was because we challenged ourselves to bring in the right people, especially as we were rapidly starting to grow.

We used an efficient process to recruit the very best talent into the team and train them up through the ranks. This philosophy came from my own experience at Onelock; I firmly believed there were probably only 8 out of any 100 candidates that would suit our style of business.

We were getting tired of intelligent people with good CV's who in reality were either lousy organisers, had no innovation or zero social skills, and occasionally, all of the above!

So, I created a speed hire type process where we would bring in as many candidates as possible and take time to cherry pick the ones that stood out.

The first rule was to tease out those special candidates who showed confidence, could look you in the eye and had a firm handshake.

If they didn't pass that simple test they would be eliminated from our process, but if they did, I'd spend some time with them.

I would spend thirty minutes grilling them, I didn't care whether they were super brainy, I was looking for someone with enthusiasm, a good attitude and those that I thought would show loyalty. We named it 'The Taylor Test'.

It was on one such occasion that a young lady called Anne entered our lives.

I notice Ben shudders as he says this and I look at him questioningly.

"Don't get me wrong, M, she had all the attributes we sought, and in abundance. I could see her value immediately and I hired her on the spot."

"I sense a but here."

Ben gives a wry laugh, "Let's just say there are hidden flaws and traits in people that can take a while to surface. We all have them, but I believe there is a chemistry clock between people that can sometimes tick for a long time before the alarm goes off."

Since the move to Southfields, I was beginning to feel Alex had taken BIM as far as I wanted it. We'd been pretty much forced into changing our own CAD engine from AEC and launching it as BIM and I now felt the need to step up and switch from a CAD driven solution to a database driven solution.

I wanted to relaunch the brand, because BIM just drew us closer into iCAD's world. They controlled the market with an industry standard CAD tool and would have everyone believe that the buildings were driven by CAD when in fact our industry was largely driven by non-graphic data.

Changing the industry perception would need deeper pockets than we had and I knew we had to be patient.

To kick this off, I quickly brought in alongside BIM a development prototype, called Strategy. It was designed to pave the way for database led products rather than those that were CAD led and we would call this XP, the upcoming product line to replace BIM.

We marketed this module at a show in Philadelphia which resulted in good starting sales and demonstrated to us that we were on the right path.

Fortunately, my views that we were being bullied into conforming to the CAD industry standard were shared with other developers.

One development group decided to take the leap by creating a look-alike CAD product that they called XCAD. We were by now well acquainted with the team behind it; Lewis and Mike from our DEVCAMP days together.

After a long legal tussle, Lewis's team were allowed to approach iCAD's main competitors, Visual, with what looked like a mirror image of their product.

Visual obviously had a keen interest in knocking iCAD off its industry standard pedestal and we were poised, interested to see how this twist would play out.

When Visual closed a deal with Lewis and his team to buy out XCAD with the caveat that they finished the development, an opportunity knocked for us.

We were approached by Visual.

We had, by now, produced an excellent all round prototype of XP and they wanted to license it as a Visual data base engine.

So, as things were taking off for us industry wise, it was with some sadness that Jessica announced she was leaving. I say sadness but actually it was bittersweet for her. She was pregnant and didn't feel she could commit to the pressures of business.

To say I was gutted would be a massive understatement, the difference Jessica had made to the company was hard to quantify, it was huge.

She was one of the most trustworthy and dedicated people I have ever met and through her control of our finances, she'd helped take the business from an overdraft nearing £250k to a surplus of £100k with a contingency overdraft of a similar figure.

I had come to rely heavily on Jessica; she would rein me in when she thought I was crossing lines, grounding me as though I were a wild child. Well, maybe in some ways I was!

Needless to say, she had become, uniquely, a good friend, and she was to be one of only a few lasting friends out of any of my employees.

Loyal as ever, Jessica helped to source her own replacement; an older lady called Leena who was technically capable but mad as a hatter.

I suppose on the surface she was pleasant, little did I know, however, what lay beneath. The chemistry clock was ticking fast on this one!

"Ooh, what happened?"

Ben laughs, "All in good time, M. Let's get some business stuff down first."

I roll my eyes, but comply all the same.

Visual eventually bought Lewis out with a great deal that was in excess of $6million, but their relationship broke down as they tried to take control and I looked on in awe as he retired at the ripe old age of forty and used his wealth to enjoy his flying hobby.

This was now our chance however. We had an opportunity for Visual to exclusively license XP into their desktop CAD product.

As a result, it was suggested that Visual would fund the development link between their CAD and our XP and we would build applications around it.

Dex, still under the Tech Group, would remain in my control with my shareholding untouched and become the main distributor for the UK and Europe, providing an outlet for the product as well as servicing all support related issues.

In a way, it would mean selling the assets and keeping the company and it was a huge decision for me.

After fourteen years of investment, of blood, sweat and tears, could I really suffer such heart ache for a price they hadn't yet put on it? I wasn't really sure I was ready to sell out the heart of my business but this was an exciting opportunity nevertheless. I could see the growth and leverage we would have if this Visual CAD system became the industry standard over iCAD.

Visual flew Alex and I out via business class to inspect their impressive operation and meet their team and I took an instant dislike to the development director, John Forbes.

He was arrogant and obnoxious and reminded me so much of Peter Coleman.

When he sat us down to make his pitch, I saw straight through his devious plan.

I knew that he saw Alex as the asset, rather than my software, because in his eyes Alex had all the developing knowledge.

It was also obvious to me that he wanted to drive a wedge between Alex and I and, to my dismay, Alex fell for it hook, line and sinker. I think Forbes had convinced him that this was something he could own; big mistake.

The offer that Forbes put on the table was an upfront $800,000 for the software license, with my consultancy and travel expenses bringing the total to about $1 million.

They also wanted Alex seconded to the US development team on a minimum two-year contract which in John Forbes eyes meant recruit him separately.

Alex and I took the offer away to consider and it became

apparent to me that he not only felt he should permanently join the US team, but that he should also get a good slice of the $800k. This was young Alex whom I had brought into the team and helped grow into his role, now being brainwashed into blackmailing me. Here was another chemistry clock with it's alarm about to go off.

Even after Stan's teachings, this still astounded and hurt me and I couldn't believe his disloyalty and disregard for me as the company owner, but I was determined that it wouldn't happen. It was my hard work, my investment that had brought us to this juncture and this deal would see my company being sole distributor and service provider.

It's incredible how greed can change the direction of somebody's moral compass and as Alex tried to resort to blackmail, I had to cut him out of any final negotiations.

It was probably one of the biggest mistakes of his career and at that point our relationship ended abruptly when he had the audacity to have his lawyer contend it.

Despite my disappointment, I headed back to Visual to close the deal with the thought in my mind that I was prepared to walk if necessary.

As a result, Alex was now technically fired from Dex, so I confirmed I would let him join Visual and we exchanged contracts on everything else that was in their offer.

"What a traitor!" I am gob-smacked at the way Alex behaved but Ben shakes his head.

"I thought the same at the time, believe me. I wanted the ultimate revenge on him for his disloyalty, but Stan had taught me to walk away before I react, to see things from a different perspective on a new day."

"And did you?"

"To be honest, if it hadn't been for his whole attitude, I wouldn't have been so opposed to him having a cut of the eight-hundred grand, but it was his sense of entitlement and his immediate involvement of a lawyer that riled me. So, no, to answer your question, I was still so pissed off the next day and the day after!"

"Ha ha, I'm not surprised."

"The thing is," Ben is serious now, "when it comes down to it, in business, everyone is out for their own gain. You really have to tread with such caution and never take anyone at face value."

"What a cruel world," I mutter pensively.

"Well you're just an old romantic, M!"

Ben is right, I am. I always choose to be trusting on things, even when I know deep in my heart that often it's not always justified.

Maybe it's why I write fiction; perhaps reality is too cruel for this old romantic.

"Are you ok, M?" Ben looks concerned but I shrug it off.

"Yeah, I'm fine," I pause. "But I'm thinking I might go away for a few days, you know, get some of this stuff written up?"

Ben looks surprised but he doesn't disagree. "Good idea, I have to go away on some business soon anyway. You're welcome to join me but it's boring football stuff?"

I shake my head with a smile. "No, no, thank you. I think I need to be alone for a bit."

"A writer's retreat, eh?" Ben winks and I suddenly think that, yes. Yes, that's where I'll go.

✦ ✦ ✦

And that is where I am now...

I have rented a log cabin beside a lake that is placid and still and, after hours of rain, the air feels thick with moisture, giving the feeling of an eerie serenity. The only sound I can hear are of the occasional passing duck and bird song. It's wonderful to have this space, this time, and some peace to just write without distraction.

I have always been comfortable in my own company, never feeling lonely. I don't understand people that need constantly to surround themselves with the company of others.

Perhaps it is the introvert in me, whatever, it's who I am.

I sip my coffee and look out across the lake as two geese skim the surface.

I think the sadness I have felt over Stan has taken its toll on me, drained me yet fuelled my need to get away, to write.

Whenever I am feeling emotional, which Ben would probably say is most of the time, I let it out onto the page. There's nothing more cathartic then allowing that emotion to engulf you and inspire your words.

Gosh, I'm driveling here! As Ben would say, "Man up, M!"

I look back to my notebook and begin to write…

+ + +

Later, having written up a storm, I pour a well-deserved glass of wine and check my emails.

There is one from Ben asking how my 'little retreat from the world' is going.

"Sarcastic sod," I chuckle, and I reply that all is well and ask how the 'boring football stuff' is.

His reply intrigues me: "Not good, M, not good at all. Remember what I said about never trusting anyone? Well if ever that truly applied, it's now. I feel like I'm surrounded by bull-shitters, seriously! My football club is being dismantled for a land grab and I'm putting myself in the thick of it to save it! And believe me, save it I will!"

Oh dear, I think, as I quickly type a response that he can tell me all about it when we meet again next week?

"Maybe..." is all I get back from him. Pfft!

It's gotten chilly out here on the deck so I grab a blanket from inside the cabin and curl up on one of the little cushioned benches, gazing out across the water as I sip my wine, drinking in the serenity of my surroundings.

My peace is interrupted by a Twitter notification on my phone; it's Jack, he's in LA, and he's obviously having a blast with someone called Milly. I quickly type a response and sit back with a smile.

I've grown quite fond of my elusive agent, I must admit, and in all fairness, he does seem to have created a lot of interest in this project. Who knows, it may just take off...

Chapter 23

They Were Baying for My Blood

1998

I was now having to cope without Alex's technical knowledge and it felt quite isolating. I'd lay awake, my head spinning, desperately searching for a solution. I was no technical expert, that's what I employed others to do. I felt again that same loss I had when we lost Nelson and I needed to act fast.

I'd only just got my head around losing Jessica and I was beginning to wonder whether it was actually possible to keep the staff boat balanced.

Whereas previously I'd had Jessica to talk about the business with, I just couldn't talk to Leena, so it was all on me.

By now, Cadgraph's momentum had lapsed and I heard that Herbert had sold out, but one day I got a call out of the blue from the company that bought him out.

They wanted to know if we would sell them the source code for BIM.

Now, in computing terms the source code is your crown jewels and should never be shared; when you sell a customer the software, you create an executable image from the source code that should never be revealed to anyone.

However, we had created a whole new version called XP and the BIM code was now kind of obsolete, so I agreed to the restrictions of it staying in German.

It was another great deal; I sold it for £150k and this along with the cash from Visual helped me to pay down some of our enormous personal debts. Just as well really, it prepared me for phase two of this incredible business journey.

> *I groan. "Was there ever a time where things were stable and you could just enjoy them for what they were?"*
>
> *Ben shakes his head, a solemn look on his face.*
>
> *"It actually felt like every time we found some stability and started to grow the business, we were thrown another curve ball. You begin to realise that's just business; if you push it, it pushes back, twice as hard."*
>
> *"I don't know how you never gave up." I'm serious here, personally I would have felt it one hurdle after another too much but Ben is smiling.*
>
> *"Well, Stan's teachings really came into effect here; the survival instinct, that throw of the dice. It's like an inner voice, constantly berating you, beating yourself up, but you can change it. Remember that song again, M, it's all about the climb? Well this time I knew it was all about finding my level of incompetence."*

In a bizarre turn of events, I got a call from Visual wanting a meeting and I instantly knew something was wrong.

It turned out they had just been taken over and they wanted me to forego my consultancy. The new business had no interest in buildings and would be unlikely to take things forward. It was actually a result for me; they'd just paid me close to a million dollars, small change for them I guess though.

But it was like a breath of fresh air; I had been cast adrift but was now a free agent to take my own approach again.

"Ah, I see, so it wasn't that bad?"

Ben shrugs, "It could have been, it could have gone one way or the other, but I saw it as a new challenge. We were facing another 're-set' situation and I felt excited about it."

"Always so positive," I intone, but Ben rolls his eyes at me.

"Not always, M."

By this time, my new recruit, Anne, was proving to be a fast tracker and with a mindful eye on The Peter Principal, I had promoted her to Customer Services Manager.

Anne was always smartly dressed, projecting an image of superiority. Something Stan had once said was if you dress smart, you feel like you can act smart and this was so true of Anne. However, although she could present well, her demo's lacked substance and she knew I wasn't happy.

I changed things around so that it was a project manager that would run the demo and she would do the smart talking. I had learned my lesson with Brian, and I explained to Anne that there were time constraints and I needed her to be hands on.

It was a steep learning curve for her and I invested a lot of my time essentially teaching her about our market and how to manage. It wasn't dissimilar to my own fast-tracked situation at Onelock and she had to deal with quite a few raised eyebrows at her quick promotion.

There was a huge under-current of jealousy which I aptly named pity parties, but just as I had, Anne coped admirably.

She was not only intelligent but sharp with it, although she could be equally cantankerous, and it meshed neatly with my desire to take on ideas and criticism.

I now felt ready to begin completely restructuring and re-thinking everything with the tools at my disposal and I was beside myself with excitement, yet still a little nervous about the Visual takeover situation.

We weren't doing anything wrong; our continuation had Visual's new owners blessing. Maybe it was just me being over-cautious, possibly paranoid. *And yes, Stan, untrusting!*

I just had horrible visions of any future success of ours raising questions that we would then have to defend. I probably wasn't giving those new owners enough credit for the situation, but I didn't want to take the risk. My first thoughts were to protect Dex from any future lawsuit that may come our way.

Coincidentally, at this time, Jessica, having had her baby, was looking for some part time work so I took her on as my assistant with the hope that in time I could oust Leena and reinstate Jessica when the time was right.

It felt so good to have a like-minded person back in the team for me to bounce new ideas off.

And boy, did I have some new ideas.

I had decided to retain Dex, the company that back in 1983 had stolen my heart, as my employer; remaining the personal vehicle for my own income, but everything else, including staff, would be sold to a new start up for a nominal sum of £1. This meant I could always keep this company, even if one day I sold out, so I pulled it away from the holding company Tech Group.

The name of this new venture was Tech X and it was all about continuing our business in management. It was really a reset situation; we had all the momentum but now a chance to completely rebuild. Ironically, this left Tech Group as a dormant company. We had sold off Dex Inc and I had now pulled Dex away which meant that the small shareholders now had a minor percentage of nothing. Whilst this didn't feel good, it did feel as though justice had been served.

The next, and far more important challenge was how I would approach the software development. I had lots of developers but no development leader. I was logical but certainly not technical enough to lead the development of this project myself. I knew what my customers wanted from the software but I needed assistance with the coding side and I didn't have total confidence in what Alex and his team had created in the new XP. We also still had customers on the BIM version, so there was no doubting it was going to be a messy situation, not only with the development but also the structure of the company.

I knew the right development team was out there somewhere and I needed to find them, fast.

To add to my woes, we were rapidly facing the year 2000 and subsequently the hype about the millennium bug in software. It was forecast as some kind of Armageddon and we all believed it.

The positive effect to this was it gave me the incentive to move away from BIM and onto XP to ensure that the code was sound.

At this point, I had decided to explore outsourcing as a preferred quick route to a solution before the 1st of January 2000, and I came across a local software house, GV Inc, with a billionaire US owner.

After an initial and positive phone call, I arranged to meet them at their offices where I was introduced to Bill Warne, the software development manager, as well as his software manager, Graham, and their MD, Jon Wyler.

Things are always so black and white for me when it comes to meeting people for the first time; look at how the bad blood with Coleman had hit me within minutes of meeting him.

Whilst my initial impression was that I liked these guys, to me, profit is a dirty word when I am spending my dollars, so I pressed for what I thought was an exceptional deal and I got it.

Hey, sometimes you have to let things take their course, and this course certainly set the scene for my new development plans.

As I got busy pulling the specification together for the all new and exciting XP, Graham from GV Inc was building a team dedicated to us and our task.

Meanwhile, we'd been approached by our customer, a well-established pharmaceutical company, who were keen to take on our software and introduce pre-planned, preventative maintenance schedules and help-desk functionalities. They were also prepared to help fund this development so it was perfect timing.

As the new development project reached its conclusion and the year drew to a close, so did the threat of the millennium bug and we engaged all of our customers in a huge exercise to upgrade them from BIM to the new GV developed version of XP before the deadline. This, it turned out, was naivety at best on my part, and with no back up plan, it was to be another hard lesson on the slippery road.

"Ben, you should set up a Master's degree for future budding entrepreneurs!" I only half joke and Ben nods, a serious look in his face. "I've certainly considered it, M!"

Whilst the software was solid, after all we had put it through rigorous testing, the data upgrade from BIM to XP caused us a hell of a lot of grief. We had customers with systems not working and with the deadline of the year 2000 looming, this was a huge problem.

"I remember when I was in banking," I interrupt. "The whole industry was on edge, and I had to work long nights and the whole

of the weekend beforehand to settle any outstanding trades, just in case. As well as New Year's Day!"

Ben shudders, "It's no different to the scare mongers out in their droves over the EU referendum now."

"It's just the unknown, I think." I like having these political discussions with Ben. We do sometimes differ in our opinion but I like that he hears me out. "There weren't computers around when the year ticked over to 1000, who was to know? Same as with the Brexit vote, lots of people believe it's better the devil you know."

Ben shakes his head vehemently. "That I can understand, but it frustrates me when, as a country, we are so negative, predicting the worst outcome ever. What this country needs is positivity; we live in a great country and I'm very passionate about being British, but I sometimes feel we need a bit of blue sky thinking, you know?"

"Blue sky thinking?"

Ben nods.

"Just think, M," he laughs, "how privileged we are to have experienced the years ticking over to a new millenium. The next time that happens I may find myself leaving Mars due to over population, perhaps I should build another home on the moon, just in case!"

I chuckle, "And here I thought I was the fiction writer!"

As the clock counted down to the year 2000, we were anxious. We hadn't managed to get a lot of our customers onto our new millennium proof XP and those that we had upgraded needed to be taken back to BIM. There was no confidence that, to use a pun, it would stand the test of time because the dates affected so much of the software code.

It was a high risk and we, along with our customers, were extremely vulnerable.

I remember seeing in the new year and thinking this one could really mean meltdown for us.

I had even started scaring myself about the outcome, all because of the media hype, but strangely, I also had a quiet confidence in myself that whatever the outcome, I would find a solution. I had, of course, assessed the risk and decided that the worst-case scenario was that I took everyone back to BIM.

There was also some relief that this was also GV's problem, and therefore their responsibility to fix it. To their credit, they did, and we got through the new millennium, though not without fixing some issues and, as a result, the loss of a few customers.

My head is always full of 'what if's' and this was no exception, but I guess it had taught me another tough lesson about the challenges of upgrading data.

Unsurprisingly, after that experience, the user group suddenly became a pressure group and to be honest it did us good. I was all out of excuses and our customers were, rightfully so, upset at being upgraded and then re-installed back to BIM while we sorted out the upgrade problems.

On this occasion the annual group event was being held at the facility of one of our customers and attendance was a record high, mainly because the customers wanted answers.

Of course, I had stood in front of groups before and spoken, but this was my biggest audience yet, and they were baying for my blood.

I've been writing up my notes in my back garden, but I'm going to stop here; I'm losing the light and my back is aching. Still, I take a moment to reflect on how Ben must have felt, stood there in front of some very angry customers.

Personally, I hate public speaking, and the thought of facing such an aggressive audience, well, frankly, I just couldn't do it. I guess that's just one of the many things that seperates those with entrepreneurial skills from those without though.

After all, Ben had to defend his product, and himself, whilst at the same time try and turn customer opinion around.

Almost like a politician really, I ponder, and then I laugh. Ben would love to be likened to a politician and actually, he'd have probably made quite a good one to be honest.

Hmmm, I'll ask him about that when we next meet, which, incidentally, is in three days. Just as well, I've written up pretty much everything he's given me and I need some more, especially how he felt at that customer group.

+2016+

Three days later, I join Ben for a pre-match lunch in the private box that he has at the football club he supports.

He had first made me promise that I wouldn't mention anything about the dealings he has had and I'm sure my sarcasm wasn't lost on him when I retorted that of course I wouldn't reveal a thing.

"This place holds so many memories for me, M." Ben explains now as we walk into the hospitality suite. "I've been coming here for nearly sixty years."

He introduces me to the staff that look after him at the club, one of which is a former player that I recognise.

"This is Mandy, she's a famous author you know?" Ben gives his usual grand introduction of me and I blush slightly.

"Oh, stop it," I giggle coquettishly as I shake hands.

We sit down at Ben's table and a young waitress approaches us with a friendly smile as she and Ben indulge in football banter, reminiscent of him and Tracey from the club in Miami.

As we enjoy a roast beef dinner, accompanied, for me, with a glass of red wine, water for Ben, I ask him about that customer group.

+2000+

The lights dimmed and the huge video wall behind me lit up, it's images moving in time to the innovative music we'd selected. I wanted to give the audience a show; to create goosebumps, and as I waited for the ten-minute video to play out, my anxiety eased a little to make way for pride.

I looked out at the sea of angry faces and I could feel the nerves from my staff at the side of the stage but I stood tall and proud.

I spoke confidently, my eyes looking around the audience, whilst at the same time stealing a quick glance at my script; there were no autocues.

Even if, inside, you feel like the little kid at school that has no friends, you just wing it.

Another important trick is to pick out somebody in the front row and imagine you are just talking to them. That's what I did and it worked a treat.

I can't deny it was one of the most difficult meetings I have ever faced though, but I was determined to face the music and take a kicking, we deserved it.

And my God, what a kicking I took.

Amongst a couple of really angry customers, John stood up; he really lost his temper and started mouthing off; his frustrations getting the better of him.

I knew I was in the wrong and I had to stay calm, so I listened, admitted responsibility and promised that I would get everyone and everything back on track, at our cost. Sometimes, perversely, it can be fun to be wrong, but this was definitely not one of those times.

I came away from that meeting doubly determined to get our inadequacies resolved and I vowed I wouldn't ever put myself in such a vulnerable position again.

"Still, quite a kicking to take?" Ben looks angry just recalling this moment when I say this.

"Oh, don't worry, M. The kicking I got was nothing to what I gave GV for putting me in that position in the first place!"

Inwardly I shudder. I know by now that Ben is a fair person but I still wouldn't want to be on the end of his fury.

By some small advantage, I had also managed to turn the situation to my gain by suggesting that that particular angry customer join the customer group committee, which he duly did.

As Stan would say, keep your enemies close, destroy them or bring them alongside you; either way you gain strength. I like to think that's what I'd achieved.

Of course, technically, the blame was with GV, but, obviously, these were my customers and therefore the buck stopped with me.

And speaking of angry customer's, there was one who had been unable to attend the user group and so demanded an audience with me.

This was Greg, the building manager at Northern Bank.

Greg was in his forties, spoke with a gruff voice and was a man of few words but dear God, he had an imposing personality.

What he had to say to me was very direct and he unleashed a torrent of carefully worded frustration at me.

Once again, I accepted what was being said and vowed I would correct it.

I liked Greg, despite his ranting, and I could of course see past his anger. Lord, if I were him I would have done the same thing and I respected him for speaking out.

I invited him to join John on the user group and he fortunately agreed.

By the very next committee meeting, things were starting to turn around and I like to think that was because we listened and were determined to fix things. I'd been doing a lot of apology writing by that time. I prefer to write rather than speak, at least that way the reader has time to digest what I'm saying. It's kind of, I suppose, like writing out of my head...

"Writing out of your head?" I've never heard this phrase but I sort of know what Ben means; sometimes I write stuff off my mind, writing for the sake of writing, I suppose you'd call it.

"Yes, M." He replies solemnly, "Like now, I'm writing it out of my head and into yours. You're the wordsmith. You sprinkle the M dust."

"Yes," I think about this briefly, "yes, I suppose I do."

Ben leans forward. "It's called imagineering."

"Imagineering? Hey, I thought I was the wordsmith here?" I scoff, but then it occurs to me what a wonderful word that is.

Imagineering; the engineering of someone else's imagination.

I guess I should now add imagineerer to my profile too...

As we bedded our customers down with the new XP software over the course of the year, it was fairly well received.

So much so, that by the next user group the whole atmosphere had changed.

Our customers were now confident in us again because we had delivered on our promise, especially John, the campaigner against a poor product. His view had, by now, completely changed and he had the decency to thank me for turning the whole situation around.

Subsequent to that, our efforts were about to be commended.

The London venue was packed and humming with excitement as everybody awaited the results of that year's Best of Business Award.

There was a real buzz around the room and I was nervous; despite the long odds, I really wanted to win this.

Nine months earlier, after making an application, we had received a visit from a magazine who ran the annual London Best of Business Awards. They explained the rules that our application would be submitted and only the strongest of all the contenders would be invited to the awards dinner. Our application was based around a hand-held unit which wirelessly connected to our software using blue-tooth. All things that today are all too familiar, however back then, not so. We had demonstrated our system as the representative took notes and a few months later we all celebrated when we received a letter confirming we had been chosen to attend the awards dinner, along with over 100 others. It was unexpected but great news; whilst we believed in our cutting-edge ideas, we never thought we could win an award, but could we?

Everybody from the team that had been instrumental in this project was at the dinner and as the chairman took to the stage with a microphone to make the announcements, we all looked at each other nervously.

A rapid silence fell over the room; you could have heard a pin drop.

The chairman announced the results in reverse order.

"In third place is..." The room was silent, as though every person in it was holding their breath, "Bluemann Group."

Applause went up and at that point I felt deflated. I think all of us had decided at this point that we wouldn't be in the top three and to accept defeat graciously.

Then the chairman spoke again.

"And this year's runners up are... Tech X."

As he said those words, we all leapt up cheering.

You'd have thought we had actually won the award, and to be honest, to us, we had.

We were just little old Tech X and we had just beaten all of the London businesses to that prestigious second place slot.

It was a momentous occasion and our statue was proudly presented in front of the rest of the team the next day, taking pride of place in our reception area.

"That's fantastic!" I say as Ben and I put on our coats to go and watch the football match.

"Not bad for someone who started from nothing eh?" Ben mutters, clearly excited to get out onto the terraces.

I quickly down the last of my wine and trot after him.

As we walk the corridor to the steps that will take us up to the directors stand, I spot a famous comedian, several former football players and a famous radio DJ.

"Keep up, M!" Ben calls over his shoulder as I gaze in awe at the people around me.

Ben is on edge and fidgety as we take our seats.

"You ok?" I ask him.

"Important game this one." He replies distractedly as he stands up to clap on his team, I stand too, well, when in Rome, I guess.

Ben is singing along to the traditional song of his club and I look at his animated face, seeing the passion that exudes him as he is caught up in the atmosphere. He is in a completely different zone.

He turns to me, his cheeks flushed with excitement.

"This is why I sit in the freezing cold and the pouring rain for at least fifteen days of the year." He shouts, trying to be heard above the noise levels of the crowd.

"This is why I still come, despite in the last few years having kicked the fence in front of me with anger and frustration. This today, for me, is why I do this, it's the ultimate rush."

I smile at Ben, noticing the tears welling in his eyes as he talks with such emotion about this place, his team, and as I now know, one of his many sanctuaries. Despite his talk of the cold and the rain, today is a beautiful sunny day and unusually hot and muggy.

There is real anticipation in the air, I can feel it washing over me in waves. The noise is deafening and almost electrifying as we take our seats when the referee blows his whistle to begin.

For almost an hour, Ben's team dominates the opposition and then they finally score.

The stadium, and Ben, erupt with euphoria and I look around me at the fans dancing on the terraces, feeling a little emotional myself as shivers go up my spine.

With just a few minutes to go, Ben's team concede a goal and he, like so many others, is furious, screaming at the players, willing them on.

Eight minutes of injury time is announced and the crowd erupt again, "Come on!"

Seven minutes later, the ball is flicked into the penalty area and we all watch in slow motion as it heads for the net. It's a goal! Ben's team have won.

Ben is screaming and jumping like a lunatic as the final whistle goes and I'm laughing at the sight. Though he's not the only one, I've never seen such a great atmosphere. I say this to Ben and he laughs, "It's rare we have the opportunity to celebrate!"

We clap and cheer the team off and Ben is buzzing as we make our way back to hospitality for a final drink.

"Believe me, M," he explains animatedly, "it's not always like this. I've walked out of here before, well stormed out actually, like a petulant child!"

"I can imagine!" I laugh.

"But games like today, rare as they are, well," Ben sighs with happiness, "they get the old adrenalin pumping, that's for sure."

Adrenaline is flooding my body too, I must admit, and I'm really pleased when Ben tells me that he's arranged it so that I can come back to a match whenever I like.

And just like the thousands of fans around me, I leave the ground with a spring in my step and a football song in my head.

Chapter 24

Things Were about to Get a Whole Lot Worse

+ 2001 +

Before we move into Bens story in 2001, it would be remiss not to mention the dreadful events that occurred that year.

Everyone remembers where they were when the horrendous events of 9/11 unfolded.

Ben was making tea in the kitchen at Southfields, watching the small TV on the wall in horror.

I worked for a German bank at the time, and I remember leaving a meeting to be told that an aircraft had apparently crashed into one of the twin towers in New York.

This was no small accident though, this was a horrific incident that was to change the course of the civilised world, and democracy as we knew it then.

It's always a sobering thought every time you tick off another decade.

When you're thirty, you're led to believe you're over the bachelor hill, at forty, it's midlife crisis time and at fifty, well, if you're lucky, maybe it's time to start thinking about the R word; retirement.

I'd wanted to do something special for my 50th; something with the family and close friends, so I arranged a weekend treat.

On the Friday night, Mary and I took everyone to what was then my favourite restaurant where we had hired a private room for dinner.

The following morning, we all re-congregated at our house to take a stretch limo to see my football team play. The limo was a complete surprise for everyone, the result, not so; we lost.

At home, after the game, there was a huge birthday cake waiting for me, and I remember making a wish as I blew out the candles and on life in my forties; simply wishing for health and happiness for my family and I.

Back at work, I had decided to start restructuring so I moved Anne in to manage and grow the sales team and brought in another manager, Sasha, to run Customer Services.

Leena still wasn't working out so I let her go, allowing Jessica to assume her rightful role as Finance Director, though this time for Tech X.

With a team of twenty, the business was starting to take shape again and I hadn't stopped believing. I never would.

At this point, I also thought about turning the run-down barn at the back of Southfields into a store. I'd call it The Annex.

But of course, nothing is ever easy and when the planners refused, I argued that the barn was about to collapse anyway. They still refused, but of course you know me by now, don't even bother saying no to me.

Eventually I got my own way, of course, and they agreed we could refurbish it, so I demolished the building and, three months later, we had a nice dry store that I, with another planning application later on, would turn into an office.

XP had also found its own little niche and was now bringing in strong sales with the outsourced GV continuing its maintenance.

I felt like we had gathered some momentum again and I wanted to bring my two strongest players together as part of my management team, so I promoted Anne to Sales Director forming a new directorship board along with myself and Jessica.

I won't lie, I was aware of the undercurrent between Anne and Jessica, they didn't get along, but they both had so much to offer.

Anne had developed fast; she was strong, she produced results and she appeared to be loyal and capable.

However, I was frequently finding that she was pushing my boundaries and I was constantly having to remind her who was the boss here.

She reminded me a little of myself with Stan but it had started to become slightly annoying too. Unlike me though, she was like a yapping dog at my heels.

I'd home grown her and was now teaching her everything I knew and whilst her sheer devilment could make most meetings productive, there were times when she just seemed to be more disruptive.

I remember clearly one day, in an emergency meeting to decide what to do with a member of staff who potentially had the rare swine flu virus, I proposed that we followed precaution-ary methods and keep him away from the office; "We don't want others to catch it."

Jessica remained silent but Anne just had to argue the toss.

"Nope, he's preparing a customer install. No one else can do it; he needs to come in."

Had she actually listened to what I said?

"Well, I'm sure someone else can manage it, he needs to stay away."

"I disagree," she held my stern gaze and I felt my temper

beginning to rise as once again she challenged my decision. "Should we just send everyone home that gets ill?"

"Yes!" I snapped, "if it's this dangerously contagious."

In the early days, we had agreed on so much but now all she seemed to do was push things too far.

"So, that's it," I stood up, "he stays away from the office."

"But…" as Anne began to protest, I suddenly snapped. I'd had enough.

I bore down on her, my voice calm but my head ready to explode.

"But nothing, Anne. This isn't a fucking democracy; this is my business."

She looked pretty shocked at my outburst, as did Jessica, and then I pointed to the door, my voice raised by an octave, "Now, both of you, get the fuck out of my office."

Anne looked at me with fury in her eyes but she said nothing; silently brooding over another lost argument.

It wasn't often I lost it like that, and I realised I'd been completely unprofessional but damn that woman knew how to press my buttons!

Sadly, I wasn't the only one who wasn't feeling the Anne love anymore and things were about to get a whole lot worse…

A few months later, Sasha, who was beginning to show huge potential, asked to speak with me, only to announce she just couldn't share the same space as Anne.

I looked her in the eye, "You can do this, Sasha," but she was shaking her head.

"Yes, you can. Stand up for yourself, don't give in. Prove to me you can do it."

To give Sasha her due, she did try, but Anne broke her. She could have been a key player but she was so young and her confidence was by now shot to pieces.

"God, sorry, but what a bitch that Anne was. Poor Sasha." I curse myself inwardly, will Ben take offence at my words?

"There was nothing I could do or say to prevent her from leaving, but happily she went on to become CEO of a huge overseas recruitment company. Actually, I met her just recently."

"That's so cool, I'm glad Anne wasn't Sasha's undoing." I like hearing how Ben has stayed in touch with his former staff. It shows his integrity and the obvious respect they must have for him.

"On the contrary, Sasha has done fabulously well."

Ben chuckles and blushes slightly.

"Ha ha, what?" I push him but he shakes his head, embarrassed.

"Well, meeting Sasha proved a point actually."

"What point?"

Ben sits back and studies me. "Well, you see, Anne always took a dim view on any staff that she considered were better than her. That threatened her, if you like."

I nod as Ben talks.

"But Sasha kind of proved The Peter Principle theory for me, with her subsequent success in a company with profits alone of over £1 million per annum."

"Wow! That's such a nice thing to hear, you clearly inspired her."

Ben blushes an even deeper red and I giggle.

"Well, you must have," I say, "no need to feel embarrassed."

Ben shrugs modestly and laughs.

"I'm genuinely really proud of her, I just wish I hadn't let such a successful entrepreneur slip through my fingers. Sasha did say that she took forward some of my advice, my little wise tips, like keeping a notebook beside the bed to record any subconscious ideas that wake you during the twilight hours."

"You were her Stan." I sit back and watch Ben as he absorbs my words.

"In fact," I carry on, "you were Stan to a lot of people. A guid-ance and an inspiration."

"No, no, M, stop," Ben is laughing as I tell him what he prob-ably thinks is flattery, but it's the truth, because he has also become Stan to me.

With my concerns about the effect Anne was having on the team, I needed to talk to her and as I explained the problem that her actions were causing, I just hoped she would take in my words and learn from them as I had with Stan.

This partnership was now feeling as though it had run its course. Sad really, given the strengths we both had to bring to the business if we could work as one.

After that discussion, Anne suggested it would be beneficial if I let her take over our Customer Services department, to allow me to focus on the development side of things. I felt uncomfortable with this, I wasn't sure I trusted her to stay in control, but I couldn't disagree that, for me, it would have its benefits. Anne helped in the recruitment of Sasha's replacement with Nina as customer service manager. Nina really impressed me. It was good to see someone as strong as Anne, someone who would challenge her, be better than her even,

Looking back, I know I took my eye off the ball when it came to Anne. I'd seen the warning signs, and not just with Sasha.

When another colleague, Gary, took me aside after a meeting that Anne had been particularly outspoken in, I should have listened.

"Ben," I'd never seen him so angry, "get rid of her, she is trou-ble. Trust me, I've seen people like her before."

As much as I respected Gary's business acumen, I also knew he could be a little pompous at times. So, I put his outrage down to the fact he felt Anne had made him look foolish. I realise now I was very much mistaken.

I was at this point hatching my plan to lift XP to another level and it was a huge project that sapped my time, and it seems, my focus.

"What a horrible woman." I'm surprised Ben tolerated this Anne person but he goes on to explain.

"Every now and again I would get a glimpse of her brilliance when she produced results and it reminded me of what I had originally seen in her."

I'm still not convinced. "Ah well, I guess if she was still producing results?"

"Don't get me wrong, M. They were just glimpses by that time, far over-shadowed by her less savoury traits. Her team had a high turnover of staff, and there were many accusations of her poor treatment of them."

"So, did you fire her?"

Ben looks angry, "If only I had, M…"

"Well, why didn't you?"

"Because things were hotting up with the business aspect of things and I took my bloody eye off that ball, didn't I?"

The software team under Graham at GV had been forging ahead with a future product version of XP, XP05, which had some amazing features and incorporated everything that the customer group had fed back to me.

That customer group at the time, was influenced by some incredible individuals and I should mention just a few here. Philip's innovation of workshops, Michael's positive character and later Don, who was a massive influence to our global customers.

The plan had been to have the software out by 2004, a year ahead of the name, but we were experiencing some delays.

As their delivery date estimate over-ran, instead of being

professional and taking it on the chin, GV decided to play tricks, dirty tricks.

When they announced that they were disbanding the UK development team and outsourcing the project to India, I was furious.

I angrily demanded that they re-think and reverse that decision but the MD, Wyler, was having none of it. He point-blank refused, pointing out that this decision didn't breach the contract we had with them. This was true, but the disruption would still delay our project, and there were no penalty clauses, so they simply committed to delivering as soon as they could.

We had no choice really but to support the change and they agreed it would be fast tracked. The revised programme would take us into February 2005 but our customers were patient as we rolled out the change of schedule.

By the end of 2004 though, the outsource had turned into a complete disaster; the Indian team had no beta product for us to test and nobody seemed to be taking responsibility.

I was so frustrated and my tolerance levels were at breaking point, so I took a letter to a meeting and handed it over to John Tyler.

The letter was basically an ultimatum; deliver the software by the 28th February 2005 or face legal action. They agreed to deliver but I knew it was impossible.

When February came and went without a response, we hired one of our customers, a legal firm, to follow this up with a threatening letter.

As a result, GV made us a settlement offer of £240k which I accepted on the basis that it would be far more productive for us to get the product to market then to wait for an elongated court case.

Two weeks passed by however, and we had still not received any settlement.

Late one evening, I was fast asleep in bed when the phone rang.

I hate calls in the middle of the night, I always think its bad news. Well, it was, but not the sort I'd feared.

My voice was still groggy from sleep when I answered the phone.

"Ben Taylor?" The brash, gruff American accent pulled me from my drowsy state and I sat up with a start.

"Yes."

"Ron, from GV." Before I could even reply he was talking again. "This is how it is, we'll pay you £130k, that's it, no more. There will be no more negotiations."

Woah! I was still trying to get my wits about me, and I couldn't believe his audacity.

"But you have just agreed an out of court settlement for £240k." My tone was firm but calm, his however became aggressive and he raised his voice.

"I've just told you what the deal is. We'll put it in writing and you have seven days to accept. Let me assure you though, if you don't accept, we will break you."

By now I had rapidly switched into angry mode as I digested the situation.

GV had already agreed a settlement and now here they were bullying me into submission. It was a typical billion-dollar corporate flexing their muscle at a small company and attempting to force a settlement by believing they had us backed into a corner.

"Send your letter," I coldly replied. "We'll use it in court to demonstrate how unethical you are."

As I hung up, I felt proud of myself. Usually I'd dwell on something before making such a reactive decision but that had felt good. This time it was straight out of my head and into his, with a vengeance.

It was now time to engage my lawyer though and the reality of a lawsuit weighed heavily in the pit of my stomach. I hate lawsuits, only the lawyers are ever the winners, but I had no doubt in my mind that court was now the only solution.

Before I knew it, I was meeting Andrew Ford and his legal team in London, and we set forth preparing our case.

We issued a writ to take GV to the High Court and Andrew assigned his assistant to the laborious task of gathering evidence.

This was a new and terrifying experience and as I prepared myself, and the business, for another year of delays, I also needed to evaluate how the software development would move forward from here.

This was my first priority; we were way behind schedule and facing major setbacks. That's when the idea hit me; what about the old team GV had laid off?

I managed to get in contact with a consultancy company called Evolution One that had been formed between two of the original GV development team, Ned and Sam.

I'd decided to use this outsource team for speed and to build my own in-house team around a newly appointed development manager and as Ned knew the brief from his time at GV, the project re-started.

Meanwhile, the months ebbed away and we drew closer to issuing papers to the High Court and to GV Inc.

The papers stated our case, as well as the level of compensation we were suing them for.

We had come up with a figure amounting to almost £800k; our lawyer had suggested this would give us more scope for negotiation and we'd have to factor in some of the legal costs, even if we won.

Within a couple of weeks of issuing the papers, we received a call from GV; they were ready to negotiate.

I would like to have told them where to stick their negotiations but as Andrew quite rightly pointed out, this would carry good favour with the court and stand us in good stead.

So, a meeting was set up in my lawyer's prestigious London offices opposite the Old Bailey and I took Anne along as a learning experience. Although, to be fair, this was a learning curve for me too.

"Ok," Andrew was calm as he explained how this would work. "I have the GV representatives in the office next door. I'll leave you here while I go and speak to them, ok?"

I nodded mutely as he left the room.

My hands were clammy and my heart was racing, pure adrenalin running through my veins.

I tried to get on top of my nerves as I paced up and down the office, taking deep breaths and trying to analyse my position.

When Andrew finally returned, I swallowed and waited for him to speak

"It's ok," he said with quick reassurance. "There are some grey areas, but they are offering three-hundred thousand pounds to settle right now."

"What?" I felt as though my head was going to explode, but this was good, because now I was angry.

What would Stan say, I wondered and then almost as though he were in the room, I heard his voice.

"Ben, get in their heads, what would you do if you were them?"

And then I knew.

Yes, that was how I had to play this.

"Why don't you take a break, have a think about this?" Andrew interrupted my racing thoughts but I was already shaking my head.

"No, I'm ready. Go back and tell them if this goes all the way, with legal fees, they will be facing an outlay close to a million pounds.

"Let them know again that we have absolute confidence in

our case, but as a gesture, we will split the difference between one million pounds and their three-hundred grand offer. Say we'll settle for six-hundred grand."

Andrew frowned at me as he put his coffee down.

"Ben, that's pretty risky…" he paused as he looked at my determined face, "well, it's your call, I suppose."

"I like risk," I looked him squarely in the eyes. "And you're correct, it's my call."

Andrew shook his head and sighed. "Ok, I'll take that back to them."

As he left the room, he stopped and looked back at me, as if about to say something more.

Then with another shake of his head, he was gone.

I sat down at the conference table and looked at the clock, its ticking sound almost menacing as I waited for their response…

It was like being in Vegas again and putting everything on red. The first thing you think of is will I regret this? Should I quickly take that off the table? Is this where they come back with a straight no and walk away? There was no going back, it was done now, we just had to wait.

The intensity was building, the huge clock ticking on the wall becoming even more prevalent in the silence as we continued to sip the coffee that was making me nauseous.

It was another twenty minutes or so until Andrew returned, smiling and nodding.

"Well, they are still here," he said jokingly, "but they don't roll over easily. They have made one final offer of four-hundred grand. That's it. They say they will walk if we don't accept and they've got their coats. They aren't hanging around."

There was silence again.

"Your call," Andrew repeated, "but I think it's a good offer and I would take it, Ben."

I took a few minutes and went to the men's room. I was still so angry.

Are they bluffing, I thought, *by saying they'll walk away?*

Yes, it's a bluff, I convinced myself.

Stan had always said when you're in a corner go with your gut feeling.

Yep, that's what I am going to do. It will be one last throw of the dice.

I walked back into the room.

"Ok, do we have a deal?" Andrew asked.

"No," I said as I watched Andrew's eyes widen with amazement.

"Ok," he said slowly, as if to add emphasis, "what do we do now?"

"Andrew," I explained, "it's a gut feeling but I feel we are still pushing at an open door. Look, I will meet them half way between my six-hundred grand and their four-hundred grand so put the ultimatum back on them, they deserve to sweat now.

"It's five-hundred grand and we will not be talking anymore. Counter offers are over, let them know we are the ones now walking if they don't accept, and make that stick."

Andrew chuckled nervously.

"Ben, I am quite enjoying this battle, but are you sure? If they walk away, there's no turning back. I would recommend taking the four-hundred grand and getting on with life, let it go."

"No," I snapped, "I've made my mind up."

That was me, outwardly portraying confidence and backing my gut feeling, yet inside a wreck, my body quivering with nerves. Andrew stood and buttoned up his jacket before he looked at me.

"Are you sure, Ben?"

I didn't hesitate.

"Yes, I have made my mind up. I am sure." I stood up and stared out of the window as I heard Anne acknowledge that this was the right thing to do.

"They will take it." She simply said.

It wasn't long before Andrew returned, and his face was dead pan…

I hold my hands up to my face, "No! You lost?"

Ben smiles and holds his hands up, "Let me finish, M."

Andrew then beamed a huge smile and I knew it meant we had it.

I remember every word he said because my relief at his words was overwhelming.

"You're a class act at negotiating," Andrew shook my hand, "they have accepted."

It was game changing, such a good feeling, what else could compare to a rush like that?

This would be an experience that I filed under 'e' for excellence.

Oh yes, that was something special.

"Wow! Quite cunning, weren't you?" I'm laughing, feeling relieved that Ben had got through and won and he looks, rightly so, proud of himself.

"God, M, that was a terrifying experience, but at the same time such a thrill! I don't know how I held my nerve!"

"Course you do, you're stubborn and tenacious and after all…"

I pause as Ben reflects me, "after all?"

"Well, you had Stan there with you."

We smile sadly at each other as we think of the great man.

"How is your friend, Barry?"

Ben shakes his head, "Not good. In fact, it's looking pretty bleak."

"Is it…?" I hesitate to say the word, because the word in itself is so terminal, and Ben blows out his cheeks and nods.

I feel bad that having ended his story on such a winning high,

I have now brought our mood to such a low. I need to cheer Ben up.

"Hey!" I sit forward and tap the table, "let's go back to Summers Wood!"

Ben groans, "Oof, not now, M, I meet planning people there every week!"

"Well, let's do something fun then," I'm giggling away and I can see Ben is struggling not to join in.

"Like what?" He's shaking his head at me, and I'm sure that short of checking my coffee for alcohol, he thinks I'm totally off my head.

"Come on," I'm up and draining the last of my coffee, non-alcoholic I hasten to add, and Ben gets up wearily too.

"Come on!" I chivvy him up, "Thanks Doris!" I shout as I race out of the café, with a bemused Ben in tow.

+ + +

We are at Southfields; the offices formerly run by Ben; a site he still owns and presides over.

"Why have you brought me here, M?"

I study his face, I can tell that coming here has stirred some emotion in him, but I don't want that to be negative emotion.

"Well, because I haven't been before," I try and bluff but Ben fixes me with a stern look because that's not the reason I have brought him here, and he knows it.

"Ok," I decide to come clean. "Because this is where you re-set the business with Tech X," I whisper, "this is where you worked so hard for all that you achieved."

Ben nods slowly, "I've been a lucky man."

I gently joss him, "Pfft! Luck has nothing to do with it, Ben. You worked bloody hard for everything you have now."

When he speaks, I witness the enlightenment on his face.

"I try to tell myself that, I really do. There were moments of sheer exhaustion and incredible anxiety, and of course the loss of quality time with my family."

"But you have that time now," I gently remind Ben. "That time to breathe it all in, to look around you and appreciate all that you have. All that you worked for."

Ben is smiling and his eyes are shining.

"I do, believe me. Now I have time, I can see the colours in the world, look at the bracken and the wild flowers in the wood. I stop to smell the flowers and savour the taste of food. You know, like I said about senses?"

I'm watching Ben as he looks again to his old offices and then turns back to me.

"You're right, M. I did earn it."

"It's strange being here," he gazes at Southfields as he speaks, "It feels weird that I'm no longer here driving the main business, but you know what, M?"

"What?"

Ben looks at me with a huge grin. "I wouldn't have it any other way."

I smile back and we sit in silence, watching a plane land beneath the backdrop of a perfect summers evening.

Chapter 25

You Could Never Let Your Baby Go

+2005+

When you work for somebody else, if you have a personal crisis you get to take time out, to ease yourself back into work when you are physically and emotionally strong again.

With your own business, there is no time out, no time to ease yourself back into things. It's ruthless; you either pick yourself up and get on with it or suffer the consequences.

After the draining, but nevertheless successful, experience with GV, I knew that's what I had to do.

I've always thought of myself as fair and generous while still retaining a frugality that I think I must have taken from my childhood years. By frugality, I mean I'll never just throw money at something, despite my wealth. I still saw, and continue to see, the value of everything, and when I'm being ripped off, whether it's to the tune of £50 or £50,000 pounds, that's when my principals kick in.

Anne was, by this time, challenging me to part with shares in what she saw as an incentive to retain her within the company.

I stood my ground for a while, I didn't necessarily disagree with her concept, but she had caused a lot of disruption with her dominating personality. Would a share incentive change her attitude or encourage it?

I decided to run it past my accountants who agreed that giving her shares was all very beneficial because it gave Anne incentive to drive the business harder and she would see the profitably.

However, they questioned whether I was being rather generous at my proposal of parting with 15% and they suggested she feel the investment a little herself by parting with some cash.

Anne and I went on to have many conversations as I tried to encourage her to buy into the company. I explained my investments of £10k in Dex and £160k in the US between 1984 and 1988 was equivalent to that current day of about £600k.

I thought about how having my own money tied up in the company had changed my attitude; the fear being the most motivating factor. Perhaps if she was prepared to take that risk it might have the same effect?

She was adamant she wouldn't buy in though. I guess some people are only happy to risk someone else's money, and I did finally agree to issue her with 10% immediately, with 5% after another three-years-service. This soon became complicated as we drew out the contracts and, foolishly maybe, albeit generously, I let the 15% share of my company go to her in the one transaction.

I'd told Anne that at some point my goal was to sell the business, but she was adamant I never would.

"You could never let your baby go," she would always say, "you will never do it. You'll leave it to your son to manage, but you'll never let it go."

I would argue back that if she really thought that, what was the point in holding shares in a privately-owned company? To which the response was always muted.

I often wondered where her thought process came from as my son and daughter were never at any time being touted to take over the company. But it was an insight into her thinking, and one that later I would use to my advantage.

But now was not the time to dwell on Anne and her views that were poles apart from mine.

With the software development still underway, things were building towards another set of events.

The pressure was on Ned's team, who were located with us at Southfields, and in the autumn of 2005 we were now a year late when we rolled the product out for testing which sadly proved that it needed extending into 2006.

I had major concerns by now so I brought in my best friend Lewis from the States, paying for him to oversee the last leg of the testing, the bug fixing and the recruitment of my replacement team.

This proved to make relations tense; Evolution One wanted to finish and withdraw, and Lewis had little regard for Sam who was CEO of Evolution One. There were lots of arguments and disagreements on where their responsibilities lay and all this time the software was languishing even further.

Eventually, I created a small team, led by my now new development head, Andreas, to take us forward and the matter drew to a peaceful conclusion.

The problem we had now was that we had cut development short and not only that but the software was being delivered with a lot of the much-planned functionality left out.

I felt so disappointed whenever timing pressured us into dropping certain elements of a software release and this was no exception.

Lewis was keen to see what could be done with the software back in the US so we set him up as our exclusive US distributor and between him and a former colleague of his, they started to gain interest and closed some US business deals, and to their credit with US clients who were a step ahead of our UK counterparts.

However, as the pressure of bug fixes and lack of functionality began to build from the UK and now our US clients, we struggled to keep up.

In hindsight, we had been too early out of the blocks with the US strategy and as we reassessed the situation, it was quite alarming to realise that, with current investment and resource, we were now predicting a two to three-year time scale to bring in all of the missing functionality.

This was yet another tough situation and I knew I had royally cocked up.

I thought the ball in play was getting the software back to the US and fast, clearly that wasn't the ball. Too over confident, maybe. If Stan had been there he would have been screaming at me.

The ball wasn't getting the software into the US without thinking, it was re-engineering it to make sure it was fit for purpose in that market. I had grown complacent, now it was time to sit up and learn.

XP05 was eventually rolled out to customers in 2006, an embarrassing eighteen months later than scheduled.

Despite much of its new functionality being missing it was still very stable and our users really liked the look and feel. This wasn't the case in the US though and sadly Lewis and I had to agree that he would cease pursuing the opportunity. We had both had the responsibility to see this coming, but ultimately it was mine. To me though, this simply showed the strength of our true friendship, in that, despite all of that, we could still move on and allow that friendship to endure.

I was now on a mission to start the process with my own in-house team to finish the job by the next release.

The cycle was usually two years to bring a major release to the market so it was game on.

Things had become even more tense with Anne now and I was constantly finding myself reigning her in, time and time again. She was so strong willed and took the view that she knew better than me. Worse, it seemed she was trying to influence the staff to believe that too.

I think this was the real turning point, the beginning of the end in our relationship.

But, I had a responsibility to continue to get things back on track and I tried to have many discussions with her, but much of these were spent with her swiping at Jessica and criticising her handling of accounts, unjustifiably so.

I really did try hard to encourage her to be accountable, and to lead by example but it was all so futile and I was running short on ideas.

At the same time, my frustrated PA, Emma, had moved on and I appointed Sylvia from our admin team, whilst another well-organised young lady, Jane, took over Sylvia's admin role.

By now, having reached the grand old age of fifty-six, I'd become open to thoughts of an exit, and, having brought my son and daughter into the business, I reconsidered if this might be something they would want to step up to.

Could this become a family business? Was Anne right after all?

In my heart of hearts, I knew this wasn't for either of my children; they had seen first-hand how business could suck the life from you. Still, I felt it only right and proper that I give them that choice.

It wasn't a commitment either of them wanted, and I respected that and was actually very proud that they decided to put their families first. Growing a business doesn't suit everyone, and I know it was Mary that had instilled in them the importance of family.

"I really wish I could tell Mary's side of things," I say wistfully and Ben almost chokes on his own laughter.

"She's a very private person, M."

"Yeah, I know that, it's just I feel I'm telling so little about her, you know?"

"It's what we agreed though." Ben shrugs and then looks at me with a smile of apology.

I sigh, I'm not going to push him. Then I suddenly remember something.

"Hey, you know the other day, I decided you'd make a good politician!"

Ben explodes with laughter, "Where did that come from?"

"Ha ha, probably your ability to withhold the details!" I reply and Ben chuckles. "Seriously though," I add, "it was the way you stood at that user group and took the flack whilst assuring people you would fix things."

"Ha!" Ben snorts derisively. "Politics and business are poles apart."

"Tell that to Donald Trump!" I retort.

Ben shakes his head. "Pfft! I'm no politician, M. I actually delivered on my promises!"

"That's true," I can't help but agree.

"And anyway," Ben adds, "there's no chance he'll be elected, surely?"

Those user groups brought a positive balance between the company and our customers, who felt not only a sense of independence in the group but that they had a united voice and we were listening to it.

We chose the next venue as the prestigious London stock exchange, it didn't disappoint.

We used this event to launch XP05, making our usual promises for the missing functionality to be included in the next major release.

I had gotten used to speaking and it was made more enjoyable when we had positive things to present. I just would not rest until I reached those personal software development targets that I had set out as my vision to my user group colleagues.

Andreas and I were in constant battles with the look and feel of the product though and it reminded me a little of Steve Jobs; a man I greatly admired. What was it about developers that think it's all about them?

I wanted the functionality to be in a simplistic form but he argued that I was just trying to square circles. The last straw was a meeting I had with him about the future strategy for the product. I had spent a lot of time scribbling pages and pages of what I wanted and in particular a detail of the way I wanted mobility to take shape.

"It's not in the manual," Andreas pompously told me.

"Andreas, do I give really give a fuck for what's in the manual? And anyway, what the hell are you talking about, what manual?"

I shook my head at the idiocy of his comment as the red mist descended upon me.

"Fine, I'll fucking spec it myself then!"

I was frustrated at his lack of creativity and I now knew this had become a problem that I needed to resolve soon. I needed a development leader that understood what it was I was trying to create and to align themselves with my thinking and it was now apparent that this was a task Andreas couldn't live up to.

Meanwhile Anne's poor management skills had come to a head, with Nina confiding in me that she was struggling to work with her. I was a great supporter of Nina, she and I got on well and she had made an excellent contribution and was popular with our customers.

I'd seen this coming for about a year to be honest. On the one hand, I had allowed Anne to manage and take responsibility for her team, after all it was clear she had no time for my opinion. Yet I still felt I should be more forceful and deal with the issues before they got any worse.

When Nina walked out after yet another confrontation with Anne, she was quickly replaced by a new recruit who left within a month under a cloud of controversy and a nasty letter of complaint about Anne.

I knew right then it was time to take action. Throughout the year, many staff had come and gone, expressing their grievances at Anne, and agencies were beginning to question our high staff turnover.

With my PA, Sylvia, also stressed by Anne, things were looking dire. I immediately realigned the admin team with Molly, a young but very confident and capable young lady but how would she cope with Anne?

However, when these events were followed by the loss of our best project manager, Dave, who sighted his reasons for leaving were to pursue better opportunities, I had to draw my own conclusions. All of this, coupled with customer complaints about Anne not servicing quotes or answering calls, made me quite certain that enough was enough.

I tried once again to discuss this with Anne, but still she insisted she knew better and once again she shunned my support.

I tried, I really did, but if I thought I could be to her what Stan was to me, I was sorely wrong.

I explained the issues she needed to address; wanting her to stop and think, to work at turning things around. I told her she had to either support me and the company or leave.

But Anne was headstrong and bizarrely the meeting ended with her telling me she was handing back her shares. I was shocked, I even argued that she shouldn't do that. How glad I am now that she insisted! It was a move she would, I'm sure, later regret, probably for the rest of her life.

It was as the backlash of staff departures gathered momentum that my mum was diagnosed with cancer.

"Oh, I'm sorry."

"It was a tough time; I'd lost my dad just two years earlier…"

It was April, and one of those middle-of-the-night calls that I dread.

Mum choked back tears as she delivered the words:"Ben, your dad's dead."

I gasped in shock, and in the dark silence I closed my eyes, the tears streaming down my face. I couldn't even speak.

"Did you hear me, Ben? Your dad has died." Her voice was shaky from the shock.

"I'm on my way over, Mum." I replied and hung up.

Just nine months earlier, my dad had gone to watch a football match and when they were short of players and jokingly suggested he play, he jumped at the chance.

There he was at seventy-nine years old running around a football pitch.

But that was Dad, he was a fitness freak, down the gym every day and achieving his black belt in judo aged seventy. The doctor told him he was the fittest old boy he'd ever seen.

So yes, they may have had their issues in their marriage but Mum doted on Dad, and his sudden death was a complete shock which broke her heart.

"And now she too was seriously ill, that's really sad."

"Ben nods, "Mum was a fighter though, and throughout her illness, she never once complained, simply got on with life."

"That must have been tough, what with everything going on with Anne and the staffing issues?"

"Ha, you'd have thought given the support I'd showed her that I would have received some back, or even a little sympathy in my hour of need."

I roll my eyes, once again loathing this Anne character, "I'm guessing that didn't happen." It's a rhetorical question and with an ironic smile, Ben continues.

"Ah well, as Stan always said, move on. And at this point I really had no time to dwell anyway..."

Chapter 26

What Recession?

I never understood why there were no big players in our market; most of our competitors were of similar size and turnover and I had seen some owners making their exit with not much more than a several million-pound sale value.

Not me though, I was determined to build a brand and would only ever consider my exit with an exceptional offer.

After we had registered a key industry leading trademark back in 1987, momentum in the market had been building, with the introduction of dedicated shows and magazines.

I always felt we were the first to innovate when it came to our competition, in fact we were the first to be different on so many levels.

Our product, even in its darkest hour, shone like a beacon what with the mobile technology, our web site with superb video content, our five-star facility, independent user group and our performances at facility shows.

From the very first facility show I had wanted to do something radical, something that would draw the crowds. We really were the talk of the town, with our competition copying our lead as we raced another step ahead of them.

Southfields was now becoming a bit of a squeeze especially as we had begun to build a serious development team.

I was open to the option of moving on and I considered two potential options.

One was to purchase a lot and build out a 10,000 square-feet new build and the other was to extend Southfields and rebuild the Annex.

Buying up the lot for a new build really appealed to me, even though we would have had to rent out some of the space, but I was personally ready to take the risk and fund it. However, the land-owner proved to be too greedy and when negotiations fell apart, it was back to plan B; Southfields.

It was weird, one morning I was driving to work and just a mile away from the office when the sun broke out of a scud of dark clouds and lit the road ahead.

There, through the rain, was the brightest rainbow I'd ever seen, and it was beaming directly down into Southfields. This, I decided, was my inspiration. But would it find me my pot of gold?

So, I focused on extending Southfields and I hired an architect, Graham, who worked with me to create an ambitious refurbishment that would add a further square footage to accommodate over 100 staff.

It was quite a challenge; three floors had to be completely gutted and a whole new ground floor created. All this while we carried on with business as usual.

In addition, I wanted to buy all new office furniture and not just any office furniture, I wanted the Mercedes of the furniture world.

Our budget was around two million and I personally funded a further £500k to ensure a high standard of finishing and furnishing, with no corners cut. I wanted my staff to have the best, though I still don't know to this day if they knew I had personally funded that level of luxury.

In hindsight, it was a high price to pay but I was a firm believer that this kind of investment was worth it if the staff were rewarded with contentment in their working environment

It was such a buzz to see staff really enjoying the workplace and our visitors taking a breath when they walked into it.

By this time, almost as though Sylvia had waited to see the completion of the new build, she tendered her resignation, sighting Anne as her reason for leaving. No matter how hard I tried, Sylvia was not about to change her mind, and the things she shared with me about Anne and her treatment of certain staff was actually quite chilling.

I immediately promoted Molly to be my new PA as she had proved to be competent and trustworthy in her admin role.

We were now ready to release the latest version of our software and what better place to do it than at Wembley Stadium with our user group.

We had called this next release, Quantum, very apt because it was that Quantum leap I had been planning since our return to the US had crashed so badly.

Software by now was being driven by a guy called Chris who I had promoted from the development team. He was bright, sharp and most importantly, eager to meet my high demands. My aim was to make the product more web and mobile based as well as ensure it was even more user friendly and to, of course, emphasise the importance of this database as opposed to the CAD element.

Wembley was the perfect event for the user group committee as a lot of us were avid football fans and I came into my own as I spoke to an audience of nearly two-hundred; a record attendance for a user group.

So it was, that just as things seemed to be going well for my business, another cloud loomed as a new recession threatened and with the collapse of some major banks, the market became dramatically unsteady. I began to wonder why it was that every time we gathered some momentum, I was suddenly thrown another stiff challenge.

"Maybe it was Stan." I say, humming the theme music from the Twilight zone and Ben laughs.
"Maybe, M. But it was a bloody unnecessary one!"

A good many articulate people sensed the loss of hope in our economy and I knew it was time for me to take stock of how the last recession had affected us and think about what I should do next. It came back to me, the thoughts I'd had during the last recession about investing when everybody else is cutting costs, and my brain began to tick.

I had to take action to protect my team and everything we had built this far, and I prepared a very severe cost-cutting plan.

Obviously, everybody was scared for their jobs; the media was saturated with news of massive redundancies happening across the UK, so I called a meeting to present the staff with my plan.

I explained to them that in my experience at Onelock, when the cuts and redundancies continued month after month, it was unsettling, therefore I knew how they were feeling.

I conveyed that I was determined to control costs but that I had confidence in our innovative ideas.

As I explained that my plan was designed to protect staff from redundancies, I could sense the instant relief around the room; like a warm rush of air. I had poured over the numbers for days, ensuring I had factored in the worst-case scenario.

It was a ruthless five-year plan but I still felt it was important to measure and reward performance.

I had promised myself that when the time was right I would try and take the software back to the US and despite our battening down the hatches as we weathered the storm of recession, I decided at the same time to kick-start my come back strategy. I had learned from the previous recession of 1990 that the earlier you can recover, the stronger you'll be against your competitors.

"So, you invested rather than cut back, like you'd wanted to during the previous recession?"

I'm impressing myself with my business talk here!

"You don't miss a trick, do you, M?" Clearly Ben's impressed too, ha ha!

We now had software that I was beginning to feel proud of and I was excited to show it off, but I had a vision to take it further still.

By now, the workshops I had created a few years earlier were really popular and with these wider audiences it was the perfect time to showcase our newly launched online training tutorials and pre-recorded webinars.

These master pieces gave online visitors the impression that the demos were live, a brilliant concept.

Innovations were flowing thick and fast and they enriched our ability to deliver more than my customers, or for that matter my staff, expected. Staff were suddenly forced to enthuse over new ideas rather than dwell on the economic storm that lay ahead. We had convinced them that we, as a company, were safe and still innovative and everyone else was surviving, clinging on for dear life, or failing. It was the perfect plan.

The only downside at this point was that there was now so much dissension in the ranks and all of it directed at Anne.

Don't get me wrong, she did have some trusted followers, in particular, Lydia who had replaced Nina's short-term replacement.

But Anne only liked to bring in subservient people. And whilst Lydia was well-organised and productive, in my opinion she was not a suitable customer services manager.

I'd always previously supported Anne on her results with UK sales but as my global sales increased, it highlighted the now apparent lacking in Anne's team. At this time, it had been brought to my attention that Anne now seemed to have it in for another of her project managers, Carla.

I had Stan's words in my head once again. *"Employ people who are better than you."*

That's what I had encouraged Anne to do but she hadn't been able to cope with the threat from staff that were as good as or better than her, as Sasha and Nina were and now Carla was.

So, having learnt from my mistake with Sasha, I decided to take Carla away from Anne, and I created the role of global sales manager for her.

I also faced the decision of firing Anne and accepting the consequences of that or to try a develop a new tact.

I know now that I should have fired her or, better still, she should have left with her dignity intact and continued her career elsewhere. To this day though, I have no idea what Anne was trying to achieve, other than to create major destruction, like an attention seeking child. Mind you, at that point, wonderful news was on the horizon, so things didn't seem all that bad.

Ben is smiling and I ask him to explain.

"Well, Mary and I got the wonderful news that every parent dreams of; our first grandchild."

"Ah," I smile and sit back.

Back in business, I decided to re-shuffle even further and attempt to rebuild things. I think my naivety must have been at an all-time high, but I foolishly believed Anne could still run the UK sales team and I thought she would either get stuck into her role or accept it was time for her to leave.

So, I brought in a young lady called Katie, that I had known from years past, as my customer services manager and took back the admin and finance, with Jessica reporting to me. It was back to basics but I seriously needed to shake things up, and that's what I did.

I also knew Katie would bring a calming influence to what had become a very unstable situation. She was a real people person and she had experience, better still she would not tolerate any nonsense from the other senior staff, especially Anne.

I set out my plans to create a new management team under the board and at the next board meeting, Jessica and I passed that motion. Unsurprisingly Anne disagreed which left me no choice but to pass the resolution by two votes to one.

Again, Anne had disappointed me in her attempt to keep control rather than let upcoming management thrive.

We now had a strong team of nine individuals representing each team, who were capable of making a good contribution. But would it be a team or a battlefield of wit, will and politics? Whilst Molly was growing well into her role as she adapted to the pace of my driven demands, I wondered if Anne would now take the opportunity to grab this with both hands, or leave, or even self destruct?

Ben seems a little quiet today, even more distracted than usual and I ask him if he's ok.

He sighs, "I'm just frustrated with a few planning things and the incredulous happenings at my football club. Honestly, M, we could write another book on the things that have been going on!"

I chuckle, secretly thrilled at the thought of our working together on another project but I gently point out to him that we need to finish this one first.

He sits up, almost as if he's surprised. "It's just occurred to me we're nearing the end of my story."

"Well, not really," I smile, "just the story of your business. Your story will continue."

Back in the business world, it was clear this recession wasn't having the same bite on us as the last one. Don't get me wrong, it did have a sting in its tail and I knew I still had to be cautious. The thing was that the cutbacks within the UK economy actually worked to our advantage because as companies dispensed with staff they became more reliant on technology. Coupled with that, my strategy to go global meant we were still attracting business from countries that hadn't been so affected by the recession.

It was the most incredible period after all those years.

The business was doubling with each quarter; profits were soaring and our margins were now ridiculously high. We still had the same overheads but were now selling volume orders of software. It had literally gone crazy!

Another high note around this time was my persuading Nina to return and work with me.

I'd always admired her, she was hard working, but I knew she wouldn't even dream of coming back if she was to be anywhere near Anne so I gave her a role in the marketing team. She was just the sort of asset we needed in that team and fortunately she agreed.

It was around this time that I had become increasingly keen to build a new home and, after some wonderful family holidays there, Miami seemed to keep looming as an option.

Mary and I had been looking at an exclusive development that was set amongst acres of forest that was teaming with wild life. The developer planned to build these exclusive homes in an area of outstanding natural beauty with three distinctive neighbourhoods surrounded by an exclusive member-only clubhouse, and a world class golf course.

It was inspirational and innovation at its best.

We selected a lot that, to this day, I still believe is one of the prime lots in the whole development. It was just under an acre with water on both sides, and was set just 500 yards from the club house. We fell in love with it.

As you would expect, the developer had pre-selected the best builders in Miami, and insisted on specific quality of materials and build.

To me, this felt like more than a second home, it was to become home from home if you like, and it was the project I had dreamed of.

It would allow me to express every little idea about design and detail that I had built up in my head when I had envisaged our dream home, especially the Italian style that I had envisaged after my party trip with Herbert years earlier.

The months that followed had me drawing up concepts and floor plans; I wanted lots of light open space, high cathedral ceilings and galleried landings.

I was like a kid at Christmas! I must have spent a thousand hours with those plans and ideas, planning the space to perfection and bouncing my ideas around the family.

Mary and I would also spend hours in granite yards, kitchen design studios and tile and lighting shops.

We were determined to get that attention to detail, from every tiny mosaic tile down to the door handles and lighting fittings.

We both loved the Italianate look with a contemporary feel and lots of light.

I was so excited and we took the plans and designs home with us to show to the family, including Mum, who by now, was in a poor state of health.

Still, it was rewarding to me that she got to see our plans, to see our dreams, and not only that, but more importantly she also survived just long enough to see our first grandchild; her first great grandchild.

"A bittersweet time then?"

"It's the way it is, I suppose," Ben mutters profoundly. "Nothing comes harder than losing someone though, especially your mum."

"I know she'd had her moments when you were younger, but were you ever close to her?"

Ben shakes his head sadly and my heart swells with compassion.

"No, if anything, as I grew up we grew further apart. I was, in a way, everything Mum wasn't and we just clashed. I don't know where my desire for the nicer things in life came from. I had dreams and when I could afford it, I indulged them. I know in her heart Mum was proud of me, but I guess coming from a life of struggle, my new world didn't sit nicely with her."

"That's sad."

"Those things I alluded to in my childhood; I can't explain them but I do know my parents had a tough upbringing coming through the war years, which probably played a large part in their struggles with parenthood. They did the best they could, I think."

I feel so sorry for Ben, but I know he would hate my pity and I try to be positive.

"Well they obviously didn't do a bad job, look at you." I gesture to Ben and he laughs but the smile doesn't quite reach his eyes.

"On her final day, I sat with Mum as, aided by drugs, she drifted in and out of sleep. When she woke momentarily, tears welled up in her eyes and she croaked, "Enjoy the rest of your life, Ben."

Her eyes drifted shut and with tears streaming down my face, I nodded.

She began to shake with what I now know is called the death rattle, and I called the nurse who confirmed that she was slipping away. I held her hand and told her that I loved her, just before she took her final breath and was still. I looked to the nurse for confirmation that Mum had gone. She smiled sadly at me and nodded, and then I sobbed."

I have tears streaming down my face and Ben looks at me with such pain in his eyes that I almost catch my breath.

"I think that's the only time I ever told her to her face that I loved her."

"She knew. You were there for her, especially in her final moments, so she knew."

I desperately want to hug Ben but he is far too proud a man to accept my comfort.

"When the clock stopped for Mum," Ben continues, "the world changed for those around her. Losing both parents is not something you truly contemplate and it was Christine, a family friend who pointed out the harsh reality to me when she said, 'Well, Ben, you're an orphan now.'."

Ben laughs softly. "And it was true. I remember choking my way through the second eulogy of my life, the first having been Dads. I had a deep sense of hope that somewhere up there, my parents and grandparents were looking down on me and that they were proud."

My tears are flowing again; I fear I'll be an emotional wreck by the end of this book!

Ben notices and sits forward.

"Hey, no tears, M. I like to think in years to come when someone looks up at the stars and utters those words; 'Grandad Ben and Grandma Mary would have been proud', our grandchildren, and children, can know that we already are."

We are both silent now; each thinking about the people close to us that we have loved and lost and I suppose of our own mortality.

"*Life's so short, M!*" *Ben suddenly says with conviction.* "*Make the most of every single day. When you wake in the morning and you see the sunlight streaming through the windows and you know you have your health, make sure you appreciate that. Just stop, take a moment and set it to your memory, because there are others that will never be able to do so again.*"

I suddenly realise this isn't just about Ben's mum, and it wasn't managing his assets, planning or football issues that were the cause of his distraction.

I don't care if I'm overstepping the mark.

"*Is it Barry?*" *I ask quietly and he looks down at the floor. I can just barely make out his words as he nods.*

"*He died last night.*"

Chapter 27

It Was Game on for This Entrepreneur

+2011+

Mum had requested her ashes be spread with Dad's at their favourite spot in the forest but I also took some to my football club. They had indoctrinated me into that club's family since I was four years old, so I got special permission to spread them in the home goal.

"That's so lovely!" I exclaim, but I see a flash of anger in Ben's eyes.
"It's also another reason why I will not let the current owner move us off to another location, but that's another story I guess."

Mum's final words to me to live my life had registered deeply and I knew now was the time to stop all the stress and devote my time to my family. I don't think anybody close to me actually believed it was possible for me to stop working at such an absurd pace.

"Well, to be fair, you haven't stopped, have you?" I jest and Ben chuckles.

"We've had this conversation, M. It's in my DNA. Now, do you want to finish my story or not?" He's joking, but I feign offence.

"How rude?" I gasp as he laughs, "as your biographer, I could change your ending, you know?"

Ben rolls his eyes at me, "At this rate there won't be an ending, now come on."

I snigger as I pick up my note book.

This is our first meeting in the three weeks since Ben's best friend Barry has died. He has needed to grieve, well he still is grieving, and to come to terms with the loss of such a close and great friend. That's as well as get through the funeral where I know Ben had read a eulogy, his third.

I want to ask him about it, surely I should, but I don't want to upset him.

I take a deep breath, put my notebook back down and bite the bullet. "How was the..." I begin tentatively.

"What, the funeral?" Ben pauses, deep in thought as I nod.

He sighs, pinching his forehead as he considers his words.

"I'll be honest, M, it was one of the toughest things I've done. The church was packed; Barry was a popular man and people clamoured to find any available space.

I sat there, right next to his coffin, and I admit I was in pieces. In fact, I think Mary worried that I wouldn't be able to go through with it."

Ben takes a gulp of air.

"But you did?" I gently ask and he nods.

"It was almost as if I could hear Barry encouraging me. 'Come on mate, do it for Jill.'

And I did, I stood and choked out that final goodbye to my best friend. I miss him dearly."

Ben smiles sadly at me and for once I am lost for words. Perhaps I shouldn't have asked?

As if reading my mind, Ben leans forward and hands me my notebook.

"It's done," he mutters softly, "he has left me realising just how precious every day is and he is at peace. And now we have a story to write."

Ben's right, the show must go on, and now it's time to concentrate on the business, or rather, the end of the business...

Even though relations with Anne were strained, it wasn't personal it was business, so as she was a board director, I shared my plans with her to exit the business.

Her response didn't surprise me particularly; she threw her head back and laughed derisively.

"Ha! You will never give this company up," she looked me straight in the eye, "I know you."

I actually shuddered at the cold glint in her eyes, how had I not realised what a calculated person Anne really was?

My hackles went up as I returned her cool gaze. "Not only do you not know me at all, Anne, but I wonder if you actually know yourself anymore."

She bristled slightly and sneered but I continued. "I'm selling the company and you need to deal with it and also keep it confidential." I knew she'd keep it confidential, she didn't believe I'd actually do it.

To add to my troubles, the breakdown in relations between myself and Anne was more than my PA, Molly, could bare and I lost yet another employee who sighted Anne, again, as her reason for leaving.

Knowing what my plans were for the business and to protect her future, I used this opportunity to bring Nina out of the marketing team and I made her my PA.

So it was, that on a warm summers evening in August 2011, I

sat with Stuart from a London accounting giant. We watched the sun set from my garden that overlooked the beautiful surrounding countryside and I shared my plans to exit the business.

I was looking for encouragement and motivation from him and I got that in spades.

Stuart was enthusiastic and certain that he could meet my expectations and the vibe I got from him convinced me I could trust him.

"Ooh, Stan wouldn't have approved," I tease Ben. "Trust nobody, remember?"

"Ha, maybe the great man wasn't always right."

I feign shock horror at Ben's words. "That's sacrilege!"

Ben smiles and then suddenly looks sad.

"I remember wishing my mum and dad could have been there to hear my plans. Whilst at the same time, for me, there was a real sadness about what I was about to do, I know in my heart they would have been proud of me."

"I'm sure they would have and I'm certain Stan would too."

Ben looks up on hearing Stan's name.

"I owe him such a debt of gratitude." Ben sighs and runs his hand through his hair, agitated all of a sudden.

"Why didn't I try and find him, to say thank you?"

I'm surprised, I had thought Ben had taken Stan's early demise in his stride. I hadn't realised it had affected him this much.

Bens voice quivers as he talks. "Why did I let that man who had given me such a gift leave my life without saying goodbye? I would have liked to ask him why. Why me? What was it that he saw in me that made him believe in me so?"

"You have to let it go, Ben. Like Stan would say; move on, learn from it." Ben pushes a finger under his glasses to wipe a tear, and my tone becomes conciliatory.

"Learn the importance of letting those close to you know how much you appreciate and love them."

Ben nods and in sudden realisation he smiles. "I suppose that's what I am doing really, M. With this book."

I nod silently and Ben continues to speak.

"And at least with this book, my grandchildren and their kids will have a detailed insight into all of this. My son and daughter may also one day to decide to write their own autobiographies."

"Be sure to give them my details." I say with a cheeky wink and Ben bursts out laughing.

"I'm sure technology will play a big part in documenting people's lives, certainly more so than in my generation. But yes, don't worry, M, I'll make sure you get first refusal."

Ben rolls his eyes as I chuckle and we carry on.

There was much negotiating to be done and, to be fair to Stuart, I gave him a pretty hard time about reaching the sort of deal that I wanted.

It was concluded that the whole process would take between six to twelve months once we got started and my target, since our colossal growth, was to sell for nothing short of seventy million pounds.

I wasn't prepared to compromise and I explained that I wanted a partner to buy me out that would agree my immediate release. I also wanted all of my staff kept in employment; I was not about to just sell all the assets and close the door on everything I had built.

I emphasised that if nobody met that criteria, there would be no sale.

It was a big ask, and I knew it, but I had done my numbers and I was determined to stand firm.

Based on my criteria, and under Stuarts advice, Project Scott, as we named it, after Scott of the Antartic, was declared top secret, only to be shared with the board.

Whilst we were confident of finding a buyer with my requirements, Stuart stressed the importance of continuing to run the business at full strength.

This made sense, if we were to come out with no sale and I had let the business lapse, I'd be in dire straits.

Anne had already been told and had dismissed it, but now it was time to tell Jessica.

She was visibly upset and emotional, after all, Jessica and I had enjoyed a close working relationship and her job with any future owner could be at risk if they brought in their own accounting team.

Unlike Anne though, as I explained the plans to Jessica, she showed true loyalty and told me she would support whatever I felt I needed to do.

It was really tough for me not to share my decision with my management team too, especially those I was close to, but Stuart strongly advised against it and he pretty much insisted I adhered to his advice.

There was one person from the management team, however, that we tactically decided to share it with. I knew I could trust Katie to keep Project Scott confidential, the reason being was that not only did she have acquisition experience but she was also respected by the majority of the team, and I knew she would inform me if she heard any leaks about my intentions.

That said, it still pained me not to share it with newly created management team.

"What are you sighing for?" Ben asks and I look up from my note book.

"Well, it's just like it's the end of an era. You'd come so far, done so much and now you were about to exit stage left."

Ben chuckles, "You're such a drama queen, M."

"Well, it's true!" I protest and Ben nods, serious again.

"It felt the same to me too. But I was tired, M, and those few years leading up to my retirement had been bittersweet."

"I understand. I can see why you were ready to get off the crazy ride."

"I was, M. I really was ready."

"I know, I know. Carry on…" I urge.

I was really appreciative of Stuart's experienced advice in managing the staff throughout the process and I trusted him implicitly.

Stuart reiterated that whilst we kept this under wraps we needed to be open to the team that there was an investment process going on, to avoid negative rumours.

We agreed that we would follow the truth but with a slight spin, so I pulled together a company meeting.

I explained that we were in need of investment and looking to move onto the next level, therefore they would be seeing a lot of Stuart's staff, as we had appointed them to drive the process. I also explained that there would be lots of various investor meetings but nothing should concern them as it was all positive and that to prepare them for that investment, we needed to create a backdrop of data. They needed to be ready to answer any potential investor questions.

Stuart's spin was absolutely accurate; we really didn't know whether I would find an investor, let alone whether they would take some or all of my shareholding.

Meanwhile, I had interviewed three lawyers and chosen one of London's finest. Jonathan was one of the partners there and he, like Stuart, was somebody I could completely relate to and had to put my trust in with what was the biggest thing I would ever embark on in my whole career; selling my business.

Stuart introduced me to his project manager, Vicki, whose

role was to source and secure prospective buyers, and we gelled straightway. In fact, we all felt that we were a winning team.

The marketing process began with a handbook on the company and setting up the data room, designed to hold every detail of information about the company. This enabled any potential buyers to carry out due diligence.

I had been warned about just how my time and effort would need to go into this by both Stuart and Jonathan but no one could have really prepared me for what was about to happen. We embarked on what seemed a mammoth task; Stuart prepared the marketing material whilst Vicki and her team focused on sourcing thousands of potential prospects.

These prospects would be whittled down from thousands to just a couple of dozen.

With everything else that was going on, this felt like an impossible job and I felt limp and exhausted next to their boundless outgoing energy.

Keep up, I kept telling myself, *you can do this, Ben.*

Somehow, with all this going on, I managed to squeeze some time in to fly to Miami with Mary.

What a cause for celebration it was to watch as the long arm of a cement truck pumped thousands of cubic feet of cement into the site; laying the foundations of our dream home.

Mary and I had spent weeks to get to this point. But they were good times, somehow an outlet to all of the other pressures going on in my life.

Of course, whilst this was wonderful, the next twelve months were going to keep us even busier as we decided which fabrics, fittings and furnishings would best complement our home.

I was also beginning to wonder what the hell I had taken on and whether maybe I should have waited until I had retired before tackling this. Those very thoughts had been voiced by Mary many a time and now resonated in my head, but I suppose with me, when opportunity knocks I don't so much as open the door but embrace it in its entirety.

It was a reality check though, I had a rebellious member of staff, Anne, who seemed hell bent on being disruptive and I had committed to sell the business while still keeping it running as if nothing had changed. I had to just keep digging in if I was going to live out my lifelong ambition of designing and building a home from scratch.

It was game on for this entrepreneur.

The priority was to prevent any disruption to sales and I had a sales team that were not performing at the top of their game.

Whilst global sales, under Carla's management, were growing at an exponential rate, this growth wasn't being matched by the UK sales.

When you consider the enormity of the global task of selling into different cultures and countries, it was inexcusable.

But I knew exactly what was going on; Anne.

I had two choices; I either fired her or I found a solution.

Under any other circumstances, I would have chosen the former and taken the consequences but now that I was selling the company I didn't want to be doing so with a law suit if I could help it. Stuart had emphasised that an ongoing lawsuit could kill any deal and was to be avoided if at all possible.

It was a decision I dwelt on for a few months as I became engaged with the data room and the constant reviewing of the status of potential buyers. The build of my dream home had to become my last priority and I was soon working into the early hours, most days of the week.

By now I was a walking 24/7 machine that was running on empty.

Whenever I did sleep, I would wake thinking of everything I still had to do, my brain felt as though it was being battered with one thousand different thoughts. I just wanted to scream out; "Stop! Stop! Stop!"

Vicki had been doing an amazing job, gradually whittling down over one thousand prospects to a short list of less than twenty.

One of those prospects wanted to meet me and, understandably, visit the office. So, I called another company meeting to reiterate that our investment campaign was well under way and that investors were visiting. Everyone clearly understood that as I was the one with my ears to the ground, my objective was to find investment and Katie, as planned, had fed back to me that they were all in support of this.

The first meeting with what appeared the most interested of all our prospects was very productive and an offer followed right on target.

The company were also willing to meet my criteria of letting me go but retaining my staff.

We were all excited, myself included, but I was also exhausted.

For years, I had felt like I couldn't step away from the business, my baby, but now I was ready. I just wanted to stop this crazy schedule and leave; my business had consumed me and I knew if I didn't get out now, it could be devastating for my health.

It was standard protocol for any prospective buyer that their offer be approved at board level but it was still an agonising two weeks whilst we waited.

I don't ever remember being so anxious, so desperate for something to happen. Every call from Vicki or Stuart shot me another injection of adrenaline. I began to feel like I had become obsessed with a sale and I knew I shouldn't be thinking that way.

It's funny how good news can follow good news and vice versa.

I was in a meeting, dealing with the exit of a staff member, when my receptionist pushed open the door.

"Stuart's on the phone for you, do you want to take it?"

Normally I would have called him back, but not this time, this time my gut instinct told me this was news, and I wanted it now.

I pushed back my chair and excused myself as I tried to walk calmly out of the office

This is it! I thought. I was shaking with excitement. I was confident about this, we all were.

I beckoned Jesscia into my office and closed the door behind us.

"It's Stu," I gestured at the phone, my excitement evident, "I think this is it."

Jessica smiled bravely, I know she was excited for me.

I picked up the phone with a trembling hand.

"Hi Stu."

"Ben, I've just come off the phone with Mathew," I couldn't pick up either positive or negative vibes in Stuarts tone.

"Go on,"

As I heard him take a deep breath, my stomach wrenched.

"The board haven't approved it."

I can't explain what rushed through my body at that time but it felt awful. Probably like scoring an equalising goal in the dying seconds of a world cup final only to realise you were offside and now it was game over.

Stuart was a master class of positivity though.

"Ben," he said in a conciliatory voice, "it happens all the time. Trust me, we'll do this with someone else."

He tried to pep me up by pointing out that we still had others in the pipeline but by now I wasn't listening. Disappointment had never felt so painful.

I came off the phone and looked at Jessica.

"Don't worry, Ben," she said calmly, "if it's going to happen, it will happen."

I knew she was right and I had to believe that. I had to get my head around taking it or leaving it. I stood tall, forced myself into a positive frame of mind and walked back to my meeting.

Nobody had an inkling of what had just occurred.

"Perhaps I really should have taken up acting!"

"Ha ha," I laugh, "I don't know how you did it."

Ben rolls his eyes at me, "Well you wouldn't, you wear your heart on your sleeve, you."

I can't argue with this.

"Anyway," Ben goes on, "that moment became rather insignificant in the scheme of things."

"How come?" I'm intrigued, but I should know now by the bright light in Ben's eyes what it is.

"My second grandchild was born, and for Mary and I, our world lit up again."

Chapter 28

I'm Not Disappointed in My Judgement

Today is Friday 24th June 2016 and Great Britain has just voted to leave the European Union.

Ben literally dances into the Little Red Café.

"Yes, M!" He punches the air with such vigour that I burst out laughing.

"Ha ha, ok, ok!" I shake my head at Doris who is looking across at Ben with an amused yet perplexed smile on her face.

"Oh M," Ben sighs happily, "I can't begin to tell you how I felt when I heard the result."

I look at Ben and raise my eyebrows. "Go on…"

Ben sits back, "You see, now there is real hope for our future and the future of my grandchildren."

"Will you please tell me now why 2077 is such an important year to you?" I ask Ben hopefully.

Ben looks suddenly drained and pale.

"I can't yet, M, can you trust me on this?"

I sigh and look at him. "It's not criminal, is it?"

Ben's face says everything and I immediately apologise.

"Sorry, I just don't want to be implicated in anything dodgy."

Ben smiles wearily, "I'm tired. Now is not the time. This book is not the time." He puts his head in his hands.

"Ready to carry on?" I ask hesitantly and to my surprise he nods, so off we go…

✦ May 2012 ✦

The next day I had a meeting with Anne. I wanted to address the lack of performance of her team and get her on board with the sale, if I could.

"Listen," I was firm but friendly in my approach, "with me gone, who knows what new and fresh opportunities that will bring for you?"

She just shrugged and smirked at me. I felt my patience, along with any hope of her playing ball, waning. I didn't have time for this.

"Anne," I tried again, "we may have our differences but this is my company and you're still working for me. Either follow my strategy or leave with dignity."

"I'm making good sales." She was so dismissive and cold, ignorant to her under-performance.

"You're not though," I was prepared for this and I passed over the sales statistics for the UK versus the global ones, Carla's results. I'd had enough now and Anne had no defence.

"I'm making immediate changes to your team. They will now be reporting to me."

Her eyes widened in genuine surprise and dismay. I got no pleasure from it but at least she seemed to be taking note now.

"You can work alongside me on the high-level accounts." Anne raised her eyebrows in clear disgust at my words but I continued, "this could still be good for you with the new owners. Just wait it out?"

I felt the need to re-iterate this but she obviously saw it all as just spin.

"You won't sell," she shook her head with a patronising smile as she stood up and left my office. I had a sense she was a little embarrassed, but maybe that was just me emphathising with her. Once again, even as I left the door open for Anne to make changes and pick up the positives with a new owner, she still thought she knew better. It was unbelievable.

After that meeting, understandably, things began to freefall; two more staff members walked out sighting Anne as the cause and commotion ensued. The alleged reason was Anne's bullying and the new management team were infuriated.

I was now under even more pressure to react but I didn't want to force anything that would compromise the sale of my business. I desperately wanted to keep a lid on it all but this management team were baying for blood. I had to take control, even if just for a few more months until I had sold up, then somebody else could restructure.

And of course, without a sale, they would hopefully look back and respect my actions.

I discussed my predicament with Stuart and we both agreed on a course of action that meant we addressed this issue head on and faced the repercussions, should there be any.

In other words, work with and support the management team as well as discuss the bullying with Anne in a fair and open meeting to give her a chance to defend herself.

Whilst on paper I agreed with that approach, at the same time I knew this could scupper my sale so I decided to seek legal counsel.

I wanted to ensure we played by the book, that we were fair to all parties; Anne, the rest of the team, and any potential buyer of my business. In fact, the whole point of our data room had been to lay bare every skeleton in our company cupboard, and this was no exception.

I had my own view of what had occurred and I needed to be open and honest but I was determined to follow due diligence by the letter and not allow myself to be emotionally drawn. Anne to me had, after all, brought this on herself despite being offered so many ways out.

Counsel advised that we held a private tribunal with Anne and a representative of her choice.

At the hearing, Anne surprisingly brought along our ex-accountant, Leena, whom she had now befriended, and a letter from the UK sales support lady that had walked, saying she hadn't been bullied; totally contradictory to the telephone call I had had with her.

Even after everything that had occurred in the last few years, I still felt some sympathy for Anne.

After all, she had been a meaningful component to our business over the years, it was very sad that it had come to this. I couldn't even begin to fathom what she must have been thinking.

When Leena suddenly stood up and leaned aggressively across the table to shout abuse, it was completely out of the blue. She had clearly lost it. Even Anne looked a little awkward. I had never seen that before in Leena and I wondered whether she really knew all the facts that had led to this sorry affair, but she was just another example of that damn chemistry clock going off.

I was of course under advice from my lawyer so I simply sat there and allowed Leena to embarrass herself.

When they both walked out, clearly very angry, I breathed a sigh of relief.

That relief was to be very short-lived; within days Anne served me her notice and with it her solicitors confirmation that she would be suing us for wrongful dismissal for what amounted to a figure in excess of £350k.

"Argh, I bloody hate that woman and I've never even met her!"
Ben laughs, "Oh, it didn't stop there, M."

What happened next was extraordinary.

As word got out that Anne had left, there was an outpouring of relief and celebration as well as further allegations against her, not only from existing staff but from more ex-employees.

Christ! How had I been so complicit?

Within days I had affidavits on my lawyer's desk to prove that there was indeed a bullying case to be heard. By taking the action she had, Anne had regrettably forced my hand.

When my lawyer pushed me to finalise my decision I had to conclude overwhelmingly with the evidence that bullying had taken place.

However, I considered myself as the one responsible, after all the buck stopped with me. I should have brought a halt to the whole sorry episode years before.

"Well!" I snort, "Even I could see that coming!"
Ben looks at me with a smile, but I can see the warning in his eyes; don't push it, M.
"The beauty of hindsight, eh, M?"
I'm suitably admonished and I allow him to carry on.

I had so many mixed feelings, all on top of the huge workload that I was struggling to cope with.

Of course, I had to take responsibility for overlooking any bullying, yet I had been so focused on the business.

Nevertheless, I still felt guilty. I had let it happen.

I had liked Anne, had with absolute sureity seen in her what Stan must have seen in me. But now but I realised Anne was nothing like me despite my being a Stan to her.

I'm feeling bad for my outburst just now and starting to see how let down Ben must have felt by Anne and his own intuition.

"You should feel more proud that you gave her so many chances, rather than disappointed in your judgement." *I offer sheepishly.*

"I'm not disappointed in my judgement, M."

Oh Christ, I think, have I offended him again?

"Far from it," *he goes on,* "Anne had given fifteen years to my company and in the main, they were good years. I don't know why or how things changed so badly. Sometimes business can do that to people."

I nod, feeling awkward now, and I make myself look busy with my note book.

"Oi," *Ben kicks me gently under the table.*

"What?"

"Why are you scribbling down a load of nonsense?"

I blush and chortle as I look at him.

"How do you know?" *Christ, how is it this guy makes me feel like a kid all the time?*

"Because Stan taught me how to read upside down, it came in handy for meetings such as this and I can see you're writing nonsense!" *Ben chuckles and I want to kick him back, hard.*

"You take me far too seriously, M." *Ben laughs out loud, obviously pleased that he's wound me up, yet again.*

"Dear God," *I mutter, shaking my head as we continue...*

Whilst the other prospective buyers were interesting, overall, they weren't in the best interest of my personal goal or of the future of my staff.

We were now nine months in and I was beginning to wonder whether I should just give up on finding a buyer.

I carefully weighed up my options with Stan in my head again.

Don't make decisions on emotions, Ben. Take time to step away and you will see it differently in twenty-four hours.

I had always taken that great advice on board and as the stress began to take its toll, I made my decision; I simply couldn't continue, I was mentally and physically exhausted.

The next day when I met with Stuart and Vicki, they brought me back from the brink of despair.

"There is momentum and real interest out there, Ben." Stuart was his usual upbeat self and Vicki too remained so positive. "It's all about timing."

Their words washed over me and I sat there numbly, wishing somebody would make the decision for me.

"Ben," Stuart tried again, "What do you have to lose? Give it another three months and if we're still in the same place, then step back."

I sighed wearily, "I just don't know."

"Look," Stuart spoke with such empathy that this time I sat up and took notice, "this is what you wanted for your grandchildren. I know you're exhausted, hell, I have no idea how you're still standing, but if you can just stand for another few months, it could be worth it."

Suddenly it felt as though Stu had morphed into Stan; giving me that motivational speech, telling me to man up, and he was right. I hadn't come this far to just give up now. This was what I wanted, I had two grandchildren to focus on, retirement was key to doing that.

It was like the penny suddenly dropped, and then I heard Stan in my head again. *Give it more time, Ben.*

I knew I had to go on.

"Yes," I said, whether to Stuart, Stan or myself I don't know. Maybe all three?

"Yes," I repeated, "Ok, I can do this. I can wait. But only three months, Stu, ok?"

I could almost hear the click of Stan's lighter as he lit up a celebratory cigarette.

+   +   +

Now that Anne was pursuing a law suit, the challenge to sell had just upped its stakes.

Stuart was adamant that we settle out of court but I knew that by doing that at such an early stage would signal defeat, not to mention an open cheque book. I knew Anne wouldn't budge from her lawsuit claim.

My mind switched into ball mode. This was going be a tough one; I was up against someone I had coached myself. It's so much harder to find the ball in the first place than keep your eye on it and for several days, as I dwelt on it, I just couldn't find it.

Was I losing my touch? Was I trying too hard? As usual, that bloody ball was eluding me, wasn't it?

Of course not, because two nights later, my subconscious did its bedtime magic and I woke up with that ball; Anne never thought I would ever sell the business and was convinced that my son would take the reins.

That was the ball; I had to convince her I wasn't selling and that my son was taking over instead.

> *"Ooh, clever!" I squeal and clap my hands, loving all the drama and intrigue.*
>
> *"Good old Stan again, eh, M?"*
>
> *"Absolutely, love that man! Now get on with it." I tell Ben impatiently and he laughs.*

I immediately spun out the news to the few sources close to Anne that I was departing to the US and that my son was taking over.

With that, I sat back and watched that ball in play as the negotiations started.

My case had already been strengthened by the affidavits that I had collected from those that had accused Anne of bullying, so it was over to my lawyer to make our case to her lawyers.

She told them we would see them in court where Anne's reputation would be brought into disrepute as well as the public eye. Of course, the fact was, had Anne pushed me, I would have had to settle at her ludicrous figure of £350k.

We simply had to wait to see if it would play out our way or simply blow up in our faces.

Of course, while everything else was going on, business always seemed to take its natural day to day course.

In my last year of running the business I felt like I was riding an express train, with life rushing past in black and white.

There was no time to stop and gaze, no time to soak up the moments as the campaign rushed forward cutting through one problem after another and dragging a wake of unresolved issues behind it.

Every day was different, sometimes we were dealing with a development, sales or personal issue which could take up half the day. All that meant for me was a longer evening in the office or even more time at the weekend to play catch up.

Of course, in that last year we were running the business as usual whilst working on the secret agenda of putting ourselves up for sale. That obviously added an incredible pressure to an already tough daily workload. Jessica and I were now not only pulling together a monthly profit and loss account and cash flow forecast, but we were frequently involved in digging back into our results to interpret them in a way that suited the flood of questioning coming in from prospective buyers.

I would meet regularly with my IT manager, Pat, to check the progress on our IT status. Pat had created a well thought through, but complex, infrastructure which we became heavily reliant upon, for its security, speed and uptime. Pat was brilliant. It was truly a critical lifeline to our business. Because of the sale, I was pushing through a new project, pioneered with Pat, to bring online a whole host of new reports to provide me with tactical information to allow me to better manage the sales and marketing teams and easy present those stats to our prospective buyers. The more sales and profit, the better the sale price, so I was pushing every single sale and restricting the spend of every single pound that I could.

This meant pushing UK sales, trying to improve results, a difficult task when at that point, shortly before she departed, I was dealing with the backlash of Anne's orientated frustrations; the will just wasn't there anymore.

Carla was still quite brilliantly driving our global sales, and despite her own personal crisis's she showed extraordinary determination. She was on a mission to prove she was better than Anne and against all the odds of selling internationally to countries on the other side of the world, thirty odd countries to be precise, she was going to prove she could sell more than the UK.

And she did.

Between everything else, I had a recruitment campaign ongoing to bring in at least two new account managers, knowing the sales team needed replenishing with new blood. Those interviews were picked up through the day as part of my five-minute interviews, the odd one turning into a full-blown interview.

There would be a daily call from Vicki to update me on the progress of gathering prospects and usually a meeting with Stuart as and when he engaged prospects.

Then a meeting with Jonathan or one of his team as they pushed for outstanding data room information.

In light of the sale, my meetings with each team were different because I was working with each departmental manager to improve their game and to engage them in bringing online positive changes. Some would improve the results and some would just improve efficiency.

I had no guilty conscience in driving them harder, it was a win- win situation; either it would result in a better sale and future for them, or simply a better and more efficient company for me to continue to drive.

Either way the staff would benefit, as would I, and believe me, I was a pretty hard task master.

Mary was brilliant during this time and so patient as quite often I would arrive home late to dinner in the oven. I'd take a couple of hours break over dinner to catch up with the news and then I'd be back in my home office, cutting through the huge pile of emails that had built up during the day. I couldn't even tell you whether I was enjoying any part of this at that point. In my mind, it was just simply something I had to get on with. To bat through as many issues as I could, to get through and survive this. It was determination not enjoyment that was getting me through, thus reinforcing my reasons behind wanting to leave.

It was like sweeping an incoming tide off the beach, it just kept coming, and after I had responded to the handful of international emails, I would finally sleep around midnight.

My mind had become highly trained and wired to sleep on problems but Stan had always encouraged me to have a pad by my bedside, just as I had told Sasha and others to do. This was now done via my phone and I would wake up during the night to type a quick note to myself. Quite often though, my subconscious would do the job for me and I would wake having miraculously solved various problems whilst I'd slept. Now when I stop and contemplate how that happened, it still astounds me. The next day would be a repeat process of the day before, with a whole set of different problems and new challenges. No day was ever the same, or for that matter, normal.

"Incredible, you didn't stop." I genuinely don't know how Ben coped.

"I sometimes felt like I was going to explode under the pressure." Ben admits.

"Could you have actually had any more pressure piled on you at this stage?"

"Oh yes, M, oh yes I could."

One of those days was actually quite extraordinary.

It had started as a fairly usual day, we had customers in for a lunch meeting and were to dine in our large cathedral-ceilinged meeting room where I was due to join them.

The sun was shining through the back of the house and lighting up the manicured lawns and shrubs which were a vista we all enjoyed, it was such an inspirational setting. I walked from my office to make tea in the kitchen and looked out at the gardens, a smile on my face as I saw two deer standing in the corner of the manicured lawn.

I felt calm and peaceful for a brief moment.

All of a sudden there was a large bang followed by the sound of panicked screams and I looked around to see one of my staff running towards the meeting room.

I quickly followed, my heart racing at what could have happened.

Entering the meeting room, I was greeted by the sight of my team and my customers sitting around the frame of what had once been the huge glass conference table. It had just exploded into tiny glass fragments and everyone was covered in broken shards. Some people were crying but some simply sat in silent shock. There was blood everywhere.

How on Earth had that happened?

Thankfully, our customers and my staff all accepted that this was a fluke incident and no action was taken. This was a great relief to our furniture supplier as well as myself, I had considered just how much this would affected the sale of the business if we had been sued.

I did, however, maybe through paranoia or stress, wonder if this was a sign. Was everything literally about to explode in my face?

During this time, Stuart and Vicki brought another four companies in for negotiations.

The two front runners that I was really excited about were a US and a UK company. To be honest I was quite overwhelmed by the interest in our business. In my heart and my head, I knew it had an amazing future but I didn't know if this was a reality or my passion making me biased.

I can only describe that summer as another bear pit. We were answering questions from every angle about every aspect of the business, I was playing out a lawsuit, the house design was still in need of weekly decisions and this was all on top of the usual business demands.

I've mentioned before how you can meet someone and feel an instant chemistry. Well, that happened when I met Richard, the chairman of Macren, and a potential buyer.

With Stuart and Vicki there to support me, I gave my presentation to him.

Once he'd listened, he talked about his company and I started to feel a buzz of hope that this could be the right buyer for the future of my business.

Once Richard had left, I looked at Stuart and Vicki as they sat waiting for my reaction.

"Well?" Stuart raised his eyebrows.

"This is my priority," I replied, and Stuart got to work on it.

Chapter 29

What's the Worst that Can Happen?

+ July 2012 +

Two weeks after my presentation to Richard of Macren, Stuart and Vicki came to see me with huge smiles on their faces.

We'd had an offer of £65million.

Immediately, with my stomach in knots, I declined, but Stuart was confident that he could raise the stakes.

I knew I was in good hands as he went off to negotiate and I was still feeling hopeful about the other prospects in the background.

I told Stuart that if we were going to get this deal, we needed to make sure every stipulation was in place. I wasn't moving until I had a £70 million plus deal, with a three year, two days per month consultancy contract in a strategic role, as well as their commitment to staying on in our premises for a minimum of two years.

I also wanted the deal to be completed by 20th October as I needed to be in Miami for the handover of our new home.

As I reeled off my requests, I paused and looked at Stuart.

"I know that's a big ask," I acknowledged, "but that's really non-negotiable. This company has been growing at an exponential rate now, quarter on quarter for three years."

"That's not a problem," Stuart took it all in his stride. Both he and Vicki were always so positive, they both had a huge 'can do' attitude. How lucky I had been to work with those two?

Meanwhile, after almost three months, we got a call from Anne's lawyers. They were willing to settle. Under advice from my lawyer, I told them I would pay just one year of Anne's salary, including bonus, and no more, and I held firm.

They accepted, of course they did, they knew they had a weak case.

Another success for me, but not a pleasant experience. As for Anne, what a pity; had she stayed, here would have been the possibility of a directorship or even CEO position within a PLC company and she could have been on a salary more than twice of that she received from me, let alone gifting back her shares. I guess she really took her eye off the ball, but this time, it wasn't one for me to find.

With the Macren deal, the one thought in all of our minds was would this be a repeat of the last offer that fell at board level.

Every single phone call had me in a state of controlled hysteria at this point. The waiting became intolerable.

Then one morning, I was in my office with Jessica pulling together the management accounts when the phone rang.

"Stuart for you," as my receptionist connected him, I mouthed to Jessica, "it's Stuart."

My heart was pounding in my chest and my mouth was dry.

Dear God, I thought, would this be déjà vu or was this it? Was this a counter offer or was this another disappointment? I tried to prepare myself for the worst but Stuart didn't mess around.

"Ben, we're in business," were his very first words, and I punched the air. Yes!

I could hear Stuart smiling through the phone as he set out the details of the Macren deal.

"Richard has come back with an offer of exactly £70 million plus all of your cash. He has also agreed to remunerate you and stay in the premises. What's more, he said they will agree to fast track the due diligence and close before you go to the States."

I couldn't believe it, I had everything I had asked for.

"Yes! Yes!" I was practically jumping up and down, then I looked at Jessica who I could see was clearly happy for me but I didn't miss the sadness in her eyes.

I knew how she felt, I suppose in a way, it was bittersweet for me too. The end of an era, but oh such a bloody relief.

I didn't fail to notice that I was selling the company itself for that £70million figure I had told Gary I would sell out for, all those years ago.

In total, though, it was a £77 million deal, and it once again brought me back to Shirley and her lucky sevens prediction. Fate or luck, who knows? It's something that would haunt me till my dying day.

But, right at that moment, who cared? I had done it and now it was time to take a bow and make my exit.

"I'm so proud of you." I beam at Ben, tears shining in my eyes.

"Ha, steady on M, this was a few years ago!"

I shake my head. "Not to me, to me it's just happened. You must have felt overwhelming relief."

"That's putting it mildly!" Ben retorts. "You know those moments when people describe something as surreal? Well that was my moment. But there was another surreal moment to come. It was bittersweet, M, let me tell you."

I'm practically on the edge of my seat as Ben continues.

I had told myself to take small steps, to solve each problem, one at a time; and, finally, I had.

The Anne issue was resolved, my new home in Miami was now pretty much sorted and I had a deal on the table that was just subject to due diligence.

And then we had further proof of my belief that good news follows good news when our little grandchild number three arrived in the world; our daughter's beautiful little girl.

The feeling was immense, Mary and I were so very proud and I was all the more determined to get this deal over and done with to ensure I could spend precious time with the little ones.

In the coming weeks, once the due diligence had been completed, we pushed to try and close the deal earlier. There seemed no reason not to, but then Stuart called me with some worrying news.

"There's something going on," he quickly blurted. "I'm told Macren's finance director is still awaiting confirmation from the bank before the deal can close."

This was a concern; bank approval wasn't something they had shared with us. In my head, Stan's words suddenly came back to haunt me – The deal's not done till the money's in the bank.

My heart sank.

I knew Stuart was worried too; he had seen so many fall right there at the winning post.

As my mind raced with a cacophony of what if's, Stuart urged me to stay positive.

"Don't forget what I told you, be prepared to carry on if this does fall over, ok?"

Stuart also went on to inform me that he'd heard Macren were also in talks with one of our competitors. To say things were looking shaky was an understatement.

"Oh no! What had happened now?" I can't believe this, I thought things were about to end on a high.

Ben laughs and pats my hand affectionately.

"Calm down, M. Like I said, it was a bittersweet time. And that was the sweet bit."

My eyes widen in shock, "Are you serious?"

The only way I could deal with this rollercoaster of emotion though, was to plan for the worst. And there was Stan again.

Ben, what's the worst that can happen?

Erm, well, Stan, the deal could fall through, my team could have a less than positive future and my family don't get to see me again because of work. Other than that, not much!

I was beginning to panic and I knew I had to tell myself some home truths; to put things into perspective.

I still had my company, this time without the baggage of Anne, I had a great team and I had the support of my family. This was not a disaster and I literally began to prepare my head for another reset.

"So that sale didn't happen? Oh, that's just dreadful Ben…"

Again, Ben laughs, "M, stop with the drama queen act and let me finish, it's not all bad, there's a twist here."

And as it turned out, it wasn't a disaster. A week before the dead-line, we got the all clear; both on the bank and the confirmation that we were a better option than our competitors.

The deal would be done by Friday.

As Macren were a public company, the city would have to be told on Friday morning. It was now all very fast track stuff.

This also meant that the value would be disclosed, something I hadn't particularly wanted but I could live with it. People could make assumptions on how much was being paid but they couldn't ever figure out what my debts, costs and tax charges were. Neither would they know to what degree my investments had increased my wealth.

The plan was to complete the contracts in my lawyer's offices when the city closed at 4.30pm on Thursday and to hold a company meeting at 8am on Friday to announce the new investor.

I needed to think about my speech but I was too excited to think, I just needed to get through Thursday first to be sure the money was transferred.

Meanwhile I announced to everybody that Friday's meeting would be a breakfast one with caterers laying on a cooked breakfast for all.

Suddenly the office was buzzing with anticipation and excitement at the news to come.

Thursday couldn't come soon enough for me and when it did, it was a strange, sweet moment, tinged with some sadness.

At my lawyer's office, we signed the papers and they were faxed off as Jonathan brought in a huge bottle of champagne and we waited for confirmation that the money had been transferred.

It seemed like an eternity and I was so tense as we sat around making small talk, but at the same time, I felt a kind of calmness, I was so near that finish line. I think I laughed more that day than I had in years. When Jonathan finally announced that the money was in, it was a moment of epiphany; quite surreal.

I wanted to hop around and scream with delight, to let out all that pent-up emotion as though I were at a football match. But I kept it dignified and we all hugged and shook hands. I let the emotion in my heart dance though, wanting to keep it there forever.

Anything is possible, I thought, *if you believe in it enough.*

We popped the champagne, clinked our glasses and enjoyed what was a very happy moment. I actually felt a bit stunned. The numbers that had, for months, been rolling around my head, were real, and sitting in my bank account.

Later that evening, I had to write my speech and what a speech it needed to be.

For nearly thirty years, I had ground away and risked everything to create my company. I had endured a multitude of experiences; some good, some not so along this rollercoaster ride to such an achievement. I took with me another positive; that I had made a difference to so many people who had worked with me.

I had felt emotions that I never knew I had and learned some valuable lessons as I grew up with the company, sometimes allowing it to drag me to the edge of my competence, but never over it.

Now, it felt like I had brought a child into adulthood and it was time to say goodbye, forever. In truth, it was probably one of the most emotional events one could ever experience, other than the birth of my children and grandchildren. This *had* been my baby. I had experienced pride and a unique and immeasurable experience, but now it was time to say farewell.

Now, as I sit writing up these notes, I feel quite sad that I am coming to the end of Ben's story. And what a story it has been; so many highs and lows, the thrill of success and the heartache of striving for it.

I have come to like and admire Ben so much over these past few months. More than that, I have true respect for him.

Yes, he's been difficult to crack and at times so frustrating I could have walked away. Why didn't I?

Because maybe in some ways he and I are the same. Of course, I'm no business guru and he's certainly no hopeless romantic, but what we share is the same will and desire to succeed; to take something and give it our best. We never give up.

I am forever grateful to Ben for giving me this opportunity and it means a lot to me that he has trusted me and shared so much of his life with me.

It's often felt like a whirlwind; flying to Miami on a private jet, sailing on private boats. I feel like I've gone from being a bit part player in the story of my own life to finally taking centre stage.

And it feels amazing.

Chapter 30

Let's Do This

It's our final meeting and as I prepare to hear the last of Ben's business story he surprises me with a question.

"M, I'm interested to know, over the course of almost two years together, what about my story stands out for you?"

"Gosh, that's thrown me," I mutter and sit back to reflect, "there's been so much!"

"Well just summarise then!" Ben says impatiently and I tut, glaring at him.

"Ok, well, here's the thing;

1 *Dex starts up, only to be threatened by closure because of Onelock going into meltdown.*

2 *You take the business and then iCAD hits your sales hard.*

3 *No sooner have you set a recovery plan, then Nelson nearly takes you out.*

4 *You dust yourself off, and then you're hit by the 1991 recession."*

Ben looks at his watch, "No offence, M, but I do actually have to be somewhere else at some point this year."

I roll my eyes. "Ok! Patience, dear boy, let me finish! You're the one that asked!"

Ben sighs but allows me to continue.

5 *Onwards and upwards you go, then Visual force another reset situation.*

6 *You rebuild again and GV threaten you with a legal battle.*

7 *Then another recession hits.*

8 *Your ex-shareholder and board director brings legal proceedings.*

9 *Then your buyer pulls out…"*

Ben simply stares at me. "Jeez, M, thanks for reminding me of all the positives!"

I burst out laughing, "But don't you see, there is a positive?"

"Really?" Ben is incredulous.

"Haha, yes," I nod. "That breakdown is made up of nine points."

Ben is confused so I explain.

"As a cat lover, I see that as your nine lives, and that's what stands out."

Ben shakes his head, still clearly not getting my point.

"You, like a cat, have fallen many times but always landed on your feet."

As my analogy dawns on Ben, he smiles at me, clearly amused.

"Where did I get you from, eh?"

I chuckle and Ben clears his throat suddenly.

"So, M, are we ready for my swan song; the final curtain?"

I nod and bite my lip to stop it from trembling.

"Hey," Ben touches my arm, "like you said, it's only the end of my business story."

"I know," I choke back tears and look across to Doris. Christ, I'm even going to miss her.

I take a deep breath, pick up my note book and look at Ben.
"Let's do this."

✛ October 2012 ✛

As I sat writing that speech, I admit I cried. Would I cry when I delivered it? I had crossed the business bridge and was left with so many memories and emotions. There had been hardship, elation and the understanding that tears can come from pain and joy. And now it was time to take a bow and exit stage left, as M would say.

The stock market opened at 8am which is when I had asked everybody to be seated.

Macren were planning to arrive at 8.30am and I would introduce them, step back and walk away. Yep, literally just walk away. Those words echoed such finality but of course it really was the final chapter.

I was nervous, not just for myself but for the staff too, especially my loyal and trusted friend Jessica and all of my management team.

I stood before them all, fighting back the emotion that was welling up inside me, the tears in my eyes blurring my vision.

I held the paper that I had written my speech on and looked across at my team; the people that had been so much a part of the success I now had. I placed the paper down in front of me.

I didn't need it; this was from my heart.

"Good morning. I hope you all had a good breakfast.

Well, today is a very exciting day for this company. As I speak, the stock exchange is releasing the news that Macren, a UK public Company, are our new investors."

I paused to allow the news to sink in and looked out at their shocked faces.

With a trembling voice, I continued.

"Macren have acquired 100% of my shareholding." The room

was suddenly filled with murmurs and rumbling voices so I had to speak even louder.

"I have chosen this company because they will continue to support our goals and that means keeping this amazing team together. Furthermore, they will bring a level of expertise beyond what we could have hoped for and with it investment. That investment will secure your future."

The room was buzzing with drama and tension and I could tell they didn't want to hear anything more, they just wanted to ask questions.

I went on to give my final statement, desperately hoping that the Macren cavalry would arrive on time and rescue me from breaking down in tears.

"As a result, I will be standing down with immediate effect. I will however be providing consultancy support, albeit on an international level."

At that moment, I looked over towards my management team, some of their faces were like thunder. It was clear nobody had seen this coming. Just like Anne, no one thought I would ever sell up.

"Macren will, in fact, be here in 15 minutes and they'll present to you and give you one to one time. Meanwhile I am happy to take any questions."

The questions came fast and furious, most of them quite probing, but I answered them openly and honestly. When somebody asked, in quite an accusatory tone, "Why have you sold and are just walking away?"

I explained with sincerity, in a slightly shaky voice.

"I am sixty years old. I have given every ounce of myself to this company since it began almost thirty years ago.

I've risked my family's finances. I've missed watching my children grow up and I want to watch my grandchildren grow up and to be a big part of their little lives."

The room fell silent and the person who's question I had just answered nodded his head in understanding, well what could anyone say to that?

A few minutes later, Macren arrived and I introduced them and allowed them to take over proceedings. Once they had delivered their vision, everybody, including myself, mingled a while in the room. Most of the team congratulated me though some were a little upset with me and I'm not sure to this day as to why.

When Richard suggested I make my way home and go and enjoy my new home and well deserved holiday and retirement, I thanked him, hugged a tearful Jessica as well as a lot of the more positive staff, and left.

As I drove away, tears rolled down my cheeks. I had no regrets for what I had done, not even for a second, I was just overcome with emotion.

The way I had left the business was the way I had started; in control and on my terms. That felt good.

The journey had been an amazing one but now it had ended. I had nurtured my beloved company, Dex, through all of this and, for her, with this sale, another journey was about to begin.

In winding the clock back it's hard to comprehend the levels of energy, advice, determination, training and loyalty, they were unprecedented. It had been the most rewarding and successful journey I could ever have dreamt of.

And now here I was facing my Twilight years, I was actually here in retirement at sixty years old.

How would I cope after being so used to life in the fast lane? Could I really just stop or would I push on with a new venture to make more millions? It made me wonder, was I still wired for wealth or ready for retirement?

+ + +

There was no time to dwell on my exit, which was probably a good thing, as we were flying off to Miami, with the buzz of seeing our new home.

We knew our builder, Ryan, had organised a welcome party and when we landed, we were full of excitement and anticipation. The last time we had seen the house was a few months ago and it had appeared far from complete.

I knew now it would be impressive; the layout and design was what I had been going to sleep with in my head and often, when I was going through those tough times, it was what drove me on. It had been a kind of therapy. In my mind, I would regularly walk through the front door and wander around the house taking in all the detail. Now I was about to see it for real.

As we dove through the front gates, I was filled with pride, not only at the grandeur of the park entrance but the fact that we had created something quite special in a very unique environment. The impressive drive up to the house was lined with palm trees and beautifully manicured gardens, all amongst the back drop of the pine forest.

A playful herd of deer fled across the road and into the sanctuary of the forest, and we drove past a lake bordered with an exquisitely precise rock garden and a water fall.

I sigh wistfully and Ben raises his eyebrows. "Ah yes, that reminds me, M, what did you whisper to that little deer when you were out in Miami with us?"

I flush bright red. "I didn't think you noticed!"

Ben gently laughs. "I've noticed everything, M. Your eye rolls when I take a call, your sadness when I talk of Stan, or anyone close to me who I've lost. Your emotion when I speak of those I love. I see it all."

I smile shyly and allow Ben to continue.

We drove across the arching bridge, through fiery clumps of Oleander blossoms that decorated the lush grass with pink and white puffs of colour and paved the way to our beautiful new home.

My heart was beating through my chest as we turned into our road and I blinked with amazement as I glanced up at our home.

It was a picture of magnificence, so pretty, so Italian looking. The landscaping was impeccable and as the daylight was fading the lighting around the house and the plants provided a soft and luxurious feel to the moment. It was a picture of great beauty and pure indulgence.

Ryan and our designer, Mel, came out with flutes of champagne which we emptied with such happiness and joy in our hearts.

They both had the whole house staged to show it at its very best. Music played softly throughout the house and the lighting beautifully emphasised every little detail.

They say first impressions last and I will never forget mine; it will sit in my head forever, not to be diluted by familiarisation.

I wanted to create long sight lines out to the lake within the house and the first line I created was from the front door down to the pool, catching the edge of the infinity pool and the lake beyond, and there it was.

We walked into the great room with its cathedral window towering thirty feet high by twenty-five feet wide and framing that masterful view. It was pure poetry.

I loved the bridge over the great room that isolated the master bedroom and bathroom, the walk across it commanding a lake view.

I felt like I was like walking into the wardrobe in the 'Chronicles of Narnia'.

And it was ours; everything we had dreamed of.

A few months later, we entertained the whole family in our beautiful home and it was yet another moment to treasure. I held a party to say thank you to the team that made it all happen, all those folks in the development team, the builders team, the suppliers and all of our dear friends out there.

It was show off time after creating something that, even if I say so myself, really was quite special.

We were so excited to share it with the grandchildren, and as their laughter filled the air and the fire pit burned like a blue cauldron at the side of the pool, I looked around me; savouring this moment.

Thirty years of business had taken me to the brink at times but this made it all so very worth it.

"Take a bow, Mr Taylor." I smile proudly at Ben and his eyes are watering as he mocks a flourishing bow to me.

"It suddenly felt like a whole new experience, having time to think, to see what was around me. Time to even get bored if I wanted to.

But it was also a shock. I had literally gone from 24/7 pressure to nothing but relaxation and I had to re-teach myself to do that. I'd forgotten how."

I nod as Ben speaks. "It's quite an extreme I suppose, but then let's be honest, you don't exactly relax now anyway."

Ben laughs, "It's how my mind is conditioned. I still feel guilty now if I sit down and do no work. I think, without the planning, managing my share portfolio, my properties and other things, I'd go bonkers."

"Speaking of other things, how are you getting on with the football club issue?"

Ben sighs, "There have been some changes there, not necessarily for the good. But I'm on to it."

"Still not found that ball yet?" For one final time, I refer to Stan.

"Oh, I've seen glimpses of it," Ben groans, "trouble is it's when it's being picked out of our goal!"

I chuckle and I know he's not going to tell me anymore right now, so I close my note book and look at him.

"Ok, I think we're done." The words sound so final, even though I know this isn't the end.

Ben looks at me, "I guess we are, for now…"

I fight back my tears and I can see Ben is a little sad too.

"Look, M." I look at him and he pushes his hand against his forehead. "I've been thinking a lot about whether to share this with you."

My heart sinks to my stomach. What fresh hell is he about to impart now? Was he about to tell me the secret behind 2077? Do I want to know?

"Wh… what is it?" I finally stammer, my heart is thumping in my ears.

"Ok, look," Ben sighs. "I'm not good at this stuff."

"You don't say!" I reply and Ben ignores me.

"I have enjoyed this journey with you, M. So much so that I'd like to begin another."

My mouth gapes open.

He smiles. "Yes, I need to finish this story, but it needs to end on another high."

"Another high?" I'm intrigued as to what he is suggesting. "Does that include your secret of 2077?"

Ben takes a deep breath and nods his head.

"The more I've revisited my past during this project, the more I've thought about what Shirley told me."

He runs a shaky hand through his hair and my heart begins to thump in my chest.

"I could write her words off as a result of too much pot, but I recently discovered something and I simply can't ignore what she told me anymore."

"Ben, what was it she told you?" I'm desperate to know.

"Well, you know, there was all that stuff about the lucky sevens, and Stan?"

"Yes, yes, and then Melony showing up in Vegas and the Grand Canyon; possibly the M Shirley referred to. I know all that, but what else was there?"

"Oh God, M." Ben sits with his head in his hands and I'm petrified at what he is about to say.

The silence ticks by until he finally speaks.

"With my wealth, and the realisation that maybe Shirley really had travelled into the future, I decided to invest in some research. I hired a guy called Matt, and we've been working on Shirley's theory for a few years now. In fact, we concluded our research just before I found you."

"And what was the conclusion?" I hear the quiver in my voice and Ben takes my hand.

"I'll never forget the day Matt called me, screaming hysterically…" Ben draws breath and closes his eyes.

"Jesus, Ben. What had he discovered?" I pull my hand away quickly, wondering whether to run; that fight or flight instinct taking a hold of me.

"M, you have to trust me on this, ok? You will meet someone in a few weeks and they will explain it you."

"What? You're not going to tell me?" I'm furious. Ben has scared the crap out of me and now he's leaving me hanging, again.

I tell him this and he mutters an apology.

"Look, you need to keep calm; all will be revealed soon."

My heart sinks but my disappointment is mixed with relief. Maybe I'm not ready to hear the secret that Ben holds so close, not yet.

I nod at Ben; I know he's not going to tell me now but it can't really be that bad. After all, it's Ben. I know him now, don't I?

Fittingly, as we finish our drinks, the radio hums into action. Never once over the course of our many meetings here has that bloody radio played a single tune.

Yet today, our final one for this particular project anyway, it plays a swan song - Time to Say Goodbye.

I look knowingly at Ben, "Shirley never mentioned a Doris, did she?"

We both shiver and stand up. With a final goodbye to Doris, not that she knows it's the last, we walk out of the Little Red Café together.

"Until next time, M." Ben says meaningfully, and he walks away.

+ + +

Later, I finish my writing my notes and I email Ben;

"All done, perhaps now I can sleep without Stan's cigarettes waking me or Shirley with her traverses?"

Bens reply makes me chuckle. "For goodness sake, M, just get some bloody sleep!"

And so I do.

Epilogue

*You are cordially invited to the pre-launch party of
Twenty 77 – The Secret Entrepreneur…*

The huge ballroom is lit by thousands, literally thousands of tiny
candles and the tables and chairs are decorated in a turquoise and
purple covering; the main colours of the front of the book cover.
There is a huge screen above the stage with a picture of the book
and of me on it.

This is it; the pre-launch party.

Jack Bourne, as good as his word, has really promoted us and
has organised this whole event. There are hundreds of people here.
I spot Richard and Judy over in the corner talking to somebody
and I shake my head and laugh in surprise when I realise it's my
dad. This is surreal.

Flutes of champagne are being carried on silver trays by hand-
some young waiters in tuxedos and beautiful models are offering
around the canapes.

I'm wearing a black satin gown that is strapless and sweeps
down to the floor in luxurious folds. I feel incredible and I shiver
in anticipation of the night to come.

As people mill about sipping their drinks and making small
talk, I feel a sudden pang of sadness that Ben isn't here. But, of
course he can't be here. Because nobody knows who he is.

I take a deep breath and prepare to greet our guests.

"Mandy, hey, over here!" I turn at the sound of Jacks voice and
smile brightly as I walk towards him.

"Thank you so much for all of this," I kiss his cheek and he laughs. "It's nothing, you'll be paying me back when you're a famous author anyway."

I laugh too, then Jack takes my arm. "Come with me, I want you to meet Milly."

My eyes widen. I've heard a lot about this Milly person, Jacks fiancé, from his tweets and I'm desperate to see what she looks like.

As Jack guides me to a table in front of the stage, I am stopped by the occasional person congratulating me on the book and wishing me success. I feel like a movie star!

"Milly, this is Mandy." A platinum blonde woman stands to greet me, a broad smile on her bright red lips, showing off her perfect white teeth.

"Well hi honey, how are you?" Milly drawls and I just about stop myself from bursting into uncontrollable giggles. Well of course she was going to be the typical Californian girl. She's a complete Taylor Swift lookalike and I can't wait to tell Ben about this, he'll be in fits.

I make small talk with Milly until Jack tells us to take our seats and then he gets up on the stage and speaks into the microphone, requesting all the other guests do the same.

After a few moments, when everybody is seated, Jack speaks again.

"Well, ladies and gentlemen, I'd like to start by thanking all of you for coming. It's wonderful to have you all here to share this special night and to celebrate the pre-launch of Twenty 77 – The Secret Entrepreneur by Amanda Armstrong."

Everybody cheers here as they raise their glasses in my direction and I blush and humbly nod my thanks. *Rah! Stop looking at me!*

Jack continues, thank God, and the attention is back on him.

"Now, there is of course someone missing tonight, and that's the secret entrepreneur. Well," Jack laughs, "he wouldn't be much of a secret if he did come, would he?"

I chuckle along with the audience, feeling another pang at Ben's absence.

"In fact," Jack goes on, "he's such a secret that I haven't even met him myself!" The audience roars with laughter as Jack shouts, "It's true!"

Once the laughter has died down, Jack becomes serious; a first for my wild and crazy agent.

"He did, however, email me with something he wanted me to read out, so here goes."

I'm confused. Apart from the initial contact when Ben hired Jack, I know they have had none since. What is it that Ben has asked Jack to read? Why didn't Ben send it to me?

I look up at Jack as he begins to speak.

"As M has stormed through this book weaving my story around hers, I have really begun to understand the hours that go into a project like this. Over the last year or so, as well as our regular meetings, I've handed over pages of notes that I'd written up and told her to go and decipher it all. It must have driven M crazy!"

I smile and nod as everybody laughs and turns to me for confirmation.

"Yet, incredibly, M is like a sponge. She's a natural at grasping what is in my head and translating it onto the page in her own very unique way. Nothing phases her. Well, most of the time…" Jack pauses as the audience burst into laughter again and I feign shocked offence but I'm laughing too. I can almost hear Ben saying that. *Cheeky sod!*

Jack continues.

"Seriously though, M. You've done a great job, and I am so glad to have you, not just as my biographer, but as my friend too. Enjoy your evening, M, and I wish our book, and you, every success that is deserved. And remember, never take your eye off that ball."

The tears roll down my face as everyone stands and applauds. I'm truly overwhelmed by Ben's words. I stand up and accept the applause, and inside I'm applauding Ben, for giving me this moment.

Later, after much champagne and lots of dancing, I'm suddenly exhausted.

"I'll get you a cab," Jack offers when I tell him I need to go home.

"Thank you." I smile, "And Jack?"

Jack turns, his bright blue eyes twinkling in his tanned face. "Yes."

"Thank you for all this," I gesture the ballroom, "I really appreciate it."

Jack gives me a cheeky wink. "You're welcome Mandy, but hey, I only organised it. I didn't pay for it."

I furrow my brow, perplexed. "But then, who…"

Jack smiles at me and I realise. Ben.

"Well, Mandy, I'll be in touch soon about the book signings once we launch, ok?"

I nod with a sigh and say good night to Jack, telling him I'll wait outside for my cab.

I've had the best night ever, but now I'm tired and emotional and as I step out into the cool night, I breathe the chill air into my lungs.

I'm waiting for my taxi when a huge black Bentley pulls up and I think it must be for one of the celebrities who has been at my party.

As the back door opens though, nobody gets out.

"Get in," says a familiar voice from the back seat.

"What are you doing here?" I gasp in amazement.

"Just get in!" Ben orders as I peer into the car.

"I've got a cab coming!" I retort, refusing to be ordered around.

"I am the bloody cab, now get in!"

"Oh, ha ha!" I quickly get into the car and Ben tells the driver to go.

"Good night, was it?" Ben asks in the darkness and I smile.

"Fabulous! Thank you, Ben and thank you for your kind words, they made me cry."

Ben snorts, "Well it doesn't take much with you." I giggle and begin to tell him all about the incredible evening he just put on for me; down to every last detail.

"And then there was my dad talking to Richard and Judy…" I'm still blabbering on when the car pulls to a stop.

"Hey," I look out of the window, "this isn't my house."

Ben laughs. "Obviously. But it's where you're staying tonight."

"What? But…"

Ben leans across me and opens the car door.

I stare incredulously at him and then at the place where I am apparently spending the night.

Just when I thought my evening couldn't get any better. I smile and thank Ben as I step out of the car.

"Oh, M," Ben suddenly says and I turn to his voice, "one more thing."

I wait, what else could there possibly be?

"Be ready for 8am tomorrow morning. You have a breakfast meeting with a guy called Tom. He has a rather interesting proposition for you."

My mouth gapes open. *Would this be about Shirley's prediction?* I'm about to ask the question but Ben chuckles softly.

"Laters, M." He says, then he pulls the door shut and the car drives off.

I gaze after the Bentley and shake my head in wonder. *Who the heck is Tom?*

I turn and walk into the Dorchester hotel and to what will be the start of a new adventure, which is apparently going to begin tomorrow at 8am.

I look at my phone and calculate that that is, erm, less than six hours away…

THE END

As an author, there is no greater accomplishment than writing those two words at the end of any book.

With that sense of achievement though comes great loss; It's over, it's finished, so what now?

Well, for me, there is a lingering sense of excitement as I now pick up Ben's ongoing story and I hope that you will join me on that journey.

Come with me as I take you 'Into the Twilight' and unlock Ben's devastating secret...

M x

A Word to the Wise – by Stan

- *You don't interrupt your enemy when they are making a mistake.*

- *Don't let your enemy read your every move, treat it like a poker game.*

- *Don't make decisions based on emotion. Take time to step away and you will see it differently in twenty-four hours.*

- *Learn to read upside down.*

- *You deserve a bloody Oscar.*

- *Keep a notebook beside your bed and record your waking thoughts as soon as they occur.*

- *The deal's not done till the money's in the bank.*

- *What's the worst than can happen? Plan your contingency, anything better is a bonus.*

- *Are you falling over yourself to be subservient? Well don't.*

- *If you run too fast you'll fall over, read The Peter Principle.*

- *File your problems in order of priority and don't let anyone force the pace.*

- *Patience is a virtue.*

- *First impressions are lasting impressions.*

- *Have a different mindset; I want you to see every person as an arsehole, until they prove themselves otherwise.*

- *Learn to control your emotions and use them as an asset.*

- *Search for the positive in every situation.*

- *Don't be afraid to be ruthless; just make sure it's in an authoritative yet productive way.*

- *Man up!*

- *Never trust anyone in business.*

- *Never say I can't; that's for losers.*

- *Don't ever be late on anything.*

- *Let the niceties go.*

- *Don't get carried away with yourself; you're only ever as a good as your next failure.*

- *You're an asset, why would anyone treat you as anything less?*

- *Surround yourself with people that you enjoy, who make you feel that what you're doing really matters.*

- *Always assess the risk.*

- *Sometimes you have to do something you hate to achieve something you love.*

- *Play to your strengths and get stronger.*

- *Don't force the pace, don't panic, solve what you can one thing at a time.*

- *Never harbour self-doubt, it's negative energy, you have no room for that.*

- *When you own something, you feel the pain in retaining it.*

- *Keep driving and believing in yourself, knowing that you deserve the gain.*

- *Recognise when the opportunity is there, and take it.*

- *Treat your obsession as something of an attribute; hone it and it will reward you.*

- *Only you alone can change things.*

- *Stop and learn from your mistakes, and never make the same mistake again.*

- *If you don't design your own life plan, you'll fall into someone else's.*

- *Keep your enemies close; destroy them or work with them. Either way, you gain strength.*

- *Stand up for what you believe, don't give in. Even when you're staring into the face of adversity.*

- *Get into their heads; what would you do in their position?*

- *Don't be afraid to move on from challenging situations.*

- *Employ people that are better than you; it keeps you on your toes.*

- *Sometimes when you fall you have to trust the fact that maybe, just maybe, you can fly.*

- *Always manage expectation.*

- *If you look smart, you'll feel like you can act smart.*

- *Anything is possible if you believe in it enough.*

And last but not least, the most important advice of all that I ever received from Stan, the guardian angel that I believe everybody needs in their life…

Keep your eye on the ball!

Lightning Source UK Ltd.
Milton Keynes UK
UKOW05f1953300417
300225UK00011B/194/P